Halcon stood so close the candle played over the leather of his shirt. He stood so tall she wondered if she reached his breast bone. Flickering light danced on the edge of his mask, revealing a white flash of a smile.

"I prayed you'd be safe," she whispered. "Halcon . . ."

Chills rained down her neck and arms—because Charity had dared to call him by name.

He took her hand to his lips and turned it palm up. As before, he kissed its very center. His lips wandered to her wrist. She answered the primitive yearning which urged her to rotate her wrist, just slightly, in invitation.

Nighthawk sighed as she flowed toward him, her other hand hovering over his hair. She cupped her palm over the back of his head and felt the thickness of his hair above the knotted leather thong. For the first time, she wasn't receiving his caress; *she* was touching *him*. . . .

She felt sure he wanted to kiss her. She formed her lips to mirror Halcon's as they opened; she felt feverish. His tongue eased into her mouth and she gasped, but his hand spanned the back of her neck, under her hair, demanding she not pull away.

She remained still until he pulled his mouth away to whisper, "*Caridad,* come out with me. . . ."

# TERRI SPRENGER
# NIGHTHAWK'S WOMAN

**ZEBRA BOOKS**
**KENSINGTON PUBLISHING CORP.**

*To My Safety Net*
*Family and Friends Who Always Catch Me*

ZEBRA BOOKS are published by

Kensington Publishing Corp.
475 Park Avenue South
New York, NY 10016

Copyright © 1993 by Terri Sprenger

Zebra, the Z logo, Heartfire Romance, and the Heartfire Romance logo are trademarks of Kensington Publishing Corp.

First Printing: January, 1994

Printed in the United States of America

# Prologue

Harvard University, 1819

Only a boy, a pup of a boy, would have tried such a thing. Charlie panted, hurdling the second landing to gain the next flight of stairs. A man would have ignored Sutton's taunts. But then, she never had been a man, only a girl who'd fooled everyone into thinking she was.

Ten minutes ago she could have walked away from Sutton. But the familiar weight of the foil's hilt had sung a tempting song. A silver sword did not recognize tall or short, bully or victim.

"You're a girl," Sutton had hissed. "A female. You've no business among men."

Charlie tripped on the loose carpet outside the dormitory room.

"Damnation!" She gasped as she regained her feet and fumbled for the key caught in the undarned hole in her trouser pocket.

Shouts echoed downstairs as she jiggled the key in the stubborn lock. It hadn't taken Sutton long to form a pack. Not pack. Wolves hunted for food and Sutton's boys stuck together with the blood lust of a mob.

She slammed the door behind her and turned the key from inside. The bolt clunked into place. But how long would it hold them at bay?

How easy, *easy* to have shrugged and walked away from the

insult. A fraction of a second, a moment's weakness had ruined years of planning. Now she could only hide.

She swung open the closet door. Dark suits dangled like bodies of the hanged. How fitting to walk down an aisle of the already condemned to hide, waiting for Nicolas or the dean to unlock the door.

As if viewing a play, she remembered how Sutton had backed away but a step at first, black boots scuffling in the yard—black boots far too dull, most days, to meet the dress code. Then, trying not to squirm beneath the stares of the fencing club, Sutton had taken his stand. He'd puffed out his pitiful bony rooster's chest in such an inviting target, he'd been irresistible.

"Bad form, Sutton," Charlie's voice had chuckled and menaced. "Bad form to taunt a man who's armed."

"But you're not a man," Sutton had gasped as Charlie flicked the sword tip to clip a button from his waistcoat. "I saw you"—he'd almost missed his footing where the grass had given way to cobbles—"In the bath—"

To pursue a person even to the bath! Leering with those fleshy, pink lips agape, Sutton had stared. Charlie's skin seemed to contract, hugging more tightly to her bones as she remembered his bulging frog eyes.

He could only have seen the pale curve of a scrawny shoulder above the tub's high sides, but—damn instinct! The very animal instinct which fascinated her, which had catapulted her into Harvard to study biology, had forced her arms to cross over her chest when any fool knew a man covered his privates!

Her shock, there in the yard, had given Sutton time to gather his courage. Lunging forward, fingers clawed as if to rip Charlie's white shirt front, Sutton had slammed against her blunted sword point. The impact sent him reeling backward to fall on the seat of his pants. No hand, not even his own, broke his fall, but plenty of laughter increased the sting.

It had been false bravado, indeed, to snap the sword in a quick salute to the other fencers before racing for the dorm.

Now she crouched against the closet wall, cornered, while the voices grew closer.

"Gentlemen, allow me to go inside alone to check on my roommate. Please."

Nicolas. That faint Spanish accent made his voice so cultured and polite, but so imperious. A sword blade dipped in honey might be just as well disguised. Nicolas had championed her—the university's youngest, smallest freshman—in the fencing club, but the hazing had remained persistent and ruthless.

How would he judge her if he knew the truth? Her fist struck the wall just as Nicolas opened the closet door.


Nicolas stood and stared down at Charlie. Seeing his roommate curled up like a kitten, with only the inky black hair for contrast against the whites, Nicolas, for a moment, believed Sutton's accusation. Curved into a protective crouch, back like a frail sapling, Charlie might pass for a very little girl, a child almost, until he stood.

"Sutton is lying, you know," Charlie challenged, feet planted apart, chin raised high. Nothing feminine about that pose. Charlie pushed gold-rimmed spectacles higher on his freckled nose.

"I know, amigo."

Charlie's attempts to learn Spanish, to master the sword, and his dreams of going to California, had assuaged Nicolas' own homesickness. Stories of vaqueros, mustangs and grizzly bear were the meat young Charlie lived on.

The sound of renewed shouting, just outside the door, caused a sag in the boy's shoulders. Nicolas circled them in a rough hug and wondered again at the light, almost boneless quality of Charlie's body.

*Jesus Maria!* He jerked back as if burned and stifled the impulse to cross himself. If Charlie turned out to be a girl—He pictured the many times he'd held the boy's waist, forcing him back against his own body, to let him mirror the proper fencing stance. Would he not have felt—something?

7

Dean Proctor, grayed, distinguished, mumbling, entered the room, flanked by Sutton and his mob. The fencers, swords at hand, followed. Freddy, Charlie's round, gregarious cousin, stood at the edge of the group, blinking and gulping.

"Now," the dean's head jerked in a series of nods before he continued. "What is this gibber-jabber, O'Dell? Sutton says you're not a man."

Nicolas stared into Charlie's face and saw his lips purse. Were his lips too red? The skin too milky pale?

"I know that, Dean Proctor," Charlie answered. "It's part of the reason I came to Harvard. To learn to act and think like a man."

He—she, whoever Charlie might be, the spirit of a man burned within, Nicolas thought.

"Yes," the dean's head bobbed again and he turned to shrug at Sutton. The bully's easy defeat drew jeers from two fencers.

Nicolas watched Charlie's eyelids droop over his blue eyes. Curly eyelashes hid behind the silvery disks of glass in his spectacles and relief rushed from his form like a sigh.

"Make him take off his shirt," Sutton growled.

Jeers stopped in mid-throat. The exodus for the door turned back on itself.

Sutton's demand signaled more than poor sportsmanship. Nicolas saw Charlie's feet widen into a combative stance. His arms crossed and his lips pressed together so hard they looked grey and bloodless.

Did he imagine the tiny sound, half whimper, half moan which caught in Charlie's throat? No one else heard.

Dean Proctor shrugged again, turning to Charlie with an off-hand gesture. "What would it hurt, my boy? If it would set this ruckus to rest?"

Charlie stripped off the soft leather fencing glove and flung it at Sutton's feet. Hard blue eyes turned chilling as sea water as Charlie reached for the line of buttons which began at the side of the high collar.

*Dios,* no girl would disrobe before—how many? twelve? thirteen?—men, just to prove a point.

"Amigo, you need not do this," Nicolas stepped in front of the boy, though he could feel Charlie look through him, fixing Sutton with that frigid glare.

"Dean," he appealed, as Charlie's arm brushed his back and his fingers loosened yet another button. "This is harassment of the lowest kind."

Charlie elbowed him in the ribs and he sighed while another fencer emitted a bark of laughter.

"Show 'im your pluck, Charlie! Don't let that bastard get you down!"

While the others gaped at the dare-devil speaker, Nicolas shook his head at Charlie. For a moment, their eyes held.

He *is* a girl! Charlie is a girl! Nicolas felt his heart buck against his ribs. It was impossible. Besides, how could he suddenly know? The same way a buck recognized a doe across a forest? The secret seared between them even as he denied it.

Charlie's fragile chin rose higher as the buttons from neck to shoulder ended and she began to release the flap covering her breast.

"Charity! No! The game is over. Stop it," Freddy, messy and distraught, his eyes heartsore instead of jolly, stepped between the crowd and his cousin.

"Dean Proctor, she *is* a girl. Charity is my fifteen-year-old cousin. I regret the masquerade. It seemed harmless," he turned to face her as the dean herded the whooping students away.

"Freddy, I'll never speak to you again."

Both hands gripped her hips as she spoke.

"They would have backed off in another moment. Freddy, where is your nerve? Where are your—"

Nicolas watched the girl's eyes drop below her cousin's belt. He knew very well what she had been about to say, but couldn't believe he'd heard.

"How do you say it in Spanish?"

She wheeled on him, all paleness gone. Now her black hair reached in thorn shapes across hot red cheeks and her blue eyes blazed.

"I won't tell you, Charlie." Why, he wondered, did he hear regret creep into his voice?

She heard it too, because she turned her face away from both males. Freddy apologized as he shuffled backward from the room.

"I'm sorry as I can be, Charity. But you knew this would happen sooner or later. Charity?" A smile quirked the corner of Freddy's mouth as he tried to catch her eye. "You beat them for two and a half weeks."

Charlie seized a suit from the closet and flung it on the bed. She grabbed a handful of silk ties which had always hung too long.

The little one did indeed have *cojones,* for there could be no feminine equivalent, could there? Not in the world he lived in and certainly not in hers. She heard his sigh and looked up. Rage sparking from her eyes dared him to pity her.

She'd better marry a pirate and relive his bloody tales by her fireside, he thought. Though it would be a pale substitute for the California adventures he'd promised her, it would have to do.

*Dios,* her sons would make soldiers from hell!

The door squeaked open and the dean sidled, sheepish and apologetic, into the room.

Charlie whirled on him, index finger pointed, voice low.

"Dean, I'll require someone to bring up my trunks."

# Chapter One

The Coast of New Spain
March, 1822

"I simply won't believe your fiancé forgot to meet your ship, Miss O'Dell. It must be that you cannot recognize him from this distance.

"Oh! Keep this little boat upright if you please, young man!" The respectable Mrs. Edward Graver flailed both arms to keep her balance in the rowboat.

"No, he's not there."

Charity pressed her hands against her knees to keep herself seated, to keep from jumping up into a wild jig which would finish the capsizing Mrs. Graver had begun.

"He must be." Mrs. Graver leaned forward, squinted and gave the young girl's trembling hand a comforting pat. "Master Freddy has always been—"

"Sweet, but totally undependable." Charity slipped her hand from beneath her chaperone's and brushed back the hood of the stifling black cloak Mrs. Graver had insisted she wear. "Besides, it simply doesn't matter."

She bit her lip to hide a smile at the woman's gaping fish mouth.

"Doesn't—matter that you're stranded? Deserted at nightfall in a strange country? Miss O'Dell be sensible. Why of course it matters."

"Madam, stay amidships. Seated, if you please."

11

A wave slapped the boat's side, underscoring the young sailor's order.

"Oh!" Mrs. Graver flinched at the spray, then crouched on the board bench like a parrot on a perch. "I'm soaked, simply soaked!"

"Well, ma'am." The sailor shrugged before he leaned back against the oars.

He probably cursed them both for delaying his supper, Charity thought. The *Leila* would have sailed on, straight to Monterey, if this rendezvous with Freddy hadn't been set for San Pedro bay.

The sleek sweep of beach glowed silver in the coming twilight. Beyond, sheds and figures stood blue before the jutting purple mountains.

California! What if she jumped from the rowboat and danced in the waves? What if she unlaced this cloak, whirled it three times about her head and cast it into the warm Pacific ocean along with every other thing Bostonian?

But no. Maintain the charade until Aunt Penny's dear friend gets back aboard the ship and leaves for Monterey. And then—freedom!

"—after all, setting up your own household. Oh dear, I'm quite queasy all at once. I fear I'll be undone by this bobbing." Mrs. Graver curled one arm around her stomach.

"Concentrate on something that doesn't move, Mrs. Graver. Your body is only responding to the movement and the shifting horizon."

"Now, now, Charity, your aunt told me you'd outgrown those indelicate studies about the—" she sneaked a glance at the perspiring oarsman and lowered her voice. "About the human form."

Ungrateful old biddy. Let her lose her meal, Charity thought. Still, she should appreciate that Mrs. Graver hadn't recited *all* Aunt Penelope's observations.

Such as eavesdropping. Certainly, eavesdropping was a despicable fault, and one she'd tried to conquer. But why shouldn't she listen at doors and lurk around corners when no one had addressed a word of consequence to her since Father

12

had died? She shouldn't, she supposed, because her snooping only caused frustration and embarrassment.

"She's domesticated nicely since Freddy's proposal," had been Aunt Penny's words to dear Dorothea Graver.

As if she were a soft, tame lap dog! She'd pressed her face hard against the door frame to keep from shrieking that her domesticity was an act, a sham. She, not Freddy, had done the proposing. But the stakes had been as high then as they were now.

"You're right, of course, Mrs. Graver." She pushed her round gold spectacles up the bridge of her nose with an index finger.

Sand grated on wood and the sailor vaulted into the shallows to steady the boat.

"At last, ladies." The sailor gripped Charity's forearm and raised a cautious hand to her shoulder, until Mrs. Graver's throat-clearing rasp turned him to help her from the boat.

His eyes had wandered back to the ocean when Mrs. Graver snapped her fingers.

"Now then, what about Mistress O'Dell's trunks?"

"They're coming, ma'am." He gestured to a long boat pulling toward shore. "Captain is seeing to them." He nodded at the figure in the vessel's bow. "Then he'll return you to the ship."

"Not until Miss O'Dell's fiance comes for her." Mrs. Graver crossed her arms resolutely and tucked in her chins.

"That could be next week," Charity began.

"They've run up the flag, Miss," the sailor nodded toward a pole and banner, barely visible against the blue-gray sky. "That's so folks waiting for a vessel can come check. Besides," he shifted from one foot to the other, "I doubt Captain will stay in the bay for long. He'll be something eager to get on his way."

Charity nodded. She'd read that Americans were not always welcomed, especially by officials from Mexico City. Such news had made her curious to know why Nicolas' family, respectable and rich, had sent him to an American university.

"The captain may be eager as he likes," Mrs. Graver replied, "But he will wait until Miss O'Dell has a proper escort."

"I have other friends here." Charity searched her mind for Nicolas's family name or the name of his rancho, anything to pacify the old harridan and speed her on her way. "Freddy attended Harvard with a boy who lives here. I roomed with him, in fact, Nicolas—"

The old woman swooped forward and clapped both hands against Charity's cheeks, pressing their faces nose-to-nose.

"Your poor Aunt Penelope will sit up screaming in her sleep, yes, even across the continent, if you so much as mention that shameful escapade," Mrs. Graver returned the sailor's stare. "Enough." She swiped at her skirts.

Charity closed her eyes and drew a deep breath. Never would she understand appearances and propriety. Raised by her father to state a fact as a straightforward fact, she constantly offended.

"Reared by a man to think like men," Aunt Penny had spat. And never could Charity grasp why this made her awkward, a misfit, wrong. Pretending was her best defense.

"Certainly, Mrs. Graver, I won't mention it. Still, there must be a coach I can hire," her eye caught the sailor's shaken head, "Or a cart to take me to the Carillos' rancho? Freddy wrote of his continuing friendship with the family. Surely they'll receive me."

Stepping from the wallowing longboat, the captain seconded Charity's proposal to set off for the nearest rancho which was, indeed, the Carillos'. Proffering a bottle of brandy and promise of payment from a rich *Americano,* he wheedled transportation for Charity's trunks before they'd been hefted ashore.

His Spanish is abominable, Charity thought. He's more worried about tax collectors descending than about me. In fact, she couldn't be sure he'd informed the two rumpled men lounging outside the hide shed that she, as well as the trunks, would be their cargo. Still, she'd stand on the shore until Christmas rather than delay Mrs. Graver.

"You're sure, now, that those two—soldiers, you say?—will convey you as a lady should be?" Mrs. Graver pulled against the captain's stronger-than-courtesy grip. She watched as one man polished the neck of the brandy bottle with his soiled shirttail.

"Of course, Mrs. Graver. You know these Californians are as chivalrous as knights of the Round Table."

Soothing, she must make her voice soothing. Freedom beckoned, only moments away. "And since the Carrillo home is the nearest to the south, I could probably stroll the distance."

She turned as the sailor parted his lips to protest. The captain gave a stifling snap of his head and the sailor's unuttered words turned to a gust of breath.

A more timid miss might worry at that, Charity thought. But what could be worse than remaining in Mrs. Graver's thrall?

The three Americans sailed. Charity sat on her tallest trunk on the twilight beach, swinging her feet as she waved farewell.

Obviously, Freddy had forgotten. Or made some silly arrangement for her retrieval which, typically, had fallen through. But in one thing, at least, she'd told Mrs. Graver the truth. It did not matter. Four years of planning, come to fruition, mattered.

This plan, unlike the one to attend Harvard, could not be sabotaged. No one could snatch her home.

The waves rippled like black velvet topped with white cotton crests. Sighing low and quiet, they carried the *Leila* out, surely beyond hailing distance.

Guffawing laughter and a spate of drunken Spanish drew her eyes back to the hide shed. The two soldiers wandered further up the shore. One stumbled, only to be pulled upright by his comrade. Then both leaned against a big-wheeled cart pulled by what, in silhouette, appeared to be oxen. Noble reputation not withstanding, she thought it unlikely these two would drive her anywhere tonight.

Charity laced the black cloak close to her throat and wrapped it around the stylish little gown, her best. Midnight blue muslin on top and sprigged robin's egg from the high waist to the white stockings at her ankles, it had been the height of fashion when it arrived two years ago in Boston Harbor. She'd worn it when she, John and a sniffling Aunt Penny had waved Freddy off to California, last spring.

"Damnation," she grimaced as she jumped from the trunk and sank shin deep in the sand. She'd likely snap an ankle tramping down the beach in these silly slippers. It would be more sensible to try to roust the soldiers before beginning the walk south.

"Excuse me."

Red eyes glowed in the light of the drunkards' campfire as the two oxen flicked their ears at her voice.

Hard to believe these enormous beasts were cattle. Their wickedly curving horns made a rack long enough to carry her body. She regarded their heavily furred legs. Adaptation to brushy terrain, no doubt. She must get about her work as a naturalist soon. But here she'd insist on the new, more accurate, title: biologist.

The oxen stamped and lowed. Only one of the stuporous men opened his eyes. He blinked, smiled and seemed to dismiss her as a player in his dreams.

"Hell and damnation." Again she muttered one Harvard gift she'd been allowed to keep. Scandalous for a proper lady and out of fashion, no doubt, the oath was still quite mouth-filling and satisfactory. And the drunkards seemed far from shocked.

She should steal their cart, she thought as she trudged down the beach. It would serve them right for taking the captain's brandy without performing the purchased service. Still, even her self-taught Spanish told her the captain had given only rudimentary instructions.

The moon hung in the sky before her, round and silver as a coin. The waves lapped softly on her right and the San Gabriel Mountains loomed on her left.

She tripped, snarled at her clumsiness and bent to remove both shoes. She weighed one in each palm, but resisted the urge to toss them into the waves.

16

Without the slippers, her walk turned to a trot and then a lope. She became a wild creature, a deer or a mustang or maybe even a bird. She filled her lungs with the salty breeze, convinced she could match this unladylike gait all night.

No Aunt Penny stood in a window shaking her finger. No brother John shook his head in sad understanding. No bonneted neighbors whispered everlasting tales of her "escapade" from behind white-gloved hands.

No one, no one! Her lope speeded into a headlong run. Her braided coronet uncoiled. It bounced and slapped the middle of her spine in time with the chant she sang to the clouds. No one.

"No," she held her breath, aimed the black kid slipper at a wave and launched it hard as she could throw. "One!" She crowed at the splash and had drawn her arm back to fling the second shoe when movement made her turn.

He hadn't said a word.

If his dark mount hadn't stamped in the sand, he might have sat there all night, a tall horseman silent as death.

# Chapter Two

The roaring, singing voices in her mind ceased. Waves lapped the shore quiet as a cat's paw feinting at a mouse. And there she stood, a silly girl with bedraggled hair and stocking feet, holding a slipper in one hand.

"Señor," she addressed the horseman.

Ghostly and silent, only his mount's restless movement, its warmth and scent, told her this phantom existed. Moonlight silvered the straight male figure, following a turn of leather at his neck, curving across wide shoulders, angling to lean rider's hips where man and animal disappeared into merged darkness.

A cautious voice in her mind counseled flight.

Run, you ninny. He is no California *ranchero* out for a moonlight ride. Do you hear chiming silver spurs? No. Does he wear a gentleman's flat-brimmed hat? No. And why hasn't he uttered one shocked word about your idiot behavior? He may not look like one of Boston's back-alley cutthroats, but he stalked you silently to the water's edge. He is something just as dangerous.

She felt a surge of energy, felt the muscles in her legs tense as the rider bent his head in a move which mocked a courtly bow. Still he didn't speak.

"Señor. I admit you startled me."

Remember your biology, girl. Act like prey and you'll be dinner. Charity straightened to her full height, head almost level with the horse's chin. She allowed her arms to float out from her sides, enlarging herself, just as a threatened cat puffs its fur.

"I've just arrived in New Spain and my fiancé, I fear, has missed my arrival." Must her words keep tumbling out in this stilted fashion? "I'm walking to the rancho of my friend Nicolas Carillo. We were chums at school." What would he make of that? Would an educated woman be safer? Could this be a joke Freddy had planned? She squinted. If she could see the stranger's face, she'd scold him for thinking her a coward.

The featureless head snapped curtly to one side, irritated, as his dark horse tossed its mane and threshed its forelegs. The very air quaked with a threat which told her this was no joke.

He reached down the hand nearest her and Charity felt the quaking shudder through her chest.

"I thank you for your courtesy, but I cannot mount a stranger's horse in the middle of the night——" She stared at her white stockings a moment, forcing her face to assume an expression which said all was as it should be. Then she stiffened her spine and regarded him directly. A submissive dog loses his throat to the leader of the pack. Look up, stop babbling and don't give the brigand ideas.

But why didn't he speak? If he sought to avoid recognition his dramatics were wasted on a newcomer. If he meant to menace her with silence, he had succeeded. But then she felt a spurt of hope. Perhaps he could not speak and offered her help in the only manner he could. California was still a wild land. Some accident——

"We have not been introduced, you see." Even Aunt Penelope could not fault her primness, yet he remained motionless. Only starlight glittered on his sword hilt.

Stillness pressed in on her. Waves moved, searching, over the sands and a coyote—wild, wondrous cry—called from the mountains.

If this wasn't a joke, if he wasn't a mute, then this ghostly rider could only be a fantasy. As she'd been part of the drunken soldier's dream, so this disarming night rider had sprung from a neglected, romantic corner of her mind. The thought lulled her for only an instant.

The hand that bumped hers aside was no dream. Warm, sinewy and rope-roughened, it clamped over her wrist.

Charity pulled her skirts and stepped closer, as if to vault onto the horse's back, then she clenched her fist and jerked, sure that strength and surprise would break his grip.

He held tighter. Damnation! Would he snap her wrist? Panic flared through her chest and arms, unleashing such power that she swung her fist over her head.

His horse snorted, half-reared, and then stumbled forward, unseating its rider.

Falling, the man loomed above her like some great bird of prey, then twisted away, and only their shoulders collided.

The sand felt gritty beneath her hands and knees. She shook off a wave of dizziness before her head snapped around at what sounded like a short breathless laugh.

Though she'd fallen on her face, he'd landed on his feet in the sand next to her. He faced her, horse nuzzling his back, and for an instant the moon tricked her straining eyes, painting a flash of white, like a smile, against the dark face.

The strength of her sword arm had dragged him down, her mind comforted, refusing to consider the import of that smile. Stolen practices with John or Freddy, even, when necessary, her own shadow, had kept her sword arm hard. But his silence didn't encourage bragging. And the rider wore a sword of his own.

"Who are you?" Weak, weak words squeaked from her throat and the smile, if it had been one, vanished.

He snatched up his trailing reins and extended the other hand with a forceful snap. His feet braced as if he expected a second assault.

Madness, Charity chided herself, madness to fight an adversary so ready. And what if she did escape? Where would she run? Or hide? And, truly, what had she to fear?

Abduction and despoilment seemed unlikely for an awkward, bespectacled bit like her. More likely he'd take her to

20

feed his wolf pack. She sniffed. An unappetizing, bony meal she'd be, too.

She had no time to flinch before his hands circled her waist and boosted her onto the animal's back.

She shuddered in disbelief. He'd forced her to sit astride the horse. Bareback. The restless, snorting beast wore no saddle and her legs draped over its shoulders.

He vaulted up behind her and his thighs clasped her so closely she felt him squeeze, urging his mount forward.

Little enough chance she'd fall with those muscled legs balancing her. No man had ever touched her waist in the dark, let alone—

Do not panic. Orient yourself, Charity. Survival depends on knowing where you are and where he is. Think. Analyze. Plan.

His left hand felt warm under her cloak, steadying her waist. His right hand moved free in front of her, holding braided reins. Her right shoulder bumped his chest with each of the horse's long-reaching strides.

She smelled the horse and felt its warm hide. It had been exercised, but not exhausted. The man smelled faintly of some herb, a faraway green odor.

Whatever clothing he wore fit tightly. No sash fluttered, lifting on the wind like the horse's mane. No hat marred the outline of his lean form. The fabric? Close-fitting, thin and soft. She moved her hand to graze his arm.

His left hand stirred at her waist.

Idiot! Why had she touched him intentionally? And what's he to make of that, Charity?

Her gasp brought another muffled sound and she turned to see his face.

He wore a mask. No wonder she'd seen only his bandit's smile. He looked steadily forward, but there could be no mistake. A leather strip covered him from forehead to the mustache. The holes cut for his eyes were blank hollows.

How much more evidence did she need to prove him an outlaw?

She could no longer fight the trembling. Boston had been

soul-deadening dull, but safe. She'd been a fool not to wait for an escort. More fool, though, to think those drunkards could match this black phantom.

Two comforting movements, like pats you'd give a frightened child, caressed her waist. What abductor comforts his victim? Never mind. Her shoulders slumped loose against his chest. Her head flopped back and her eyes absently tracked the starry smear of sky. She swayed with the rhythm of the galloping horse.

A shame, truly a shame he'd needed to frighten her so.

He'd only intended to take her off the beach, to protect her from her own foolishness. A sigh so deep it shuddered through them both racked her frame. He hadn't meant to break her spirit.

Yet it seemed he had. Was that why she reminded him of Tempesta? He remembered watching a mustang herd, then picking out a red filly so wild he'd known her as the equal of any stallion, even this black beast he rode tonight.

He slapped his horse's neck affectionately before he looked down the empty beach. He'd named the filly Tempesta, Storm, and held tight to the reins, her mane, and finally her neck as he'd tried, one summer morning, to teach her to bear his weight.

Darkness had fallen by the time the filly stood listless and beaten, mastered at last. And had he felt triumphant? Victorious?

No. He'd felt regret, just as he did now, for frightening this girl into submission.

An amusing shortcoming in a miscreant.

Shortcomings were luxuries for those with time. He had little time and none to waste on a distraction like this simpleminded miss. The sooner she disappeared, the better.

Suddenly the stallion stood, still as a rock. His nostrils vibrated in the greeting he'd been schooled to stifle. But no horse could be trusted not to hail his own kind.

Riders. He listened, eyes closed in concentration, since it

would do no good to stare into the blackness. Fewer than—probably only two. Still, the wise course, especially with this burden curled against his shirtfront, was to hide. He reined the stallion behind a rock outcropping.

The girl started alert and he covered her mouth. He spared no instant for regret. Even as she drew away from his bruising fingers, he pressed his hand closer, pinning her loosened hair against his chest. After one enraged squeal she quieted.

"There'll be the devil to pay, Lieutenant, if those pigs are responsible for her drowning." The voice, heavily accented as that of a peasant, seemed almost within reach.

"The American who bought them off with drink is to blame, Francisco." The second voice corrected, clipped and official. "Of course the Yankee-lovers will not see that. Bah!" It sounded as if he spat at their feet. "It will be a bright day for Mexico—yes, for these Californios, too, though they're too foolish to see it—when these shores are again forbidden to foreigners."

He felt her lips move, straining against his hand. The wench would make him smother her if she didn't—He felt again that resigned sigh, that shudder. He loosened his grip.

Without warning she pounded the stallion's ribs with her heels. One, two, three drumming blows forced the horse to bolt forward with a low, surprised neigh.

"Halcon!"

"After him!"

The two riders, Mexican soldiers, of course, were upon them. The bewildered stallion had stampeded into their path.

No choice but to grip this struggling, stupid girl with his left arm and free the sword with his right. *Dios* would have to guide the stallion, though it seemed the animal, abashed at its mistake, maneuvered him into perfect position.

The silver sword sung free of its scabbard. If it nicked the girl as it passed, he had no time to care. He braced for impact as the horse careened toward the nearest soldier.

The stallion's chest slammed the soldier's mount, knocking the smaller horse to its knees. The girl slipped as the horses collided, hanging to his left, as if she rode sidesaddle. *Jesus Maria,* the wench was a curse!

Afoot, the peasant Francisco reared his unwieldy cutlass, and tried to parry the blade from above. The weapon's weight and the descending blow knocked the man backward.

Francisco rose to his feet, shouting to the lieutenant who circled galloping behind.

"It is him, Santana! It is Halcon, the Nighthawk. He's got the girl!"

So, the lieutenant who spoke in clipped military tones was Guerro Santana, the Spaniard come from Mexico City to lend much-needed intellect to California's occupying army. He'd guessed as much, but hoped he was wrong.

Santana was smart, Halcon thought as he urged his stallion closer, but the Spanish lieutenant couldn't guess he'd faced his opponent before, unmasked and fencing in sport.

Halcon held his sword steady, moving its tip in tiny feinting swings. With a blade, Santana knew what he was about.

"So, Señor Nighthawk," Santana taunted. "You're not the saint your devoted Californios think, eh?"

The soldier struck, metal ringing metal and kept his sword arm flexible, even when Halcon forced him to lock hilts. Santana refused to return the steady pressure that might lure him into falling forward if the stronger sword withdrew.

And yet Santana stared, frowning slightly, as if his glare and derisive words could pierce the mask.

"Afraid to speak, Señor Halcon?"

Halcon slid his blade along the Spaniard's, then jammed his hilt close once more. Let the bastard think he had but one trick.

"You so adore the Americans that you're not above stealing some sport with their women, is that it?" The Spaniard drew an audible breath and snatched at the girl.

The black stallion spun away as his rider sheathed his sword and shook out a loop in his reata. The horsehair rope felt limber and able, and he had only an instant to wonder at the girl's stillness before the moment came when he must cast.

Santana charged. Now! The loop sailed over the lieutenant's sword arm and torso, and tightened. Santana slid down his horse's extended neck and slammed to the beach. He tried to gain his feet, ran a few steps, then fell cursing while his rump plowed a deep furrow in the sand.

Nighthawk slowed his stallion with gentle, gradual pressure on the reins. The reata was a good one, too good to waste. Still, Santana showed skill with his sword and he would know a trick or two. It might be foolhardy to ride closer.

Halcon let his stallion work the rope, keeping it taut, jerking Santana off his feet as if he were an errant calf. Should he close in and save the reata or cut it and leave the man entangled and humiliated before his underling?

The stirring of the accursed girl decided him. Halcon drew a bone-handled knife from his boot and leaned down an arm's length to saw through the rope, lamenting the waste as the last hairs twisted apart.

He clucked his tongue to the dancing stallion, urging it to trot off a good distance before halting.

She would hate this, but it was necessary. Necessary because he had remembered why this wench reminded him of Tempesta. It wasn't the fiery spirit in every angry line of her pale face, not the challenging eyes which showed, now, just a hint of worry.

He remembered that the filly, two days after pretending to submit to the life of a domesticated animal, had repaid his consideration and regret by dumping him at the edge of the great desert—neighing and swiveling her heels in a feigned kick, a last insult as she escaped.

*This* filly, he determined as he fingered the rope, would not escape. He clenched his teeth in resolve and smiled when her eyes flicked to his tightened jaw, then widened.

He held up one cautioning index finger, swept her skirts aside and took two quick turns of rope around her stockings.

"Oh, no!" She started several thoughts and left off each one with an insulted squeak. "I won't—Don't you—? Señor, I will not try to escape again."

He pulled the rope tight, then slipped a finger between the coils and her legs so that it didn't bind any more than it must.

25

Her ankles felt trim and strangely muscular beneath the battered stockings. He fought the ungentlemanly urge to investigate, then succumbed. Devil take him if a patriot didn't deserve an occasional privilege! Patriot or not, a man would have to be a gelding not to explore such treasures from behind the anonymity of a mask.

His hand covered the whole of her lower leg, from the tight calf muscle to the delicate peak of her ankle bone.

"Stop it!"

She kicked against her bonds and swung her shoulders against him. So she would tolerate punishment for her transgressions, but resisted worshipful fondling? He could not blame her.

He ducked his head in apology and felt the sting of her loosened hair as she whipped her head to face away from him.

By the Virgin, he had no time for this! Admire the way she looks, the way she feels against the V of your legs, Halcon, but leave it at that.

He kicked the black stallion into a full gallop.


Charity leaned against the gatepost outside the whitewashed rancho walls. Wordless, they had ridden the entire night. Dawn had lightened the sky to pearl gray before he'd let her slip from the horse to find her legs wobbly and weak.

She rubbed her right ankle, watching the dark horseman gallop away and vanish in the half-light. She sniffed. The dratted rope had sawed right through her stockings and they hung in tatters. She'd ponder the fate of that other slipper when she regained her wits.

Her wits had obviously ridden away with the outlaw. She knew, because a tiny crescent of skin across the back of her hand still vibrated from his touch. And, whether she looked at the sky, the ruined stockings or the house inside these gates, she knew why her hand trembled. Not from weariness, but because her captor's mustache has brushed it as he bade her farewell.

How did he dare? She scrubbed the hand against her skirts.

It had not been farewell, either, a logical and measured voice within her mind, corrected.

*"Hasta luego,"* the man in soft leather had whispered, and the Spanish dictionary she had all but memorized said that *luego* meant later.

## Chapter Three

Shimmering pristine white, the stately house within the plastered adobe walls radiated reproach. Charity's straggling braid, shredded stockings and twisted gown would be pitifully unacceptable, here. Charity shivered in the watery sunlight and pulled the wrinkled sleeves of her gown to cover her elbows.

Alone in the morning quiet, disturbed only by a gurgling courtyard fountain, she would seize the time to create order in her appearance. Charity clawed fingers through her hair and rebraided before she realized her hairpins had showered across the landscape and she had no way to fix the braid atop her head.

" 'Welcome, señorita.' " She gritted her teeth to mimic the greeting she expected from Nicolas's proper family, if this was, in fact, their home, " 'And do you perform your toilette in the barnyard at home in Boston, too?' "

She smoothed both palms down her crumpled skirt and recalled the pink satin ribbon woven into the edge of her petticoat. Might it serve as binding for her braid? She glanced furtively within the hacienda gates. Still no movement, though she heard the pawing of restless horses. A cock's crow made her hands jerk from their task before she scolded herself for such silliness.

In only a moment she slipped the ribbon loose. Another moment and the outer skirt would have been flipped down to cover petticoat and lower limbs. But the rush of hooves and scattering sand made her look up first and push her skirts down second.

The young rider's lips rounded into a circle and Charity clamped her lips firm, lest she mirror his astonishment.

The boy, perhaps fifteen or sixteen, drew himself straight and calmed his jigging white horse.

"You must be Señorita O'Dell."

"I admit it," she sighed and shrugged. Either her sarcasm or Spanish must be wrong. The boy's brows lowered in confusion.

"Pardon me, Señorita?"

"I *am* Charity O'Dell." She softened her words with a dip of her head. "I apologize for my unorthodox arrival—"

"And what was that, Señorita?"

She hesitated between bemusement and laughter. Could she explain her rescue, kidnapping and abandonment by a masked man?

She lowered her forehead against her fingertips and forced her sleepy brain to sort through appropriate Spanish phrases.

When she raised her eyes, the boy had slipped from his horse and stood beside her. "You are faint. Let me help you inside."

"I'm fine, really. I can certainly walk alone," Charity shrugged off his encircling arms and started toward the white house. A man and woman stood at the porch railing. Focusing on them so she wouldn't wince at the prick of pebbles through her thin stockings, she strode across the yard.

"It's Señorita O'Dell," the boy called. "She's being quite brave, but she's actually faint."

Charity half-wheeled to upbraid the boy for his inaccurate assessment.

"Then let us not leave her standing in the courtyard," the man with a lion's mane of waving white hair and sun-darkened face ordered as he clattered down the steps.

"Señor Carillo, truly, I'm only disheveled, not injured." She felt herself swept along by his hands.

"But the sergeant who rode by this morning—" the boy began.

29

"Enough, Arturo. Señorita O'Dell, we must see to your comfort at once," the woman said, black hair gleaming as she nodded brief introductions, "My husband, Don Carlos, and I am Doña Anna Carillo, this one's mother," she glanced at the young horseman with an indulgent smile.

"I only wanted to ask—"

"No more, Arturo," Don Carlos frowned as he gripped the porch rail. "And yet I would lie, Señorita, if I told you *I* am not curious to learn how you traveled the distance from San Pedro Bay to our rancho."

Charity watched Doña Anna's hands twitch toward the sky, as if to say the father could not teach manners to his son.

Had they ridden so far? She felt again the rocking of the dark stallion, the warmth of its hide against her legs and the other warmth. Her stomach bucked within her, seemed to drop down and away. The warmth of the outlaw's chest, beneath his rough leather shirt—

"I—I don't remember." She listened not to their gasps, but to the splashing courtyard fountain.

"But Señorita—" Arturo broke off, shaking his head.

Charity's eyelids felt heavy and she wished she could just go to sleep. A meadowlark's warble wove through the fountain's song. Couldn't she just ignore their questions, ignore the fact that her kidnap had brought Halcon, no doubt a wanted man, one day nearer the noose? She needed sleep.

*Indeed.* The frail little lady must sleep. Or faint. Fainting would be a nice touch, her mind sneered. Sweet dumpling of a girl arrives to find her fiancé absent and—oh heavens! is snatched by a nasty bandit. Is this how you greet opportunity in a new land, Charlie?

Charity's eyes snapped open as if her shoulders had been shaken until her teeth cracked together.

"Excuse my distraction." She straightened her spine and breathed deliberately. "I meant to say, I don't quite know how to describe the hombre who brought me to your gates."

The Carillos relaxed as she turned her sentences from English to Spanish. A smile touched Doña Anna's lips and faint approval showed as she straightened her neck above the collar of her green gown. The lady stood taller than her husband.

"He wore rough leather clothing and a mask and rode a tall horse that moved like a deer." She swallowed as her stomach dipped once more. Again, she felt the nimble haunches swing to place his rider just so, heard the stallion's gutteral neigh, the clash of swords in the moonlight. And the soldiers called him Nighthawk. She didn't say it. If Nicolas's family didn't know, well, she'd been honest enough. Why convict him with a name?

"Halcon," Arturo breathed.

Charity shrugged, then her knees buckled in spite of her resolve.

"Get the child inside, out of the sun." Doña Anna smoothed her fingers over Charity's clammy brow and Arturo slipped his shoulder beneath hers.

The hacienda proved a haven of coolness. All three Carillos departed to provide for her, leaving Charity to examine cove ceilings and arched doorways, silver crucifixes and mahogany furniture. Not her imagined colonial outpost. Centered on a carved sideboard, a white china bowl sat heaped with oranges.

But their scent faded beneath a cloying wave of attar of roses. Even as she identified the essence, Charity heard skittering female feet, rushing taffeta skirts and twin gasps.

Their costumes might be foreign to her, but Charity felt weary at their familiar expressions. "Aghast" might be a bit strong, "put out," too weak. Aunt Penelope had said her niece "offended gentle sensibilities." Judging by the short girl's arched eyebrows and the taller one's suddenly covered lips, California sensibilities were no different from Boston's.

Goose, did you think they would be?

Charity pinched her shoulder blades together and met their gazes. The tall girl must be Nicolas's sister. Though her face mirrored Doña Anna's, she lacked the lady's serenity. Her white lace mantilla billowed. Her skirts swished. Her eyelashes fluttered. Her brown eyes sparked with curiosity.

"*Buenas días,* you must be Señorita O'Dell from Boston."

The girl's fluting voice matched her incessant movements. "And you've had a rough journey, have you not?" She half-turned to her companion. "She is the one the sergeant spoke of—"

"Excuse my sister for the twittering little bird she is."

Charity felt a warm hand between her shoulder blades. For an instant, she knew it for Nicolas'. He'd tried to rescue her before, unnecessarily—

But, no. The hand and voice were Arturo's. Did all *Californios* handle women so? She didn't dislike it, really, but it seemed—possessive. Even now, Arturo's narrowed eyes and tensed jaw made him seem a hunting hound protecting a bone that might be tasteless and, she looked down at her ruined stockings, well-chewed, but none the less his.

"My sister Barbara, and Esperanza Ortez, Nicolas' *novia*," Arturo bowed toward each.

If she were a wild creature, alert for predators, Charity thought she'd mark Esperanza as the most threatening being here. Heady rose perfume, thick coiled hair, black brows and furred lashes were lavished on a voluptuous figure which reached only, Charity judged, to her own shoulder. But Esperanza's unmoving topaz eyes warned all those dressings were protective coloring. She neither spoke, nor nodded at the introduction.

*Novia.* The word echoed as if from a distance. This confection of a girl could not be Nicolas' fiance! She mustn't trust her self-taught Spanish.

"Charity."

This time her ears were not deceived. Framed in the curved doorway, silhouetted against the sunlight outside, stood Nicolas. Relief surged through her. His strong fencer's body still widened only in the shoulders. His lustrous black hair fell across his forehead before being brushed back to touch his white collar. Nicolas was the same. Even his chivalry remained. Within the hand holding a flat-brimmed hat, he clasped a crimson rose.

His arm moved away from his chest as if he'd enfold her in a hug and Charity bolted forward.

"Nicolas!" His name on her lips felt like welcome. *Her* welcome, though she spoke it. She'd blend in, survive, in this foreign place if, on occasion, he'd shelter her under that arm.

She pretended to trip when his glittering eyes dimmed, when he turned away from her to tuck the rose into Esperanza's twisted hair. For the barest second, tears pricked Charity's eyes and a strong hand of betrayal gripped her throat.

"Well, truly, Nicolas," she drew herself into the boyish, hands-on-hips stance which had served her well at Harvard. "Is this how you greet your old roommate?"

The sliver of silence which followed her words was broken by the ching of silver conchos which ran from hip to ankle on Nicolas's leather breeches. She wished for a grin to transform his face into the one she knew, but none came, only a quick lightening, a trick of reflected sun. His arm encircled her shoulders in a brief, comradely embrace, the same warm move which had followed hours of raucous swordplay four years ago.

Doña Anna took a silent step closer and shook her head. Charity felt Nicolas' hug loosen, then cool. She looked up to see his brows draw together in a line both paternal and stern.

"You have had, I hear, an unsavory welcome to California."

"Surprising, unsettling, perhaps, but you told me—" she slowed at the memory of the Doña's reprimand, "before—that California was still raw and exciting."

Nicolas' jaw tightened and his head snapped in the same irritation his mother had shown.

"Eventually, the bandit will hang for his treachery. You cannot know, Charity, of the injuries he's inflicted on our soldiers, preferring to champion *Indios* and disloyal *rancheros*—those who would enrich Americans rather than trade with vessels from their own mother country."

Chills skittered down her arms. Priggish, vindictive and, unless she mistook the sudden jut of Don Carlo's jaw, at war with his family. Nicolas looked the same, but he had changed.

"Nicolas, it is hardly like you to offend a guest."

Arturo's voice interrupted, strident and protective, and now his hand went to his hip as if touching a sword hilt.

"Miss O'Dell and all of those who visit California are welcome. It's only those who would sap the vitality of the Crown—" Nicolas began.

"Like Freddy?" Charity's voice rose, too sharp for propriety. Freddy had been sent here to establish a bank. And if Nicolas' aversion touched all American ventures, her ebullient cousin could hardly escape condemnation.

"Freddy," Nicolas's face brightened and his hand rotated palm up as he turned to the rest of his family, all suddenly relaxed and smiling. "In fact, I have a letter for you from Freddy. Congratulations on your engagement."

Nicolas pulled the tawny glove from his hand, finger by finger, and reached inside his jacket to withdraw a letter.

"Besides, Lieutenant Santana will snare that traitor before he causes more trouble." Esperanza crossed the tile floor, brushing Charity from Nicolas' side.

She won't let it go, Charity thought. Nicolas had turned conciliatory, his family had sighed their relief, but this little creature had her teeth in an argument and refused to let go.

"Señorita Ortez is the daughter of a great Royalist," Arturo's tone goaded Charity beyond the reach of her conscience.

"The last I saw of Lieutenant Santana, he, himself, had been snared," Charity tried to bite back the words when all eyes but Esperanza's widened. "The unpatriotic Nighthawk roped him from his horse and left him sitting in the sand."

For the second time in minutes, Charity's words cut a swathe of silence in the formal room of mahogany and china and silk. Yes, and was it worth it to see Esperanza's rage? Was it worth the approval in Arturo's grin or Don Carlos's consternation?

Although his expression remained unchanged, something in Nicolas's eyes reminded her of his words that night at Harvard, the night she'd been ordered to leave after snatching up Sutton's challenge when she might just as easily have walked away.

34

"Well amigo,"—Nicolas had ruffled her hair that night, forgetting for just a moment that his friend was female—"I would say you missed a good opportunity to keep your mouth shut."

# Chapter Four

"Perhaps Señorita O'Dell would appreciate some time to compose herself, and see that her things are in order," Doña Anna's voice slipped between the echoes of the lapping courtyard fountain.

Charity's eyes faltered then studied the polished floor surrounding her shredded stockings and curled-tight toes. She'd felt this disabling confusion before. Charity excelled when she argued with men—marshalling logic, statistics and examples, seasoning her intellect with desktop pounding to emphasize her point. She easily sparred against kittenish girls like Esperanza who mouthed her father's politics. But Charity knew she would never match the cool female power of women like Doña Anna.

Only mothers imparted that ability to girl children who pressed against their skirts like nestlings under a wing. Charity's mother had died after suckling her once, and her only legacy was independence.

Charity bowed her head to Nicolas's mother. The hastily braided tail of hair flopped over her shoulder.

"Maria will show you to your room." Doña Anna said, beckoning a servant to leave off hovering in the doorway.

A room? After such rudeness, Aunt Penny would say she deserved neither kennel nor corner.

"Please, Señora, you are too generous," Charity protested, "When Freddy arrives, I feel sure he will have made arrangements for my—our—lodging."

"These are the arrangements," Nicolas told her, stifling Esperanza with a quick hand on her shoulder. The girl's drawn breath ended in a huff as Nicolas handed Charity the letter he'd pulled from within his coat.

"Freddy must have mentioned that he stays with us much of the time."

Nicolas's brown eyes flicked to Charity's so briefly, as he extended the letter, that she pretended his words needed no response. She examined the gray-green blob of wax marring the folded parchment. It wunmarked by any signet that proved it Freddy's, she decided the typical omission served the same purpose.

The maid padded on low-heeled leather shoes, leading Charity to a room dominated by the most luxurious bed she had ever seen. She spared only a surprised glance for her trunks before sliding her fingers over the blue silk coverlet, decorated with pink and lavender embroidery, and peeping from underneath, lace-edged pillows. She pressed one palm hard against the bed and heard, not the expected rustling of straw, but the sigh of duck down.

"Gracias," she thanked the maid.

The girl had retreated only a few steps down the hall when Charity heard Arturo order "their guest" a meal of *carne asada*, *frijoles*, tortillas, chocolate to drink, and, of course, fruit.

Charity tapped the letter against her thigh and thought that if she were the lady Aunt Penelope had schooled her to be, she'd call out that, really, she ate no more than a bird, and a repast of such proportions—roast beef, beans and corn cakes—would only go to waste. In fact, she wished the languid Maria would run—not walk—toward the kitchen.

Charity popped the bilious green wax free of the parchment and read Freddy's bubble-round lettering.

Welcome, Charlie, Welcome! California is the most Wonderful Place. Your arrival was indefinite and there was the Chance to go Trapping with a Russian and a Kentuckian. Good Investors for the family bank, I vow. Nicolas will see to your Needs until my return. We will have Such Times here, Charity! I remain your affectionate cousin, Frederick.

And what of our damned betrothal, she fumed. She loved Freddy dearly, but he seemed determined to remain a boy.

Another, smaller note, much folded and grease-stained to transparency in one spot, had been placed inside the sealed letter.

Nicolas,

An Unmarried, Unchaperoned Lady is out of the question. You know Charlie will Never Hear of a duenna dogging her about. So, it falls to you, Amigo, to arrange one of those Marriages By Proxy we discussed. No doubt you'll be an Excellent Substitute and Charity has ever been a Good Sport. Freddy.

What in the name of God did he mean, "marriage by proxy"? Charity stared at the whitewashed wall above the room's single window, scanning her mind like the close-copied page of a book. Nicolas a substitute? For what? And why must she be a good sport?

"Freddy, you idiot!" she railed at her absent cousin. "I don't even have any bloody shoes!"

She gathered both sides of her skirts and would have flounced from the room to demand clarification from Nicolas if the doorway hadn't been blocked by the servant Maria and Nicolas's sister, Barbara.

*"Que?"*

Barbara's inquiry could only mean she'd heard the outburst.

"It is nothing. I'm just having difficulty understanding these letters," Charity flapped the missives, but her eyes tracked the tray of food Maria carried.

When Charity looked back, Barbara's head had tilted to examine her from the wrinkled pink ribbon wrapping her braid to the ripped white stockings. Caught, Barbara straightened and resumed the girlish twittering she'd displayed in the *sala*.

"Nicolas reads," Barbara offered, nodding at the letters. "But of course, you know that."

For just a moment, blatant curiosity shone from Barbara's eyes, but discretion quickly shuttered her interest. Barbara would never be forward enough to ask about Harvard, nor give any indication—other than this tiny lapse—that she suspected such outrageous goings-on.

"I can read." Her words sounded perfunctory, maybe abrupt, but Charity ached with hunger. She lifted the steaming cup of chocolate, sipped and closed her eyes to savor it. "But the words make no sense. What, do you know, is a marriage by proxy?"

"You might ask the padre, a priest?" Barbara moved to the table, rearranging the meal. "Too, Nicolas might know of it."

"I was on my way to ask Nicolas when you came in, but—"

Charity grimaced as her stomach gurgled with hunger. The aroma of spicy beef and beans wafted past her anger with Freddy, but she saw no utensils.

"Please, Barbara, could you explain how to eat this delicious meal without appearing impolite?"

The girl preened, delighted, Charity thought, to be asked something she could answer. Seated across the table, Barbara gave directions like a governess.

"Place a bit of the *carne, si*, like that, on the tortilla. A bit of *frijoles*, too, if you like, then roll the tortilla—"

Charity mastered the technique and had slid her chair back to look, somewhat chagrined, at her empty plate when a cat landed with a thump on her lap.

"Oh, Princessa!" Barbara scolded the animal as it rose on hind legs to sniff Charity's face. "Careful, Señorita O'Dell. She bites," Barbara warned.

Cream-colored, with a brown mask, tail and legs, the cat uttered a gutteral yowl before curling on Charity's skirt.

"I've never seen a cat with such markings." Charity rubbed her hands with the linen napkin, then stroked the purring cat.

What sort of adaptation did such coloring indicate? Her biologist's mind tugged her on and her fingers itched for her sketch book to record the strange beast.

"She's from," Barbara's brow furrowed, "China? Canton? One of the *hermosos Americanos*, married to my cousin Catalina, brought her to me from his ship."

Each word seemed dredged from the girl. Nicolas's sister

tucked a curl beneath her lace mantilla, fighting the jealous pout which marked her as much younger than Charity had thought.

"Well, Princessa. You're a cunning little animal." Charity scooped up the cat's limp body and deposited her on the coverlet. "But I think it's time I tracked Nicolas to his lair and asked him about this—arrangement."

"*Que?*"

How despicably rude of her to mutter in English. Charity had leaned forward from her seat on the bed's edge, to explain, when the ringing of spurs made her turn to the doorway.

In the time it took her to blink, he'd moved, but just as she'd looked up, Nicolas had leaned, indolent and relaxed, against the doorway, watching. And, once more, Charity felt pressure like a reata tightening around her chest. She wanted to tuck herself beneath that upraised arm.

Grow up. You were a child when he held you like that, teaching you to move a sword with your body instead of your hand. Do you think, *Miss* O'Dell, that he would have pressed you against the front of him, ankles, buttocks, back, teaching you to mirror a proper fencing stance, if he'd known you were a girl? Would he have gripped your wrist and flapped it—mocking you as a weakling unworthy to wield Toledo steel—until you fought back?

Besides, that graceful moment had passed. He stood tall and handsome, outlined in black velvet, not the laughing caballero of her dreams, but tense as a thoroughbred hunter on tight rein.

"Señorita O'Dell said she would track me down like a wild animal," Nicolas told his sister.

"As if *you* were a wild animal," Charity corrected.

Barbara's eyes widened then flashed to her brother to see how he accepted the revision of his sentence.

"Charity must always have the last word," Nicolas explained.

It rankled that he talked around her rather than *to* her. And, he'd never called her "Charity" before. Always, even after he knew the truth, it had been "Charlie." Today, he'd used her wretched name, twice.

"Nicolas, what is this foolery from Freddy?" She widened her legs into a boyish stance, hands perched on hips. "I appreciate the note you included—his to you—but I studied biology, not law, remember? What is this 'marriage by proxy'?"

Nicolas tugged the bottom of his vest, squaring it on his shoulders before he answered.

"It is a legal matter." Nicolas held up an index finger to silence her before she could interrupt. "But Freddy wants a priest present, too. A proxy marriage may be performed when one of the contracting parties is absent, if that person has named a substitute to participate in the ceremony in his place."

Charity nodded. It seemed sensible. In fact, Freddy might have thought of this idea before she sailed from Boston. Her brother could have stood in. That would have suited far better.

"His letter names you his substitute?" Charity's stomach lurched in protest. Had she bolted the meal too quickly?

"You—instead of Freddy—are marrying Señorita O'Dell?" Barbara leapt to her brother's side, wringing his hand.

As if it were a fate worse than death, Charity thought.

"In place of Freddy," Nicolas smiled at his sister's horror. "But what of Esperanza?"

"I won't be taking the vows," Nicolas continued. He glanced down at Princessa, who'd left the bed to bat Nicolas's boots with her forepaws. "Freddy will be."

"You're loco, Nicolas," Barbara crossed her arms at her waist. "I don't think this will be approved by the church. Or Mother, either."

"Both will approve." He bent to unhook the cat's claws from his velvet trousers, "Besides, Lieutenant Santana arrives tonight to perform the ceremony."

Tonight? Sensible as a dowager's shoes, Freddy's arrangement still pinched. Must she be married, irrevocably and permanently, tonight?

41

Nicolas turned with almost military precision to address her. "Perhaps you'd like to rest until dinner?"

"Rest? It can't be noon yet," Charity peered toward her window.

"Still."

His black brows arched, reminding her of the indiscretion she'd committed upon arrival. *Really, Charity, to be abducted by a brigand mere hours after putting ashore,* the look admonished.

"I didn't walk the twenty miles to your rancho, you'll recall." Charity's pulse lurched. If he wanted to act the prim maiden aunt, she'd give him opportunity. "And I'm certainly not tired from riding with your outlaw Nighthawk."

Nicolas regarded the gloves he'd pulled from the sash binding his waist.

"Perhaps we could talk in the *sala* then."

Oh, he'd grown so proper. He'd hadn't put even the toe of his boot over the threshold of her room. Instead, his words had drawn her to the doorway. And now he labeled their conversation unsuitable for the hallway, where servants might overhear.

And yet, when he touched her elbow, from arm's length, she matched steps that led toward the *sala.*

"Barbara, put this cat in your room, where she'll do no harm." He stopped to shake the cat free of his ankle.

"I don't know why you're so mean, Nicolas. You're the only man she likes." Barbara cradled the cat beneath her chin, and watched them move away.

The *sala,* with its carved sideboard and white bowl of oranges, stood empty. Nicolas moved a sandalwood screen across the doorway to guarantee their privacy. Again, Charity felt her pulse quicken as he turned to meet her eyes, talking not around her, this time, but directly to her.

"And now, Charity O'Dell, tell me when you grew to be such a brat?"

"I? A brat? When did you become such a—peacock?"

"That's just what I mean." Nicolas' voice stayed smooth and cool as the silver conchos that marched down the seam of his breeches. "I'm surprised by your rudeness, Charity."

"Never once have you called me 'Charity,' until today. Even when you *knew*." She cursed her childish retort until she saw her words made him pause. A dark line scored his forehead, a line of worry ill-suited to his fussy performance.

"Still," he began. His expression softened as he cocked his head. His bound black hair curved inside the white collar to brush the side of his neck.

"I'm sorry if I've been rude," Charity rubbed her fingers between her brows as if she could erase his frown. "I would never embarrass you on purpose, Nicolas."

The corner of his mouth twitched with the start of a smile.

"Of course not," he said, and the white smile appeared, in spite of his gruff head shake.

"I *wouldn't*," she insisted. "I might bait you a bit, but only to make you act like yourself."

"We must all grow up, Charlie." Resigned, he shrugged and the smile faded.

"Except for Freddy," she put in, stepping closer.

Instead of the open hand she would offer a shy dog or cat, she evoked her cousin's name. It had lightened Nicolas's mood before; perhaps it would work again.

Nicolas gave a short laugh and nodded in agreement.

"Except for Freddy. He'll be truly sorry he wasn't here to greet you."

"He won't be sorry, Nicolas," she joined his laughter.

Her surge of joy felt quite out of proportion to the mere appearance of Nicolas's smile. She squeezed his arm as she continued.

"Freddy will be far more excited to hear of my adventure with a masked night rider—"

Nicolas pulled away. Though he strained to the end of her arm, she didn't loosen the fingers clinging to his sleeve. When he looked up from her ill-bred grip, his lids hid any warmth she'd imagined in his brown eyes.

"The man is no joke, Charity. If he isn't stopped, he will ruin colonial California, surely as plague or a conquering army."

When she released his black velvet coat, he patted her hand twice.

"Guerro—Lieutenant Santana, that is—will be here tonight. If it seems appropriate—"

Nicolas broke off to caution her, and Charity thought his tone treated Santana as a friend. Somehow, she'd equated the lieutenant with the bully boys of Harvard, and thought Nicolas would stand against Santana as he had Sutton.

"Not all gentlemen discuss politics with ladies," Nicolas lectured. "The 'bluestocking' concept is singularly Bostonian—but if he cares to, Guerro can explain the dangers of Halcon."

Beyond his frown, levity hummed in Nicolas' voice. Alerted by the incongruity, Charity studied Nicolas as if he were a creature she'd sketch for her notebook. He threatened like a watchdog whose growl sprang from duty and whose wagging tail revealed his heart. At school, most boys had hidden vulnerability behind swearing and swaggering; Nicolas had withdrawn, masking himself with regal reserve. But, always, for her, he'd been warm, accepting and *charming*. Even Aunt P. had admitted it.

"That Carillo boy is too charming for his own good," Aunt P. had sniffed once, when Nicolas flashed a swordsman's salute and smile from outside her parlor window.

Damnation, why, now, had he turned his coldness on her?

They must remain friends, if only because Freddy had as little skill wielding a sword as a cooking spoon. She'd pined to duel with Nicolas, a real opponent instead of a shadow in the corner of Aunt P.'s basement.

To that end, she should never allow him to fade off into the glacial recesses of his mind, as he had, now.

She knew their friendship dangled from the thin thread of his good humor, but before she could stop herself, she spoke.

"Do you know the most despicable thing about you, Nicolas?"

"Only the *most?*" He asked.

"Maybe the only despicable thing," she amended, undeterred by his amusement. "You are so damnably controlled. It makes mere mortals furious."

Nicolas went still and all bantering vanished, spinning beyond reach, down the dark well of memory.

"I never called you Charity?" Nicolas frowned, harking back to her earlier remark, forking fingers through a lock of black hair upon his brow. "Not later, fencing on your aunt's lawns when we were supposed to be taking a turn about her garden?"

Nicolas evoked memories fragrant with lilacs fat as lambs' tails, with sun-warmed grass and turf springy beneath her feet. Although she stood staring at this Nicolas, seeing the sun-etched lines at the corners of his eyes, her mind presented a vision of a younger Nicolas and of herself, constantly backing.

*. . . Parry. Metal glides on metal. Parry again. Gracefully, but much too slowly, she turns his sword aside until gliding shaves into grating and suddenly she misses a parry, her weapon dipping into open air. She struggles to regain balance, to retreat from Nicolas's relentless blade . . .*

Now Nicolas balanced no blade. Fatigue made her yearn for afternoons when he had.

"Never." She shook her head and the untidy braid wiggled. "You called me 'Charlie,' never 'Charity.' Do you remember—"

The smile hardened on her lips when Nicolas yawned.

"I find that curious," he said, "Because it's as 'John's sister, Charity,' that I've remembered you."

Nicolas granted no rebuttal. His curt bow and extended arm ushered her from the room. Deftly as he'd once flicked aside his blade and left her floundering for balance, Nicolas withdrew.


Charity licked the faint salt of sea wind from her lips. Dusk had grayed the *rancho* walls and the Carillo family moved about inside the candlelit hacienda with suppressed excitement over her wedding.

"Señorita, don't chill yourself."

45

"I just needed to breathe, Pilar. Thank you."

Charity smiled at the square-bodied Mexican woman who served as Barbara's duenna and lady's maid.

"It amuses her," Barbara had explained, earlier, "to speak in old Spanish proverbs. She doesn't think we've had a proper education, you see."

The older woman—who had played nursemaid to both Barbara and Arturo in Spain—had sniffed at this.

Now, hands on hips, Pilar silently reprimanded Charity's insistence on submitting her person and hair arrangement to the night air. Clearer than words, Pilar's crossed arms told Charity the woman had no intention of recognizing such a clumsy excuse.

As deferentially as possible, Charity turned back to the wooden rail of the upstairs balcony. Barbara had bragged that Rancho de las Aguas Dulces boasted the only two-story structure south of Monterey. Don Carlos had insisted on the complicated construction because the added height made it possible to scan the sea he'd yearned for while in Spain.

Two long strands of hair had already strayed from Charity's coronet of braids and they waved on the breeze. This time last night she'd been sitting atop her trunk, kicking her heels with the pleasure of watching waves roll in. She hadn't worried Freddy wouldn't come. She hadn't worried her friend Nicolas would scorn her. And certainly she never dreamed of a man like Nighthawk.

Charity inhaled the salt-sharp breeze. His leather clothing and his hair, as he'd bowed to kiss her hand farewell, had smelled of sea wind. Not like Nicolas, scented with a civilized combination of Jerez sherry and velvet! Charity crossed her goosefleshed arms and nodded.

The renegade Nighthawk would never chide her "brattiness," nor sneer at inappropriate manners, she told herself. Then again, the man didn't even speak.

He didn't need to. She got on with beasts, and they didn't talk. Charity's fingers tightened around the rail as she remembered the bandit's touch on her leg.

The memory started as a chill between her shoulder

46

blades. It shivered in a spiral down her spine and curled warm at the small of her back. The touch had been curious, not threatening.

Aunt P. would have considered her ruined, if she'd glimpsed the nightrider's hand beneath Charity's skirt. Even his half-smile, granting a flicker of respect after she'd pulled him from his horse, would send a proper Bostonian scurrying for the altar.

Fiddle. She picked a sliver from her finger and shook her head. The altar, indeed. Might as well consider marriage with the phantom she'd first thought him, silent on his black horse.

A rustle of petticoats sounded in the doorway behind her. "Señorita?"

Barbara stood silhouetted against candlelight from within.

"Pilar, if you will excuse us, *por favor?*"

When Pilar showed no sign of moving, Barbara added, "I would have a word with Señorita O'Dell, before the wedding."

"I dance to the tune that is played," Pilar inclined her head in mock submission and shuffled from the doorway.

Could it be so late?

The priest, Father Salinas, had arrived just as Pilar wove the last hair pin into Charity's coronet. He sat chatting inside with Don Carlos, but Charity had heard no announcement of the alcalde, Guerro Santana.

Careful, Charity warned herself at the surge of derision she felt at his name. He may be Nicolas's friend. There's no need, none whatever, to let the man know you witnessed his humiliation last night. To plow the sand with one's rump—

An unseemly gurgle of laughter burst from her lips before she stifled it.

"Are you crying, Señorita?" Barbara took a rustling step to touch Charity's shoulder.

"No, I—"

"I'm sure this isn't the wedding you dreamed of," Barbara sighed. "No solemn ceremony, with a proper gown and satin slippers, no happy guests and gifts."

As Barbara took a breath, Charity looked askance at her.

Charity had dreamed no such thing. She counted herself a realist.

"No decorations, no wedding feast—"

"—no husband," a voice Charity recognized as Arturo's cut in. "Now, little sister, if you've made our guest feel sufficiently pitiful, perhaps you will hush and reconsider. Señorita O'Dell has both a priest and, if he deigns to appear, an alcalde to preside at her ceremony. Dignitaries enough, I should say. She has the Carillo family as joyous guests and tomorrow," he bowed and Charity noticed that Arturo alone, of the Californians she'd met, had hair colored mahogany brown, not black. "Tomorrow, Señorita, you will have a fine gift, if not from your *novio*, at least, from an admirer."

Barbara touched the fingers of one hand against the heel of the other in a mute parody of applause.

"My courtly little brother," Barbara rolled her eyes.

"Is he? Yet he calls you his *little* sister. Who is younger?" Charity saw the two regard each other with long-suffering eyes.

"Alas, we are twins," they groaned in unison and Charity guessed they had recited the words a hundred times before.

"How interesting!" Her hands clapped of their own accord. What an opportunity for study! She'd never met twins, never even seen a pair, except the twin kids of a neighbor's milk goat.

Hooves on rock, a clink of brass-buckled harness and the grunt of a tired horse sounded at the rancho gates.

"Ah, Barbara's future *novio* approaches." Arturo pretended to straighten his sister's mantilla, but she swatted his hands away.

"In his dreams, perhaps," Barbara sniffed.

Charity leaned over the balcony rail. The hacienda's front door opened and Nicolas stepped to the center of the light washing the courtyard.

Arturo stiffened like a hostile dog. When Charity looked straight into his face, for they were of a height, she saw his eyes narrowed as Nicolas's had been. Arturo's glare targeted Santana, but she almost imagined it aimed at Nicolas.

"You don't like Lieutenant Santana," Charity hazarded.

"Heresy," Arturo's lips barely moved with cold humor.

"He is a very powerful man," Barbara began, but then she faltered, brushed the white lace shading her yellow underskirt and resumed her earlier butterfly fluttering.

"Oh, none of that is important! Politics have nothing to do with your wedding. Don't chew at your lip so, Señorita. You will make it bleed." Barbara twined Charity's errant hair back into place. "Come inside, dear Señorita O'Dell."

"No need to worry who will take command of the hacienda after Mother passes on," Arturo grumbled at his sister. "Not so long as Barbara survives."

"Arturo, run ahead and inform Father he must pour Señorita O'Dell a glass of sherry," Barbara said grandly, "And you must put a smile on your face, Señorita, before you pretend to wed my brother!"


Nicolas Carillo straightened his shoulders with such stiff precision an onlooker might believe a bar of iron had been welded along his spine. His body paid with burning muscles for the contrived posture, but Guerro Santana had come to expect lofty carriage of his royalist friend and supporter.

"Señorita O'Dell, let me introduce Lieutenant Santana of Mexico City, our alcalde," Don Carlos said, stepping to intercept Charlie as she entered.

Ah, Father's charm never flagged. Don Carlos tucked Charlie's hand through his arm as if her garishly flowered dress were the height of fashion. He ignored the fact that she and Santana had encountered one another under politically, embassing circumstances. Don Carlos hesitated not a heartbeat when he gave Santana the title alcalde, though he'd usurped it while the title's proper bearer attended the Emperor Iturbide in Mexico City. At best, Santana was a stand-in.

A stand-in. Nicolas adjusted the crease in his linen cuff, pressing it flat against the dove gray velvet of his coat. Were any in this room not pretenders? The bride had uttered no word of concern over her absent groom. His parents and siblings substituted for a church full of guests and he, Nicolas Carillo, would act as Charlie's proxy husband.

"Enchanted, Señorita O'Dell."

Guerro took Charlie's hand. It drooped limp from her wrist until the Spaniard kissed it. Then she seemed to suppress a shudder, rolling her shoulders backward as she freed the hand to push gold-rimmed glasses up her freckled nose.

Both the alcalde and Charlie glanced his way. Guerro smirked at the girl's discomfort, while Charlie's eyes, almost obscured by the reflecting disks of glass, begged him to end her confusion. Nicolas swallowed.

Charity O'Dell would only make trouble for him. Crowned with black braids and lips so red they must have been rouged, this girl wasn't Charlie, the child who'd hidden her tears in his Harvard closet.

No, this Charity was a young woman, even if she still radiated boyishness. Though the top of her head didn't reach the first button on his vest, she looked to be half legs, and too thin, except for an acceptably—no, be fair, Carillo—an alluringly full bosom. Her legs and shoulders, under his exploring fingers last night—and what, in the name of all that's holy, had *that* been about?—had swelled taut with a swordsman's muscles, yet she displayed no athlete's grace.

Upon entering the room tonight, she'd tripped on the edge of a rug, then accidentally rapped her hand against the door frame, just trying to pass through it. She'd stood sucking the sore finger until she noticed his stare, then she'd wiped the soggy thing on her skirt and clasped her hands behind.

Nicolas took up his glass of burgundy and twirled it. By age twenty, Charity should have outgrown her two bad habits.

Worst was her rampant curiosity. Those insistent mooncalf eyes followed his every move. Not by way of female flattery, either. Her drive to *know* could kill them both.

Less deadly, but so irritating he almost preferred the spice of danger, was Charlie's sassiness.

Pray *Dios* she kept her painted lips shut tonight. At least through the introduction. And, ah, she did, lowering her forehead at Guerro's title, allowing candles to glint on the intricate meshing of her hair. She dipped a curtsy so proper, he smiled.

Then he stepped close enough to see beyond the spectacles to her assessing blue eyes.

His little roommate had taken in Guerro Santana and found him attractive, Nicolas thought. Her eyes skimmed Santana's gold mane, brushed back in waves and cut bluntly over his blue collar. Her eyes feinted left, right, back again as she examined the broad shoulders and expanse of uniformed chest, complete with gilt cording, sash and medals. She saw not a man whose form promised beefy bulk past middle age, but a great golden lion of Castile.

By the Saints, Carillo, the girl harbors no such thoughts. No Boston-bred miss could guess that Santana, exiled to colonial California by the floundering emperor of Mexico, planned to use the assignment as a last chance to prove his worth.

Very well. Let Santana act the lion of the Castle. Nicolas recalled a painting, brown and red and gold, which showed the eagle of Mexico, curved beak and talons ripping a viper to bloody shreds. Even lordly lions could be bedeviled by a brazen bird, and California hid just the avian to do the deed.

"Señorita, your sherry," Don Carlos offered, pressing a fragile glass into Charity's hand.

"You look a little pale," Doña Anna's tone, as she addressed Charlie, seemed half exasperated, half kind.

"She's had a long journey, and no food to speak of," Arturo defended, sweeping to Charity's side.

Despite her boyishness, Nicolas scoffed silently, Charlie had made one conquest.

"Charity will be fine." Nicolas forced his inflections flat. What sensible older brother would allow Arturo to pursue such pointless chivalry? He'd insist Charlie leave the rancho within the week.

As his father stepped back, Nicolas cut between Arturo and Charlie. Her skin shone milky and moist under the splatter of

51

freckles. Waves of hair had straggled loose from her braided coil, and clung, pasted with perspiration, against her temple.

"She suffers from nothing that alacrity with the wedding ceremony won't cure. Don't you agree, Padre?"

From the tail of his eye, Nicolas saw Santana and the priest nod to each other. Then he watched Charity's fingernails turn white and heard the snap of crushed glass.

# Chapter Five

"Damnation!" Charlie snarled. Her fingers darted apart and the goblet plummeted to the carpet. It lay there, whole except for a C-shaped shard that freed the amber wine.

No one questioned the mysterious rage which had moved her fingers to snap the glass stem. Maria swooped to blot the rug and Barbara covered her rounded lips with an edge of mantilla before turning to the padre and alcalde. Arturo and Nicolas bumped shoulders accidentally, then again, aggressively, as they lunged to her side. Doña Anna commanded both out of her way.

Ladylike fainting might be preferred over smashed glassware and cursing, Charity decided. As Doña Anna inspected her for injury, Charity willed her hand to stop trembling like a captured rodent.

"There are no cuts?" Nicolas' mother slid her thumb over Charity's palm, then glanced up.

"I—?" Charity shrugged apologetically. She could have at least bled. Preferably blue blood.

"She reacted too quickly to be cut. I neglected to tell you, Mother. Charity is a schooled fencer, with a fighter's reflexes."

For one instant, he was her Nicolas! No sardonic quirk lifted the corner of his mouth, no cold tension chilled his face. Only a wide smile flashed under his black mustache!

"I did not know." Doña Anna's cool fingers turned the

hand to examine its back. "You're all right then, Señorita O'Dell?"

How kind of her, exceedingly kind, not to mention the accursed trembling. But Charity felt her belly shrink against her backbone as Doña Anna's eyes skimmed her gown from square neck to waistline. Perhaps the flowered print *was* too gaudy. But Charity had deemed it less than sensible to waste money or trunk space on a wedding dress, when the same money and space could go to books, a year's supply of paper and two bottles of ink.

Doña Anna's inquiring look vanished. The others closed in, supporting her almost bodily as the alcalde and priest read their ceremonies. The room still spun as it had before, but she focused on Nicolas's arm, grazing hers as he stood at her side.

*Don't wonder why you're having the vapors like a proper Boston miss, instead, feel that soft velvet, gray as dawn. Concentrate on the ceremony and resurrect your Latin.*

The priest, in a rough-textured gray habit, motioned them to kneel. A pink wing-shaped birth mark crossed Padre Salinas's cheek, as if an angel had gently slapped him.

"—the ring?" Lieutenant Santana's tone indicated he had spoken before. But what had he asked?

She looked to Nicolas, wetting her lips.

"I apologize for not asking earlier," Nicolas leaned so close he stirred the hair against her ear and she shivered. "But, did Freddy send a ring? He left nothing with me." Nicolas took a breath, and shook his head when she didn't respond.

"Never mind." He drew the gold Harvard ring from his hand. "Hush," he anticipated the protest which had already gathered at the back of her throat.

The ring, warm and smooth from his hand, comforted her cold sticklike fingers, but it swung upside down from the spot where Nicolas positioned it. A poor fit.

Charity sighed and swore to return it after the ceremony. Tomorrow at the latest.

Nicolas's hand curved beneath her elbow and urged her to

stand, apparently by order of the priest. Damnation, had she gone deaf?

His right hand remained as his left reached across to cover her clenched fingers and pin her arm against his side. Her breath must have been coming in pants, for now she felt it slow.

"To be absolutely official, amigo," Santana's voice joked, "I believe you must kiss the bride."

Charity felt a blush flood her cheeks. Another coast, another culture, but she recognized Santana's tone. She'd heard the same derision from suitors who coveted the O'Dell banking money. Impeccable manners hadn't hidden voices which assured her they courted money, not a bookish, bespectacled spinster.

Nicolas's grip shot pain through her arm to her fingertips. Her body took warning, tensing before she looked up at him.

A bulge appeared at the turn of his jaw before he gave her hand two pats. Santana's mockery had angered him as well. Nicolas turned her to face him.

*It's just me,* she imagined him saying. Nicolas's forearms underlay hers as his fingers cupped her elbows. Those arms became the walls of a haven. *Just me, your roommate Nicolas. Remember how I protected you from the big boys' hazing? How I taught you to fence? Helped with your studies? It's just me.*

And before Charity could give herself a mental shaking to end such idiocy, Nicolas kissed her.

Ambrosia, food of the gods, existed in California. Charity hovered in limbo between invigoration and lethargy. She'd eaten far past the point of hunger, making a meal of appetizers Doña Anna called *chalupas,* before white-gowned maids offered salads, tureens of vegetables, and meat. Meat in pit-roasted slabs, in tiny red-sauced cubes and meat shaved to paper-thin slices, rolled into tortillas and called "enchiladas."

She touched the white napkin to her lips. It was just as well she'd concentrated on dinner, since conversation had not ebbed to the female end of the table. It might be her wedding feast, but there at the foot of the long table, bracketed by Barbara and Doña Anna, Charity was ignored.

Horse talk had dominated the men's conversation. Straining to hear the rapid, idiomatic Spanish, it seemed Nicolas had argued the merits of imported bloodstock over the native mustangs Don Carlos favored. Arturo had challenged Father Salinas's vow that mules bested horses when facing grizzly bear. Only Santana found no one to debate his assertion that heavy Spanish bits rendered hackamores, the bridles used by Indian vaqueros, outmoded.

Speak of Halcon, she demanded silently. Nicolas had promised to encourage Santana to discuss the bandit, but now Doña Anna had granted the men permission to withdraw. What could she do? Follow Barbara off for a rousing hour of needle work?

"Guerro, you know Señorita O'Dell is from Boston. . . ."

Charity stopped, half risen from her chair. Imagination did not create the humoring tone of Nicolas's voice. ". . . and she would hear us address the problem of the outlaw Halcon."

"A boy might find such tales diverting, but, truly, Señorita, the man is only a self-aggrandizing peasant." Santana's words rolled with the satisfaction of a man savoring the honey of his own phrases. "Before I could begin to explain his twisted motives, Nighthawk will—" he stroked his tawny beard in mock regret, "—have had his wings clipped. Permanently."

"Oh, Señor—"she broke off as Arturo, standing just past Santana's shoulder, gave a quick shake of his head.

What? The topic? The form of address?

"Alcalde, please." Charity saw Arturo's wink and took a deep breath. "I don't seek diversion. I'd like to understand. I am, after all, planning to live in California."

Don Carlos laughed.

"A discussion of *bandidos* has no bearing on your life here, *hija*. Better you should talk with my wife about setting up a household, hiring servants and," Don Carlos tilted his head to smile, "Children?"

Doña Anna and Barbara rose as if it were settled.

How could she insist, without offending? Nicolas refused to meet her eyes. Again, Arturo came to her rescue.

"Pardon me, Father," Arturo lowered his eyes in respect. "But we have forgotten Señorita O'Dell is now *Señora* Larkin."

And able to do as she pleases, his tone implied. How strange that she'd forgotten. The food, the talk of horses, her yearning to hear of Nighthawk, had wiped it from her mind: Freddy, absent two years and not even present at this wedding, was now her husband. She touched Nicolas's ring and made a fist so it wouldn't slide from her finger.

Doña Anna dropped a half-curtsy and Charity gnawed the painful spot on her lip. Had she gained permission or condemnation? Charity pushed her glasses up. They passed the bridge of her nose and then fell back with an audible thump. Give me a scientific treatise, a translation from French to English, she prayed, but please, spare me the intricacies of society.

Doña Anna and Barbara departed. After urging Santana to stay the night, and being refused because the alcalde must return to check the watch before midnight, Don Carlos departed to make his own rounds within the *rancho* gates.

Charity perched on the edge of a dusky green velvet chair. Ankles crossed so only the toes of her slippers showed, assuming an air of polite feminine interest.

Santana made himself at home in the *sala*'s chair-cluttered corner. He poured a deep glass of brandy, unbuttoned his blue coat, shrugged it off and folded it to show gold-fringed epaulets. He sprawled on a small couch with a weary moan.

Charity willed Nicolas to stir this conversation from where he leaned, still in his gray velvet jacket, one arm stretched along the mantelpiece. Only his fingertips moved, twitching like a cat's tail, tapping the stone surface inches from his full wine goblet. But it was Arturo, standing behind her, who baited the *alcalde*.

"Are the reports true, *Alcalde*, that you met Halcon last night?"

Charity's throat went dry and her fingers itched for her

57

sketchbook. If only she could take down every word to match, later, with her memories.

"A brief encounter of little consequence," Santana shrugged. "Señora, just what do you wish to know?"

Santana's eyes blamed Nicolas for this irritating interlude, but Charity snatched at the faint encouragement to speak.

"First, I suppose, what is it he steals?"

"Steal?" Santana frowned, "Rarely objects. The occasional necklace or purse of gold, but his quarry is more often the good name of the hidalgo, the *gente de razón* of California.

"You see, Señora Larkin, Spain only recently released these lands to the control of Mexico. And now that the government is changing, colonies are in a state of," his hand tipped from side to side, "Instability.

"So. Who is in control?" Santana asked rhetorically, cocking a gleaming black boot over his left knee as he warmed to her interest. "The Emperor of Mexico? The missions? The Governor of California? No. Control has been awarded to the local alcaldes, humble men like myself who are close to the people of each district or pueblo."

Humble, indeed. Santana's high cheekbones slanted beneath imperious eyes bluer than her own and he seemed to aim his broad chest like a battering ram.

"It makes sense, no? To let one who knows the people rule them? But not to Halcon. He desires anarchy. Each *Californio*, he believes, should decide with whom he will trade—the Russians, the English, the Americans—" Santana ducked in apology. "Each *ranchero* should discipline his own *Indios*, that *Indios* separated from the missions should be allowed to go their own ways."

Santana drained his brandy. Before he wiped its final droplets from his mustache, Nicolas tilted a crystal flask to refill the glass.

"But how do you know all this about him? Surely he doesn't give speeches or publish tracts?" Charity's eyelashes brushed her glasses as they always did when her mind threatened to outdistance her lips. She blinked quickly and repeatedly.

Unattractively like a rabbit, Aunt P. had commented more than once.

"The brigand never speaks, but his actions are loud enough." Santana pressed his outstretched fingers on the knees of red breeches which fit like the skin of a chili pepper. "Carillo, you tell her the stories. You've studied his habits.

"Nicolas is highly educated, as you know, Señora. His mind assembles facts and sets strategies to stalk Halcon. I supply only gunpowder and blades. For the truth is," Santana admitted, "I care only that the outlaw is hanged before the old alcalde returns, and I am recalled to Mexico."

"You are too modest, Guerro." Nicolas said. "The rogue may possess cunning, but no great intellect. His offenses fall into three simple categories.

"First," Nicolas directed his conversation past Charity's left ear. "He champions the Indians. He feels the native people have been—what, Arturo? You appear eager to explain."

Arturo moved nearer Charity. "Halcon feels, Señora Larkin, that the Indians have been victimized by both soldiers and missions. It's not a popular view, especially since the *Indios* are our best vaqueros and farmers. But there are signs that our civilization doesn't set well with them.

"The recently reported death rate of their babies—What was that troublesome figure, Alcalde?" Arturo frowned. "Seventy-five out of the last hundred baptized were dead?"

Charity felt a stroke of admiration for Arturo's daring.

"There is no shortage of *Indios*," Santana snorted, sipping his brandy as Nicolas interceded.

"His second cause is the independence of *Californios*. As Guerro said, Nighthawk would have *rancheros* trade with whomever they chose, even form contracts or marriages with outsiders."

"And those things are illegal?" Charity asked.

"Not exactly," Nicolas's eyes almost met hers before his fingers pushed the wine glass an inch farther down the mantlepiece.

"Least harmful—in fact, the blackguard never harms a

soul, never gives soldiers the satisfaction of an out and out fight—"

"Saints! I've men who won't forgive him for that," Santana agreed. "All his 'stealth' hides the heart of a coward."

"As you say," Nicolas continued. He snapped his head in a nod that might have been a salute. "His most annoying habit is harassing the troops stationed at both the Presidio and the mission," Nicolas concluded.

"Harassing?" Charity asked. She must commit the night-rider's three-point plan to paper. Indians, independence and harassment. This revolt sprang from the mind of an intellectual, not a brute.

"Harassment, Señora, like unlocking the *presidio* jail to free a *ranchero* arrested for trading with Russians," Arturo paced, looking up as ideas came to him. "Thwarting the whipping of renegade Indians by—how was it?—stealing every *latigo*, every whip," he added, in explanation. "In the *presidio*."

Arturo so gloried in the outlaw's escapades, Charity knew that if she hadn't met the bandit last night, she might have guessed Nicolas' little brother to be Halcon. But she'd been near enough to take Nighthawk's physical measure, and Arturo was too small.

"Guerro," Nicolas' grim voice intruded. "You are too generous to say he's no thief. You neglected to mention he captured the payroll for your soldiers."

"And then turned around and gave it to the *renegados*—the Indians hiding in the Sierra!" Arturo added. "And the devil feels moved to write the Emperor, bragging of each misdeed."

"Those ensconced in the capitol have no idea what it takes to control a primitive province such as this!" Santana gestured with his hat. Its embossed eagle flashed a dismissal.

"Señora," Santana snapped his boot heels together. "Congratulations. Perhaps at our next meeting your husband will have returned and we can talk of more entertaining subjects."

Arturo escorted Charity down the silent hallway while Nicolas walked the alcalde to his horse.

Charity closed her bedroom door and stepped to the window, listening for the lowered voices of Nicolas and Santana.

60

At first, their words fell beneath footsteps and the rasp of a match. Then she smelled the acrid scent of tobacco.

"Will we be treated to her presence at the Vargas wedding?" Santana's muffled tones told Charity he clenched something between his teeth.

"Unless her husband returns and I can be shut of her sooner."

Could Nicolas really feel so? Charity closed her eyes in concentration, but caught only snatches of the conversation.

"*Jesus Maria* . . . didn't even recognize me . . ."

Santana's voice vaunted with self-importance and she wished she dared correct him.

". . . ankles . . . skirts twisted up . . ." the voice faded under creaking saddle leather. ". . . does have a glorious throaty voice, which, in its place could be . . ."

Could be—what? Charity pressed her knuckles against her lips to stifle her impatient growl.

Santana's laughter chugged low in his chest. The smoke singing her nostrils signaled he'd moved closer.

". . . much too serious for one such as Freddy Larkin. That look, *amigo*, that expression of intense concentration that grips her little face . . .

"I had a cook once, a conscientious old hen, who inspected her children's scalps morning and night, looking for—what are they called? The young of lice?—nits! That's it. Your house guest has the very look of old Juana, scratching about for nits."

Hooves clattered on adobe bricks. Nicolas called a quiet farewell and Charity stood beside the window, her back against the wall. She stared up at the ceiling and told herself Aunt P. had been right. Eavesdroppers heard only ill of themselves. Charity crossed her arms over her chest. A brand new bride, alone on her wedding night should not be called a nitpicker.

Grateful there'd be no labor for gallant, masked patriots this night, Nicolas tilted the chair on its back legs, careful not to kick the lantern beside his book and glass of burgundy. He propped his boots on the porch railing. Ay, his back hadn't been built for such posturing.

Having peeled off his dandy's coat and sash, Nicolas savored the ocean's distant rush and decided he'd follow Santana's example and drink his fill of the mission's fine dark wine.

He should sleep. Last night at this time, he'd been racing along the beach with Charlie slung over Hamlet's withers. No restful errand, that.

He must get rid of her. Curse Freddy for slinking off with those two from New Orleans. And Freddy's note had told her the trappers were Kentuckians! Not that Freddy knew or cared for the difference. Which just proved—

And they were married. *Cristo*. Might as well wed two children for all the means they had to survive in California. With one word of encouragement, Santana would exile them both. The lion of Castile distrusted foreigners.

Satin quilts rustled inside the hacienda, and he heard the overstuffed mattress shift on its frame. Charlie felt restless this first night in California.

Too damned bad. Just as her bedroom stood close enough for him to hear her every move, Nighthawk hid that close to her prying eyes, ears and analytical mind. A hazard waiting in pretty ambush, Charlie could rip the careful, painstaking fiction of his life.

More rustling, then the clink of the water pitcher against a glass. What did a girl with a man's mind wear to bed?

Nicolas gulped his wine without tasting, then inhaled and reminded himself how much he'd craved this drink during Santana's discourse on Halcon. He'd heard Guerro's lecture time and again, but never before an audience attentive as Charlie.

Eyes still as a painting's had fixed on the *alcalde* and then, each time Guerro drew breath or stroked his chin, Charity had half closed her eyes, as if inscribing notes on her mind.

Perhaps he'd pack her off to the *pueblo* until Freddy returned. The town of Nuestro Señora de los Cielos Azules— our Lady of Blue Skies—lacked Santa Barbara's cosmopolitan bustle, but Charlie, Barbara and Mother might be convinced to go shopping. If Charlie's flowered "wedding gown" were any example, she possessed no proper attire for the Vargas wedding.

Mother understood what was at stake, though her incredulous glances said she thought him a fool for worrying. Two weeks ago, when Freddy departed, Nicolas had confided that he didn't want Charlie about. When no polite escape from obliging Freddy had presented itself, Doña Anna had agreed to keep the girl at bay.

Mother might be right, he thought, arching his spine away from the chair's wooden back. Perhaps he overestimated Charlie. Hell, it had been four years. Maturity might have magnified the weaknesses of her sex. Already she'd shown herself nervy as a mare, snapping the stem from her wine glass.

"Oh. Hello."

His boots slipped from the rail and thudded against the porch as he heard Charlie's little girl voice, quiet on an intaken breath.

Midnight darkness hid all but her toes and a white flounced hem. The lantern's orange glow faded as it stretched toward her, but its pale light illuminated her from below, dancing beneath her gown.

"You can't come outside in your night dress!" He hissed. Even as the words left his lips, he cursed himself for forgetting his icy hidalgo tone.

"I couldn't sleep."

Charlie moved across the porch, graceful as a ghost until the flounce snagged on a rough board. She bent straight from the waist, like a boy, not dipping her knees as a girl should— *Jesus Cristo*, he *could* see her legs, outlined all the way up to their joining.

"That's all very well, Charity—"

"Nicolas," she heaved a weary sigh and moved closer. "I thought I'd be alone."

Charlie settled at his feet. She pulled her knees up under the gown, circling them with her arms before resting her chin on their shelf. A curtain of loose black hair hid her face, then dropped rippling, curling, tangling past the lantern's light.

"When will Freddy return?"

Nicolas knew he should smile at such melancholy longing in a homesick girl. But he didn't smile.

"How should I know, Charity?"

Damn. Get it right, hombre. She's said nothing to provoke proper Nicolas Carillo to snarl through his teeth. Poor little bride.

"I haven't meant to embarrass you, Nicolas. I know quite well what a poor female I make."

She kept her head bowed and pushed her burden of hair over the shoulder furthest from him. His hand could span that pale neck. *I know what a poor female I make.* Jesus. But he wouldn't correct her. No one would be safe until she left.

"I don't suppose with Freddy it makes much difference." Charlie's rueful laugh still didn't turn her toward him.

"The men he's with are from New Orleans, not Kentucky, and they've crossed the Sierra before. They're experienced trappers."

"I'm not worried."

Without spectacles she looked softer. And that mustang's mane of black hair! Four years ago, it had been chopped short, not reaching her chin.

"There's nothing Freddy likes more than playing—certainly not banking—and I suppose playing is what he's after. I would have gone, given the chance."

You won't be, he started to tell her, then realized as Freddy's wife she might do any number of mad things. Fun-loving Freddy would let her sidesaddle a grizzly if she pressed hard enough. He should have the ceremony annulled and send her home.

Charlie watched him, waiting. Her eyes didn't look a bit owlish, just wide open and wary. Their expression recalled the instant he'd known she was no boy, known it as a buck knew a doe. For all her awkwardness and doubt, Charlie looked very female.

"That was a nice kiss."

64

She said it with the same enthusiasm she'd awarded the *chalupas*. Very tasty. No wonder they'd chased her out of Boston. And she didn't have the decency to drop her eyes and blush. He wrapped his hands hard around the arms of the chair.

"Since I grew up—no, really, since Daddy died, I don't think I've been kissed." She stared into the black courtyard, leaning a shoulder against his knees. "Robert used to kiss me sometimes, but then he decided I was too old, and Aunt P.—"she chuckled, "Aunt P. wanted me to believe me she was only doing her Christian duty, so she pushed me away."

As I should, he thought. I should jerk my legs back and let her fall sprawling on the porch if that's what it takes. But the urge to stroke that glossy hair pulled his hand like magnetism. He cleared his throat as if he could clear his head.

Suddenly she rose up on her knees, close. Her eyes traced his throat and loosened shirt. A man could not mistake such behavior. She wanted another kiss. Fine. A brotherly kiss would be—fine.

"You've been drinking wine," she observed.

Take that, all-knowing Halcon. The child wasn't waiting for a kiss, just sniffing his breath or eyeing the glass, over there, like Princessa on the prowl.

"I have."

Is that *quite* all right, he wanted to demand of her, but the insult had leveled his feelings.

Insult? No. He'd made an idiot miscalculation of the sort he could not afford. She was simply Charlie, in spite of those violet eyes and torrent of hair.

"I only noticed," she twisted his ring on her finger "that you left your full glass on the desk, before the ceremony, and then left another on the mantle, afterward."

Si, simply Charlie. The Charlie he'd warned Mother about. She didn't have to suspect anything to begin scratching for facts. How long from this first night until the lightning instant in which she realized he didn't drink so his wits would be sharp. How long from then, until she knew he required quick wits to remember all the lies? Si, simply Charlie.

"Shall we fence tomorrow?" He asked, leaning forward, certain she'd take the lure.

"Oh, yes! It's been so long," she squeezed his arm hard enough to hurt. "You must be patient, Nicolas, but I'll work."

"In the afternoon, if you like. I ride out at dawn, with Father. But, perhaps after the midday meal?"

"Whenever you say." She rose without the wobble he expected, then stood fidgeting with his ring.

"Oh! Your ring! I should give it back." She slid it from her finger and held it outstretched.

A gentleman would rise, and Nicolas Carillo was nothing if not a gentleman. He unwound from the chair.

"Keep it until Freddy returns and gives you a proper one," he waved her hand away. "It will make everyone more comfortable."

"No, really, Nicolas. I must have packed some trinket I can use to signify I'm married." Her arm remained extended and he saw her shiver in a breeze that coursed through the patio. "I really should—"

"Probably you should."

Again he felt a pull that made him imagine folding her palm around the ring and pressing it safely against her chest. No. He'd lasted twenty minutes, perhaps thirty, without touching her. He rubbed his palms together as if warding off the night chill.

"But why don't you keep it?"

"I will then." With a high-headed grin worthy of that feisty Harvard freshman, she squared her shoulders. He felt so certain she'd turned to go, his shoulders drooped in relief.

"How is my Spanish, Nicolas?"

A girl of twenty shouldn't stall like a child dreading bedtime.

"You inspired me to learn, but Aunt P. would allow no tutor. I had to teach myself," she prattled, "but I think I'll improve, hearing it and speaking it all of the time."

His teeth locked over the answer she wanted. You're doing fine, *querida*. Your progress is brilliant. I'm honored to have inspired your learning.

"Get to bed, Charity."

Her sigh stirred the gown. She lifted her hand in a boyish gesture, half-wave, half-salute, and left him.

Get to bed, little bride. His eyes followed the last edge of white hem as it trailed through the doorway. Get to bed and be glad the man on this porch is stuffy Nicolas Carillo and not the outlaw Halcon. Be glad, for a man behind a mask can say or do whatever he likes, no matter who gets hurt.

# Chapter Six

"You insult me, Señorita. I know you don't intend it, but you insult me, nonetheless."

Arturo dropped the reins at her feet. He turned away, allowing no reasoning looks or sensible discussion to interrupt his ire.

The horse tossed its head and swiveled pointed ears as if following the argument.

Charity didn't want to turn away Arturo's gift. The animal shone like satin in the morning sun and its small tossing head and delicate hooves showed Moorish blood. It shifted, unsure, and she noticed the dappling, fine as gray lace, over the bunching muscles of its deep chest and haunches.

Beautiful and strong, the horse appeared perfect for carrying her into the country for research. Those tiny hooves could pick a path up shale-strewn hillsides. That long sloping shoulder guaranteed a gentle ride for a novice such as she.

Arturo had presented this beauty as a wedding gift and insisted she'd be rude to refuse.

"It's your husband's job to give you a fine horse and a saddle decorated with silver as a wedding gift." Arturo's judgmental tone softened. "But, since Freddy is absent, and, as a *yanqui* he can't be expected to know, it falls to your host. A *ranchero* often gives such gifts to his guests."

Arturo removed his rust brown hat and seemed to speak to it as he brushed imaginary dust from its brim. His movement scattered the yard dogs which had followed them to the corral, and Charity held out a hand behind her back, beckoning their return even as she watched Arturo.

Arturo's hair had the same rebellious curl as Nicolas's, twisting loose from its ribbon, it twined into the boy's collar. Arturo looked and acted like the Nicolas she'd known at school. No, she corrected herself as Arturo risked a sidelong glance; the little brother was sweeter.

A slick nose nudged her fingers as one of the dogs ventured near.

"Very well, Arturo," she gave in, eyes lowered to encourage both boy and dog, "If you promise this animal—"

"Luna, because he is the silver as the moon," he supplied.

"—Luna, then, is even-tempered enough for one who's only ridden bridle paths, I accept."

Charity bent to take up the reins, and though the sand-colored dog darted away, the horse stepped close, misting her spectacles with grassy breath.

Charity gathered a handful of skirt and poised to accept Arturo's offered knee up into the saddle, when the dogs, led by the inquisitive sandy one, barked welcome to Nicolas's chestnut.

Only the animals exchanged civil greetings.

"The porch would be a better mounting block, Señora Larkin," Nicolas advised.

Charity stopped her hands from perching on her hips, forced her fingers from fists and regarded him.

Had she imagined last night's friendliness? Imagined that they'd discussed her bridal kiss? Imagined his affectionate acceptance as she leaned against his knee to talk? This morning, *hidalgo* haughtiness rested like a mantle on the man who sat the side-stepping, sweat-marked chestnut.

Deliberately, Charity nestled her knee in Arturo's interlocked hands, pushed off her earthbound foot and thrust herself onto the horse's back.

Don't look up, ninny. Don't listen to Arturo's laugh, gloating as if he'd won some contest. Just hook your leg into the sidesaddle, before Luna dumps you on your backside.

"Where are you riding?" Nicolas dismounted and dropped

69

his reins, loosening his cinch before squinting over the saddle toward his brother.

When Arturo remained silent, Charity noticed he held the bit shank of the strangest horse she'd ever observed. Its coat glowed the yellow-brown of tanned deerskin, with mane and tail of black, but its markings were oddly primitive. From forehead to Roman nose, a black sash bisected its face. Black stripes angled across its forelegs. How, she wondered, greedily, could she investigate this animal's ancestry and unravel its mysteries?

"Tigre and I will take the Señora on a short ride, to see if she and Luna suit each other," Arturo answered Nicolas.

"Just see that she's back in time for our fencing session." Nicolas's tone, more than his words, raised Charity's eyes from Tigre's legs. Like the fabled zebra, she'd mused, until Nicolas's commanding words caught her up short.

Arturo answered his brother's directive by jamming one boot into a stirrup. His hiss sent the horse into a plunging run and Arturo balanced there, leg in a straight line to the stirrup, until Tigre passed the rancho gates. Charity bolted after.

Only when Luna drew even with the yellow horse did Arturo raise his right leg in a leisurely manner to the other stirrup, and settle into his saddle.

"You did that on purpose," Charity gasped, sawing her reins until the gray slowed to a trot. She glanced back to see Nicolas, standing hands on hips, and almost lost her balance.

"Sí," Arturo answered, eyes shadowed by the dark hat, "Stay a few weeks and I'll teach you how."

"I don't believe so," Charity answered primly, but her thoughts were less sedate. If Arturo and she had been children, they would have exerted bad influences, one upon the other.

When they returned, Nicolas saw Charlie's wind-flushed cheeks and loosened coronet of braids and wanted to punch his little brother until he bled. Not only had the intruding pup made her a present of Luna, Arturo had been first to show

70

Charlie California as it should be seen, from the back of a fine horse.

Silent, Nicolas stood at the sideboard, turning an orange in his hands, as he watched her.

Charlie's open smile faltered into a frown, as she stepped into the *sala*, but not because she'd noticed him.

Her ungloved hands tucked up tendrils of hair. Tidying herself for a chance meeting with him? Or did Charlie sense Esperanza's critical presence in the *sala* air thick with Esperanza's rose scent?

Esperanza's appearance, two days in a row, surprised him. Nicolas weighed the orange in his palm. He couldn't name another time, since their betrothal, that she'd been so attentive.

A year ago, *si*. She'd been at his elbow each time he turned. Esperanza's father, Don Esteban, had encouraged her pursuit of Nicolas, heir to Spanish bloodlines untainted by Mexican *cholos* or foreign sailors. Esteban Ortez had braved the frowns of doñas and duennas who whispered he granted Esperanza too much freedom ensnaring the eldest Carillo son.

The same mothers and chaperons allowed that Esteban's eyes showed not a glimmer of gloating when he rose at a children's Posada fiesta to toast his daughter's betrothal. Even as her father raised his glass, Esperanza had stroked her fingernails down the spine of Nicolas's jacket. Breath spicy with cloves, she'd whispered she preferred a long courtship to a headlong rush into marriage before the onset of Lent. Her torrid pursuit had cooled and, now, five months later, they had yet to set a wedding date.

Just as well, Nicolas thought. A man in his precarious political position couldn't risk an attentive wife.

Today, Esperanza's eyes had swept the *sala* in quick inspection. Then, dotting a sisterly kiss on his cheek, she'd fluttered off with Barbara, speaking only of the Vargas wedding.

Nicolas replaced the orange in the white china bowl. As he watched, Charlie's stern, silent lecture to herself ended.

"It would appear you enjoyed your ride."

Startled, then embarrassed she hadn't noticed him, Charlie tried to disguise the surprised bunching of her shoulders.

She had looked perfectly content to bustle through the room on some errand of her own. Why the devil had he detained her?

"Luna is a wonderful horse," Charlie said, standing so close he felt coolness rushing from her skirts. "He'll be perfect for pursuing my studies. But then," she studied him through her spectacles, "I haven't told you of my research, have I?"

Her fingers dashed back the tendrils around her face and she wiggled a bone hairpin through her braids.

"Where is Esperanza?" Charlie's impatience interrupted his response. She abandoned the wayward plaits and jammed the pin into her riding habit pocket.

Her gesture drew his eyes to her attire. The ink-blue serge, too small and rusty with age, had rubbed a pink mark on her throat. Both arm and shoulder seams had frayed where Charlie's growing bones, pressing the flesh of her boy-thin body, had forced the cloth to make room. A generous man might say the costume lent Charity coltish charm, but the same man would be rendered speechless by the entrance, behind her, of Esperanza.

"I'm here, Señora Larkin. How kind of you to inquire."

Cut like a man's shirt in blood red silk, Esperanza's blouse flowed into the waistband of a black riding skirt. Her garments floated while Charlie's bound. Her voice throbbed while Charlie's rasped. Her skin showed smooth as white rose petals while Charlie flaunted apple-red cheeks and freckles. If a painter were searching for models, Esperanza's rich beauty would make her the aristocrat and Charlie would be cast as a maid.

Poor little—no. Nicolas crushed the thought before it formed. Charlie deserved no pity. She could no more rival this wealthy royalist's daughter than become a Californian. If Nicolas Carillo found himself too tender-hearted to show Charlie the way of things, Esperanza would not.

"Señora, since your Señor Freddy has not given you bridal

clothes, what will you wear tomorrow?" Esperanza toyed with the black leather quirt looping her wrist.

"I—" Charity's voice creaked to a stop and her teeth worried her lower lip. "What *is* tomorrow?"

"Surely the Vargas wedding is not so soon?" Nicolas asked.

"Of course it is, *tonto*, silly one," Esperanza flicked the quirt so its lash soundlessly circled his leg and fell back. "Can you keep only cattle and politics in your handsome head?"

Nicolas's back tightened, but he cautioned himself to ignore this rush of disbelief that just last week he'd counted Esperanza a bonus. No doubt he'd recall that feeling as soon as he felt her naked, beneath him, once more.

Now, her cloying sweetness seemed one more layer of lies.

"Mother will help you with a gown," Barbara's clattering heels, invisible under frothing lace, signaled her arrival even before her damned kitten began batting his spurs.

"Mother says she sews because we have no decent seamstress, but truthfully," Barbara confided to Charlie, "She likes it. She's talented, Señora Charity. She'll think of something."

Princessa spun the rowels on his spurs with irritating rapidity. Nicolas bent to scoop up the little beast, but she skittered away, feinting sheathed claws at his hand.

"I do have a few gowns," Charlie said, squatting and trailing her finger along the floor until Princessa pounced, allowing herself to be captured. "Perhaps one of them would do."

Curved over the kitten, Charlie missed Esperanza's smirk.

"As you like." Nicolas dismissed the subject. "Just now, we have a lesson," he snapped a bow, telling himself he had no intention of protecting Charlie. He yearned to spar with her only because it had been years since he'd wielded a sword for pleasure.

Arturo took swordplay as a challenge to his burgeoning masculinity. Fencing with Santana, Nicolas used half his mind to record strategy for future battles. The other half remembered to falter.

"I don't understand—" Esperanza began.

"Nicolas and I attended school together, you know." Charlie squared her shoulders as she offered the kitten to Barbara.

"I learned to fence there, and I've had no decent partner since."

"What attire does one wear for that?" Barbara wondered.

"At school, a uniform of fencing whites. When I outgrew them, I took to wearing my brother's castoffs," Charlie said.

"Men's clothes?" Esperanza sputtered.

"The idea in fencing is to present the slimmest silhouette possible." Charlie ignored the outrage, turning sideways, skimming a flattened hand past her chest, ribs and belly.

Had he really done that, at Harvard, without noticing her sex? *Dios*, he must have. The explanation she used was his own.

"A skirt's loose fabric would catch the sword tip rather than allowing it to pass," Charlie drew breath to go on.

"How fortunate Nicolas has his den, to hide you from view."

Tobacco brown and expressionless, Esperanza's eyes met his.

"Are you going to dress, now? Let me help," Barbara slung the kitten over one arm and tugged Charlie's sleeve. "I want to see you in boys' clothes!"


"Let's see what you can do."

Charity had paused uncertainly in the doorway, but as soon as Nicolas spoke, she saw him standing at the sword rack in the long room Esperanza called his den. Long and narrow, with a row of expensive glass windows in one wall, the room had been built on one end of the *hacienda*, Barbara said, to hold family portraits and suits of armor. But the prized objects never materialized and the room became Nicolas' private gallery.

The room's history mattered little. The sound of a blade slipping free of its wooden rest and the perfect weight of it across her palm—those things mattered.

Charity rolled her wrist, testing the unfamiliar sword as it dipped low, curved high. She'd heard fencing compared to dancing, but never by a swordsman. Power nestled in her hand.

Charity raised the sword hilt even with her chin, as if to kiss the cross-shaped intersection, then snapped it toward the floor, saluting her opponent as he saluted her.

She drew a deep breath, expelled it and settled her torso between her thighs in a balanced crouch. Nicolas's face stayed impassive as she advanced, front foot raising on its heel to move her closer, back foot advancing an instant behind.

She moved close enough to tap his blade. He retreated a step. Again, a beat meant for his sword, but he flicked his blade aside so she met air instead of steel.

Charity extended her arm, aware suddenly, that he'd discarded his velvet jacket and vest for a white shirt. At her extension, their skirmish kindled, but before she drew a second breath, she found herself disarmed.

"Ow!"

Steel rang on the wooden floor and the sword rolled like a wheel on its hand guard.

Charity snatched the sword up awkwardly with her left hand and stood shaking the fingers of her right.

"You held too near the hilt," Nicolas lowered his blade parallel with the floor, before giving her jammed fingers a cursory glance.

"How do you know?" She grasped the sword once more.

"No control. You were batting about like it was a paw instead of a fine instrument. Try again."

He nodded patiently and she thought she must have heard him say those words, "Try again," one thousand times.

She tried, this time sliding her hand back on the grip, keeping her fingertips far from the hand guard. Once more, the sword flew ringing from her grasp.

"No, you moved your hand back too far. You extended your reach, just a little, but then you had no strength. A tiny move with the weakest spot on my blade, and you lost it."

Placing his sword on the floor, he strode toward her.

"Like this, remember?"

Nicolas took her sword, tucked it out of the way, under his arm, and cupped her hand in his.

"No, too tight," he flapped her hand from the wrist until it relaxed. "The sword's grip goes here," the edge of his hand sawed across her palm, between her thumb and index finger, and Charity tensed against a shiver.

"One grows sloppy, dueling with shadows, that's all," he told her. "Show me your grip, now." He slapped the sword back into her hand and shook his head. "Let your hand remember, amigo. It will, even if the mind doesn't."

Amigo. He'd called her friend, as if she were a boy. Hers were not the only thoughts lingering in the past.

Charity glanced up and saw Nicolas's patient frown.

"Charlie. Remember Critter, that evil-tempered raccoon of yours? Remember how you said to hold her? Gentle, but don't let her escape. This is the same." Nicolas's hand rested under hers, molding her hand.

"There. As if you hold the breast of a wild bird in your palm. Don't let her fly, but don't crush the life from her."

"Good. Perfect. Your grip is back. Try again."

Nicolas's blade slapped hers, first on the right, then the left, taunting her to follow, letting her parry, extend, parry, extend, staying just a half step too far away for her to hit him.

Charity pressed her lips over labored breaths, humiliated by her tortured thigh muscles. Nicolas was right. Dueling with shadows hadn't prepared her for dueling with a man.

"That's it, Charlie. Come on, come get me. Try a lunge, *amigo*. Not that I'll let you touch me." He parried her blade so hard the shock ran from her wrist to her elbow. "I don't want you marking me for my lovely Esperanza.

"What? Some fire? yes! Beat my blade out of your way and come get me. Yes! The feet remember and so does the arm! Good, Charlie, good!"

And this time when he circled his blade around hers, wrenching her grip loose, she held a heartbeat longer, and then he stood next to her, hugging her shoulder against his chest.

I won't wipe the sweat from my eyes, though salt stings so

much it makes me weep, Charity thought. No, I'll lean here against his chest for a moment, for the moment it takes him to remember I'm not his amigo.

It took more than a moment, but by the time he'd slipped the blades back to their wooden rests, Nicolas's stiff hidalgo bearing and hard-set jaw had returned. Charity felt a sigh building, expanding, paining her chest, but she would not vent it.

They walked an arm's length apart through the den's arched doorway, toward the *sala*. The echo of their footsteps on buffed tiles, the honey scent of candles, created a mood so formal, her breaths, ragged from exertion, rasped rude and intrusive.

"It's quite true, Anna," Don Carlos' voice reached them. "Guillermo said the parchment is posted at the bodega. Messengers are riding the Camino Real with the news."

Nicolas stopped, every line of his body intent. "Father, what is this news?"

Don Carlos took in the trousers outlining Charity's limbs, and, disconcerted, he stared straight into Nicolas's eyes.

"Lieutenant Santana has issued a proclamation stating that because Halcon has become a molester of womankind—" Don Carlos frowned at his wife's sniff, "seems he attacked a peasant in Cielos Azules this morning—because of this, the Crown offers a reward for the renegade's body."

Don Carlos's voice continued, but concentrate as she would, Charity could no longer discern every word.

"Since no one knows his identity," Nicolas scoffed. "What is to keep some miscreant from presenting the corpse of—"

First the *sala* wavered. As shimmering heat distorts a distant horizon, so Doña Anna and her husband bent and rippled. Buzzing deafened her and the hallway narrowed to a dark tunnel.

"Nicolas. She's fainting again."

Doña Anna's impatient words pierced the cacophony within Charity's head. Fighting, she flailed for the support of the wall, furniture, anything to stave off weakness.

"Truly, she never used to be so delicate."

Nicolas's annoyance sighed next to her ear, as his arm circled her waist.

"I can stand." She shook him off, straining to focus past the pinpoint dots crowding her field of vision.

"Get her!" Don Carlos's warning rang from the walls as Charity's knees buckled.

"Of course you can stand," Nicolas soothed, lifting her, one arm around her shoulders, the other beneath her knees. "You just haven't quite mastered walking yet. Let me be your beast of burden, Señora, just as far as your chamber."

# Chapter Seven

Still as the sheltering oak grove, Nighthawk sat his stallion. A breeze sifted through the branches and he welcomed the leaves' dusty shower. That, and his change of clothing might, if *Dios* were merciful, banish Esperanza's scent.

"I could not see the brigand's face," he imagined a victim confessing to the alcalde, "but he reeked of attar of roses."

He grimaced, then studied the clustered *carretas* and saddle horses, below. Further on, rancho walls resounded with music.

The Vargas wedding had attracted guests from as far south as San Diego and as far north as Santa Barbara. The Bandinis, Vallejos, the Munoz, even Uncle Jose, nearly a recluse these days, all celebrated this last fiesta before Lent.

The fiesta offered fine pickings for the leader of a movement rich in spirit, but poor in funds. The women fairly clanked with heavy gold chains and ropes of pearls, and the men carried bulging pouches of gambling gold. Nighthawk's harvest would do more than warn royalist sympathizers: it would supply the renegades who fought Santana.

Tonight his timing must be precise. At midnight, after hours of dancing, a lavish picnic supper had been served. He'd peeled Esperanza from his arm with the excuse of joining Santana indoors for a night of high-stakes gambling.

Exactly one hour into the game, Nicolas excused himself to meet the groom's godfather. In minutes, he'd left the old man nodding with wine, and escaped to the woods where he'd tethered Hamlet.

So far, the plan had proceeded on schedule. Now, dressed in Nighthawk's leather garb, he must swoop down on the fiesta, sword persuasively drawn, and make off with as much booty as he could take without risking a fight. Next, he'd trust Hamlet's years of painstaking training and send his horse running for home range. All evidence of the bandit would disappear with the horse. Nighthawk, transformed by velvet breeches and silver lace back to Nicolas Carillo, would join Santana's hopeless pursuit. The riderless stallion would rejoin the mustang band near Rancho de las Aguas Dulces and vanish.

Nighthawk's precise planning never failed. The night's events would be risky, but worth it. Still, gold and jewels weren't the stimulant making his pulse thrum loud as the flameco guitar in the patio below. No, he hated the staid, stuffy peacock—wasn't that what Charlie had called him?—Nicolas Carillo had become. He lived for these nights of danger.

"The man without honor is worse than dead," Cervantes had written. And though Nicolas sacrificed his *hidalgo* honor to keep faith with his people and his land—no one knew.

He drew his spy glass from his scabbard. Few *Californios* agonized over patriotism. Made complacent by their idyllic existence, they resented Mexico's grip only when taxes increased. No more than the few encompassed by the circle of his spyglass resisted, though many gossiped in quiet support of Halcon.

The glass wavered as Nighthawk scanned the crowd. Mother, cool in her emerald gown, talked with the bride. Tonight's enterprise would be impossible without his mother. Doña Anna had agreed to act as his voice, even though she simmered with anger. Over Charlie.

"The girl is either madly infatuated with Halcon, or pregnant." Mother hadn't looked up as she'd spoken this morning.

Speechless, Nicolas had watched her set a pin in the

blue-green dress she altered for Charlie. Her deft hands had trembled slightly as she'd flipped the garment right side out.

"Truly, I think it is the latter. A girl stuffed into tight stays might faint as often as this one, but yesterday she wore only men's clothing."

He watched his mother cross her sewing room to a dressmaker's dummy. As she pulled the dress over the shoulders of the headless form, he cursed the rigid upbringing that kept him from calling his mother a madwoman if she believed such a thing.

"It would explain why she came to California, would it not?" Doña Anna glanced back over her shoulder and raised one eyebrow.

"It could, Mother, in another girl, but you've seen her. She's clumsy, and outspoken. No man's attracted by that. You saw Santana's reaction—"

"And Arturo's." She'd held a pin in her teeth as she knelt at the gown's hem. "And your own. Don't bother to argue, *chico*."

He'd almost choked when she'd called him a boy, but she'd pressed on, still intent on her handwork.

"That first night you allowed her to see Nighthawk. That was ill-advised, stupid, really, but I explained your actions as boyish curiosity. But when you might have allowed Santana to 'rescue' her, you offered her a place on your saddle and hours to examine the outlaw Halcon."

"Mother, the night was cloudy. No moon shone. She saw—"

"Enough," Anna snipped a thread and twitched the hem into place. "You heard her—ignorant as a sheep—but still defending her abductor to you, and Santana. And then you encourage her schoolgirl fantasies by fencing with her.

"Nicolas, if Charity Larkin is as smart as you would have me believe, how long will it take her to guess?"

His mother's voice hadn't risen, but he'd seen her hand jerk back quickly, seen her regard the bright drop of blood drawn by a badly, but vigorously aimed, pin.

"When you set out to do this, Nico, when you wrung support from me," she blotted the finger on a white lace hand-kerchief, "you said it demanded selflessness and complete dedication."

For the first time since she'd started to speak, Mother's tidy blackhead raised from its work and her eyes met his.

"See that you don't forget."

And then, she'd demanded that he inquire of Charity if she were pregnant!

*Cristo,* biologist or not, Charlie would have no idea what he was talking about. Nicolas Carillo knew a virgin when he kissed one. At the end of that farcical wedding ceremony, her lips had been still and unresponsive as a peach, a flower—as a *virgin's,* damn it! Last night, there'd been no trace of guile as she thanked him for the kiss, no awareness of him as a man when she leaned against his outstretched legs.

And Mother hadn't watched while they'd fenced. No woman who knew where physical closeness led would let him hold her hand, and pound her on the shoulder.

Let Halcon explain, his traitorous mind chuckled. Some things should be shown, not described.

Hamlet shifted and snorted, ears pricking forward as a knot of deer picked its way from the woods to the meadow below.

"Shh, boy. We'll ride down a bit closer. Graze with them while I lighten a few purses. You'll be home before dawn."

But only if he concentrated. His mother had promised to signal him, by repinning her mantilla, when most of the men had finished eating and followed Santana to the *sala.*

He wanted to scan the crowd for Charlie. Why did she trip and stammer when she didn't have to? Last night on the porch, and again today, fencing, she'd floated, graceful and lovely. Tonight, she'd been painful to watch.

Laughing Dario Vargas had kissed her extended hand, and Charlie's confusion showed she'd had every intention of shak-ing hands, manfully. Then an irritatingly handsome boy, some gypsy-eyed cousin of the Peraltas, had crushed a scent-filled eggshell, a *cascarone,* into her freshly washed hair. Charlie had stopped, wide-eyed with bewilderment. Why hadn't he, or any member of his family, remembered to explain the holiday custom?

No sign of Charlie, but there he saw Esperanza. Hair center-parted and loose in thready serpentine curls, she passed by his mother on Santana's arm. Why in hell was the man back on the patio? Nicolas refocused his glass. Laughing into the alcalde's face, Esperanza traced her fingertips along the neckline of her gown. Santana's gaze, of course, followed.

Doña Anna raised her eyebrow as if looking directly through the night to meet the eyes of her hidden son.

"Yes, Mother," Nicolas said, though only the horse's ears flicked back to listen, "I see what a bitch she is."


"I don't know, Charity!"

Barbara shouted to be heard over the band and dancers. Her eyes darted past Charity's shoulder, and she ducked. An eggshell filled with bits of brightly colored glass, shattered on the patio.

"It might be as you say, something about birth and Spring. But it's the custom at Christmas, too. Would that still make sense?" Barbara whirled Charity from the path of a dozen children rushing past in rustling skirts and slapping shoes.

"Possibly," Charity mused. "It just seems so senseless," she began, then covered her head as footsteps stopped behind her and a hand seized her elbow.

"But so much fun." Arturo's laughing eyes held hers, and Charity didn't flinch until she felt the delicate shell crumble against the intricate six-strand plait Pilar had painstakingly braided over her shoulder.

"And see?" he said, "This one is filled with bits of ribbon." Arturo drew Charity close enough to whisper, "Would you believe that in the pueblo it cost me—" he squinted one eye closed as he calculated, "a dollar! For one egg! Don't look horrified, dear Señora Larkin. I would pay ten times that to stand this close and apologize for my impetuous behavior!"

"Arturo!" Barbara shook her twin's shoulder and regarded him with a pout. "Shame on you for flirting with the Señora!"

83

"Come walk with me." Arturo shook Barbara off and took Charity's arm. "I guarantee it will be more amusing than clattering about with Barbara."

They had walked several steps when Arturo confided, "All the talk is of the scandalous Señora Larkin, you know."

"What?" Charity's slipper caught a crack underfoot. Only Arturo's hand kept her from falling. "You're joking, of course."

"Of course I am not. Be sensible, Señora." Arturo tilted his head. "A pretty American lands here, is married by proxy— how many times have I explained that?—to my sought-after, engaged brother. Add to that rumors of abduction by the crusader Halcon . . ." Arturo laughed and wagged a finger at her, as if the facts comprised irresistible gossip.

Charity glanced over her shoulder to meet the eyes of three women who turned away amid fluttering fans.

Damnation. Charity braced her arms around her middle and reminded herself to behave as a veteran of such looks. Then she scolded herself. Curiosity, not condemnation, *might* have shone in those dark eyes. Curiosity she could understand.

"My mother will silence any unkind words, Señora. She plans a *bailecito casero*, a little house party, after Lent, when Freddy returns. That will satisfy most of them.

"I, however—boorish younger son!—remain unsatisfied. You are almost a member of the family, *si?* And Halcon is as close to a hero as *Californios* have. So, tell me, Charity. Tell me every word he spoke. Describe his every move."

As if Nighthawk's restless stallion pawed the earth beneath her, Charity felt again the outlaw's hand on her leg, shameless as he bound her, and she could not stutter a response.

"Señora, I must give you a fan to hide those blushes!" Arturo scolded. "Then you will tap me on the sleeve with it and tell me I dare too much. But," he shrugged and smiled, "You have no fan, so I must be a gentleman and speak of other things."

Arturo asked proper questions and Charity tried to ignore

thoughts of Nighthawk while she marshalled adequate responses.

She talked of the bride's saddle, festooned with ribbons, and hundreds of tiny copper pieces jingling like bells, but she thought of Halcon's strong sword arm, his bareback horse and teasing smile that lit the very light.

Charity admitted that she'd been startled when the wedding couple, riding tandem into the patio, had been greeted with musket fire, but silently she asked herself why she should care whose face hid beneath Nighthawk's mask? Charity Larkin, married woman and serious biologist, had no time for such skullduggery. A brigand's kiss on her hand meant nothing at all.

Arturo paused and, before she could apologize for her inattention, held Charity by both shoulders. He regarded her so intently, thought of Halcon receded.

"You look beautiful, Charity, like an *hija del pais,* a daughter of my country, not a *Yanqui.*"

"Your mother did wonders with my dress," Charity agreed.

Doña Anna had transformed the blue-green taffeta from a day dress to a party gown with tiers of ruffles from knee to hem, and a tight waist circled with a shot-silver sash.

Charity's fingers curled so tight under the top ruffle, a quick movement might cause it to rip, but Arturo ignored her embarrassment.

"It is not the dress, Señora," he assured her.

And if I were Esperanza, Charity lectured herself, I would return the flattery and tell Arturo how handsome he is in his russet velvet trousers and embroidered vest.

"Those spectacles just won't stay in place, will they?" Arturo watched her push them up her nose. "Do you need them?"

"Of course!" She snapped.

"Arturo!" Giggling girls, lurking behind a hedge, beckoned.

"I forgot!" Arturo smote his forehead, clowning as he tugged Charity's arm. "These bad girls slipped away from their duennas because I promised you'd tell stories of Halcon."

85

"Arturo, I can't," she whispered.

"They're just little girls, Charity."

"He's in enough trouble because of me." Charity swallowed against an absurd grabbing, like the beginning of tears, which threatened to close her throat. Thank goodness the glass lenses hid her misting eyes.

"All right, Señora." Arturo patted her back. *Dios,* I swear you unman me, Charity O'Dell y Larkin." Arturo shook his head, then lowered his brows sternly. "But I will only put them off until tomorrow night. Then I will insist."

He bowed and strode off to console the disappointed girls.

Arturo's formality reminded her of Nicolas, who had disappeared inside the hacienda. Deserted, she bristled because Nicolas hadn't acted the gracious host and squired her about the fiesta. After all, she knew no one.

Nicolas had hardly even greeted her. His eyes had dissected her blunders, until she felt relieved by his strutting departure. Now she missed his comforting familiarity. Even if he scorned her, he let no one else do so.

Esperanza had tensed, surely ready to pounce on some flaw in Charity's appearance, when Nicolas had tightened the hand on his *novia's* arm. Esperanza had pretended to misunderstand the gesture, and surreptitiously raked her pointed fingernails down his back. Tawdry behavior, Charity judged it, and she'd gritted her teeth, later, when she'd noticed the pattern of scratches still marking the fine velvet jacket, marking him Esperanza's.

Stranded among a hundred guests who'd known each other since birth, Charity drifted toward the fountain and the voices beyond. Waxy pink camellias banked an alcove sheltering women—including Doña Anna, Barbara and Esperanza—who had gathered to enjoy their picnic supper in relative quiet.

Charity braved the sudden attention her appearance caused, working her way, eyes downcast lest she stumble on some *señorita's* skirts, toward Barbara. Just before Charity reached her, Barbara shrugged an apology and disappeared toward the music on the arm of an amber-scarfed man.

Doña Anna shifted her skirts to make room, and Charity settled there, hearing the conversation's lull lap around her.

Had they been speaking of her? Before she could ponder further, Charity heard the unmistakable whisper of a sword.

"Halcon!"

Doña Anna gasped on an indrawn breath even as the name formed in Charity's mind. The torches lit him like day.

This is your chance. Memorize the man. Determine what he would look like without the mask. Charity's mind chattered directions, but she saw only two things: the smile that flashed from below his mask and mustache, and the glittering hilt of his sword as it rolled to aim its point at the base of Señora Martinez's plump white throat.

"Please, please, don't hurt me," Señora Martinez shuddered, her voice a faint quiver from beneath her collar of rubies.

She seemed a captured pigeon, quaking and cooing, when any fool could see the sword point lifted the necklace with perfect precision and control. She's in less danger, Charity thought, than if she were slicing lemons in her own kitchen.

Señora Martinez unhooked the ruby necklace and placed it in the *bota*, the hide bag slung from the outlaw's waist. Next, the sword point indicated the heavy gold chains—treasures from primitive Peru, Ysibel del Valle had bragged all night—adorning the teenage wife of an elderly *ranchero*.

"No, Ramon would kill me!" Ysibel del Valle set her fingers, like claws, through the chains. "They have been in his family for generations!"

Halcon smiled, keeping the girl's eyes on his as he stepped close enough to place one ungloved hand on the back of Ysibel's neck. Charity could swear Ysibel shuddered in reaction. And she did not appear repulsed.

Keeping his sword pointed toward Doña Anna, whose outrage flared like heat, Halcon dropped the chains into his *bota*.

Why didn't anyone scream? Or run for help? Fascination, Charity answered herself. They couldn't wait to see what Nighthawk would do next.

An imp of perverse curiosity whispered that she should run

for Nicolas and see how Halcon fared against a swordsman, instead of a flock of spellbound hens.

"This is an outrage! I would throw this ring to the *Indios* before I'd give it to you."

The voice spat with fury and it belonged to the only woman with backbone enough to break Halcon's spell: Esperanza. Nicolas's betrothed leapt to her feet when Halcon's blade indicated her silver engagement ring. She surged forward, and only Halcon's swift movement saved Esperanza from impaling herself.

"Esperanza, don't be a fool. Give him the ring." Doña Anna ordered. "The bauble is not worth dying for."

"Take it, then," Esperanza hissed, "But you'll have to crawl like the animal you are, to retrieve it."

She flung the ring down. It struck the adobe bricks, underfoot, and when it bounced ringing up, Nighthawk's blade pierced its center, displaying it aloft before slipping it into the *bota*. In that instant, Charity heard the women around her rustle in appreciation for the desperado's skill.

*And I rode with him.* Before the smug, possessive thought had finished, Nighthawk turned on her.

"I have no jewels, Señor," Charity kept her voice level. What could she have to fear from a man who nodded politely as he deprived each victim of her valuables?

The icy sword tip insinuated itself between her finger and the loose gold band of Nicolas's ring.

"No!" She snatched her hand back and pressed the ring, against her lips. Calm down, ninny, she shamed herself. Think. Take a deep breath and think. "No, Señor. I am sorry, but the ring is not mine to give."

Esperanza's scornful snort made Charity stiffen with resolve. *He made you give in, but damnation, I will not!* Charity set her slippers in a wide, unladylike stance and sought to catch the eyes beyond the mask. Before she could, the sword lifted and whistled down in a brief salute.

"Such audacity!"

Nighthawk probably never heard the *doña's* gasp, and Charity never knew which had spoken, because even as the salute split the air, there'd been a rustle of camellia bushes and Halcon vanished.

*Californios* were charming, cordial and enthusiastic, but Charity would never understand what drove them to stay up for hours on end, just to celebrate a wedding.

In the twenty-four hours since Halcon's disappearance, she had been head-throbbing witness to Santana's furious gathering of a posse, to a flurry of gossip, more music, more dancing, and daring horseback games which culminated with the bridegroom galloping at full speed to pluck a crowing rooster from premature burial in the sand.

All night, long tables were replenished with food and wine. Though Charity's throat felt parched from thirst, she refused to drink more wine.

Anyone who expected her to uphold the *Yanqui* reputation for an iron constitution would be sadly disappointed, Charity reflected. The muscles between her shoulder blades ached. Her eyes felt gritty. Worst of all, her mind felt fuzzy with fatigue.

She craved escape from incessant questions about Nighthawk. Only Nicolas's uncle, Don Jose, had spoken of anything else.

Better still, the courtly old man send a maid in search of orange juice. And, when the other *rancheros* stampeded after Santana, Don Jose declined.

"I much prefer your company to such foolhardiness, Señora." Don Jose had kissed her hand quickly, then stared past her, sipping brandy. "It was just such madness that killed Reynaldo."

"Reynaldo?" she asked, eager for the distraction of an exciting local tale.

"My nephew," Don Jose looked at her sharply. "Nicolas's older brother. You did not know? Were you not Nicolas's friend at school?"

"I was," Charity faltered, shock roughening her Spanish. A

brother. Nicolas's brother, dead, violently dead, before he
came to Harvard? "But he never mentioned—"

"I don't wonder that he kept it from his new friends. It was
a tragedy. And a travesty," the man snorted. "Useless. It
nearly drove a good boy to drink."

And now he drank only in private. What did that mean?
Charity's teeth worried her bottom lip as she tried to decide.

"Nicolas was my *mayordomo* for a time, while Carlos and
Anna were in Spain and Reynaldo acted as *patron* at Aguas
Dulces." He gestured at South, toward the Carillo
rancho. "*Dios mio*, Nicolas was hardly more than a boy. Never
should I have asked so much of him. But—" Don Jose shook
his head and his lips twisted in a self-deprecating scowl, "I
had problems of my own.

"Reynaldo's death, on the heels of the Sanchez girl's
disappearance—" Don Jose broke off, as a couple locked in a
dance which seemed a mere excuse for embrace lumbered
past. "Rumor said Nicolas loved her, the Sanchez girl who
ended so badly, but I tell you true, Señora, he loved my
Catalina—"

Catalina. Charity's mind swirled like whirlpooling water.
Had she heard the name from Nicolas himself? *Had* he loved
her?

"Ah! But who am I to speak of evil drink," Don Jose
toasted his own intoxication. "When I bore a beautiful young
woman with rambling, it is time I switched to orange juice!"

"No! Don Jose, I am far from bored," Charity protested,
"Truly!"

Don Jose turned at his sister-in-law's approach, "Anna,
does this one not remind you of my Catalina?"

"Jose, Catalina was a child when she left for school." Doña
Anna shrugged in a dismissal so near rudeness that Charity
felt a warning prickle over her scalp, before the two departed.

Charity rolled her shoulder muscles, trying to loosen them
within the sea-colored gown which bound her like a shroud.
*Cascarones,* her mind grumped. She couldn't imagine a more
obnoxious custom. There was nothing for it but escape.

Charity slipped through the dancers and practically ran from the perfume-soaked gathering.

Voices became murmurs and the fading strains of guitars were replaced by insect voices and the padding of her slippers, on dewy grass. Even if Barbara or Doña Anna called her, she'd gone far enough to pretend she didn't hear.

Charity stopped when she reached the horses and carretas. One animal nickered. She stroked its nose, then rubbed her bare forearms against the chill and gazed up at the sky.

One never saw such stars in Boston. Street lamps were lighted at dusk, and the stars paled by comparison.

"Keep Halcon safe," she whispered to the midnight sky. If she was wrong to pray for an outlaw, God would sort out her plea from the deserving.

Faint swishing drew her eyes back to the surrounding grasses. Charity raised the spectacles from her eyes and squinted into the darkness. A herd of deer, mystical silver shapes against the hulking carts, left the sheltering forest to join the horses.

She could hardly study them by starlight, but she felt drawn to steal nearer, as close as she could.

Several deer had dropped their heads to graze. Their teeth ground more softly than the horses'.

Those nearest her were wary, switching tails showing white. Could that be their leader, thicker-bodied and watchful, beyond?

She tiptoed toward the animal. Here, where the horses hadn't come, the meadow grass stood tall, wetting her stockings to the knee. Her second pair of slippers would be ruined, too.

The deer fell silent. Grinding stopped and each head flew up, ears erect. The form before her took shape—no guardian buck, but a horse, cropping just beyond the tree line. The deer herd moved away, parting, trotting, then running silently past the horse. Through the deep grass they'd deserted walked a man.

Did the stars shine brighter? Was she less fearful? Whatever the reason, she saw Halcon quite clearly. Though darkness bled away color, she saw he wore the tight-fitting leather garb of a common *charro*. As he stepped through the high grass, she made out buckskin leggings. Then he stood before her and a flash of white smile showed beneath the ragged edge of a thin leather mask.

Again she felt a jolt, as if some fluid rushed through her arms and legs, shrilling an order to flee. Her leg muscles tensed as she swallowed against a scream. Screaming made no sense. Neither did running. He stood close enough to touch her and his movements did not threaten.

Damnation, he kissed your hand two nights past, Charity O'Dell. He spared Nicolas's ring and slashed you a salute just hours ago.

Could he have turned cutthroat in a few hours? Unlikely. Didn't you half come looking for him? Perhaps.

Logic didn't always work. She stood alone with each breath rushing louder than those of the horse who rumbled a low nicker to his master.

Weariness. She could only blame weariness, for her inability to think. She could smell the grass and the horse and the leather of his clothes. She could see the waving meadow beyond him, the horses and carretas, some blocked by his looming form, blacker against the blackness. She heard the insects who'd resumed singing in his wake. She heard her own breathing and his, as if he'd run up the hill to her.

To his *horse*, she corrected herself.

"I'm sorry if I caused Lieutenant Santana to set a bounty on you, Señor." Her voice didn't sound like her own.

He shook his head, glanced down the hillside toward the festivities, seemed about to speak, but merely shrugged.

"Will you talk, this time?"

He'd begun shaking his head before she finished, and his expression turned rueful. Stupid, stupid girl. Don't make his rascal smile fade to regret.

He stepped back, under the sheltering trees and blacker shadows.

"I don't mind, really," she swallowed, taking two steps after him, knowing he heard the lie as clearly as she.

He held both hands out to her, as one who coaxes a babe taking its first steps. His hands were ungloved and so were hers, and when he clasped the hand she extended, he gripped so tight she felt another surge of prey instinct. *Run!* The command rang so strong she almost turned back.

She would have, but the shadows which had made the eye-holes in his mask blank hollows, disappeared. Splayed leaves overhead allowed moonlight to glimmer on his eyes. A tremor of relief touched her and before she could stop, she squeezed his hand, as if, stupidly, she congratulated him on being human.

Did he understand?

He pulled her forward, and then his arm relaxed, telling her she must choose to take the next step. He wouldn't force her. She hung back until his arm stretched in a line. Why did she want to? Why stand closer to a brigand? Why go to him?

Charity's teeth locked against her bottom lip until she tasted blood. She faltered a half step closer.

His mustache brushed the top of her wrist, slid to her curved knuckles and then he turned her hand. He paused and she strained her eyes in the blackness, wishing she could see the man who took such liberties.

As if a star marked the place, he kissed the center of her palm, then slipped her ruffled sleeve up. His second kiss touched the pulse at her wrist. She took the second step.

Halcon captured her other hand, forming a bridge between them. If she leaned forward, her chest would touch his, but she noticed suddenly, as if a cow bell clanked next to her ear, that he'd begun easing Nicolas's ring from her finger.

"Oh, no!" She didn't step away, only snatched her hands from his and joined them behind her. "I told you, it's not mine."

Faintly, she saw his smile and it turned her giddy.

"Besides, both Nicolas—Carillo, you know?—and Lieutenant Santana said you were no thief. At least, they believed that before tonight."

She filled her lungs with the grass-sweet night air. There. She'd implied a sort of criticism. She'd broken his spell.

Much better. She exhaled and straightened her shoulders. Whoever he might be, Halcon had no magical powers.

She had both hands back, and along with them, her wits. Now, she felt more like herself. Another deep breath and she'd once more be Charlie. Smart-mouthed, clever, Charlie.

Damnation, for a few moments she'd reminded herself of a bird, a weak, idiot bird hypnotized by a snake. She'd read of such things and—

His hands cupped her face and her yammering mind fell still. Charity felt each of his fingers touch her jaw. One, two, three, four, along the jaw bone until his thumbs met in the center of her bottom lip. They stroked out toward the corners of her mouth. When she leaned forward to meet his kiss, he stopped.

Cretin! She felt hot, confused and ashamed. She wanted to shield her face with her forearms, but he held them, even as he glanced away.

Noise rolled up the hill from the direction of the wedding.

"They're after you, aren't they?" Her voice sounded raspy low, and embarrassment faded under the threat of muskets.

Halcon nodded and took a long stride toward the stallion. The horse danced into silver dappling that filtered through the trees as Halcon grabbed the reins and mounted.

"Before, you told me goodbye."

He'd wheeled the horse on its haunches and couldn't have heard her childish taunt. He couldn't have, but the white flash that lit his face made her idiot heart tumble from her chest into her belly.

"*Hasta luego, Caridad.*"

*Hasta luego*—until later. Later! *Caridad*. Who could dream plain, Puritan "Charity" sounded beautiful in Spanish?

"*Hasta luego, Halcon.*"

She echoed his whisper, then wrapped her arms against her shivers, and ran, stumbling only once, back down the grassy hillside.

# Chapter Eight

*Bare shoulders—brown and muscular covering smooth ivory—showed through skeins of hair like black silk. Her head tipped, arching to bite the back of his neck. She tasted faint salt on his skin. He pulled her against him. A golden glow of light illuminated them both before a heavy weight crushed her foot.*

"Pardon me, Señora. I had no wish to disturb anyone, but you squirmed right into my path!"

Nicolas's mother apologized in a whisper. One of her hands held back the tent flap to admit a flood of sunlight.

My golden glow, Charity thought, rubbing sleep from her eyes.

"Will you never call me Charity?" Her voice sounded like a querulous child's, but Nicolas's mother dipped. Her skirts pooled around her and she dropped a kiss on Charity's dishevelled hair.

"Of course I will, Charity," the woman patted her cheek, then the tent flap fell close behind her.

She should go back to sleep. Charity stared blearily until she found the blanketed hump of Barbara's sleeping form. Already she'd accomplished more than she did in a usual day, calling to hand a haughty *doña* and having a dream which warned infatuation with a phantom—was only that, a dream.

When Charity had returned to the wedding fiesta last night, she'd learned where Halcon had been before they met on the hill.

No wonder he'd been out of breath, she thought as she

95

snatched at her pack of fresh clothes. According to every wagging tongue, Halcon had struck again, swooping down to rob a card-clever *ranchero* whose luck had run out. Rumor said Halcon threatened the man with a pistol. Not even a sword, she thought, shaking out a yellow calico gown, but a noisy, dirty pistol.

She started to pull the gown over her head, became bound in the yards of fabric and stood, blind to all but the butter-colored swathing. Just so—blind as a bat—she thought, and jerked the dress into place. She yanked tight the laces that crisscrossed beneath her breasts to tie at her waist, then grabbed up a brush and ducked into the sunlight.

Attacking her snarled hair in the open air probably strained propriety, but she couldn't bear the tent's confinement.

A horse raised its head to neigh and was answered from the other side of the encampment. Three cook fires crackled and smoked with a hazy autumnal smell, and the dozen white tents standing plump in the meadow reminded her of corn Aunt P. had popped—in a rare burst of gaiety—one All Hallow's Eve.

Charity knotted a bit of yellow satin at the end of her braid, observing that few people were awake to see her outdoor toilette. Doña Anna spoke to a nodding gray-haired woman who stirred a black cook pot. Two men raced their horses far out, near the woods. An infant cried and was crooned to silence.

Since no one would notice, Charity left her soggy shoes to dry, plucked up her skirts and picked her way to the stream, barefooted.

She drew a deep breath. Could a smell be green and gold? If so, this morning was both. Nighthawk smelled green, she thought. Some herbal scent, one she'd caught that first night, had clung to him still, last night.

Ouch! She stepped on a jagged stone while skirting a pile of horse droppings. And that should teach a lesson about spinning fancies, she scolded herself. The Nighthawk you

96

want is a fantasy. The real man is—perhaps not horse drop-pings, but a thief—a far cry from what you want to imagine.

But that dream? Charity's fingers slackened their hold on her skirts. She stared across the meadow grass and wild mus-tard.

Usually she delighted in unraveling dreams, using a scien-tific approach which said the mind knit dreams from incidents during the day. What incident did her mind mirror to show her twining around a man to bite his neck?

Male cats held she-cats by the scruff while mating. She'd seen it, and judged it barbaric. Cats had needle-sharp teeth, and their screeching had shot chills up her arms.

Did her brain warn that Halcon was no better than a tom-cat?

She sighed, recalling the honey-thick languor of her dream.

"Go scrub the moon dust from your eyes, Mrs. Larkin," she muttered harshly, hauling her skirts above her knees. "That man is no part of your real life."


What had she seen, pausing there in her yellow dress, knee-deep in mustard flowers? It couldn't have been much, for she'd forgotten her spectacles. Yet she'd swayed a bit, staring far off, before storming in his direction.

And what impulse had sent him up this oak tree? He'd left Halcon behind on the plains near Agua Dulce, and had been stuffing his shirttail into Nicolas's dark velvet trousers when he looked up to see Charlie mincing across the meadow. Now he lay full length like a cougar on this wide branch, and he liked it.

In spite of the determination in her step, Charlie hummed as she came, and her dress trailed atop the grasses and flow-ers.

He'd never seen this Charlie. He'd known her as a feisty boy, a sharp-tongued young woman, but never as a barefoot, freckle-nosed girl. Softness haloed her unguarded face, the same softness he'd sensed while touching her.

Tentative, but eager, she'd come to him. Knowing Charlie,

97

she'd only come out of curiosity. But what if she'd felt more? What if her yearning had built, every night since that pathetic wedding kiss?

Nicolas jammed his cheek against the chipped mosaic bark of the branch, molding to its silhouette in case she looked up. Halcon could recall her lips parting at the touch of his fingertips. For Nicolas Carillo, no such memory existed.

Carillo would see a slender dark-haired girl approaching the brook below him, and only recognize her as his former roommate, now his good friend's wife. A middling fencer, perhaps, but, without a sword in her hand? Intolerably clumsy.

Charlie dropped to her knees, brushed back her braid and splashed water on her face. She had to lean far down. Rain had been sparse and the stream ran well below its banks. As *ranchero* Nicolas Carillo, he bemoaned the fact. As the unprincipled brigand Halcon, he thought the drought forced Charlie to present an admirable view of her yellow-calicoed backside.

She raised her face, lips still dripping, and he saw she'd drenched the front of her gown. She scanned the empty meadow, then rolled onto her back, eyes closed against the sun.

He remained still, barely breathing. He knew what it looked like inside her eyelids. She'd see red laced with crimson, and she'd feel hot and cold at once, from the morning sun and the faint breeze fanning the wet calico over her breasts. Eyes still closed, she raised her hands.

For an instant he thought she conjured him, but Charity only held her chilled palms to the sun, before letting them fall back on the grass above her. She nestled her hips more comfortably.

He swallowed past his constricted throat.

What had years of fencing, of poising *en garde* and lunging, done to the muscles that drove those hips?

*Dios,* it would be so good when they finally joined!

No.

Nicolas heard the words echo as if he'd moaned aloud. He could never allow it. Never.

"Despicably controlled," she'd deemed him, and he would be, but he ached with wanting her. How long could he savor Charlie's throaty voice, taunting eyes and eternally fraying braid, and still send her home?

It was a good way to drive himself insane, trying to be two men: one who loved her and one who feared her.

Why not tell? The question fell into his brain like a stone in water. Charlie's quick mind had already assembled enough facts to lead her to support his cause. He could teach her revolutionary politics along with love-making.

But what of Freddy? And Esperanza?

Charity wore his ring, but she belonged to her cousin. Charity Larkin, not Charity O'Dell, lay below him.

God's blood! He wasn't some young stallion filled with the juice of his own *cojones!* Why didn't his body accept his mind's mandate that mortal sin was reason enough to keep himself in check? Why did every sinew clamor to leap from the tree and pin her where she lay?

The rebellious, corporal part of him needed scourging. If it kept Franciscan priests mindful of duty, why should it fail for Halcon? He forced his eyes to the bone-handled knife in his boot. No wire flail or hair shirt being readily at hand, he reasoned that one slash across his thigh, just deep enough to draw blood, would impede lustful thoughts.

No. Pick a fight with her, Carillo. That will ease the blood hammering in your head. And elsewhere. Make both of you furious and there'll be no room for desire. It's not you she wants, anyway. It's Halcon. Start there, if you need a spur to prick your pride.


In the heartbeat it took to spring to her feet, Charity knew it wasn't Halcon. But just as her eyes snapped open it had been. Backlit and hurtling from the branch, it *had*.

She took three deep breaths. In the first, she reminded herself both men's bodies had been shaped by the saddle and the sword. With the second, she thought two temperaments could not be more different. As she held the third breath, she wished she could recite the spell that would fuse the two men into one.

"*Buenas dias,* Charlie."

"What were you doing up there, Nicolas?"

He shrugged, as if he knew, but wouldn't tell.

"A better question is, what are you doing out here, alone?" He took a few swaggering steps, then paced, a thing she'd never seen him do.

"I came to wash my face and clean my teeth, Nicolas. I believe that's allowed in California."

"Si, but you wander off too much. Last night, when the bandit Halcon stripped Señora Martinez of her ruby necklace and Señorita del Valle of her golden chains, and took Esperanza's betrothal ring, where were you?"

"I was there," she insisted. "It was later I—now, why must you look so satisfied? I took a chill," Charity explained. "And went to find my cloak in the carreta, Nicolas." Charity met his eyes with a liar's conviction.

Again, his insolent shrug. If Nicolas Carillo had probed her mind for a gesture guaranteed to irritate, to abrade her nerves, that shrug was the gesture he would have found.

"I told you: California is still a wilderness. Beasts and men who'd be caged in Bóston roam freely, here. It is not wise to go off, unchaperoned."

"But that was the purpose of our—'proxy' wedding, wasn't it? So I wouldn't require a chaperon?"

"In one sense, but—" Nicolas shook his head as if the conversation had veered onto a track he refused to follow. "Truly, Charity, the reason I waited to talk with you concerns your health. And my mother's worries about it."

"My health." Charity watched him resume pacing, but now his hands gripped the lower edges of his vest. He looked like a banker, and she had seen her fill of bankers. "Nicolas, what are you about? Is it my behavior or my health you want to discuss?" She swatted grass from her skirts and yawned.

"My mother wants to know if you're pregnant."

The words stopped her hand in midair.

"Of course, I'm not pregnant!" Her face fired hot at the

suggestion and she began to unravel and rebraid her plait rather than look at him. "Whatever made her think such a thing?"

"Your fainting spells. And, she thought it might explain your sudden decision to come to California."

"Nicolas!" She searched his face for a sign of a joke. "You, of all people, must know it was not sudden! I came because you—"

How could he kindle an ache, deep beneath her breastbone, with a few careless words? And then forget.

"Besides," she regathered herself, gripping the half-braided plait in one hand. With the other, she patted his shoulder as if he were an obedient dog. "It would be impossible."

Cross one strand over the center, and tighten. Cross another strand over the center and tighten again. She wouldn't give him the satisfaction of meeting his eyes.

"It's not impossible, Charity." His low voice sounded maddeningly patient. "You are quite old enough to have become a mother."

"We both know age doesn't necessarily have anything to do with it, Nicolas." She retied the scrap of ribbon and tossed the smooth black braid over her shoulder.

"I have only just married." She spoke soothingly. "I have not been around my husband, and so I cannot be pregnant."

Agog. Agape. That was now Nicolas stared at her.

"Charity, you don't know what you're saying. You could still be with child."

"I *do* know what I'm saying, Nicolas." She tried to keep the anger from her voice. How dare he address her with that confusion of pity and humor? "I'm a biologist, remember? Just because I'm self-taught doesn't mean I haven't read and observed. Widely. You're trying to embarrass me, but it won't work.

"Human females are like some other mammals," she told him. "They do not come into season, into heat, if you will, unless they are exposed to their mates."

Why hadn't she noticed before how devilish he looked with

101

his thick black hair and sinister mustache? *Diablo,* she believed, was the correct Spanish name for him.

"Or to another male?" he prompted.

"Of course not!" Her words held more shock than she'd intended. Was Nicolas testing her? She strained to enjoy this rare scientific conversation, but his manner was combative.

"Are you telling me, Charity, that you believe a woman can only get pregnant by her husband? When she is," Nicolas shaded his eyes with one hand and firmly compressed his lips before continuing. "When she is"—and then he cleared his damned throat!—"is in heat?"

"That's correct." She nodded. "I hardly thought I'd have to explain such things to you, Nicolas. It's all right. Wise, in fact, since you're set on marrying Esperanza."

Before she continued, he faced away from her. His shoulders jerked as if he coughed. Or laughed.

"I don't think we should be having this conversation, Charity."

"If that's what you want, Nicolas."

Oh! He'd grown into the most maddening of men. Just when she'd warmed to the topic, he grew squeamish and turned his back.

Walk away, Charity. This is the same thing, the same thing as Sutton baiting you in the Harvard yard. Do it, this time. Walk away while there's still time.

Instead, she pointed her finger like a sword tip and reached above her head to jab between his shoulder blades.

"I knew you'd become a snob," she taunted. "But I didn't take you for a coward."

His shoulders stiffened and she knew, too late, the urge to flee.

"A coward, am I?"

Smoldering predatory eyes, not his, stopped her even before his fingers, which moved fast as a striking snake. His grip crushed her hand, holding it fast against the sash at the top of his trousers. Her pulse pounded so loudly she almost missed the words that matched his narrowed eyes.

"I could teach you such things about *mating*, little girl, that would make you beg for mercy."

She'd been right. This alarming man was not the Nicolas Carillo she knew. Something had gone badly awry. She would discover what. And she'd start by asking Doña Anna. Now.

Charity jerked her hand free and strode away.

"Charlie, I'm sorry. I didn't mean to do that. Stop, please."

She stopped, partly because it hurt to walk so quickly through the high grass without picking her way among the rocks and stickers. Partly because he'd followed her and, for some insane reason, she quailed at the thought he might touch her.

"Come back and sit down, please?" His dark brown eyes were wide and his hair disordered. He didn't look a bit devilish.

A flash of memory brought her that dream picture, projected an image of her, nipping the back of a man's neck.

"No." She continued walking.

"Charlie, I didn't mean to frighten you."

"I'm not afraid," she gritted her teeth. "And you're not a coward. I take that back. And if you think my understanding of reproduction is—" God! How hateful it was when words floated beyond her tongue! "is rudimentary—"

"*Pequena*, it's worse than that. You're just wrong."

He stared down, as if watching a marmalade-colored butterfly scale a stalk of mustard would reduce her embarrassment. "You do have it about half right," he conceded.

One lustrous section of hair curved around his ear and she remembered his boyish boasts that someday he'd have a gypsy pierce his ear and wear a gold ring, just as Shakespeare and Lord Byron had in their portraits.

"Why don't you get your ear pierced, Carillo?" Charity slung her hands on her hips and kicked a lone poppy with her bare toes. "You take life too seriously."

"Charlie, I—"

She met his eyes for an instant before he frowned and looked away. If she'd been a sop for romantic nonsense, she might have guessed Nicolas had almost blurted he loved her.

103

Instead, she felt again that curious falling away, the same unbalanced feeling of lunging to catch his blade with her own, only to find it vanished, off somewhere else entirely.

"I'll sit down and listen to your lecture, but I don't promise to believe you," she cautioned.

Nicolas sat cross-legged, facing her.

"I wish someone would deliver coffee," he glanced across the meadow to the tents and cook fires.

"But, no. Now, you have come to the conclusion, from your reading and observation," he snorted gingerly through his words, "that a woman cannot become pregnant except by her husband, when she is in season. Do I have it right?"

Was he trying to trip her up? He'd repeated it so often, even she began to doubt. Where *had* she read it? She nodded.

"Charity. A woman can become pregnant by any man— husband, friend or enemy—who lies with her," he broke off, massaging both temples as if he couldn't possibly continue, but then he did. "And as for being 'in season'—That's partly true, but it happens often and it happens, whether or not she's chosen a mate." Nicolas rubbed both hands together, regarded them, then glanced up from beneath his eyelashes.

"But that doesn't make any sense!" she protested. "From a survival standpoint, perhaps, but to improve the breed—"

Nicolas's hands tipped away from each other and he raised both eyebrows.

"It may not be the best for the breed, Charlie, but it's the way of things. Truly. Choice is not always an issue. It's why husbands and fathers don't let their women wander among strange men."

She didn't want to believe him. It could damage her thesis, at the very least.

"And, about fertility," Nicolas broke off a mustard stalk and twirled it, not looking at her, "People don't only— humans—" He cast the flower spinning back into the field. "They don't only mate when the female can become pregnant."

"But Nicolas!" Charity heard her own voice break his
104

name in disappointment, as if descending a scale. "That makes even less sense! Why else would they do it?"

She fixed her gaze on him, and even though he looked down several times, drawing a breath and then hesitating so long he had to draw another, finally he met her eyes and held them.

"*Pequena,* you must trust me. As for other animals, they were never my area of study. But for humans, you may take my sterling *hidalgo* word of honor: they do it because they like it."

She could formulate no response. When Nicolas stood and offered his hand to pull her upright, she walked beside him, matching long steps to his, feeling her skirts twine and cling. Her head spun with the information he'd dumped over her. She longed for a scientific library to verify or disprove his words.

They'd walked halfway back to the tents and the aroma of roasting beef tantalizing her when she snatched at his sleeve.

"Nicolas, have you mated only with Esperanza? Or have there been a variety of women?" She waited, aware it was a personal question, but convinced their conversation had propelled them past flimsy propriety.

"Charity. Charlie. *Pequena.* My dear, strange visitor from a star," he gestured at the firmament before grasping her shoulders and shaking them gently. "Is there nothing that comes into your mind that you don't say?"


Later in the day, Nicolas regretted his words. He swore beneath his breath when Charlie ignored him. Brisk and competent as a man, she tossed full leather pouches over the skirts of her saddle. Had his candidness about reproduction embarrassed her? She knotted saddle strings to hold the bags in place, then stood behind the horse, checking the load's balance. Charlie's glance flashed from the animal's right to its left. Nicolas positioned himself near its head, but still her eyes skimmed past him. *Carumba!* Was her silence supposed to be proof she didn't speak every thought that entered her head?

Let her try to teach him a lesson! Charlie's childish behavior would make it downright pleasant to banish the little troublemaker, even if his brother had been the one to provoke her into this improper outing.

Around midday Nicolas had been examining his chestnut's legs, making ready for a race against Santana, when Arturo had ridden into camp.

"Charity!" Arturo's improper summons drew not only Nicolas, but all within earshot, as Charlie's head emerged from the tent she shared with Doña Anna and Barbara.

"If I come out, you're not going to shower me with more eggs, are you?" Charlie had asked.

"No, far better. Señora, I have the answer to your dreams," Arturo boasted.

"As always," Charlie flashed Arturo a wry smile, then gestured to Luna, tethered nearby.

"See? You're learning to flirt!" Barbara burst from the tent at her twin's admiring laughter.

"Not really."

Shock had been Nicolas's reaction until he judged, by Charlie's drenched-scarlet blush, that her coquettery had been accidental.

"I was only joking," she explained. "Tell me, Arturo, what is the answer to my dreams?"

"Father, old Señor Vargas, some other guests and their *vaqueros* are not staying for the dancing tonight," Arturo had watched Barbara wrinkle her nose and flounce away. "Instead, they're riding out to gather hides for our mission tithe. It's a chance to turn a chore into a party," Arturo held up one palm to silence her impatience. "But that's not why I tell you. Better, it will be perfect for your study."

Nicolas had felt hot irritation that Arturo, and not he, knew of Charlie's study.

"Since only the hides will be taken, this time—Don't frown your disapproval, Señora, usually we take the meat as well," Arturo soothed. "This time we leave the meat, and the grizzlies and wolves and other wild dogs, all of them, come to feast on the skinned cattle."

Nicolas had watched Charlie from the far side of his horse, crossing his arms on the animal's back, wondering why Arturo thought the tithe killing, a bloody, violent business, would fill Charlie with anything but disgust.

And then her face had lit with eagerness, and she'd babbled of feeding behavior and mingling species as she ran to find the sketchbook she'd packed among her gowns.

"I suppose I should consult your mother," Charlie's voice had come muffled from inside the tent. "Oh, I do hope this will be enough ink—still, it is polite to explain."

Still ignoring him, she'd emerged from the tent and addressed Arturo with a voice near a whisper.

"Arturo, are other women going? It's not all men?"

"I would not invite you, if other women were not present."

Arturo had huffed with offense and Nicolas smothered a chuckle. Charlie's quicksilver reversals confused even him, a man familiar with women's ways; small wonder she mystified a pup such as Arturo.

Now, as Charlie stood judging her horse's load, Nicolas felt all smugness drain away. No one had asked him along, so he stood, nursing the petty hope that she'd forget to pack something vital, which he'd remind her to bring. Charlie squatted to roll her black cape, then draped it like a serape across the back of her saddle. She'd forgotten nothing.

Even her attire was right. She'd borrowed his mother's split leather skirt and tucked in a full-sleeved white shirt, ready for serious riding. Nicolas crossed his arms so abruptly Luna shied, and words burst from his lips before he could stop them.

"Charlie, you won't enjoy this. I've seen it all my life, and it is never pleasant."

Charlie stroked Luna's shoulder, then regarded Nicolas through her spectacles, as if he were a specimen.

"They call the cattle to them for slaughter," Nicolas continued. "Did Arturo mention that? Then a rider hacks the nerve at the back of the steer's neck, felling him. One vaquero pulls up the chin to cut his throat and another rips the hide off."

Aghast at his lack of control, at the sensation of being out of breath, Nicolas stopped.

Charlie's brow creased and her tongue wet her lips.

Good, his description tested Charlie's affection for animals against her scientific curiosity. Nicolas pressed his advantage.

"At night, grizzlies and wolves battle for the carcasses. In their fight for meat, there's more carnage. Can you truly find this preferable to a dance?"

Charity's lips twitched, but when Nicolas searched her eyes, his reflection bounced back from the mirror of her glasses.

"Scientific study isn't always pretty," she agreed. "But this is an opportunity I must seize. Freddy could be back any time. Who knows what he'll want to do, where he'll want to go? I must gather information now, before I'm interrupted."

Charlie rubbed her fingers beneath Luna's noseband and Nicolas felt he'd been dismissed. The afternoon seemed to cloud over. He would have left if Charlie hadn't cleared her throat.

"Are you going with us? Or staying?"

Still she didn't look at him, but his stubbornness had outlasted hers.

"I'll stay," Nicolas told her. "I must mend things with Esperanza."

*Jesu Cristo.* Charlie twisted him in knots. He'd been panting for her invitation. His mind had pictured a leisurely ride: he'd point out strange beasts and unfamiliar terrain; she'd ply biologist's skills to his land, sketching and making notes while the wind whirled her black hair around her sunburned face.

Charlie wouldn't see the homesick student he'd been, nor the stiff royalist he mimicked. She'd see Nicolas Carillo, *hacendado*, who loved California enough to protect it with his life.

And what had changed his mind? Charlie's obvious wish that he ride beside her. Where did it come from, his perverse desire to hurt her?

"She still blames you for the loss of her ring?" Charlie asked, flicking her eyes to his for the first time since morning.

He nodded. *Dios,* if only the breech with Esperanza could

be final! But a girl of such exalted blood would not tarnish her reputation over a quarrel.

Although such privacies weren't discussed, only the most naive believed betrothed couples held off intimate relations until after they'd recited their vows.

He and Esperanza hadn't, and, until the last few days, he'd been satisfied. Now he could not stop contrasting Esperanza's "virginal" protestations with Charlie's innocent calf eyes.

He saw Charlie watch him shrug against the tightness in his back. Perhaps she'd pity him, and leave off questioning.

"Where were you during the robbery, Nicolas?"

Ah, sensitive Charlie. Her curiosity never slackened.

"Inside with the groom's godfather, Señora. A good Californian whose loyalty to Mexico and—"

"I didn't ask for a lecture, Nicolas," Charlie snapped. Then she smiled. "If I had, I would have requested your treatise on your biology, not politics."

She slid her hands into the skirt's deep pockets and leaned her weight on one foot.

"I found that discussion both informative and amusing."

Charlie ducked back into the tent before he realized the truth of Barbara's earlier assessment. Charlie might, indeed, be learning to flirt.

# Chapter Nine

Time for the noon meal had come and gone as she sat on the dry golden hillside, chewing a strip of jerky with her pencil still between her fingers. No Bostonian would look at her sun-reddened face and believe she'd just lived the best twenty-four hours of her life.

Carnage, just as Nicolas had predicted, spread below her on the plain, but she had forced herself to remain an observer. She filled the pages of her sketchbook, thinking that even if her worst nightmares came to pass and Fate snatched her back to Boston, she had pictures to fill all her rocking chair days.

Her favorite, sketched while Luna capered sideways, ears flicking to catch the sound of wind-ruffled pages, showed Don Carlos' five top *vaqueros*.

Toro first. Within his plain brown poncho, the man named "Bull" sat stiff-backed as befitted a former soldier. His neat black beard jutted forward and he kept his horse a nose ahead.

Next rode three Indian vaqueros wearing leather breeches and fringed leggings, silver spurs, white shirts and tight red sashes.

The fifth vaquero, Pancho, sported a drooping mustache and large sombrero which might have made him comical, except that he never smiled. Ever vigilant, she thought, so she'd sketched him, not looking forward with the others, but staring straight at her.

Charity popped the last shred of jerky into her mouth. The second drawing, done from a distance, lacked life. She'd tried to catch a grizzly's fluid lumbering, the flash of light through silver-tipped fur, but failed.

Here, she'd caught movement better, the cattle, heavy-headed with far-reaching horns, rumbling up out of arroyos, crashing through manzanita brush high as the horses' bellies.

She pushed her spectacles up. The bridge of her nose felt wet, and Arturo had laughed at the white racoon's mask they'd left across her sunburned face.

She'd sketched herself that way, adding a self-portrait to the group scene around last night's campfire. The fire's glow showed her next to Don Carlos, squatting on her boot heels, braid straggling, sharing coffee and stories so colloquial her textbook Spanish only hinted at their meaning.

Her good cheer after eight hours twisted into a sidesaddle had impressed the other riders. Her unconcerned acceptance of a manzanita bush as lavatory, a canteen and the hem of her shirt for performing her toilette had earned Don Carlos's smile.

Her work, however, was beyond his comprehension.

"My part of biology is probably the simplest. I make lists of different kinds of animals and describe their behavior," Charity had explained that morning. "It's called cataloguing."

"And you do this by sitting, without moving, and watching the animals," Don Carlos verified.

"It takes a lot of patience, and, well, with the bears and wolves I've seen, it's difficult to catch animals acting naturally, so, I'll scout your rancho for caves and den sites and then sit all day and watch to see how they really behave."

"And this you would rather do, than ride, or sew or play the guitar?" he asked.

"*Much* rather! Don Carlos, it can be exciting—Why, even last night, inside my tent, the sounds I heard from the bears were far different than during the day." She saw his face harden with the same coldness Nicolas wore.

"Never, never approach them at night. Not on foot. Not on horseback," he ordered. "You should not be in bear country

111

at all, as poorly as you ride. Even the best rider may be surprised. Even the best horse spooks at a grizzly's charge."

Don Carlos' eyes skewered the intention that had grown in her mind since she'd heard the bawling grizzlies last night.

Now, riding back toward camp in the orange-skied twilight, she weighed her responsibility to Nicolas's father against curiosity and the chance of a lifetime.


If her belly hadn't been stuffed with Roberto Espinosa's notorious beef and bean stew, Charity thought, silently pulling on her boots, she might have slept through the grizzlies' feast. In the tent's darkness, she untied her black cloak from the saddle she'd used as a pillow.

Night's chill cleared her head of the tent's stuffiness and noise. Her tentmate, Doña Ronda Crespi, rode like a centaur, but snored so stentoriously Charity's ears could hardly differentiate the Doña's grunts from the feeding bears.

Damnation! She swore only in her mind, leaning down to grab her twisted ankle. Why must she have freckles and be clumsy, too? She'd caught her boot toe in the reata Arturo had circled around the tent, swearing it warded off rattlesnakes.

Luna nickered as Charity slipped past the rope corral. Hours ago, she'd decided it would be quietest to walk. Vaqueros had dragged the carcasses off from the skinning place, dumping them into a nearby ravine where wild beasts could quarrel and gorge without unduly disturbing sleepers.

Although the chance of waking most of them rivaled that of waking the dead, Charity thought, stepping over—oh hellfire!—Arturo, face down and spread-eagled on his poncho, a victim of the fabled *aguardiente* of a *ranchero* named Sanchez.

"It is none of that raw, gut-eating swill sold in the pueblo," Sanchez had boasted, producing several jars of the clear liquor, to pour for all but the two females.

Right then, Charity's plan had been born. The *rancheros* had delayed their return for a day. At first she'd worried, knowing she should polish this idea. But there was no time. Nicolas would arrive soon, trusting her less than his father and brother. And Freddy! He could return and demand she act like a wife. She had no time to refine this excursion.

Besides, she'd executed many exciting sorties without using the four-step plan which had allowed her Harvard fortnight.

Think-Analyze-Plan-Act: her private strategy was the surest, but certainly not the only way to enjoy an adventure.

The moon lighted her path bright as noon, but Nicolas watched as Charlie stumbled over the reata. Mooncalf, he'd called her once. *Cristo*, she managed her legs worse than a newborn calf. And, she'd forgotten her glasses again.

Charlie *would* try something like this.

He'd been right to flail himself with desperate images of runaway horses and vengeful Indians as he galloped away from the wedding.

After failing in his half-hearted seduction of Esperanza, he'd ridden out as himself, not Nighthawk. His father expected Nicolas, and no threat worthy of Halcon existed outside his imagination. But then, not an hour ago, he'd succumbed to mind-gnawing fear, looped his reins about a manzanita, and pulled on Nighthawk's leathers and mask.

Such illogical behavior could get him killed.

Tracking Charlie along the ravine's rim, he tightened his reins, demanding the chestnut's slowest walk. Moonlight didn't reveal Charlie's bear-stalking garb. Did she wear the buckskin skirt or a night rail beneath that cloak? God help her if she had to run, unless Nighthawk swooped down to raise her.

Why, when he'd made an absolute fumbling ass of himself not two hours ago, did he itch to touch Charlie's arm? She stopped at the ravine's edge, squatting gracelessly among the rocks. *Cristo*, she gave no thought to snakes, or her clothing. Could Charlie and Esperanza possibly be the same sex?

He'd lured Esperanza from the fiesta's raucous second night, promising a replacement for her stolen betrothal ring.

"A sapphire, Nicolas, please? The other ring was so plain," Esperanza's arm had snaked around his waist as they walked. The uncertain flare of patio torches lit her rich beauty in a pout.

Nicolas had moved to touch her hair and Esperanza had grimaced. Because she didn't want her hair mussed? He only knew his irritation faded when she'd stroked the seat of his trousers.

"Don't frown so. I only want to look nice when we return," Esperanza purred, sidling against him.

"And people will talk," he'd grabbed her hips just as unceremoniously, feeling the taffeta bunch beneath his hands.

"Nicolas!" Her reprimand quaked with amusement as she restrained his hands with hers.

He'd stopped her complaint with his mouth and felt the abrupt, matched thrusts of her hips and tongue. Esperanza mimed the moves of passion, and he rose to them, stroking white breasts spilling from the neck of her gown. But when he half opened his eyes to assess her willingness, she stared abstractedly past his shoulder.

He'd let his fingers move too roughly, then.

"This is a new gown, Nicolas! I don't want it ripped."

*Dios!* True anger he'd understand better than this conversational reproof.

"I'll be so glad when we have rooms of our own," Esperanza had slipped the string of her fan down to bracelet her wrist. "Then we needn't indulge these open-air longings of yours."

She'd tapped his shoulder with the folded fan.

"I never bargained for marriage with a savage, Nicolas." She'd straightened the lapel of his jacket. "Perhaps when you're paying for them, you'll think twice before crushing my gowns."

And then—as he told himself far too often—because Nicolas Carrillo was nothing if not a gentleman, he walked Esperanza back to the fiesta before flinging his saddle onto the chestnut and galloping headlong home, toward the plains of Aguas Dulces.

Here, where he'd planned to rendezvous with Father and dutifully escort hides to the mission, *here* crawled Charlie, ripping her cloak free from a snag. Not a fit match for Don Nicolas Carillo, this girl who cared best for beasts, but—*Dios*, he craved Charlie's sweet honesty.

Dante had not described such a hell as this pit of gorging beasts. Bears, at least seven of them, held the center of the ravine, leaving the coyotes to feint in and grab. Wolves sat back, watchful and regal, waiting for an opening. Charlie crouched, transfixed, oblivious to Nicolas's approach.

The heaving backs of the bears, even silvered by moonlight, were grotesque. In mountain meadows, grizzlies reigned, fierce and alert. Tender with their cubs, the giants rolled with liquid grace within glossy pelts. But here, choking on the false bounty of slaughter, greed made them quarrelsome and ugly.

A roar erupted amid the growls. He heard a shower of rocks, and the heavy buffeting of bodies followed by a coyote's yelp.

*Sangre de Dios*, if she had fallen—No, she'd edged closer, but a young bear, slapped away by his elder, had caused the commotion. Shaking his cumbersome head from side to side, the chastened youngster scrambled toward the top of the ravine.

Good girl, Charlie, stay still. Her low form might have been part of the rock-strewn ledge. The bear should be so stuffed with beef, he'd lumber on his way, even if he scented her.

Scenting the bear, Nicolas's chestnut grunted, and took two rushing steps backward before Nicolas's legs stopped him. The grizzly rose on hind paws, swaying side to side, nose jerking upward, testing the air.

Stay put, Charlie. He's too full to spend his energy searching for you. Oh bloody hell, what could she be thinking to stand and face the beast?

"It's all right," she crooned. "I saw what he did to you. I won't hurt you." Her low tone might have soothed a child or a horse, but the bear swiped one paw at the ground and rumbled.

*Dios,* he didn't dare move until the bear decided.

Charlie had sealed her fate with *him,* if not with the bear and her Maker. At dawn, if she survived, he'd get rid of her.

At least she'd stopped babbling. If he rode between them, he'd sacrifice the horse, when it was equally possible the bear would lose interest. Damn Charlie. Those claws would cleave her to the bone.

The grizzly charged.

"Drop! Play dead!" He shouted as he jammed spurs into the chestnut.

Without a word, Charlie dove to the earth.

Nicolas slung a loop into his reata, but the bear's lowered muzzle made a head shot impossible and darkness hid its churning rear legs. With no time to wait for an opening to throw, Nicolas lashed the rope across the chestnut's haunches, forcing the horse to ram the bear, broadside.

The horse screamed, but the grizzly only stumbled a step and galloped on. Nicolas saw it draw back a paw to swat her. *Cristo!* Even a seasoned *vaquero,* a man who knew bears, who knew they'd likely grow bored with mauling and wander away, rarely had the bravery to feign death. But Charlie tried.

Nicolas drew the knife from his boot and tumbled from the running horse. For a foolhardy instant he thought of stabbing the grizzly, but by the time he reached Charlie, he knew her only chance lay in continued limpness. He dropped the knife and cast himself over her motionless form. Circling her arms and legs with his own, he might shield her.

"Don't move. Don't move and he'll go away."

Did he shout or whisper? The grizzly's next swat was lazy. He nosed the new form covering the old and grunted a breath heavy with meat. The next swipe ripped through Nicolas's leather shirt, rolling them over like children tumbling down a hill.

Heavy paws shuffled after them, then stood. Charlie's breathing mixed with the bear's, but she remained slack as a corpse. Maybe the bear had finished, sated on such a full belly. Merciful Virgin, let it go away.

Impact, as if a horse kicked him in the shoulder and then,

116

*Dios no,* dragging. The grizzly's jaws grappled for a tighter hold, gripping flesh along with leather. Whuffling growls so loud they wiped out the world, the bear tugged them along the ground.

With each step, Charlie's head hit the ground. With each step, the wild smell clogging his nostrils and the raging pain in his shoulder clamored for Nicolas to fight back and escape. Instead, he let the grizzly drag them. Not to the ravine, pray God, not to the ravine.

The dragging stopped and the grip loosened, released. The grizzly's frustrated moan came from a few steps off. Charlie tightened from ankles to shoulders as the heavy paws charged back. One slap rolled them over, then the grunting moved away.

The quiet of the night pressed in, and Nicolas' ears rang with a jangling like a dozen mission bells.

Probably it had gone. Nicolas assessed his body without moving. Feet, ankles, legs, all fine. His chest and back ached, but breathing didn't cause the jabbing pain of broken ribs. His neck and head, and *Cristo,* his shoulder, felt hot and weighted.

Charlie's head burrowed so tightly beneath his chin it almost choked him. He felt her breath against his throat, otherwise, she felt dead.

Paralysis? Not for quicksilver, everywhere-at-once Charlie. He remembered the day she'd arrived. He'd held a rose, plucked for Charlie, meant for her, until he'd remembered who he was, how she could destroy *Halcon,* and he'd given it to Esperanza. He'd seen Charlie pale and fade, but only for an instant.

God would not be so cruel. He couldn't bear to see Charlie's life end that way, could he? Fading . . .

Nicolas turned from the darkness and pressed his cheek against her hair.

Charlie's forearms tightened and her fingers flexed, as if her arms pinned beneath them—oh, sweet relief—were only numb.

117

"Are you all right?" He whispered through strands of hair stuck to his lips.

Still, she didn't speak. What, did he believe Halcon deserved a miracle? Her arms might have twitched only in reflex. That first swipe had been powerful enough to snap her spine.

Nicolas worked his hands between her back and the earth. Closing his eyes to concentrate, he felt gingerly from the base of her neck, down her back, to her hips. No wetness, no blood, just the accursed cloak, wadded beneath them. But what of her head? He'd felt it smash the ground time after time.

"Are you all right? *Pequena,* talk to me."

The pulse in her throat raced, and then her heart—or was it his?—bucked against his chest. Alive, but why so still?

"I'm all right."

Her whisper rubbed rough lips against his neck, flooding him with thanksgiving. But even as joy crested, he remembered his mask.

*Cristo,* he might explain away Halcon's costume as rough clothing, appropriate for the cross-country ride, but what of the mask? And he rode Nicolas' chestnut horse, not Nighthawk's black. Worse, he'd spoken, using Nicolas's endearment.

Never before had he made such mistakes.

And here came the chestnut—completely recognizable with blazoned forehead and flaxen mane—nickering concern now that the bear had departed. Nicolas flipped a stone at the animal, and recoiled at the pain wrenched from his ripped shoulder.

Charlie struggled to raise her head. No broken neck, then. Alive and strong! And so, dangerous. If only she were too dazed to unravel the mishmash of identities, if only he could keep her trapped with his body, he might invoke some lie to satisfy her.

Think fast as you ever have, Halcon. You'd better decide who you are and what the hell you're doing.

Things would progress more smoothly, if he quit thinking

118

with his crotch. Small consolation that he recognized it for a reaction, only a response to the fear he'd lost her. Small consolation when it rendered him incapable of thought!

He swallowed back a groan. Could there be hope for California's future when the patriot Halcon disregarded his threatened identity, his mauling by a grizzly, and focused on Charlie, squirming between his legs?

Decide who you are, *cabron*. But he only decided to clamp his legs closer and press his hips against hers. He inhaled the scents of her hair: sun and wind and madness.

"Señor? My head is spinning, but I don't think I'm injured."

Her lips brushed his throat again. God, the whole scene mocked lovemaking—their entwined legs, her breathlessness and lips moving gently against his neck. Madness.

But what had she said? *Señor.*

"*Señor Halcon,* you understand I appreciate your attempt to protect me. And I would be lying if I said I wasn't—" she drew a deep breath and held it, "elated to see you, but I assure you, I can take care of myself, and I can stand, now."

No, you can't. His mind raced. Can't take care of yourself and can't get up. He drew apart from her just enough to raise her hand to his mouth. The knuckles he kissed were dry and scuffed. Little husks of skin pricked his lips. No laved and lotioned Esperanza, but when he nuzzled her fist open, her palm felt smooth and there, at the juncture of her wrist and thumb, his teeth closed slowly, into the softest cushion of flesh—

A shudder like the flick of a bird's wing shook Charlie from shoulder to ankles. Telling himself only self-defense drove him—he was distracting Charlie, no more—he tilted her chin and let his lips fall on hers.

He'd sworn never to kiss her. Never.

Quiet and questioning at first, her mouth suddenly answered his. He widened the kiss with a savagery intended to tell her she could not take care of herself. He wouldn't allow it.

She started away. Heaven curse him for a brute! But when he would have withdrawn his lips, Charlie strained back against him.

As if the moon shattered and rained shards of light, he felt it. For the first wonderful time—not acceptance, not curiosity—*passion*. Carillo, call it by its right name. Charlie's first passion rendered him reckless.

Let her feel the leather of his mask, since she'd taken him for Nighthawk. Let her learn that there were dangers worse than grizzlies for girls who wanderd a wilderness in the dark.

Hardly aware his hands traveled her, he stopped when she winced away with a sharp intaken breath. Blood, not much, but there, stickiness oozed through her blouse. *Dios,* those massive paws might have ripped her arm off.

He wanted light and water and soft cloths. He wanted to minister to her, cover the wound with salves or—He must get her help. Now. And that meant help from the camp.

*"Mi corazon,"* My heart. He said, wanting her to remember his words, instead of what he did next.

Nicolas tugged the sash from his waist, felt the flash of surrender, then puzzlement in Charlie's movements, and blindfolded her. She struggled beneath him, but he knotted the sash viciously front, then back. It would hold until he'd ridden into camp and spooked Arturo's wretched Tigre.

Nicolas sneered at the irony of it. Arturo, again.

But their kiss and Charlie's head-tossing response had surely branded her his.

Charlie's knee jerked up between his legs and he twisted away.

*Jesus Maria!* If not for that tangled cloak, she'd have gelded him, just because she didn't fancy the blindfold!

Nicolas lurched toward the chestnut, gripped the stirrup leather and hung a moment, sickened by the pain flooding from his mauled shoulder. He pulled against the saddle horn and gained his seat as he heard Charlie's vaunting "Ha!"

The chit had worked the sash loose.

Nicolas spurred to the tents, gave Tigre a rump slap to

make him squeal, then galloped away. For all the recognition Honor had earned him tonight, he might as well have been born a swine.

# Chapter Ten

"Ay! Charity, reckless little fool! Let me be your Halcon, next time! Señora, look at you!"

Charity tugged the edge of her chemise down to cover the long wounds gouged over her ribs by the grizzly's claws.

Since her return, Charity had played hide and seek with Pilar, refusing to let the woman attend her. Instead, she'd cajoled Arturo with a secret errand. He'd delivered the pottery bowl of aloe vera, a pad of folded bandages and a goblet of wine to treat the riding injury she'd invented, and then withdrawn.

Only he hadn't. When she'd raised her lace undergarment, to inspect the gouge puffing yellow at her waist, Arturo gasped.

Charity met his eyes in the pier glass.

"Arturo, you promised to help. Please."

"I promised to help tend a scrape from a 'riding accident.'" He crossed his arms and regarded her coldly.

"Just help me, or go away," she snapped.

Arturo's lips compressed and he shook his head, unaffected.

"If I'm to help, tell me the truth. It is from a grizzly, *verdad?*" His voice wavered with horror when she nodded. "It will become inflamed, then—*Jesus Cristo!* You could die, you know, with no more treatment than this." He sneered at the meager supplies he'd brought, then reached, as if to shake her. "I begin to think Nicolas is right. You—Never mind," he

122

stopped himself. "Nicolas is not here, and I am. Sit down, and drink the wine."

He ignored her protest and lowered his head in thought.

"I know what you need, now, but who to ask?" He ruffled his hair, stood, then pressed his lips against the part in her braided hair and sighed. "*Carumba*, girl, you are a pest!"

The pine door closed behind him, and Charity sat on a corner of her bed, stunned. A month ago she'd never been kissed by a man not her relative. She touched the spot his lips had grazed, then reached for the goblet.

Heated and sprinkled with rosemary, the wine warmed her hands as she tightened her fingers, one at a time, counting. One: on her wedding day, she'd been kissed by Nicolas. Two: that same night, her hand had been kissed by Santana. Three: the young Vargas bridegroom. Four: Arturo.

Yellow sunlight flooded through her window, but she might as well have been stranded in a Boston downpour.

Moody. Helpless. Guilty. *Stupid.*

Under cover of the commotion created by Halcon's departure, she'd ducked inside her tent, hidden the blood-soaked blouse and bathed the wounds with canteen water, knowing it wasn't enough, but unwilling to tell anyone what she'd done. What he'd done.

She might have braved Nicolas's scolding and asked for help, but when the *rancheros* departed for home, he still hadn't returned. Gingerly, she'd pulled herself into Luna's saddle and gritted her teeth, trotting to catch up.

Now, she set down the goblet and pulled her quilt close against an illogical chill. The two-day-old memory of Don Carlos' flattery as they'd ridden home, might have warmed her, if guilt hadn't slipped through her guard once more: *Don't let Freddy come for me. Let me stay as I am. Free. Free to be with Nighthawk.*

His were the kisses she hadn't counted, hadn't dared remember—on the back of her hand, the palm of her hand, and her mouth. . . . That kiss, as if his lips still held hers, jolted down into her belly. It worked every time. She'd saved the memory, concealing it at the edge of her mind, then drawing it out so suddenly it nearly made her catch her breath.

Though the moon had outlined his looming shoulders, darkness had hidden his face. No matter. Vision had been unimportant. She'd breathed the green-grass scent of him, felt the rub of his leather mask and hot lightning zigzagging from her lips, through her chest to the pressure of his hips.

She drained the wine glass. Arturo said the drink would soothe her and she'd never needed soothing more. Because she found it impossible to think of him as just—Halcon.

This meeting couldn't be dismissed as coincidence. The bandit stalked her. Or courted her. At the very least, watched over her.

*That isn't your worry at all,* her mind taunted. *Not his pursuit, not guilt over the sort of female you've become, but curiosity quaking on the edge of conviction. You're not stupid. There's a thesis here which might easily be proven.*

Charity welcomed the ache in her side as she set the goblet down. Arturo's second remedy should be here soon. In the meantime, she refused to consider the theory hammering her mind.

Charity pressed the heels of her hands against her eyes to block out the afterimage of the horse. Swimming with rainbow flashes, her mind refused to serve up the image of the thick-muscled animal she'd seen on the beach, then again in the deer meadow. Halcon had flipped a rock to drive the horse away, but she'd seen: a tall dancing animal with pale mane and forehead.

Neither could her hands block the echo of his voice.

"Are you all right?"

"*Pequena,* talk to me."

A biologist employed her senses to record information and the biologist in her knew neither sentence had been spoken in Nighthawk's rusty whisper.

"Charity!"

Clacking heels, rustling skirts and her bedroom door swung open to Barbara. The girl wore her hair twisted high, but

Princessa, held like a fur muff against Barbara's smocked skirt, marred the formal effect.

"You look terrible, *chica!*"

Barbara pressed her hand against Charity's brow. "You're sick. And sunburned, too. But I see Pilar brought aloe for your skin. Ow! Princessa, ungrateful little animal!"

The cat writhed, twisted to bite her mistress' hand, then landed on the floor with a thud. Princessa licked her shoulder haughtily, eradicating Barbara's very scent.

"I told you to stay for the dancing," Barbara continued. "I knew the ride would be too much."

"The ride was glorious. It wasn't that," Charity slumped forward. Too weary to dissemble, she allowed one hand to cup and guard the wound on her ribs.

"Ahh ..." Barbara glanced back at the door before she continued in a knowing whisper. "Your monthly flow?"

"Perhaps," Charity bit her lip. As if the wound were not enough, Barbara had guessed at her other malady, one subject she could not discuss with studious detachment. " 'Perhaps'?" Barbara's brows disappeared into her black fringe of hair. "Surely, you know."

"It's happened only twice," Charity admitted.

"Twice? *Twice?* But you are—how old? Almost Nicolas' age?"

"Twenty."

"Twice? At ten years old, I—"

"Of course it's odd," Charity scratched behind Princessa's ears as the cat curled in her lap. "And it verifies what I've always known. I'm not a very satisfactory female."

"You don't want to be," Barbara shrugged. "You are clever, Charity. You have fine eyes and your hair is thick and wavy. But you care more for that cat than you do for clothes. Your trunks brim with books and papers, not dresses."

Barbara would be forced to continue on her second hand if she was set on enumerating flaws on her manicured fingers.

"You refuse to dance. And flirting? I could do better at the age of twelve, maybe eleven."

Charity's mind showed Halcon, moving like a fox through

125

the flock of well-dressed women. He'd charmed them out of their jewels, making them smile at the privilege. *If I could flirt*—

Her memory erased the other women, replacing them with a scarlet-gowned Charity O'Dell who danced seductively, head thrown back, one arm aloft, high and white.

"It's too late, Barbara."

"No," Barbara's voice drew the word out, considering. "I could do it!" She rubbed her hands down her skirts and used two fingers to lift Charlie's simple braid.

"What?" Arturo strode through the doorway, tucking a bowl behind his back. "Must you set upon her each time she's alone, Barbara? Must I protect her every instant? I have other jobs, you know."

"Then why aren't you about them? Arturo, whatever you're hiding—" Barbara grabbed for the clay pot, regarded its contents and wrinkled her nose. "*Yerba de jarazo?* That's for arrow wounds! You are so *loco*," she giggled, then cocked an eyebrow at Charity, surprised she'd confide such an intimacy. "You can't cure her with that, though you are sweet to try."

Barbara had shooed Arturo away and stood to follow when suddenly she whirled back.

"Ohhh! The fainting! Has it happened before when—?"

Charity nodded.

"I see, I must tell Mother," Barbara said, lips drooping. "Esperanza will be disappointed, but Mother will be weak with relief! She thought you were pregnant!"

In a rush of skirts, Barbara disappeared.


"Doña Anna, I know Nicolas. I lived with him for two weeks, and something has gone badly awry. He is not himself!"

Charity used her foot to trap the rolling embroidery hoop. Her words had caused Nicolas's serene mother to drop her sewing.

"Charity, you must never speak of that," Doña Anna rear-

126

ranged her skirts to cover something red and square in her lap. "And remember? You may call me Anna."

"She'd been determined to correct Anna's impression that she could be with child, but when memories of Nicolas's procreation lecture had flooded back to her, Charity found he was the only subject she wanted to discuss.

"Anna, you must know nothing untoward happened when Nicolas and I roomed together. It's just—" Charity flattened her palms against each other, tapping the index fingers on her lips.

"Nicolas took me for a freshman boy with no idea of how things went at Harvard. He helped me knot my neckties and arrange my shirts and trousers in the highboy. He introduced me to fencing and warned off the bullies." Charity wrapped her skirt close and settled on the sewing room floor.

"Hazing was fashionable among upper classmen, but Nicolas wouldn't stand for it.

"And best of all, he told me tales of California—of *fiestas*, wild mustangs and long-horned cattle. When I couldn't sleep, he told me to close my eyes, then he helped me pretend I was warmed by a California sun, gold as a pirate's doubloon, and that the canopy above me was no dormitory ceiling, but a sky so blue it seemed you could drink it."

Anna shaded her eyes. Charity looked discreetly toward the dressmaker's form in the corner, hoping Nicolas's mother suffered from more than a seamstress' headache.

"Can you imagine Nicolas, the Nicolas who lives with you, saying such poetic things?" Charity asked.

Anna's needle pierced the cloth with an audible peck and her fingers drew a strand of green silk out to arm's length.

"I wonder—" Charity paused, tempted to discard the obvious possibility of youthful rebellion. "I don't suppose Nicolas could be defying Don Carlos?"

"Of course not," Anna continued to sew.

"Still, I noticed at the *fiesta* that Nicolas is one of only a handful who speaks in favor of Santana. Might Esperanza have influenced Nicolas unduly?"

"I think a newlywed girl should fill her hours with pretty

clothes and parties, not politics," Anna flipped two loose ends of linen across the center hoop.

"I know. Barbara thinks she ought to make me over, teach me to act like a lady," Charity laughed.

Looking down at skin peeling from her sunburned hands, Charity noticed the book hidden in the folds of Anna's gown.

"What is it you're reading, Anna?"

"Reading?" Anna's voice cooled. "Ladies in California do not read, Charity. I use this book as backing for my needlework." She let the leather-bound volume slip to the carpeted floor.

"Charity," the upcurl of Anna's voice snared Charity before she could identify the fallen volume. "What harm would there be in going along with Barbara? I have a length of turquoise satin. With your hair's reddish lights, it would look exquisite."

"Anna, I have in mind a project much more interesting. I've decided—"

Charity swallowed against a throat tight as if it had been closed by a drawstring. "—to uncover the secrets of Halcon."

The doña's dubious eyes and pressed-tight lips made Charity embellish the nascent thought.

"He's someone else during the day, don't you think? He can't hide in a cave—a nocturnal beast on the verge of humanity—" she laughed and held her fingers in fierce claws.

Anna stood, needlework clutched in one hand, not quite successful in hiding her disapproval. Charity felt a surge of desperation. She wanted Anna to like her, wanted it with an ache she'd thought she'd outgrown.

"Do you understand why I'll refuse Barbara's help?"

Pity shifted beneath the irritation in Anna's eyes and it shot Charity's best intentions full of anger.

"I won't be like this fashionable form," Charity draped her arm over the wooden shoulder of the dressmaker's dummy. "Because you'll notice something rather striking about these ladies who dress so well," she reached over as if to pinch the mannequin's invisible cheek.

"They have no heads, Doña Anna," she patted the form's

wooden stump of neck. "No head and so, no mind. I won't be that way. I'd rather be dead."

Still shaken from the confrontation with Anna, Charity settled, with paper, ink well and pen, in a corner of the patio. She must prove, logically, that Halcon was no one she knew.

Charity's only audience was Luna, grinding grain as he watched, blinking, from his sunny corral across the patio.

"Think, analyze, plan and act," she instructed the horse, then donned the student demeanor which fit her much more comfortably than that of a lady.

Habitat. In analyzing any wild thing, she identified the creature's territory. Every animal, the California cougar, the gentle deer, and the ground-nesting bird from which Nighthawk filched his name, had territories.

She'd observed Halcon at the fiesta, the shore, and the ravine. She listed them all. Guerro Santana had admitted Nighthawk harrassed his troops at the presidio and the mission. Charity let her eyes lose focus. Mountains, shore, mission, presidio. A map. She would ask everyone she met where Halcon appeared, then record sightings on a map until a pattern emerged.

Jingling spurs heralded the arrival of Toro, whistling as he crossed the courtyard, polishing a silver concho against his rough leather trousers.

"Toro, where have you seen Halcon?"

"*Jesus Maria*, Señora!" Toro's right hand flew to cross himself: head, breast-bone, shoulders. "I did not see you! What is this, now?"

Charity explained.

"For me," Toro answered, casting his gaze around the patio as if confused, "I do not believe in Halcon, having never seen him."

"Well, I've seen him and he's real enough."

The words passed Charity's lips before she recognized the taunt in Toro's eyes. Why must she always snap up the bait?

"But, you are the *mayordomo*, here, si?" She watched him

129

square his shoulders and decided Toro, too, could be lured. "You know the land, and I need a map."

Working quickly before daylight vanished, they sketched a rectangular area bounded by Eastern foothills and Western sea.

"No, no," corrected a *vaquero* who'd entered the courtyard and spied their project.

A third rider and a fourth, hanging their saddles for the evening, offered stories extending Halcon's territory South to San Diego and North to Santa Barbara. The rectangle had expanded into a roughly star-shaped plot filled with x's signifying Nighthawk's attacks and tricks, when the vaqueros turned silent, parting a path to Charity.

"I would speak with my guest. Excuse me."

Had Nicolas returned? Charity scrambled to her feet, swiping a dust smear from a skirt covered with them.

Her smile stiffened at the appearance of Don Carlos.

Damnation! These Carillo men—Don Carlos, Nicolas, Arturo—all paced their words the same: smooth as poured cream, forceful as *aguardiente*.

Don Carlos' mannerly request dispersed the *vaqueros*. "Señora Charity," he shook his head, aggrieved, as he took her under the wing of his arm, "You must know it is not proper to sit in the dust and joke with men. You are a lady and my guest. It is only because you are a *Yanqui* and foreign, that the men forget themselves."

Charity found herself gulping like a fish.

*This is not fair,* she thought. Don Carlos's eyes were soft, and though she easily fought scorn or criticism, he managed to make her feel as if she'd insulted him.

Stripped of her anger, she apologized and allowed him to juggle her writing materials as he led her back to the hacienda.


Still bemused, Charity stood, biting her lip against the painful pulling of her wound as she raised her arms to braid her hair before dinner. Without knocking, Barbara entered, waving a message addressed to them both.

Señorita Carillo and Señora Larkin, the missive said, were invited to tour the Presidio, tomorrow, as the guests of Alcalde Guerro Santana.

Nicolas blamed fever for forcing him to remember, to see again how it started. Though he lay in cool dimness now, nursing his wounds in the safety of Refugio—grand name for a dark cleft in the earth—he felt the heat waves which had radiated like dancing serpents from the baked earth of Los Cielos' plaza.

How could he have felt so confident in those days? Stirrup to stirrup with his father, Nicolas Carillo had ridden tall, college-educated heir to Rancho de Las Aguas Dulces, assuming when he thought of it at all, that California's troubles had ended when strict Spanish rule had faded into Mexican laxness.

Across the plaza had stood Guerro Santana, a uniformed dandy leading columns of soldiers back and forth from Mexico City to Los Cielos. Too many soldiers deserted military life for pastoral serenity. Why polish brass buttons and march endless, sweating drills, when rancheros sat in shady patios, quaffing fine wine after a morning's canter over their endless properties?

Santana, just a sergeant then, stood at his horse's head.

"Who is he?"

Don Carlos's head had snapped up and Nicolas had seen his father's concern over the undisguised growl in Nicolas' voice.

"Some bantam rooster of a sergeant who shepherds troops from Mexico City to the colonies. He's had his fill of our provincial ways. No doubt we'll see no more of him."

A primeval flash of communication, primitive as clubs and stones, told Nicolas his father was wrong. The tall blond sergeant gripped his horse's headstall as his men eddied around

131

him, awaiting orders to mount. But their blue-clad leader had no eyes for them. He stared at an Indian.

Dressed in mission uniform of baggy white trousers and blouse, shock of black hair wrapped into a bushy horse's tail, the man had turned up his sleeves and bent to splash water on his face from the plaza fountain. He gathered the waters, raised them, then shook his head like a mustang, flipping a loose lock of hair back from his eyes. And he returned the sergeant's stare.

"Sabana? Santoro?" Don Carlos sorted through his memory for the name. "His father is rumored to be a Spaniard."

Later, Nicolas tried to convince himself that Santana had caught his eye by chance. But now he knew better.

Instinct alerted one to a situation—like the moment he knew Charlie was female—and etched its importance, fine as patterning on crystal, into your awareness. And then, just in case you missed your lesson, some force drove it home, shattering the crystal so its shards drew blood. The moment of *knowing* Charlie had been followed by watching her dreams destroyed. The moment of recognizing Santana for an enemy, feeling tension vibrate among the three of them, was followed by an event that still shamed him.

The Indian had been the apex of the triangle, and Santana had mounted, then jogged lazily within a horse length of the man.

"Nicolas, this won't end well. Ride on." The tension had been palpable even to Don Carlos.

It might have been the first time Nicolas ignored his father.

*"Indio,"* Santana had uncoiled the whip from his saddle as he hailed the man. "This fountain is for the use of horses."

"I've ridden in from the mission, Señor. I only wash the dust from my face."

The words were so casual, so uncowed, Nicolas felt warning rage through him. If Salvador—later all California had reason to learn the Indian's name—had fallen to his knees, if he had tried to slink away or failed to meet Santana's blue eyes, would their three lives have run off in separate directions?

*Quien sabe?* Now, in Refugio's blackness, Nicolas shrugged his shoulders, heard his own gasp and then deliberately rolled onto his back, meeting the pain firing from the slashes on his back. A grizzly's claws were benign, the force of impartial Nature; Santana had wielded his lash with cruelty.

Nicolas stared through the lantern-lit darkness, following the black fractures in the gray stone ceiling.

The first crack of Santana's latigo had stilled the plaza's bustle and bargaining.

"You wish to share with horses? Perhaps you should be disciplined as one," Santana's voice rose, calculated to draw an audience.

The whip's second crack had made women pause in their marketing, drawing rebozos to cover hesitant frowns. Most men turned away in distaste. One spat before mounting and turning his horse from the spectacle.

But Nicolas saw the whip slash like a bandolier from Salvador's shoulder to waist. The Indian didn't flail to be free, nor did he run. The lash snapped a third time, slicing across a copper face which refused to bow.

That third crack had split off Nicolas's impulse to help from a stronger desire. Santana's cruelty and Salvador's defiance personified colonial arrogance—whether it flowed from Spain or Mexico.

Since his return from Harvard, Nicolas had ignored politics. Then, the dazzling light of the plaza had presented him with a scene so vivid he could no longer ignore the truth.

Salvador had stood unflinching, fighting what must have been an almost irresistible compulsion to press his hand against the blood pulsing from his nose and cheek.

*He's waiting for another day, when the odds are closer to even,* Nicolas had thought, and the tension coursing among the three of them ignited. Nicolas would help even the odds.

"The man without honor is worse than dead," Cervantes had written, but this *Indio* showed a kind of honor Cervantes had never championed. This buried honor humiliated Nicolas Carillo, but it created Halcon.

133

Nicolas Carillo had finally obeyed his father's hand on his sleeve.

Some, such as Shakespeare's Hamlet, took madness as a disguise. Jogging his horse along the trail home, Nicolas had dismissed such a ruse. For his mask, he had selected patriotic devotion to the wrong cause, and vowed to end his charade better than the Prince of Denmark.

Professor Langley, at Harvard, had struck the podium, startling nappers awake.

"Intellectuals," Langley had sneered at his white-collared, black-tied pupils, "Make poor men of action."

What the skinny academician knew of action puzzled all, but Nicolas had named Halcon's black stallion "Hamlet" as a reminder.

Was there a difference between sleep and unconsciousness? Nicolas reached for the wet cloth he'd been applying to his brow.

Salvador had chosen an equally ironic reminder of duty. The Indian's cheek had knit along a faint, flat seam, but his lash-split nostril had healed in two pieces. Two months ago, when Nicolas had last seen the renegade, Salvador had worn a stud of Spanish gold through the loose flap of skin.

Salvador claimed that some *Garbieleno* tribes administered just such cuts to the nostrils of unfaithful wives. Salvador hoped his mutilation would keep him faithful to his cause.

Salvador had stood as leader of a proud race fighting to take back its land. On nights he allowed himself to think of such things, Nicolas felt the *Indio* had chosen an easier course. Salvador's people knew who he was and what he stood for; Nicolas Carillo pretended to champion self-indulgent rich men.

Only in California's wild places, or here in Refugio, first gouged from the earth by wolves, then expanded by Nicolas's own hands, did he feel like himself. Refugio hid candle stubs, a store of jerked beef and dried fruit, Hamlet's bridle and a collection of rags and medicinal herbs. More than the hideout of Halcon, it held relics of Nicolas Carillo before Nighthawk.

A book case carved in the dirt wall cradled three prized

volumes: the Bible, his student copy of Shakespeare's works and his book of Cervantes, sent by ship to the first Carillo born in New Spain, from a Spanish grandfather he'd never met.

Nicolas lowered his gaze from the earth ceiling to the protruding tree roots he used as a sword rack. Next to Nighthawk's sword hung an ancient cutlass he'd found on a solitary trip to San Diego.

He lurched from bed, now, and clutched the cutlass. *Jesus Maria!* He'd never felt so weak. The cave spun, streaked with smears of light. When he clamped his eyes closed against dizziness, his mouth filled with moisture. Nausea threatened. Still, Nicolas braced his feet apart, letting his hands recall the weapon's weight and balance.

Heavy and worn, chipped by use and years, the sword testified to another man's dedication. Nicolas didn't open his eyes to read the flowing script which reminded the possessor of his promise: "Do not draw me without reason; do not sheathe me without honor."

Balance. For a moment he felt the centered balance the sword always lent him. Then he imagined her face and the heat which suffused him had no origin in fever.

Nicolas swayed as he rehung the cutlass, then collapsed on the cot. Even after two days, even here, as he meditated upon his most sacred possession, Charlie intruded.

What had conjured her this time? The simple word "sheathe"?

*Sheathe me—Dios*, with his back flayed bare to the muscles and a murderous grizzly on the prowl, his body had begged, pleaded, *demanded* sheathing within her.

What fracture in his mind had transformed her from companion to temptress?

All through the feverish hours, once he'd crawled into Refugio like a wounded animal, the physical pull persisted.

Did she recognize my voice? A logical question. Let his meandering mind chew on that.

*You were atop her, gelding, and did nothing.*

Will she ask unanswerable questions when I return?

135

*You felt that sweet, waiting space between her thighs, capon, and rolled away.*

What cruelty will drive her off before she ruins the only accomplishment of my paltry life?

*From lips to ankles she curved up to you, like a bow in the hands of its master, but you, coward, failed to nock the arrow!*

Nicolas took a lung-filling breath and tried to release his body's tension by exhaling. Tomorrow he must be strong enough to find the chestnut. One night at the mission, in the care of Alvarado, should enable him to make the ride home.

He'd have plenty of saddle time to catalogue his errors, just as Charlie listed her wild animals. Now he must sleep, must gather the strength to battle Charlie's curiosity and the he-goat lust of Halcon.

# Chapter Eleven

The looking glass in Charity's room showed her cheeks normal rose pink, not flushed with fever. Her fingertips detected no heat on her brow, none along her grizzly scratches. She'd almost enjoyed the presidio excursion, so why did she feel ill?

Her only explanation—though it defied all logic—was *his* illness. Halcon had suffered worse injury than she and he lay sick, perhaps dying, cursing the night he'd first seen her.

Seeking signs of him—his wandering horse, a dropped glove, a careless word from a stranger, or Nighthawk himself, held captive in Santana's jail—she'd given in to Barbara and accepted Santana's invitation.

She hadn't found Halcon. Charity sighed, wringing a cloth dipped in orange blossom water. Still, she'd record three new facts in her notes: Santana considered Nicolas—but for one flaw—fit for public office. Her own clumsiness was enough to compromise the presidio jail's security and, most interesting, Esperanza had confessed an attraction to Guerro Santana.

"Esperanza was furious Nicolas didn't fight Halcon for her ring!" Barbara had gossiped. "She ordered him to ride after Halcon, but he wouldn't. Nicolas never relinquishes control."

Almost true, Charity thought, passing the damp cloth over her forehead as she gulped back the memory of one instant, at the edge of a mustard field, when Nicolas had seemed ruthless as Nighthawk.

Then Barbara had whispered that Esperanza sneaked away

with Santana, just to make Nicolas jealous. Too, Esperanza had confided in maudlin fantasy that if some disaster—and they were many for those who lived amid horns and hooves—befell Nicolas, she could think of no man she'd sooner seek for comfort than the handsome young alcalde.

Charity felt her heart flip over now, just as it had this morning. Before Barbara had offered more details, though, Santana had crested a rise, galloping to greet them.

Dressed in dark blue with gold cording and flashes of scarlet, Santana had kissed both their hands, showed off his new palomino and allowed Charity a glimpse of something she couldn't, at first, identify.

As he'd bent to kiss her hand, Charity had covered her discomfort by focusing on his white gloves, gold-bordered sleeve and the gap between them. There, a sort of bracelet—twisted horsehair?—encircled Santana's wrist.

Removing his cockaded hat, allowing the breeze to ruffle his customarily smooth blond hair, he had begged their assistance in naming his palomino.

Gold as a new-minted coin, the stallion pranced and whickered, shaking his snowy forelock from dark eyes. They discarded names like King and Prince. For all his beauty, the palomino lacked majesty.

"What of 'Paloma'?" Barbara asked. "He has a dove's gentle eyes, and he seems to float rather than canter."

Santana accepted the name, then talked of the drought and the *Indio* prediction that dryness would bring the worst sort of California summer, rife with leaden skies and earthquakes.

Construction din surrounded their arrival at the *presidio*. Charity sketched every object in sight—the alarm bell, flag pole, drilling soldiers—to hide her true interest, Santana's jail. Whenever a soldier glanced her way, then turned aside, Charity followed his eyes. Did he look toward Nighthawk's cell?

Finally she asked to see the jail.

"Señora, surely something else?" Santana had offered. "Even my cook's little herb garden would interest you more."

Santana's tone sent her pulse racing. Had she guessed right?

"I've never seen a jail, alcalde," Charity said, flourishing her pad and pencil. "I'd love a chance to draw it."

The single cell stood empty. About twice as big as a coffin, it held only a besmeared Indio, applying whitewash.

"*Andale,* out of here, *muchacho!*" Santana banished the artisan, calling him "boy," though the man looked fifty.

Santana pointed out a cross of pale brick, below the window.

"A humble masterpiece," Santana bragged, with a confusing smirk. "Make sure to include it in your picture."

She had, but when he left them alone, to investigate a gunshot and cackling guinea hens, she'd nearly destroyed the brick creation.

Standing tip-toe, trying to peer from the window, Charlie felt her skirt snag. With a rip and scrape, it pulled loose.

"You've torn your skirt, and—" Barbara broke off, and Charity followed her pointing finger. "The alcalde's cross!"

"Damnation."

Jerking her skirt free, she'd loosened a brick in the cross's intersecting lines and pulled it inches out of the wall.

"He's coming," Barbara had whispered at the crunch of approaching footsteps.

"Hell and damnation," she'd muttered, crouching to rock the brick back into its niche. Hollow grating and then, when she butted it in with the heel of her hand, a tinkling like brass.

"You've broken something! Did you hear? And look at your hands!"

Charity glanced at the scuffs and bloody scratches on her palms. Before she wiped them on the ruined skirt, Barbara shook her head in admonition.

Barbara wheeled to greet Santana and his frown faded to an amused wink.

"What was it, Lieutenant? The gunshot?" Barbara asked.

Santana bowed them from the cell.

"Nothing of consequence, Señorita—" he led the way toward a long, low building, also under construction.

Once inside, Barbara spared no glance for the meal, but Charity saw nothing else.

Golden chicken breasts, banked by unpeeled wedges of lemon and orange, glittered under a citrus glaze. A pinkish meat—rabbit? pork?—shared an earthen dish with tomatoes and green peppers. Centered among the delicacies sat a slab of gray mutton, big as a pumpkin, stranded in a congealing puddle of fat. A faded sunburst of overcooked carrots fanned the edges of the plate.

Santana couldn't have chosen a more typical, less appealing, example of winter fare from Boston. Yet Charity felt touched. He had served a meal he hoped would please her.

She and Barbara sat at the alcalde's left hand, but the place laid at Santana's right remained empty as he regaled them with the state of California politics, with the differences between Hispanics and Yankees and the secret traps awaiting one misstep by Nighthawk.

"Nicolas is helping you with all this?" Charity finally interrupted.

"Immeasurably," he nodded, "In fact, I thought he'd join us today," Santana doffed his hand to the undisturbed place setting, and once more his cuff gapped back, revealing a patch of rubbed raw skin. "Nicolas will help all the more when I convince him to enter the service of his country."

Nicolas in Mexico City? To serve a foreigner ruler? Charity had felt bitterness gather at the back of her throat.

"Do not look so aghast, ladies. You will not lose him soon, unless I wash his mind free of—" Santana smiled ruefully at Barbara.

"If I had to name your brother's only shortcoming, Señorita, it would be his soft heart over *Indios. Dios*—" Santana's genteel chuckle made Charity's neck crawl as though covered with a hundred rough-legged insects. "He acts as if they were human. But even great men are allowed a blind spot."

Blind spot indeed, Charity yawned. Bathed with scented water, and nearly ready for bed, Charity braided together the information she'd gathered, as she plaited her waist-long hair.

140

Esperanza and Santana. Nicolas and Santana. Then, she kept circling back to it, her clumsiness, the loosened brick and Santana. The cool, blond alcalde remained the center strand in all she cared about. And yet . . .

Charity dropped her brush in sudden recognition of the bracelet rasping Santana's wrist. The alcalde only pretended to be full of himself. Santana wore an irritant to goad him on—a knotted fragment of the reata Nighthawk had used to drag him from his horse.

Crawling under the embroidered coverlet, Charity imagined the twisted horsehair as a little funeral wreath to the honor of Guerro Santana.


For two weeks, the secret grated on her as well. Recovered from the grizzly attack, she pulsed with the demand for activity. Her muscles knotted, though she taxed them mercilessly. Her veins throbbed as if clamoring to burst free of her skin. For relief, she sought exhaustion.

Charity sat out past dark, befriending the feral yard dogs. She rose early, draped herself in a black rebozo and bowed her head for mass in the family chapel. Crossing herself, she rose from tingling knees, to peel off gentility with the rebozo.

Flanked by vaqueros, or accompanied by Arturo, Charity rode the boundaries of the rancho and Don Carlos's iron propriety. She catalogued three canines: wolves, coyotes and a gold-dun creature with prominent shoulder hackles. She listed cloven-hoofed mammals ranging from antelope to longhorned cattle, and sketched two bears smaller and darker than open-range grizzlies.

Spring carpeted Rancho de las Dulces Aguas with mustard and red-orange poppies. Beasts cavorted, giddy with sunshine and green shoots, and *rancheros'* wives patted out *asaderas*, white cheese so fresh it must be savored the day vaqueros robbed the milk from nursing cows.

Amid it all, Charity resisted the yearning in her belly, ignored the ringing hollow beneath her heart.

Only spring fever, she told herself, nothing whatever to do with Nighthawk. Or Nicolas.

She mastered weapons to battle the ache: rise earlier; ride farther; focus harder on books and notes; force heavy eyes to stay open later.

Never linger in the *sala*, where scents of oranges and beeswax curled into images of haughty Nicolas. Never pass the doorway of his fencing den, where glittering racks of swords spoke their clashing language in silence.

At all costs, avoid twilight balconies angled toward the ocean. Headier than *aguardiente*, the sea wind stirred dreams of dark stallions, masked lovers and riptides dragging her to caverns hidden beneath death-black waves.

"Penance! You empty-headed animal!" Nicolas shortened his reins as the pinto rolled its eyes—one blue, one white—and ducked down to buck. In a heartbeat, he loosed his grip, before the animal's sky-pawing rear overbalanced and toppled them.

"He'd go over backwards, kill us and never suspect what went wrong. *Sangre de Dios*, quite sniggering, Salvador. You scare him. Whatever possessed the padres to confine him to the mission yard? He shies at every accursed thing that moves or makes sound."

Shrugging an apology, Father Alvarado said that the animal was the best he could provide—to a Royalist swine. The latter words remained unspoken.

The pinto hadn't allowed him two uninterrupted sentences with Salvador, and now they'd crossed the boundaries of Rancho de las Aguas Dulce, perilous territory for the renegade leader.

"What do you expect when you give an animal such a name, Nicolas?"

"I might have called him Hair Shirt. It would have suited him as well." Nicolas smoothed the rumpled black and white mane.

"Tell me about this girl." Salvador's voice seemed imperious, but his pierced nose and faint smile gave the lie to his command.

"She's trouble: too curious, too smart and too impetuous." Hot pain slashed over his back as the pinto crow-hopped past a windblown manzanita. *Dios!* Two weeks he'd nursed this injury! Two weeks with Charity running amuck without his supervision.

"We watched, during the herding, and she seemed fine." Salvador said. "Only an adequate rider, but clever in anticipating the cattle, in letting the horse work."

"Then you watched the wrong woman. Charlie is never patient." Nicolas looked away, fearful his face betrayed him. He might have used her impatience to his benefit. The way she'd arched up to him with only the plain for a bed . . .

"And she'll become Halcon's woman?"

"*Cristo,* no!" Nicolas thought of the hours he'd spent raking through his mind as he healed. All his thinking, lusting, and philosophizing, had come down to one question: could any association—call it love, desire or gut-wrenching curiosity—survive daily scrutiny which demanded, "Is it worth it?"

Is it worth endangering her life and mine?

Is it worth sacrificing California as it struggles toward birth?

Is it worth eternal damnation for adultery?

He'd sought an honorable motive for his longing and found none more noble than this: mind, spirit and body, he wanted her.

"What trouble?" Salvador asked, and Nicolas strained to remember he'd called Charlie a troublemaker.

"She forces me to make mistakes," he admitted. "Nothing serious, but, I robbed those rich *señoras* in sight of Santana. I spoke when I thought her injured. Masked, I rode the chestnut." He forced his words between gritted teeth. "I want her gone.

"My strategy is two-headed. Halcon might frighten her away," he paused and swallowed. "By seeming to stalk her. If that fails, Nicolas's insults will freeze her out."

143

"So, you play both the good Spaniard and the bad bandit," Salvador drew rein, eyes focused toward the horizon.

"I just want her to leave, but, *Dios,* it's a shame. She could be of such use. She's brave enough to bring supplies to your *renegados,* not too squeamish to doctor wounds, and she looks like a schoolgirl. No one would suspect—" Nicolas paused as he made out a horse within the approaching dust cloud.

"Is it a runaway? Or just a bad rider?"

"Tell me, Halcon. He's one of yours." Salvador backed his horse to leave.

"Don't go. He won't reach us for a while. When he's near enough to see, pretend to attack me." Nicolas played at drawing his boot knife, and the pinto shied so violently he stumbled.

"I'll just leave it to the horse," Salvador muttered.

They sat silently until Nicolas heard the quiet broken by his own breath.

"No man who rides like that is worth such a sigh. Who is it, amigo?" Salvador's grim voice rekindled his savage reputation.

Nicolas knew he had only to hint, and Salvador would ride into the canyon below and slit that white throat. Any pause would come later, not for regret, but to wipe his blade against his buckskins. Nicolas also knew the hint could never come.

He'd prayed for a way to be rid of Charlie, and his prayer had been answered.

"Her husband," Nicolas's lips moved as if numb with cold. "It's Charlie's husband."


Charity loosed the leather strings around her throat. Her braid uncoiled and the flat-brimmed black hat fell to the middle of her back as she strode through her long swirling skirts.

Doña Anna had requested the return of her divided riding skirt and suggested Charity avoid further gossip by dressing conventionally.

Charity flipped a swathe of the black fabric over her arm. "No matter"—her whisper blended with her boots

144

scuffing—"that my skirts are so long a running horse could place a hind hoof through them and crush his rider to a ladylike mush."

Galloping her horse, today, had been a mistake, but not because of the skirts. If she'd ridden Luna at a sedate walk, Sable might have stayed crouched and watching.

Charity's notes demanded a specific designation for the she-wolf who seemed equally eager to watch her observer. The dark brown wolf had the teats of a nursing mother, Charity had noted.

Charity stripped deerskin gloves from her sweating hands and wondered why she suffered the discomfort. Though they protected her from chaffing reins, she hated the confinement. She flexed her fingers and closed her eyes. Halcon's lips had played across those rough knuckles, her leather palm and then set his teeth against the flesh at the base of her thumb.

Her chest tightened when she forced herself to remember what came next. Have you forgotten, ninny? He blindfolded you so he could escape.

She'd flung down the gloves and stooped to plunge her hands into the fountain when she heard riders at the gate. She squinted through the sun's glare on her glasses, then lifted them to see.

A man she didn't recognize, and—Nicolas! The chinging of spurs and the rhythmic striking hooves—Nicolas! But it was the other rider who dropped from his mount and ran toward her, circling her waist, whisking her onto her toes.

"Freddy?"

Were her words strangled by surprise or the hat strings?

Dizzied by his appearance and frenzied dancing, Charity shook her head, planted her feet and gripped the wide shoulders. She gasped for breath to speak. All the same, he beat her to it.

"Hellfire, Charlie! You look just the same!"

"Well, you don't."

Freddy squared his shoulders in mock manliness and laughed. How long since he'd bowled her back with his

145

booming, improper laughter? Hens ran squawking as she grabbed his hand.

"A few months hauling traps, wading creeks, chopping down trees—It pared the civilization right off me, Charlie. Never had enough to eat and we hardly dismounted, even to sleep!"

Could this be soft, sweet Freddy, gloating over such hardship? He retained his barrel chest and red face, but now his cheeks were sunburned, not flushed from overindulgence. His dark brown hair had been bleached chestnut, and the faded blue cotton shirt and trousers matched his eyes. And there, Charity decided, the real change had occurred.

"Not too smelly to hug, am I?" Freddy pretended to swoon.

Charity nuzzled against him. Self-conscious buffoon or blustering outdoorsman, it didn't matter. Being with Freddy was like being home.

"Hellfire, I didn't really think you'd come," he laughed and bounced his chin on the top of her head, "I should have known better, right amigo?"

If Nicolas had kicked her feet out from under her, he couldn't have weakened Charity's knees more effectively. His nose and mouth twisted as if he'd eaten rotten fish.

*But you're Freddy's friend, his best friend,* her mind protested, and her fingers dug convulsively into Freddy's waist.

"Ow! Careful there, little one. I'm tough, not indestructible!" Freddy unwound her arm from his waist, then raised it to flaunt her toward Nicolas.

"What do you think *amigo?* Didn't our little Harvard boy turn out nice?"

Disgust vanished so quickly from Nicolas's face that she might have imagined it. Freddy gave no sign he'd seen it, and now Nicolas's eyes shone with indulgence. Curiously stiff, he swept off his hat and bent over the hand Freddy relinquished.

*He must feel he's kissing his horse. Sweating, smelling of deer hide. His lips touched down briefly. Not like—*

The quick brush of his mustache, coupled with the sun-

146

glint that turned his hair russet-rainbowed instead of black, muddled her mind so she hardly understood him.

"Freddy, you're right." Nicolas straightened and his smile bypassed her for her cousin. "I've worked day and night keeping suitors at bay. None would believe a bumbling *Yanqui* bear such as you could win such a charming *esposa*."

But if she'd imagined that look, why did Nicolas's eyes avoid hers? She'd missed him these long weeks, and he wouldn't even look at her! Charity buried her face against Freddy's shirt. She'd be damned if she'd let Nicolas see the ache beneath her joy.

Freddy kept her hand trapped in his as Doña Anna summoned them into the *sala*.

"Are we peasants, that we keep our guests standing in the courtyard?" She chided. "Señor Freddy—" Anna raised her cheek for a kiss as he shambled up the stairs. "I know you will not refuse some *dulces* while you tell of your travels."

Freddy protested that he needed to bathe, first, but Anna dismissed his excuse.

"Nonsense. Your cousin has not seen you in years and we have missed your company for months. We'll let you bathe—"

"We'll insist," Nicolas added.

"—but first, some news."

Freddy gushed tales of his early squeamishness. Baiting traps and skinning prey had, at first, sickened him. A freak snowstorm and a crashing fall through thin ice had lamed and almost killed him. He described the death of a packhorse that stumbled off a narrow trail, laden with hard-won furs.

"I climbed down there to shoot him, Charlie," Freddy shook his head with regret. "I had to. The poor bas—beast was screaming with pain."

Most of all, he told of the high Sierra Mountains.

"If that land were a woman, I wouldn't have come back to you," he told Charity. "I know that sounds idiotic, but it's the most incredible place—not even a place. A world. Charlie, it's a whole life away from Boston and banking. You'll love it."

A thin glaze of tears shimmered in his blue eyes, and she wanted to turn away.

*Damnation, are you never satisfied,* she asked herself. You left Boston for adventure, for wild California freedom. Yet, here it is, served up on the proverbial silver platter, and all you see is moonlight flickering on a sword blade and the flash of an outlaw's smile.

The silence stretched tight and still she couldn't look at him. Or Nicolas.

"I will be merciful and grant Señor Freddy's wish to bathe," Barbara's voice lilted from the couch she shared with her twin. "Hush, now, Arturo," she elbowed her brother. "As they rode through the gates, Mother promised we could have a *bailecito casero*—a little house party," she explained to Charity.

"Arturo, you'll hear everything when Señor Freddy's friends arrive—you did say they'd return from Los Angeles? Tonight? And one is a Russian?" Barbara's head whipped back toward Freddy in a rush of black curls.

"As soon as they've sold the furs," he assured her. "I thought, Don Carlos, they might sleep in the stable."

"Because I offer such cold hospitality, Señor?" Don Carlos' mock ferocity included a gentle punch against Freddy's shoulder.

Charity's eyes widened. Even among the other *rancheros* Don Carlos hadn't displayed the humor Freddy evoked effortlessly.

"Well. I must see to the rooms," Doña Anna rose, smoothing her skirts."

"Really—" Freddy protested.

"I mean yours, Señor, not your friends'. You're not so enamored of your horse, surely, that you plan to sleep outside, when you have a bed?" Doña Anna asked.

"Anna, surely there's no need for another room—" Don Carlos began.

Charity flushed as Anna beckoned her husband into the hall.

*Talk someone, talk,* Charity's mind pleaded, but no one did.

Without pressing her palms over her ears, she couldn't block the voices.

"—most uncivilized," Anna's voice dropped below a whisper.

"But they are married in the eyes of the church and the Crown. They will share a room sometime. It might as well be now."

"Shhh!"

Charity hid her face in her hands. Her blush burned her fingers.

Freddy chuckled and she felt him separate the fingers covering her eyes.

"Take your hands down." He held her wrist, planted a mock-gallant kiss on it and raised his voice to his host and hostess.

"What if Charity stands in the hall outside while you decide and I bathe? Just talks to me, keeps me company? Very proper. I'll stay seated and all."

Charity's eyelids clamped shut once more. Humiliation. He meant it in the most helpful way, but she wanted to shrink until she disappeared. Her stomach hurt from sucking it in so hard.

In the arched doorway, Anna's mouth trembled against tears or laughter, then her hands flew wide in a dismissing motion.

"I think," Nicolas said, "that she has washed her hands of the both of you."


Parry, extend, lunge.

At least she hadn't trotted behind to watch Freddy bathe.

Parry, extend, lunge.

*Dios*, would his back never heal?

Parry, extend—*there*, even with his lightest foil, the extension pulled the muscle painfully tight across his back—lunge. Lunge, lunge, lunge, his sword tip ripped the cloth-covered target.

If Santana were here, Nicolas Carillo would harness this

149

anger and mince the false alcalde into dog's meat. He'd forget Nighthawk, forget patriotism, just kill the royalist bastard, hope to God the *rancheros* were smart enough to embrace democracy or something like it, and end the whole charade.

Such foolhardiness sprang from Charlie. He'd been talking to her in his mind, these two long weeks, recovering. Now, she was here, clearly upset with the bargain she'd made, but not because she wanted *him.*

*Charlie,* he told her in his mind, *open your legs to Freddy or me, but Nighthawk doesn't exist—*

He stopped and barred his mouth with the back of his sword hand. *Jesus Maria,* what if he'd spoken?

Silence reigned, except for his breaths, heavy with exertion. Wind rushed past the edges of the window set in adobe. It wheezed and hushed and a gull wheeled screeching for the garden. He hadn't spoken. Charlie was driving him mad, and into mortal danger.

Nicolas shouldered the foil like a musket and walked to the window. Strong enough to cool the sweat on his face, the wind gusted again. A gull settled among a flock of his fellows, squawking a warning to a solitary crow. A spring storm was brewing and they knew it.

Freddy had kissed Charlie's hand, though he hadn't a clue how to do it properly. Nicolas had almost cringed at his friend's loud lip smacking and the bone-wrenching squeeze that had caused Charlie to flinch. Properly done, such a polite gesture could make his lady moan. And not from pain.

Which was why he'd taken Charlie's hand, Nicolas admitted. To remind her. He'd been too cunning to meet her eyes, but her fingers, for the barest instant, had spasmed around his.

Her hand knew his touch. So? What did it prove? That her body recognized his in any guise? It changed nothing.

Nicolas watched the crow beat his wings, cawing raucously, to drive the gulls from his feast of fallen blossoms and spring insects. Gray and white and graceful, they rose in a hovering cloud, then dropped to surround him once more.

* * *

A scuff, like a leather slipper on adobe tile, sounded in the hall. Turning from the window, he willed her to be framed in the doorway.

Nothing. Sunlight, unnaturally bright before it was reconquered by the clouds, flowed like spilled honey over the polished wood floor. Then grayness.

No Charlie stood biting her lip, dead set against apologizing, but doing it, all the same, by her presence.

No Charlie burst the den's silence by railing against his studied coldness.

No Charlie studied him with bewildered radiance and murmured, "It's you, isn't it?"

Christ! He'd give Refugio, his books, even the antique sword if he could banish daydreams of her as easily as clouds blotted out the sunlight!

Nicolas held the foil at arm's length and worked his shoulder in huge circles, until pain almost convinced him the grizzly had swiped him again.

This afternoon had been a test. His pitiful plan had worked. Hidalgo coldness had driven her right into Freddy's arms. *Cristo* it ached. He tossed the sword, caught it with his left hand and continued the circles.

Better. The claws had wreaked less damage on his subordinate side, and that was a mercy, since Santana had offered an irresistible challenge. Mother had pulled him into her sewing room and whispered that Santana had doubled the reward set on Halcon. The funds would be deducted from the large gold shipment expected, any day, from Mexico City.

Since his mother had her information from two elderly *señoras* who were not usually privy to military secrets, the rumor could only be a trap.

Santana possessed the bravery of a driven man, but he clearly needed a strategist. Such broadcast hints would make even the unwary suspicious. Just the same, Nicolas thought, whipping a lightning-quick riposte with his left hand, Halcon relished the chore of springing the trap.

The thought of such daring made his pulse jump and strengthened his resolve. Halcon was not so weak he would trade his followers' hearts and minds for a bespectacled spinster. He craved the thunder of Hamlet, running hard, whirling and dodging, beneath him. He longed for the sweet ring of sword upon sword and soldiers' oaths splitting the midnight sky. He wanted a fight, damn it, a fight worthy of Halcon.

If Nicolas Carillo could bear his people's scorn to save them from tyranny, he could sit at the *bailecito casera,* and watch Charlie curl next to Freddy, her *husband.*

Nicolas Carillo could yawn as she smiled and pushed her spectacles up her nose, entrancing rough men who hadn't spoken English to a girl for years.

Nicolas Carillo could easily ignore Charlie.

"No great feat," he told himself. "A simple matter of patience, like training a horse," he muttered.

But it would take *cojones,* not brains, to beat the Spaniard.

# Chapter Twelve

Charlie looked heartbreakingly like a Boston lady. Her black hair had been pinned so high that the lashes at the corners of her eyes showed dark against her temples. Her face, neck and the corset-flattened tops of her breasts had been powdered dead white. She stepped down the hall as if her legs were straight sticks. *Cristo,* if this was his sister's idea of fashion, wiping away the freckles and rose-cheeked liveliness to make her a blank slate, Barbara might at least have told Charlie she was allowed to bend her knees.

The wind had risen and spatters of rain gusted against the windows. In his eagerness to greet his trapping companions, Freddy had left the front door ajar.

No candles had been lighted against the storm's premature darkness, and he wore no spurs to ring out his presence, so Nicolas watched her from the shadows.

Charlie stopped, as if instinctively aware of his presence. The breeze that chased down the dusky hallway created the only movement about her, rotating her wide skirts a half turn to the left, then leaving them to rock and settle.

Nicolas listened to the rough laughter from the courtyard. Arturo's voice rose above the rest, calming a dog which added its raucous bark to the excitement.

Still Charlie didn't move.

Somewhere Barbara tittered and his mother's calm command—the pumpkin *empanadas* required more nutmeg—echoed from the kitchen.

He and Charlie stood alone. Was this how she stalked wild creatures? He wondered which of them she'd label predator and which prey.

"Nicolas."

His heart bolted wildly and he felt an insane instinct to run. But she only fumbled among the pink billows of her dress and continued, "I have this for you."

He ground his teeth together and strode closer to the hand she extended.

"Si?"

Her hand trembled as she tugged at the lace fingers of her glove. It fluttered away like a leaf and, when she bent to retrieve it, she gasped as if stabbed.

Had the bear injured her, after all? *Cristo,* he'd worried, but known he couldn't ask. Nicolas Carillo knew nothing of a grizzly attack.

"Damnation, I hate corsets." She stamped one foot and dug her fingers into the satin at her waist. "I can't reach it, Nicolas. You'll have to help me."

Only the corset, good. He looked at the fragile scrap of white lace and nearly smiled at its owner's blasphemy.

"Or you can leave it there—" her blue eyes flared behind their porcelain mask, "though I have no idea why you're treating me this way. The last time we spoke you explained mating to me. And a fine job you did. I—suppose."

Nicolas watched her eyes dart toward the door and he wanted to bar it against Freddy. Boisterous Freddy would teach her—no, that thought was too charitable, but Freddy would have her. Here, under the same roof, in a room steps away from his, Charlie's blundering cousin would be the first. *Dios!* The thought was past bearing!

Charlie's haughtiness cracked. She bit her red-rouged lip and her eyebrows arched high on her naked forehead.

"Is it because Freddy is here? Has he ruined everything?" She swallowed audibly and her white neck shuddered all the way to the hollow of her throat.

The seducer Halcon would have overflowed that hollow with kisses, but Nicolas Carillo could not.

"I'm afraid I don't understand, Charity." He linked his hands together behind his back.

"Of course not." She lifted her chin. "But, before Freddy comes in, I want to return your ring."

He almost fell back a step at her vehemence. *Keep it,* he wanted to say. For a few days he'd half pretended the ring proved his claim over her.

"Step lively, Nicolas," Charlie's demand quavered as she snatched his fist and folded the ring into his palm. "I don't want it anymore."

He shrugged, "It was only meant to rescue you from embarrassment during the ceremony."

"Then it has served its purpose." Her jaw jutted forward and her eyes stared past his shoulder.

"Then it has," he echoed, but when she tried to sweep by him, he didn't move aside.

She growled in frustration and sidled down the narrow corridor, facing the wall rather than look into his face. He might have kissed the defenseless nape of her neck as it passed.

Nicolas waited until her voice twined with Barbara's, until he heard her call a joking caution to Arturo. Then he plucked up the white lace glove and tucked it into his black satin sash.

Halcon would ride tonight. He could carry a worse favor to bring him luck.


"I'll come in, then, I suppose."

An hour had passed since dessert and fruit followed dinner. The mountain men, Sergei and Ambrose, had repaired to a chamber adjoining the storeroom and now Freddy closed her bedroom door.

White curtains had streamed in, blown by high sea winds which followed the storm. When the door shut, they fell abruptly limp.

"I wonder why they didn't put you in my room when you first arrived," Freddy mused.

He wandered the perimeter of her bedchamber, exploring. His hand hovered above orange poppies and purple lupin stuffed in an earthen jar. He centered the water carafe on her nightstand, examined the wooden crucifix nailed to the wall, and finally ran his hand over the bed's quilted blue coverlet.

*Damnation, there's hardly enough room in that bed for one,* Charity thought. Her cousin had lost flesh enough to make a whole other man, but he'd still overflow her bed. The vinegary taste of the *barbacoa* soured at the back of her throat and she faced the window to draw a breath of wet adobe wind.

"Aren't you cold?"

Freddy stood by the bed, rubbing his hands together, as if trying to get warm. All evening he'd joked and told stories spun to remind Charity of their easy friendship. She'd remained silent. The tension, stretched tight as cat gut on a bow, was her fault.

"So, we're well and truly married." Freddy resumed pacing. "Nicolas told me about the ring. I'm sorry. I'm afraid my school ring went to—we'll see about another one, later."

"Freddy, it doesn't matter."

"I can tell you're angry, Charlie." He waved off her words. "If it wasn't the ring—oh, what I said about letting boys win—? In front of Ambrose and Sergei? I'm a lunatic! Too old to be showing off for my friends—"

"No, Freddy, it's not you." She turned from the window. "You don't mind if I take my hair down? I've developed a murderous headache."

Charity plucked out the bone hairpins, scattering them next to the jar of wildflowers. She threshed stubby fingernails over her scalp, then tossed her head back.

"It looks like a witch's mane, doesn't it? Oh, but it feels better." She sighed. "I'm not angry. It's just a damnably strange situation."

"Don't let it be strange," Freddy ordered. "You've got your hair down. Now, take your shoes off and come over here. We haven't had a chance to talk."

He tugged her hand, while Charity hopped on one stockinged foot. He released her so suddenly she almost fell. Oblivious, Freddy flung himself backward on the bed.

"Oh Lordy, a real bed," he groaned, shucking off his

cracked leather boots. "That's better." He stretched full length on the coverlet. "Now, let me bore you with tales of the high Sierra."

Charity sat, knees gathered under her skirts, wiggling relieved toes inside white cotton stockings. She closed her eyes and followed Freddy's memory to a place of mountain mornings and wood smoke, of snow-melt streams and pine scent so addictively sweet a man felt testy anywhere else.

"Swear to God, Charlie, I don't think I can live down here anymore." Freddy crossed his arms behind his head.

"Don't you mind—sharing?" She'd spoken before forming a decent question, and wished she could chalk up her clumsy tongue to weariness and wine, instead of animosity.

"You don't like my friends?" Freddy chuckled. "Well, I'll tell you, I'm not good enough to go out there alone, Charlie, even with you to identify the birds and beasts for me. You'll see. They're not so bad away from civilization."

She'd liked the black-bearded Russian, been struck by his bearish movements and inquisitiveness, but she'd loathed Ambrose.

Not only had the lank-haired Southerner boasted of furs stripped from thousands of dead creatures, he'd lumped Nighthawk in the category of "dangerous vermin"—same as, he'd drawled, wolves and coyotes.

"Sergei seems nice enough," she offered.

"But Ambrose is something of a weasel, huh?" he suggested.

"*Weasels* are nice enough," she began.

Freddy's booming laugh made her giggle in return. She'd missed the easy verbal skirmishes she'd had with John and Freddy. With Arturo, there was the language difference. With Nicolas, the confusing tension which sapped the fun from the simplest conversation. With Freddy, she felt at home.

"You've guessed, haven't you, that I've shown a decided lack of industry in founding the bank." Freddy steepled his fingers and looked at her sideways.

"I guessed." She pulled her knees higher and sat facing him. Freddy looked embarrassed, but damnation, he looked

157

far more comfortable than she felt. Should she ask him to help her out of this fussy gown and stays?

"It would have been more sensible to buy up hides for Boston shoe factories. All this cheap leather, even with shipping costs, could have made us rich. Trying to start a Western arm of the bank, when people here live on barter and trade—?" he shook his head dubiously.

"It's probably a lost cause. But I have a plan. There's a ship due within days, that'll be heading for San Diego. I figured we might have a sort of honeymoon, let you see some of the coastline, too, and there's an American banker down South that, well, I'm not sure, but—"

"Freddy, do you know how glad I am that you've changed?" She leaned forward to touch his cheek. "You used to be so stuffy and worried. You'd go along with me, like the time you loaned me your breeches to ride your father's stallion? Remember? You gave me the pants, helped me sneak into the stable, then looked so guilty, we got caught anyway." Laughter bubbled in her throat as Freddy looked sheepish, even now.

"And I could have brazened it out, you know, at school! Oh Freddy." She took a breath and pressed a hand against the bare skin above her neckline, trying not to laugh because the stays threatened to suffocate her. "You got me kicked out of Harvard just because I loosened a button on my fencing jacket?"

Freddy snatched her wrist and trapped her palm against his cheek. She blinked once, twice, and understanding flashed through her: she'd made a serious mistake.

The hacienda had fallen silent. A mourning dove cooed, melancholy against the sound of a dog lapping from the courtyard fountain. Freddy's eyes seemed to bore through the surface of hers.

*This isn't right. It's awkward and makes my stomach hurt.*

He pulled her down next to him. The bed rustled and creaked and she wondered how the mattress was supported. By interwoven ropes? By leather thongs lashed to the bedposts?

Freddy's face loomed so close her eyes crossed. His face had two noses and three eyes. The three somber blue eyes made her want to giggle. His hand covered the nape of her neck, then fought through the tangled mass of her hair, snagged, and jammed into a pin she'd missed.

"Ow! Freddy, let me just get this." She reached her arm back, straining against the stays to pull the pin free.

Damnation, his eyes seemed fixed on the pink bodice as it tightened, protesting her contortions to reach the pin. His hand played up and down her throat as if urging her to swallow.

Freddy's blue eyes glazed, then closed and she felt embarrassed for him. His hand flattened against the back of her bodice and she knew he felt the stitches straining. In spite of Doña Anna's fine needlework, the gown had never been fashioned to withstand the stays' pressure or Freddy's clumsy caresses.

He's trying to be a proper husband, she thought. He raised his hand to the back of her head again and pressed their faces together in a kiss.

Idiotic. She felt detached, as if she dangled from the ceiling, watching them make a rat's nest of the bed and roll wrinkles into her dress. She felt Freddy lift his knee, reach it over her skirts and use the muscle in his lower leg to pull her toward him.

So stupid. His lips felt loose and fleshy. Movable. How humiliating for him to try this! His mouth wiggled closer and his lips squirmed over his teeth.

She must tell him such heroic efforts weren't necessary.

She parted her lips to speak and his tongue, thick as a sausage, eased into her mouth.

"Ugh! Freddy, what in the world—" she sputtered in surprise and then began laughing. Charity rolled onto her back and stared at the whitewashed ceiling. Her stays stabbed her, but she couldn't help it, couldn't contain it, until she realized her giggling was the only sound in the room. She took a deep breath and swallowed a sort of hiccup.

159

"I guess it's not working, is it?" She rolled back toward Freddy. He stared into her eyes so directly, her smile died.

"It sure as hell was working for me." Freddy swung his legs off the end of the bed and stood.

He yanked his trousers up at the waistband, grimaced and tugged them away from his crotch. He took two strides toward the door, looked down at his bare feet and stopped.

Faintly, Charity heard Arturo bid good night to someone.

Freddy picked up one of his boots, stood as if he'd pull it on, then glanced at his disheveled image in the pier glass and tossed his boot at it.

He made a sound that was half groan, half growl.

"I think I'll sleep on the floor, Charlie."

"On the floor? It's a narrow bed, but I'm sure—"

"Yes, on the damned floor, if I've your permission, *cousin!*"

If he were an animal, she'd have understood the message Freddy's posture sent her. His hands locked onto his hips. He leaned forward from the waist and his lip curled away from his teeth in a snarl. He displayed an aggressive stance, a threat, but why had he turned it on *her?*"

Freddy's snarl faded into a sigh and his hands dangled loose and defeated against his thighs.

"Shit, Charlie." He blew his cheeks full and round, and a worried look from their childhood drooped his mouth into a frown. He expelled the air, clenched his eyes into a tight grimace and raked his fingers through his hair so hard she felt sure he'd bloodied his scalp.

"Shit. What have you gotten me into this time?"

# Chapter Thirteen

Into the wind, along the sand, wet hooves splatting, he galloped the pinto at the foaming margin of the waves. Storm smells of wet vegetation, salt mud and wind filled Nicolas's throat and chest.

If Freddy thought the Sierra addictive, it was because he'd never galloped the midnight shore, blinking off wind-whipped tears, hearing the metallic rub of blade against sheath, riding taut as a threatening arrow, thighs and knees clasped to balance over thundering hooves.

Foolish horse, to run till his sides heaved, hooves hitting so fast the four beats drummed as one. Nicolas felt the gelding draw its first labored gasp even before he heard the breathing change from rush to grunt.

Nicolas leaned low, relinquishing the safe upright seat which let him sight between the animal's ears. He pressed his cheek to the hot, furry neck and eased his hands down the reins.

"There, Penitencio. So, boy, *despacio*, go slowly."

Gently he tightened his grip, no tugging, just closing his gloves around the reins until the gelding stopped.

Penance had been the first animal Nicolas had seen when he'd fled the hacienda. Rear hoof cocked and bony hip jutting at an angle, the pinto had flicked an oversized ear toward Nicolas, then jumped back, eyes wide as if he'd seen a serpent. The Franciscans had displayed good judgement in one thing at least: gelding the animal.

Would the dare-devil Halcon leap astride this bewildered creature and gallop him bareback, headlong into darkness?

The challenge had tantalized him.

Nicolas kept his right rein short and the jittery animal stepped in circles. Should he ride toward Refugio and screech the hawk's cry that summoned Hamlet? Did he dare risk Penance inland, where the earth bulged with ridges and rocks and a skittish horse might find plenty to trip over? Inland to the presidio, where failure to follow the directions of hands and knees meant death or discovery?

He dared, by God. This night, he dared.

Nicolas settled the sword in his belt sheath, and braced against the pinto's startled bucking.

*Jesus Cristo,* he'd risk a hundred muskets' roar if it deafened him to the memory of Charlie's lewd laughter.

Fool he'd been, to tell Father he'd serve his turn as *hacendado,* tonight. He'd pace the courtyard, check the gates and settle the trappers and their horses. Still in velvet and pale linen, he'd done it all, so fast it seemed he raced.

Finally he'd stopped, pushing Arturo's yellow-eyed yard dogs off his legs, dragging one away from regal Princessa who minced provocation in Barbara's bedroom window. Then he'd lowered himself to the porch and, ashamed but determined, listened. He'd recognized Freddy's low rumbling, but strain as he might, he couldn't hear Charlie's voice.

Ramble on, Freddy. Bore the poor wretch to sleep, he'd urged as he caught occasional words, "Sierra . . . meadows . . . run-off . . . magnificent . . ."

Nicolas had smiled, then, confident his friend—no matter how trim and toughened—wasn't pushing up Charlie's pink skirts while he babbled his obsession.

And then there'd been quiet, a tinkling outburst of giggles and more quiet. That second silence had unnerved him.

He'd crouched there, muscles tensed, setting his teeth against his fist.

What had he hoped for? A scream? And then what? No man interfered in another's dealings with his wife. Especially

162

not his virgin bride. But why hadn't she protested? Why hadn't he heard whimpers of invaded outrage?

He'd grown just as still now, and Penance snorted, confused.

"Hah!" Nicolas urged the pinto with voice and legs, threading him through a line of trees.

Had he wanted Charlie to be fearful? Did he care so little for her as a *friend, por Dios,* that he preferred her suffering? Would he prefer the image of Charlie staring wide-eyed past Freddy's heaving shoulder into her room's darkness, crying silently—for him?

No, but what a shame it was. He might have had her right there on the plain, both of them breathless, embracing life after the grizzly had threatened death. What a shame, when he'd felt her eagerness and known how good it would be. *Cristo,* his body still believed it.

Trouble. Nothing balmed jealousy and lechery like trouble. A fight would make him forget. He seethed in readiness. Fury had goaded him to exchange his clothing for Nighthawk's, his light dress sword for the iron-hilted broadsword and metal scabbard. Nicolas sent the pinto up a sandy path to the bluff.

"Run, *amigo,* but save a little fire," Nicolas muttered to the horse's flattened ears, then fell silent, communication with body and mind.

When you fly with Halcon, he told the animal, your nostrils will burn with the hot gray stench of gunpowder. Your eyes will be dazzled as it flares yellow against the blackness. You'll hear the clash, and smell the cool silver of fresh-honed Toledo steel. Your pricked ears will swivel to locate men's shouts—surprised and frightened, insulted and quarrelsome, defeated and vengeful, then distant, growing quiet, fading softer behind.

No female could rival the glory of such solitary gallops, the sudden, hammering jolts of danger and the hot pride that he, polite Harvard scholar, could meet mortality with a swordsman's skill and a rogue's cool humor.

On such nights, he imagined the ghost of an old-time highwayman stormed from his dank grave and sighted Nicolas

Carillo's horse and blade. Mad for a lark, the shade might cast out Carillo's polite hidalgo spirit, seize reins and, whirling silver sword hilt, shriek his power to the moon.

The presidio lay silent and unguarded.

"I've let them grow complacent," Nicolas told the horse.

No sentries. He'd ridden close enough to smell cook fires and horse droppings, and not even a dog had marked his approach. *Cristo*, there was little thrill in this invasion.

Wind flapped a rain-damp flag against its pole. Inside the barracks, a soldier coughed.

He let Penance continue at a flat-footed walk until he stood at the very entrance to the presidio.

Not much of a fort, compared to the installations at Monterey and San Diego. No real fortification protected the square of connected rooms. He rode past a blacksmith shop, a row of boarded windows supposed to keep vermin from the food stores, a rough kitchen, a room stacked with boxes of ammunition and pikes and two cannon so incredibly heavy it took a dozen soldiers or a yoke of oxen to move them. Beyond, sat the barracks. Behind them, a corral of dozing cavalry mounts.

Salvador's renegades could wipe out the entire lot before one man wakened enough to stagger toward the bell.

The bell. Sidestepping the deserted stone bowls and metates which would grind corn for Santana's breakfast tortillas, Penance rolled his eyes at the gray hive-shaped ovens, and walked to the center of the square. The bell.

The rope bell pull swayed in the cutting breeze, striking the thick brass dome in gentle pings.

Halcon shouldn't stoop to a boy's prank.

What? Ring the presidio bell and ride away? Beneath him.

How much more subtle for Penance's hooves to thump along the board walk beneath the alcalde's chamber, sending Santana upright in panic.

Nicolas walked the pinto another lap around the yard. Christ, he wanted a fight. He craved the release of savagery.

What if he pulled Santana from his bedclothes, pressed a sword into his palm and shouted "Have at you, pretender!"

Or perhaps Francisco. The lumbering sergeant had proven a vicious foe. For all his bulkiness, the man could ride.

But no. Cold necessity forced even Halcon into circumspect behavior. There'd be no blood and steel tonight. This solitary ride must engender plans, not relief.

His mother had talked of a wedding fiesta for Charity and Freddy. Bile spewed in his guts at the idea, but he'd take that poison and use it. Let it push him into springing Santana's trap. Anything to wake the sleeping *Californios*.

He'd push. Push Santana into a confrontation. Push Charlie and strength-sapping passion into memory. Push himself into the people's awareness. Every night he'd wreak mischief. Every night, until the approach of dusk made them search the horizon for his silhouette. Inside a month, Santana would be gone.

Yes!

He kicked his heels against the horse's ribs, clinging low and eating mane for two tearing circuits around the courtyard. Then, even as he heard soldiers snorting awake, Nicolas grabbed the bell rope and swung it wildly, whooping to the sky, until the pinto's speed snatched the rope from his grasp and he rode into the night.

Dratted Pilar had been granted her wish. Charity stood before the pier glass and sniffed. Each night as she'd leaned against the balcony rail, straining for sight of the sea, Pilar had predicted disaster.

"You'll be sick, if you keep that up."

Charity's eyelids puffed over itchy eyes. Her throat felt stuffed with cotton. She dabbed the lace-edged handkerchief at her nose for the tenth time since waking. She could feel Pilar—old witch!—sitting in Barbara's room, racking her mind for the perfect proverb. For, clearly, Charity had taken cold with a vengeance.

Moments before hearing Nicolas's spurs, she'd wakened behind swollen lids, mind registering her dripping nose. On opening them, she'd noted the blue quilt on the floor, but no

Freddy. She'd just begun to wonder, could she and Freddy settle this like comrades? Or would they flounder in the tongue-tangling male-female language which made Spanish complexities seem simple as a lesson from a child's primer?

"—plague me every time I approach my own room?"

Nicolas's mumble and the picking of claws ripping free of velvet had made Charity's eyes close in a drowsy smile. Nicolas pretended to despise the little cream-colored cat, but when Barbara protested Nicolas was the only man Princessa tolerated, Charity noticed his grudging pleasure.

"Nicolas, I would have a word with you, when you smell less of horses and cigarillos."

Doña Anna's chill voice had brought Charity upright in her tangle of blankets.

"Certainly, *Mamacita*."

Little mother, indeed. Charity had wobbled to her feet, kneading her brow and sniffing.

Now, Charity tugged the white camisa over her head and swiped the handkerchief one last time under her nostrils. Black hair, blue eyes, red nose. A pleasing contrast, she sneered at her reflection.

If she held off snuffling while she loitered outside Anna's sewing room, she'd surely hear a most interesting conversation. The heavy wooden door had just closed behind Nicolas' booted steps moments ago.

Consider *that*, she cautioned herself. Polished floor tiles were less forgiving to the eavesdropper's tread than Aunt P.'s Turkey carpets. Should she go shoeless? Carry her slippers as if—in case of discovery—she'd been about to put them on? Too risky, too rude. Completely illogical.

And yet, temptation tugged at her. Arrogant, coldhearted, critical Nicolas might get a tongue-lashing from his mama. She settled her spectacles firmly, gave a last satisfied sniff and padded barefoot into the corridor.

"Si." Nicolas's voice sounded patient and weary. "Pilar is right. I did return just before dawn. And, si, I reeked of tobacco. What her informants did not know, because I spoke to

166

none of them, except to ask for coffee, is that I spent the time not with Esperanza and her father, for Christ's sake—"

"Why you insist on blaspheming—"

"But in El Pueblo"—Nicolas's voice only continued over his mother's—"playing monte at the bodega with a few respectable *rancheros*. It was a long ride in and a longer one home, but I did quite well, Mother. My winnings almost equal the value of a ruby necklace."

What did he mean by that? Charity pinched her nostrils against a sneeze. Why a ruby necklace? The example seemed rather pointed.

"And were you drinking?"

Doña Anna's voice quavered so faintly Charity thought the effect might have been created by her own clogged ears. But no, Nicolas's tone softened and silk rustled as if the prodigal hugged his mother.

"A bit. Never to excess, Mama. You know that. I keep such promises."

"Well, I admit you look more presentable. Like a vaquero prince, if such a thing exists."

Doña Anna's voice dropped. Damnation. Charity glanced down the hall and edged closer. Someday she'd be caught. But not today.

"—cordial to your guests. Freddy's companions are annoying, but he is your friend."

And then the doña stopped. Charity held her breath, urging the woman to continue.

No! The door swung open. Hell and damnation!

She sneezed and covered both nose and mouth with a flat palm that made her next, uncontrollable sneeze sound like a watery sob.

A dark avenging angel, he burst from the room, blacking out her view of the corridor. Stride by stride, he loomed closer. Merciful Mary, he looked angry, violent. She'd never seen him so. Now he'd trapped her, but his brow contracted in concern and one hand touched the tender flesh below her ear.

"Are you all right, *pequena?*"

167

Nicolas's hair still shone wet, tied high and braided with a thin black satin ribbon that curled along his neck.

Charity's mouth opened and closed like a fish on a riverbank.

His open-necked shirt was so pale a blue, it seemed a shadow of his embroidered royal blue vest and breeches. Charity forced her eyes down from his face, his chest. Even then, her lowered eyes watched the tasseled ends of the gold cording that circled muscled legs just below the knee.

His fingers lifted her face.

"You've been crying, Charlie. Don't tell me you haven't."

She swallowed and tried to make sense of it. Angry, but tender? His breath came loud, like a chuffing bull's, yet he hadn't upbraided her.

Nicolas's index finger slid her spectacles down to the tip of her nose. Damnation, she'd lose them, shattered on the adobe tiles, like her sneaking eavesdropper's heart should be.

*Don't be a weak-kneed ninny. Answer him like the boy he knew at school. Show some bloody backbone.*

"No such luck, I'm afraid." Charity squared her shoulders and pulled away, tossing her braid down her back. "I've taken a cold. Nothing more than that. Pilar will rail and scream, but I'm out to catch up Luna, so I can bring Freddy to see my wolves. Like to ride along?"

An exhalation like that, one that caught in his throat before it finished, should have made him seem smaller, softer. But Charity could have sworn Nicolas grew.

"I regret I have other responsibilities."

His hand fell to his vest, and his fingers flew so emphatically, fastening the front of it, she thought the copper buttons would pop loose and jingle across the floor.

"One bit of advice, Señora Larkin."

He regarded her bare toes, and Charity curled them, seeking the shelter of the camisa's hem.

"If you've taken a cold, wear your slippers. Even in California, there are conditions more unpleasant than not knowing your host's business."

He awarded her a brisk pat on the shoulder and strode

down the hall. And if she'd been holding her slippers in her clenched fists, Charity would have landed at least one right between his shoulder blades.

Desperados should live as hermits.

Nicolas relived the conversation in his mind as he greeted his sister. He did it again as he thanked the cook for the early cup of coffee. As he swallowed fresh tortillas and chewed a handful of figs, sun-warm from the orchard, he remembered it again.

While talking with Mother, he hadn't said a word amiss. He knew it, and yet he might have. And Charlie would have heard. More strongly than ever, with more conviction than he'd felt as he lay feverish at Refugio he knew: Charlie must leave.

Wretched little sneak—up to her old tricks! The corner of his mouth twitched in amusement. But Charlie's intriguing was not funny. The stakes were too high, but she'd never know how high until someone died. Murder was one mortal sin Nighthawk must never commit.

And yet, he'd wanted to. *Dios*, when he saw Charlie's reddened nose, her swollen lips and eyes swimming with tears as she tried to avoid his, hiding behind those absurd spectacles—A mercy he'd grabbed her face instead of his sword! Because all he'd seen, for an instant, was blood. Freddy's blood. His amigo's blood spewing like a fountain because—and he'd *known* it, felt it hot in every vein from wrist to heart—he'd *known* Freddy had raped the sweet bride . . .

And he'd been wrong.

Nicolas surrounded the pottery coffee cup with both hands and shook his head like a man in the throes of a nightmare. His eyes stared through the twisting wisps of steam.

She'd driven him that close. *Sangre de Dios*, he must get rid of her, before he did something irreparable.

"Nicolas, still breaking your fast?" Arturo paused as the elder brother brushed a spot of coffee from his blue cuff. "You've missed family prayers! An infraction I've—"

"Enough, Arturo. I'm still a good enough Catholic to escape damnation, I think," Nicolas snapped, but felt the chastisement sorely. He hadn't made an honest confession for two years.

"Nicolas, I was only joking."

"It's nothing," Nicolas aimed a stiff smile at his brother. "Forgive my distraction, *hermanito*."

*Cristo*, could Charlie be blamed for this, too. He wanted nothing more than to hug this dandified cub, his little brother.

"Do you know the trappers' plans? How long they will stay?" Nicolas rapped out the questions in a fusillade he hoped would maintain their distance.

"I don't." Arturo's mouth twisted in scorn. "I'm fairly disgusted with them, myself. This morning, as Freddy came forth, they harangued him for details of his wedding night."

"It is a primitive reaction, but not unusual," Nicolas held his brother's gaze. "It is almost—traditional."

"I suppose it could be worse. They might have asked for bloodied sheets," Arturo spoke with the false bravado of a boy.

"Not in this house," Nicolas enunciated.

"You like her more than you show, Nico."

"Charlie's a nuisance."

"I know, I know." Arturo's smile stretched toward his ears. "But I tell you, *hermano*, had Freddy not returned, I would have been in line to marry her."

"What?" Nicolas's jealousy receded before amazement. "Arturo she's—seven? eight?—years older? And a *Yanqui!* A girl with little breeding, and even less sense of decent conduct."

"But could a man ever be bored with her, Nicolas? What will come out of those charming lips next? An American curse or praise for a lumbering grizzly? Do you know," Arturo offered an example, "I told her how bears are frightened by mirrors, by seeing their own reflections. Everyone believes it, vaqueros and *rancheros*. And do you know what Charlie said? 'No. They're not afraid of their puny reflections.

It's because you're flashing sun in their eyes!' She never complains of dust or heat—"

"But, Arturo, Freddy has not ridden his horse off a cliff or drowned in his beloved Sierra streams," Nicolas hardened his voice when Arturo would have pressed on. "He's home, and he's her husband." Nicolas crossed his arms over his embroidered vest.

"So it seems," Arturo snarled. "Even Sergei seemed embarrassed . . ."

*You don't want to hear this, Carillo. Stop him now.*

". . . but Ambrose spurred Freddy on when he implied . . ."

*Concentrate on that white bowl of oranges, sitting serenely on the hand-buffed sideboard.*

". . . just by hints, you understand, not specific details . . ."

*Their round globular shape, those oranges, the right size for a man to encompass with his full hand.*

". . . but he said that when he helped unfasten her gown `. . ."

*Sweet to the tongue, oranges. Just a nip of tartness biting through the skin, but then, one could be so sweet.*

". . . when it slid off her shoulders—it was that pink gown, remember . . ."

*And the color of the fruit, how glowing in that shaft of sunlight, how beautiful . . .*

". . . how beautiful—"

"I needn't know such things about my houseguests!" Nicolas slammed his fist on the sideboard. The white bowl jumped forward to teeter at the wooden edge.

"Nicolas! Mother loves this bowl!" Arturo leapt to push it back. "You had only to tell me to shut my mouth."

Arturo's voice was too comforting, his eyes too damned knowing.

"Then shut your mouth. Please." Nicolas took a step away, then turned back.

"You have duties today, *hermano.*"

"I'm riding out with Charity and Freddy. To watch her wolves." Arturo said.

"No. You'll accompany Ambrose and Sergei to Los Cielos

and help them spend their money. And while you drink and gamble and seem very much three grand amigos, you'll discover their plans."

"*Carumba*, Nicolas, I told you—"

"I heard what you said. But I want the Americans gone," Nicolas demanded. "All of them. Even Freddy and his wife. Knowing their plans will make it easier to—hasten their departure."

"Isn't it ironic?" Arturo mused, but his boyish voice held more regret than sarcasm. "You are so wrong about the *Yanquis*. Three-quarters of the *gente de razón* have no opinions. About foreigners or anything else.

"If they may ride, dance, have the occasional duel and, of course, their squabbles with the church, they're happy!" Arturo's voice soared in amazement. "But you and I, Nicolas, we think! Si, a radical concept, but we do! What might we be, the two of us, if we joined forces with Halcon and Salvador's *renegados?*"

Nicolas longed with the desire to *tell*, to assure Arturo, puffed up with conviction and faith in his elder brother, that his devotion was deserved. But even as he watched, Arturo's faith faded.

"I try to find the irony amusing," Arturo passed a hand over his sleek brown hair before donning his hat. "But it's not. It's shameful. Among hundreds, we're two who think, and you're wrong."

Spurs ringing, Arturo strode from the room.

The sunlight warming the bowl of oranges had shifted to a pale, watery shadow. The *sala* turned cold, and Nicolas felt his chest tighten as if he'd been wound in a shroud and motioned toward his grave.

# Chapter Fourteen

If a giant had gripped her by the ankles and cracked her spine like a whip, Charity would have felt the same. In fact, she sat on her aching tailbone, hidden from her chuckling husband by a vast field of mustard. Luna hadn't even bucked her loose, she'd fallen, while Freddy and Don Carlos watched.

She knew better than to let her mind wander while riding in open country, but Freddy's company made her careless. She'd praised the physicking ability of blue skies and wildflowers, of beef and beans breakfasts, and she'd rhapsodized over her gelding, Luna.

"Gray lace over moonlight," she'd described the horse's coat, then pulled her soggy handkerchief from her sleeve, shaken it out, and Luna had exploded.

The spindly forest of mustard stems whispered and bent as Freddy's roan approached. An ant scurried across her hand.

"The handkerchief," Freddy explained, before she even saw him.

He cleared his throat to dispel his unwelcome levity. As well he should, Charity nodded to herself.

"Luna saw it from the corner of his eye," Freddy added. "Horses' eyes are on the sides of their heads, and he saw you flap it."

"I *know* where horses' eyes are, Freddy!" Charity struggled to her feet, hampered by layered petticoats. "It's a damned—" she gasped for breath through her congestion, "survival development. They're prey. Things eat them. I *know*, Freddy! I'm the biologist, remember?"

She lifted her skirts to rub her knee as Don Carlos cantered, swinging his reata in lazy loops, after Luna.

Stuff! Could any but the worse puling weakling list bear-scored ribs, fainting spells, a head cold and twisted knee as ailments?

"Damnation," she snarled, dropping her skirts at Freddy's appreciative leer. "Riding sidesaddle is a waste of time and cursed dangerous."

"Charlie, it wasn't the saddle," Freddy began.

"Don't you dare!"

"You weren't paying attention, the horse—which demands every bit of your equestrienne skills, Charlie—bolted, and you fell. Now put your foot in my stirrup, and climb up behind."

From the corner of her eye, she saw Freddy extend a hand to help her.

"Get up behind yourself," she puffed, slogging through the weeds toward Don Carlos and dancing, unchastened Luna.

"Stop indulging your sulks and get up here." Freddy crossed his horse in her path and lowered his voice. "Act like a lady. You make Don Carlos insane. He shakes his head when I assure him you studied from Harvard textbooks, the same as Nicolas and me," Freddy's storytelling voice wove its power, reeling her close, "But he says he's too old to understand you—a beautiful woman with the voice of a seductress, and the words of a sassy boy."

Charity stood with her hands on her hips. She sniffed, fought the urge to wipe her nose on her lace-trimmed sleeve and glanced at Don Carlos. He'd stopped the horses to watch her challenge her new husband.

"Really, Freddy? He said that? About—my voice?"

"Ask him," he offered, gesturing toward Nicolas's father.

Devil. He knew she didn't dare.

"Freddy," she jammed her boot into her cousin's stirrup and swung herself astride. "You are such an ass."

* * *

174

Soon enough, Freddy's ability to play the simpleton served them both. They'd been afoot, seated in a tumble of rocks Freddy declared unstable.

"It could go any moment, Charlie," he'd pointed up the ridge behind them. "And if there were an earthquake—"

"This rockslide happened centuries ago, and it's the place Sable expects to see me. Her den is there, across from that huge boulder with the crack," she pointed, leaning close to let him sight along her arm.

Sable hadn't shown herself, and Charity squinted with concentration as she searched for the she-wolf's brown-black coat in the newly christened Split Rock Cleft.

"There she is." Charity whispered.

The wolf trotted across the sandy area between her cave and the split rock.

"See how she sniffs there? Something about the rock or the vegetation—and, see, she's marking her territory."

Don Carlos cleared his throat as the she-wolf squatted to urinate.

"Charlie," Freddy regarded his host with a quick grin, "Male dogs do that, of course, but isn't it unusual in females?"

Charity sucked in her breath and frowned.

"I'm not sure. She's a lone female," Charity ticked off her fingers, "She hunts by herself and ranges far. She knows I'm here—see her ears point this way? Then she gets low on her front paws, haunch end up, tail-wagging as if she wants to play."

Don Carlos, listened and nodded. Freddy rolled his eyes and mouthed silent words. 'You're crazy,' she thought he said.

"Sable will select a mate, soon, I think. Dust keeps flying from her burrow as if she's preparing for pups."

Sable abandoned tail-wagging to stalk home. Charity bit her lower lip in concentration. No one else would notice, but she felt certain Sable was pregnant. Sable stretched before entering her den and Charity saw that beneath her glossy fur and prominent ribs, the wolf's belly swelled.

"You think the female selects her mate?" Don Carlos ventured.

"That's my theory," Charlie told him, distracted by Freddy, who snatched her twig to scrawl something in the dirt. "They bear the young, feed them, protect them, teach them to survive. It makes sense that they would improve their species by choosing the strongest and smartest mates."

"I don't know, Charlie," Freddy shook his head, still writing. "Are you applying this theory to all species?"

"Probably. Eventually." Charity's tone dared him to challenge her. She'd not endure another lecture on procreation.

Don Carlos stood from his cramped position and took two quick strides to his horse. She heard nothing, saw nothing, but the white-haired patriarch mounted and immediately swiveled his wrist, limbering his reata.

Hooves rang on rock. Lieutenant Santana, blue, red and gold in his imperial uniform, rounded the tumble of boulders, with Sergeant Francisco. Don Carlos dropped the loop from its poised position, but didn't recoil and strap the reata to his saddle.

*"Buenas dias Señora, señores."*

Santana nodded as impersonally as if she'd never shared his table, nor named his palomino stallion, whose dark eyes peered past a flaxen forelock.

Freddy and she stood. He moved close behind her, one hand resting at her waist. She felt the broad solidarity of him, and thought his gesture implied protection, as well as possession.

Santana exchanged pleasantries, asking Freddy of his travels, remarking to Don Carlos that some Indian fortune-teller predicted three more years of drought. He complimented Charity on improved Spanish, and begged her tell Doña Anna he would attend the Larkins' upcoming marriage fiesta. But he failed to dismount.

As if he enjoyed the horseman's superiority over those on foot. Uncowed, she rubbed the palomino's muzzle.

"How goes Paloma's schooling, Alcalde? I see he no longer plays with his bit."

176

"He—it goes well, Señora Larkin," Santana indulged her, allowing his charger to be coddled like a pet. He unfastened his high hat and held it under his arm like a knight's helm.

Barbara had compared him to the golden lion of Castile. His blond hair glittered like the shako on his hat, and the flat planes of his cheeks were commanding.

"If I thought Paloma would tolerate a lady's saddle, I'd offer you a canter," he smiled, then added to Freddy, "Your charming wife named my steed for me, some weeks past.

"And, though I have never married, myself, I would advise to encourage her blossoming interest in horseflesh. This is an obsession far healthier than meeting up at strange hours with Halcon! That I would curtail at any cost."

Freddy's hand tightened and Charity looked up to intercept an angry glance. He might have conspired with Luna, as the horse shoved with his nose, knocking her hand away from Paloma.

"I regret my ride out from Los Cielos is not entirely for pleasure." Santana's blue eyes focused on Freddy's.

"My recent communications with the governor at Monterey have underscored the importance of expanding trade with Mexico. This dictum concerns you, Señor Larkin, since one way of assuring this is to require long-term California residents to become citizens."

"I see," Freddy answered, his tone fading to the boyishness he assumed while storytelling. "And what length of residency would constitute 'long term'?"

When Freddy shifted his weight from leg to leg, Charity stepped back to watch his performance.

"Señor Larkin." Santana seemed almost embarrassed by Freddy's question. "You have been here over a year, *no?* In anyone's terms twelve months would constitute 'long term.' "

"I see, I see." Freddy tapped an index finger at one temple as if focusing his thoughts, "And what—if one were, stupidly, to flout such orders—what would be the consequences?"

The last sibilant syllable hung in the air when Francisco rammed his priming rod home, plucked it out and raised his musket to his shoulder.

177

"Hellfire!" Freddy shouted.

But Charity followed the lesson which had enriched her field observations. She didn't stare—along with everyone else—at the beefy Francisco; she looked the other way.

*Not Halcon, please dear God*—Sable!

"No!" She leapt forward and snapped the back of her hand against the flared metal musket.

"Ow! Oh! Ow!" she tried not to moan, but she just knew she'd shattered the delicate bones webbing the back of her hand.

"Señora, you could have been shot!" Santana's voice shook at Francisco's stupidity, at Charity's, and at Freddy's outrage.

"A wolf, Señora," Francisco protested. "I wanted to shoot the wolf." He pointed toward Sable's den.

"I know," she spoke through gritted teeth, and would have continued, but Freddy caught Luna by the bit and motioned her to mount. Shaking with reaction and pain, Charity obeyed.

"Perhaps, Sergeant, you will lower your musket now," Don Carlos said. "The wolf is out of range."

"They're horrid things, Don Carlos," Francisco shuddered. "Worse than rats. Vicious and dirty. I hate wolves."

*Small wonder.* Charity set her teeth over the comment and stared at the discoloring back of her hand, *when they are so much smarter than you.*

"Sergeant! Even a peasant knows better than to shoot, without warning, in company," Santana's cheeks flamed at Don Carlos' rebuke.

"Your hand, Señora, it is all right?"

Charity emitted a deprecating laugh and raised the hand from the knee on which she'd cradled it.

"You must have one of Don Carlos' Indians make a poultice for it. Some are quite skilled at such things." Santana stilled his side-stepping palomino and turned to Freddy.

"Nevertheless, Señor Larkin, your continued presence in California, and that of your wife, depends on your quick application for citizenship. If you intend to become a merchant here, you must apply. And become a Catholic, of course.

"The law, in fact, forbids your marriage if you have not converted." Santana rubbed his saddle horn, frowning. "A detail I should have considered—"

"Lieutenant, I feel the very devil for complicating your job," Freddy smote his forehead in dismay and Charity thought his playacting had turned to melodrama.

"I just assumed that the law of converting before marriage—of which I've heard, of course—applied only to foreign men marrying *hijas del pais*. I had no idea, *no* idea." Freddy flung his hands apart, Luna shied and Charity nearly lost her seat again. "That the order included marriages between non-Catholic foreigners."

"But, Freddy—"

Both Don Carlos and Santana silenced her with threatening looks, but damnation, she *was* Catholic.

"I vow, Lieutenant, I'll give the matter serious thought." Freddy made a tsking sound. "And I'll tell my companions, too."

"Ah, but Señora, before we part—how goes your study of the outlaw *Halcon?*" Santana asked.

"Slowly, *Alcalde*." Charity forced a ingenuous smile.

"I only ask, Señora, because I've found a clue!"

Charity drew in, going still as the sun-baked countryside. A cicada chirred, bit off its call, and chirred once more. Dust shimmered in heat waves on the horizon.

"A clue?" She infused the words with girlish enthusiasm.

Santana flipped open a leather pouch buckled to his saddle and withdrew a white lace glove.

"The careless blackguard dropped it in the presidio patio! Right outside my room! What does that tell you of Nighthawk's intelligence?"

Her heartbeat raised to her throat, then pounded at her temple. The world shrank to only Santana and her glove.

"When?" she tried not to choke on the single word.

"Last night, Señora!" Santana gloated. "Could it be you recognize it?"

*Last night. He lived, last night. And though he wasn't under the gun*

179

*when Francisco aimed, now he was. Charity O'Dell, you better lie more brilliantly than you ever have before.*

"I recognize it, *Alcalde.*" She giggled and shook her head disparagingly. "I fear you have no clue at all. That style of glove is the very rage among California ladies, Barbara says. She had two pair, and made me a gift of one set. Esperanza has a pair, too. And, if I'm not mistaken, that little friend of Arturo's—I believe her name is Lucia?—but they might have been blond lace instead of white—"

Santana motioned her to silence.

"Please, Señora, no more! You've broken my spirit, entirely," Santana's smile was rueful, but indulgent. "Do you know. Señor Larkin, this is the first time I have heard your *esposa* chatter like a *Californiana,* and it's quite becoming. Were I you," he chuckled while replacing the glove in his pouch, "I would consider the issue of citizenship, very carefully, indeed."

Halcon told himself, galloping the palomino away from the presidio, that he'd stolen Santana's horse to humiliate the *alcalde.*

He told himself the theft would create gossip—a sure way to push Californios toward awareness.

He imagined how talk would stir to life by dawn, when a vaquero, in line for the day's first griddle-hot tortilla, whispered to the cook news heard from outraged Nicolas Carillo at the bodega. The cook would tell *la patrona* of the theft. Her daughters would titter it to their friends. The tale would ferment in creaking *carretas* full of doñas and daughters traveling to Rancho de las Aguas Dulces, then bubble over at Charlie's wedding fiesta.

He told himself a number of sensible things, when, in truth, Halcon acted from lust, with as much logic as a buck in rut.

"Quiet, amigo." Nicolas slowed the young stallion to a walk.

He could rationalize the theft, but what guerilla errand

180

could take Halcon inside the gates of Aguas Dulces, besides taking Charity for a midnight ride?

He'd known he would do it when he saw her on the beach.

Chafing against their third day of civilized living, the mountain men decided they'd succumb to Los Cielos's new monte tables, and convinced Arturo to ride along, so they might stay the night in the Carillos' townhouse, near the new church. Freddy, the *attentive new husband*, Halcon snorted mentally, had accompanied them.

Christ's blood, had they done it or not? The question gnawed his bones, burned his stomach like smoldering coals. In spite of the bawdy conversation Arturo had reported, the bantering relationship between Charlie and Freddy didn't seem—conjugal. He'd have no way of knowing until she showed pregnant.

*Dios*, Charlie pregnant? What would he give for one night with her, ten hours—even two!—of kissing, touching, exploring, before she began the descent into domesticity? Halcon reached to the back of his mask, assuring himself the knotted leather held.

Charlie would domesticate as poorly as one of her wolves. She yearned to please, tried to follow the rules, but she hadn't learned to disguise feelings which led her outside propriety. She followed her instincts like a wild thing, and that very failure to dissemble had drawn him back tonight.


After an early supper, Charity and Barbara had joined a covey of bucket-carrying Indian girls sent to the shore to dig clams for tomorrow's fiesta.

"Nicolas, those girls went off chattering like hens," Don Carlos had chuckled. "They wouldn't hear of an escort. Still, you should ride down and be sure they start back before dark. Just days ago I told Señora Larkin the path was treacherous, but she would take it."

"That's why she took it, Father," he'd told Don Carlos, and his father had agreed he was, no doubt, correct.

When Nicolas and the prodigal chestnut had arrived at the

base of the bluffs, girls in white *camisas* had scattered like a handful of shells, over the wet gray beach.

The tide rippled far out on the horizon, leaving the beach bare and perfect for clamming. Heads bent, eyes searching for tiny clusters of bubbles indicating clam beds, the girls wandered from the rocky shoreline, across the exposed sea bed.

Safe from disapproving eyes, many girls had tucked skirt hems into their sashes, freeing bare legs and feet to swing in long, natural strides.

He'd stalked Charlie as he had that first night, and though no darkness hid him, Charlie's stubbornness made her an easy target.

Ignoring those who'd gone farther out, Charlie squatted next to a bucket of seaweed, spectacles and hem tucked into her red sash. Her *camisa* skirt hiked up her thighs, almost to the joining with her body. She used a pronged wooden fork to dig between her feet, occasionally blowing away wisps of hair waving loose to brush the sand.

"Having any luck?"

She'd yelped and bounded up, spouting curses on a gasp.

"Nicolas! Damnation, you're lucky I'm the 'good sport' you—you—" She batted her hair back, smearing grains of sand across her forehead and cheek. "If I were a mean puss like your Esperanza, I'd have had at you with this!" She brandished the clam fork.

Charlie held a cocky schoolboy's pose, and if he'd been Halcon instead of Nicolas Carillo, he'd have shattered it. His fingers had splayed on the reins, imagining how he'd loosen her hair, wrap his hands in her unruly mane and pull her into a kiss, or launch a flying tackle from the horse and hold her captive until the sea soaked her clothes and she no longer struggled.

Then Charity remembered her skirts.

"You sneaking—" she'd sputtered, jerking the material free with such energy her spectacles fell loose.

Set against the evening sky of pearl and pink, puffing her cheeks full to blow sand from the lenses, she ignored him.

182

*Dios*, the tension had crackled so strong between them, he'd sucked in his stomach until it surely touched his backbone.

"Charlie, ride back with me."

Who spoke? Not Nighthawk; he had no voice. Not Nicolas Carillo; the words were too soft. *Cristo*, despite Freddy, despite patriotism and the laws of his church, he did love her.

He closed his eyes, wishing he could snatch back the thought. When had Charlie stopped being his comrade? When had he first seen her as mistress? When he looked again, she'd been studying him.

"I want to Nicolas. I do," Her voice flickered and he knew she saw him not as a friend, but a man. She retrieved her bucket, hoisting it to her hip. "I want to, but—no."

With a few cruel words, Charlie saved them both, and turned to shout down the beach.

"Barbara! Barbara!" She raised her free arm in a hailing wave. "Your spoilsport brother's come to fetch us home!"

Charlie took a dozen swinging steps away from him, before turning. She ran back, bucket rocking madly in her hand.

"Nicolas," she clung to his stirrup as if it were a lifeline. "I have to know—you have to tell me—"

Charlie had begged, beseeching him, and he couldn't— though he threshed around desperately in his mind—he couldn't find his hidalgo reserve for armor.

"Yes, Charlie," he'd ached to cup her face in his hand, but past her shoulder, he saw Barbara jogging closer. "What is it you have to know? What?" he'd demanded. "*What* would you have me say? *Cristo*, girl, you're married!"

Only his chestnut's hooves, sucking at the mud as the horse shifted, had broken the silence for two heartbeats, three.

"I know it!" She'd shouted, furious, and she'd backed into the bucket. She kicked it, watching the arc of sea weed and clams spill as the bucket rolled on the slick sand.

He'd left her to walk home with the other girls, but as his chestnut picked its way up the path to the bluff, his mind vibrated with questions.

What had she meant? "I have to know—you have to tell me—"

183

Yearning and frustration had shuddered between them. Her blue eyes turned pale, so widened to search his face.

Even if Freddy had lain with her, he hadn't created Charlie's longing, her new, untested passion. Halcon had kindled it first, on that night of the grizzlies, and her body, her heart, *something* in her, recognized him as its source.

Now, Santana's palomino moved beneath Halcon, fluid as water. Now, Halcon walked the horse to Charity's bedroom window and dismounted.

Nicolas Carillo could never answer Charlie's desperate questions, could never discuss fidelity and desire with a married woman. But Halcon—?

*There* rode a man to answer Charlie's questions, and he would do it without uttering a word.

# Chapter Fifteen

Charity knew she should feel exhausted. The trail up the cliffs had twisted high as the magic bean stalk in the child's tale. Pebbles had rolled underfoot and her wet toes, rubbed raw by her leather sandals, had stung at each step.

Preoccupied with anger at herself, he'd hardly reacted when Doña Anna, emerald earrings glittering, embraced and kissed first Barbara, then Charity, as they stumbled into the hacienda.

"Pilar has chocolate and hot baths waiting. I insist you drink the first while enjoying the second. Then go to bed." Anna held up a finger to silence Barbara's protest.

"Tomorrow, beginning at dawn, I need your help. Charity must learn to prepare a fiesta, and you, *chica,* can use a reminder. Off now," she'd fluttered her hands as if scattering chickens.

Charity tried to drown her irritation in the bath, but Pilar wouldn't allow it. Before the water cooled to comfortable warmth, the woman swept in, gray braids flapping, instead of pinned up.

"I, of course, cannot retire until the señoritas deem it time to wander home," she suffered.

"Oh Pilar, have mercy!" Charity moaned.

"You're tired, are you?" Pilar had stroked a sympathetic hand across Charity's brow.

Charity closed her eyes, banned all images of Nicolas and leaned her head back against the tub's edge.

"I am tired," she sighed.

"It's been just a few days since you took a chill," Pilar crooned, "and you wander the beach in bare feet and damp dress!"

"Pilar—" Charity's outflung hand foiled the woman's addition of attar of roses to the bath water, but Charity could not fend off Pilar's gloating.

"'Punishment is a cripple,'" Pilar quoted, "'But it *will* come.'"

Before the bathwater cooled to the cloying warmth of the spring night, Charity knew her body's exhaustion wouldn't black out her mind's repetition of the scene with Nicolas.

Charity swallowed the tears gathering in her throat and dismissed such weakness as fatigue. Still, as she climbed from the tub, she allowed herself one self-indulgent complaint.

*Oh Nicolas, don't ask me what I want! If I knew I'd seek it out. Think. Plan. Act. Like I always have.*

Nonsense. Charity stood, yanked a white night rail from her trunk and jerked it over her head. She reminded herself how touchy Critter had become, upon reaching sexual maturity. She weighed the irritating possibility humans might experience the same unpredictable emotions.

Stuff and girlish foolery!

The fainting and tears, Charity O'Dell? The yearning for Nicolas and incessant fantasies of Nighthawk . . . didn't it make humiliating sense?

Very well. Whether biology, heat or exertion had led to this missish melancholy, she must shrug it off. Tomorrow, she'd be so brisk and efficient, Nicolas would believe he'd had a nightmare.

She'd start erasing the embarrassing scene now. All she needed was a book. She'd relight the candle and read.

Princessa's cry, outside the door, sent Charity tiptoeing across the floor. Since Freddy's return, the cat had been elusive. Now, Princessa scanned the room, blue eyes inspecting every corner before she deigned to cross the threshold. Meowing once more, she launched herself onto the bed.

Charity joined her, settling on one side. She should snuff

the candle, but she felt so comfortable and warm. Her eyelids drooped as Princessa curled purring against her chest.

Two blows rapped against her shutters.

Princessa's claws ordered Charity still. She held her breath, straining to hear past her pounding pulse.

Might she have dreamed the impact at her window? No. A hoof nicked adobe and a dog issued a sharp bark.

Charity slid from bed, ignoring Princessa's lashing tail and guttural protests.

Like unresponsive pieces of meat, Charity's fingers fumbled to unlatch and open the shutters.

Halcon stood so close the candle played over the sand-colored leather of his shirt. He stood so tall, she wondered if she reached his breastbone. Her eyes rose to the laces crossing just there, at his breastbone, and then she looked higher. Flickering light danced on the uneven edge of his mask, shadowing his mustache, revealing a white flash of smile.

"The grizzly didn't kill you. I prayed you'd be safe," she whispered. "Halcon . . ."

Chills rained down her neck and arms, because she'd dared to call him by name. She tried to remember what she'd resolved to do about girlish fantasies and runaway emotions.

He took her hand to his lips and turned it palm up. As before, he kissed its very center. His lips wandered to her wrist, warning Charity to maintain her scientific distance, to observe and identify him if she didn't want to lose him again.

She should be the biologist she'd trained herself to be, but the biologist only marveled at how very thin the skin must be, there over her veins, to allow such sensation.

Just for now, she edged aside biology and sense. Just for now, she answered the primitive yearning which urged her to rotate her wrist, just slightly, in invitation.

He remembered. Nighthawk sighed as he bowed his head to the flesh at the base of her thumb.

She flowed toward him, her other hand hovering over his hair. Butterfly quiet, she cupped her palm over the back of his head and felt the thickness of his hair above the knotted

187

leather thong. For the first time, she wasn't receiving his caress; she was touching him.

Holding her breath, Charity let three fingers reach from the thong to the collar of his leather shirt.

Soft. So roughly fashioned it might have been ripped from leather, the shirt still felt like velvet under her hand. But leather and velvet were not the textures her senses sought.

Charity closed her eyes at her boldness, then, with her smallest finger, she stroked the skin of his neck, so gently he couldn't have felt the touch, but he did.

He shuddered, circled her wrist with his fingers, and slid the sleeve of her gown up, to kiss the tender flesh at the bend of her elbow. Charity gritted her teeth, but she couldn't hold in a soft whimper. She tried to cover her reaction with a laugh.

Halcon didn't smile as he raised his head and watched her. "Yes?" she asked.

He clasped both hands around the back of her head. She felt so sure he wanted to kiss her, she swayed against the window frame. Instead, his hands slid to the freshly washed braid, down to the very end, and yanked loose the blue satin ribbon.

Brash. Inexcusable. Shameless. The condemning litany came scolding in Aunt P's voice. And the words weren't for him. *Charity, you should know better.* And she did, of course, but when Halcon's hands settled on the white cotton over her shoulder blades, then rose to the back of her neck, she wanted to lean into him, resting her cheek against his neck. She wanted to breathe his scent of leather and green herbs, while his fingers lifted the shattered braid again and again, spreading the woven strands of hair. She agreed it made her shameless, but she simply didn't care.

*Let me stay here forever.* But even as she thought it, burrowed against his neck, Charity felt a thrumming in her veins that demanded more.

Her mind echoed to the thud of her heart, *what now, what now, what now?*

A horse nickered behind him. A vaquero's? His black? The flax-maned chestnut?

She screwed her eyelids closer, driving out that analytical twit still struggling to control her mind. Tighter she closed her eyes, ignoring Princessa, whose front paws rested on the window sill as she rubbed her face toward Halcon.

As if the horse had fractured the underwater slowness of their movements, he kissed her. First soft as her bridal kiss, their touching changed abruptly.

Did he think she recognized him, that he closed their distance so suddenly? Did she?

She formed her lips to mirror Halcon's as they opened. Her head twisted sideways, closer to him, and she felt feverish, knowing she changed the tempo of the kiss. Their teeth met in a click before their lips widened. His tongue eased into her mouth and she gasped, but his hand spanned the back of her neck, under her hair, asking her not to pull away.

*Not like with Freddy, not sloppy and laughable but hot, flushed, eager—enough to make her curse the hacienda wall between them.*

She leaned so ardently from the window that he stood closer to keep her from falling.

*I want to be next to him, against the whole front of him. I have to.*

Her smothered frustration froze when his hand deserted her neck and curved around her breast. His fingers closed, warm as if the gown had disappeared. Surprised, she remained still until he pulled his mouth away to whisper, "*Caridad,* come out with me."

Before she gathered her gown and swung her legs through the opening, his lips jolted forward again, as if he had no control of them, and her lips surged forward too, even as she nodded "yes," she would come out, would go with him, would do whatever he wanted.

Sabotaging all thoughts of respite, her hands surged from his shoulders to his face and the same heat that made her want Halcon's hands against flesh instead of cotton made her fingers snatch at his leather mask as if she'd rip it loose.

*Stop, stop, stop!* Too late her mind, long since subordinate to her body, shrieked a command. And though she threw her

189

hands wide, away from his mask, away from any leather or flesh, he stepped apart.

Embarrassment at her shuddering breaths, at the hand that had touched her breast, flooded between them. Charity forced herself to look up because she feared—if God were merciful it wouldn't happen!—but she feared if he moved out of reach he'd never return.

"Don't go," her fingers caught his shirt, but he stepped back. "No," she hissed. Her fingernails buried in a desperate grip before he collided with his startled horse, out of reach.

Nothing, no words from his lips, no white smile. What was he thinking?

"Damnation, Nicolas!" the words erupted from her. "I know, I *know.*"

But if he cared, if he even heard, she couldn't tell. He didn't kiss her, didn't shake her, didn't spur savagely from the courtyard. He glanced at a glow from the hide shed, guided the horse across the adobe tiles at a walk, faded to a dusky blur near the gates, and disappeared.


Tendrils of mist drifted from the scrub oaks. The trees crowded the inland valley, hiding him among knotted trunks as thick as mythical serpents.

Nicolas's mind writhed as he urged the palomino through wet veils of fog. How quickly he'd deserted his lofty ideals. How easily he'd committed himself to a path both selfish and dangerous.

He'd seen Santana's punishments carried out against Indians, against *rancheros* who traded with foreigners, against an adulteress. Why in God's name had he risked Charlie?

"Damnation, Nicolas, I know," she'd sworn, her hair wavy black and swirling around her. He'd already started moving away from her inquisitive fingers—no, that wasn't fair. Her seeking hands hadn't been curious or set on scientific exploration.

*Sangre de Dios,* he ached at the thought. They had been eager and passionate. Charlie had wanted him, and he'd

190

soaked up her adoration greedily. As much as he'd wanted to strip her free of her gown, he wanted to revel in her searching hands. He knew she hadn't tried to unmask him. Charlie just wanted his face bare to her touch.

Discovery and danger had freed his mind of drugging emotion before he heard her angry whisper. It wouldn't have wakened a soul, but he'd understood clearly as if she'd painted red letters on the whitewashed hacienda walls.

Charlie knew.

Banishment or imprisonment would be the best Charlie could wish for if Santana brought her to trial. Whipping was generally reserved for Indians. But jail, certainly, and humiliation.

Charlie would never soften her punishment by telling what she knew. Although most hidalgos would scoff at the idea of a female possessing Honor, Charlie did. She wouldn't taunt Santana with her knowledge, but if he confronted her, Nicolas knew she'd push her glasses up her freckled nose, cross her arms, and dare Santana to wring a confession from her.

Whipping would follow stubborness. Would they shear off her cloak of hair? Would they bare her torso to lewd eyes before the whips descended? A true patriot would let Charlie suffer for the greater good, but Nicolas Carillo would confess.

Dense fog rolled past as he aimed the horse for higher ground. Nicolas patted the young stallion's neck and wondered why his feelings for Charlie were so foreign. Always before, he'd been expert at separating emotions from reality.

With Esperanza, he'd enjoyed mindless thrusting like a boy's—explosive and all-consuming for moments, but easily forgotten until the next opportunity. For Catalina, his vanished cousin, he'd felt love based on admiration. The two times he could have had her—once when she curled into his arms in pure weariness, once when too much tequila and a fight with Matthew made her seek him for comfort—nobility won over desire.

"Nobility" was no match for Charlie, nor would his need for her be relegated to the background. Mating—she'd used

191

the word, and, it fit. Theirs would be no blind rutting, nor a cozy coming together. Between them, there flashed a current like lightning, an instinctive knowing and anticipation, an insistence and completeness he couldn't have if he remained Halcon.

Night insects, chirring on the hillside above, stopped. Alert and aware, Nicolas felt Halcon invade his senses.

Like the true nighthawk, flying alone, he smelled sagebrush, freshly crushed and pungent. A disturbed rabbit drummed its paw in alarm. Wings whispered overhead and the palomino quivered on the verge of a neigh. Halcon knew another horse was near, before he saw the silhouette on the skyline above.

"Alcalde, I have it. The message."

The rider panted like a hound, as if he, not the horse, had traversed the hillside. Only good fortune made him draw a breath in time to hear Halcon's reata singing toward him.

The messenger spilled beneath the palomino's hooves, rolling and launching into a run before the loop sailed over his neck. The man hit the end of the rope, gagging, as his horse thundered on.

Coughing and choking, the shadow twisted into a crouch and clawed the reata at his throat. His thrashing evoked strong scents of sweat and garlic.

How fortunate the stranger wouldn't recognize the voice of Nicolas Carillo! Halcon needn't rely on force to drain facts from this silly messenger; this night, Halcon could speak.

"Señor, I regret this abrupt end to your journey."

"Who are you?" The man's voice rasped.

"I think you would not believe me if I told you I am an amigo of Santana's, who has borrowed his horse?"

The man spat in disgust.

"I thought not," Halcon continued, "But you must feel free to convey your message to me, as if I were the alcalde."

The man crossed his arms.

"It is irritating," he told his captive, "but you must understand my position, Señor," Halcon kept the reata straight as a spoke while circling the palomino around the seated man.

"You must understand: I do not like wasting an evening. If you refuse to speak it will be the worse for you, amigo——"

"I'm no amigo of yours, Halcon! Yes, I know who you are, and I can see you well enough——" the voice broke as if he reconsidered the wisdom of admitting he could identify Halcon.

"Santana may reward you, but," Halcon sighed, "the alcalde is suspicious. And if he doubted your silence . . ." Nighthawk tsked as if he'd spilled a drop of wine on a fresh tablecloth.

When the messenger's jacket crackled with movement, Halcon jerked the neck-encircling reata snug. Even fools carried knives. Then he recognized the sound as crumpled parchment.

"The alcalde's correspondent would not be so indiscreet as to write the message?" He laughed aloud at his luck.

"Of course not." The hesitation rang clear as admission.

"I see. And will you surrender this non-missive to me, so I'm not be forced to take it from your breathless body, later?"

The man scrambled to his feet and lurched toward the palomino.

"Señor, I'm sure you're a man of honor, but I feel it fair to warn you I am unsheathing my sword," Halcon rattled the blade against its scabbard as the messenger approached, " . . . and will keep it leveled," Halcon heard a gasp as the sword tip grazed the man, "Ah yes, just there, at your throat."

Halcon grabbed for the parchment, slipped it into his waistband and elevated his hand so that the sword point moved harder against the man's throat.

"And now, señor, since I fear I cannot read, please reveal the message in words."

"What? Halcon cannot read? I thought—everyone thinks——"

The man's guffaw jiggled the sword point. Eager to save his pride, the clown believed the worst of his captor. How convenient, if he chose to spread the tale that Halcon was an uneducated peasant! Why explain that only an owl could read by such faint moonlight?

"When you have enjoyed your joke, Señor, let me remind you of this: Halcon is known for his mercy, but it is not unswerving. If you have heard rumors of Nighthawk at Santa Barbara, believe them."

"But you—" The buffoon's laughter turned to stammering. "You hung that man upside down in a tree, with his own reata. He might have died!"

"He might have," Halcon agreed.

He gave the messenger time to remember what he'd heard of Halcon's cruelty in Santa Barbara. Some had called the act evil, but the power and justice of it had been intoxicatingly sweet.

*Dios*, the swine had been so near to raping her—

"And do you know, señor," he probed, "what the man's infraction was? The man hung upside down?"

"Well, he was a soldier, and Nighthawk despises Mexican soldiers—"

"He attacked a woman. Just 'a God-forsaken Indio' he called her, and he'd hardly noticed her nursling son crawling and crying, nearby," Halcon explained.

"And that is why his uniform pants were down," the messenger realized, "hobbling his knees together, even in the tree."

The messenger scrubbed one hand back and over his lips.

"You knew help was near—for the soldier. Halcon never kills. None of the stories—"

"Señor, there is a first time for everything, and I raised the story only to prove Halcon is not all-merciful," he snapped, "My patience grows short."

"The *alcalde's* plans have been approved," the messenger's words rushed out on an exhalation. "He has permission to implement them."

Greed, approved by a subprefect in Monterey and implemented by Santana in the south, was the theme of the messenger's revelation. Money and goods would be wrung from foreign vessels, land from disloyal rancheros and gold from Indios whose villages sat on rich lands. Though the ideas were not new to him, Halcon knew the precise names and numbers would be invaluable in converting uncommitted *hacendados*.

"I don't know if I've truly helped you, Señor Nighthawk," the messenger ended.

"I appreciate your courtesy all the same." *Halcon's* voice stayed noncommittal.

"The rope, señor?"

"Remains a bit longer. I urge you, though," Halcon nodded at the messenger's returned mount, and his voice held friendly advice, "approach your horse carefully and keep pace with this headstrong palomino, if you do not wish to walk the streets of Los Cielos like a hound on a leash."

They were almost too late. As they turned the horses onto Calle Principal, Los Cielos's main street, Halcon noted the tar smell of the *brea* roofs, and the stillness.

His eyes tracked past the saddle shop to a solitary lantern hanging outside the bodega. A door opened to emit light and the clinking of gold coins. Two men, their steps jaunty but sedate, walked from the bodega, spurs jingling as they sought one of the town houses ringing the Plaza. Behind them, the door remained ajar. Shuffling feet and flickering cards became background to the indulgent voice of the bodega's proprietor.

"Last glass, gentlemen. The monte tables are closed," his voice rose over muttered complaints. "My eager young bride is both a blessing and misfortune, hombres. What can I tell you? She cared for me well enough a month ago, but if I am late to her bed, yet again, *quien sabe?*"

A chorus of knowing moans underscored his query.

"Last glass, gentlemen. Count your winnings and go home."

Halcon recognized one of the departing men as Ramon del Valle, possessor, himself, of a much younger wife whose buxom charms had been displayed the night he'd relieved her of del Valle's family jewels.

Rancheros like del Valle, men with enough leisure and

money to spend their evenings in wine shops and town houses, could be his best allies. Independent men like his father, they mouthed loyalty to Mexico, then went about business, as they liked.

If the messenger's confession fired their *Californio* honor, he must be sure Mother invited each of them to Charlie's *bailecito casero*. Fiestas provided the quiet corners and brandy that fostered hidalgo rebellion.

Through the bodega's open door, Halcon saw other influential acquaintances. Sitting back, heels propped on a monte table covered with glittering towers of coins, sat Sanchez, California's best brewer of *aguardiente*. Rising to his feet, hands supporting the small of his back as he stretched, was Ibarra, a victim of the alcalde's campaign against "smugglers." The others were beyond his vision, but, given the men he could see, none were likely to be King's men of the same chauvinistic stripe as Esperanza's father, Juan Ortez.

Farewell your quiet evening, señores, Halcon shrugged his apology, then froze.

Could he have forgotten Freddy, Arturo and the trappers might be within? Damn Charity for so scattering his thoughts, he'd forgotten the presence of four more men who knew him.

Too late to worry, he shrugged fatalistically. With luck they would be drunk. Nicolas smacked Mancha's horse with the flat of his hand and sent it bolting into the bodega.

A wild flash of light rocked and flared as the horse upset a lantern.

*"Diablo!"*

Halcon saw a cigar shower sparks as it dropped from the corner of Jaime Tiburon's mouth, saw a sword glint before the careening, neighing horse, and then the blackness inside the bodega rivaled that of the streets.

Halcon held the long reata taut, like a fisherman. *Cristo,* it took much of his nerve to only turn and nod at del Valle. The old man had wheeled from his meander home, and stood wheezing and waving a pistol as long as a colt's leg.

"What's the meaning of this? A horse in my bodega!" The proprietor flapped a white apron at the weary bay and it

196

stumbled backward, it's rump appearing again in the doorway.

"Keep it away from tables—oh! My floor!"

Lanterns flared inside.

"Finally I put down planks over the dirt—"

Jaime Tiburon gripped the bay's reins just below the bit, clucking and easing the animal backward. Somehow he had retrieved his cigar, and its tip glowed orange as he regarded the rider controlling the messenger's leash.

"Halcon."

Nicolas nodded at his old friend, wishing he could clap his cocky shoulder, wishing his masquerade as Carillo-the-royalist hadn't sundered their friendship two years ago.

"He doesn't speak? I'll make him speak!" del Valle flapped his pistol perilously close to Jaime's face.

"Ramon, for the love of *Dios*, put that thing away!" Jaime brushed the gun aside and continued staring at the dark horseman. "I want to know why the Nighthawk has come calling."

Six rancheros and the proprietor stood outside, and though their voices had rung off the walls of the new church, and roused a dog to staccato barks, no one else stirred in the streets of Los Cielos.

Halcon tugged at the reata. Pray God, Santana's messenger repeated the tale he'd told in the toyon bushes. He did, and Halcon couldn't have arranged a better audience.

Sanchez had the memory of a priest. He'd learn the tale like a litany and recite it far and wide. The proprietor would stimulate his patrons' appetite for food and drink by showing them where he'd held at bay the dreaded outlaw, Halcon. Ramon del Valle, eager to find a cause, brandished his pistol, bemoaning absentee rulers and false alcaldes.

Jaime Tiburon asked questions. He listened. He pressed the messenger past vague suppositions and Nicolas saw Jaime would lead them in whatever they planned. Nicolas leaned from the palomino, surrendering the parchment which supported the messenger's words.

Alarmed, he braced for an assault to accompany Jaime's

197

movement, but Jaime only grasped his forearm and squeezed. Warning faded and Nicolas returned the grip.

"*Gracias*, Halcon. We appreciate your actions and would not have you think that all Californians are Mexican cattle."

Grudging nods underscored Jaime's words. For emphasis, del Valle fired his pistol into the night sky.

As Nicolas wheeled the palomino toward the presidio, Jaime's grip lingered. It would be pleasing to believe his old friend knew him, knew what he did, and understood the pain brought by the end of their friendship.

## Chapter Sixteen

The day of the engagement fiesta, Doña Anna insisted on a full midday meal, attended by the entire family and "the bridal couple."

"Señor Freddy, you will please try a bit more of the *pozole*." Don Carlos motioned a maid to ladle thick pork stew into Freddy's bowl. "And you"—he aimed a critical eye at Charity—"are quiet as never before."

Charity raised her eyes from their apparent study of the tablecloth. Truly, she'd watched the veins over the back of Nicolas' hand and wondered, with that empty falling away of her stomach, how she could have allowed—

Ha! *Allowed,* is it, this morning, Charity O'Dell? Very well. How could she have *reveled, delighted, soared* as that hand stroked the underside of her breast?

At his father's voice, Nicolas's fingers tightened on his spoon, but he didn't look up at her. He hadn't favored her with even a passing glance, when only hours ago she'd allowed him—

"As you will," she mimicked him, silently. She had the skills to stalk wild prey. *I've nearly got you, Halcon, and I'll snare you whether you will it or no.*

Before answering Don Carlos, she swallowed a sip of water and glanced around the table. A portrait artist would have itched for a pencil and sketchbook.

Grim and green, Freddy obviously suffered from his overnight visit to Los Cielo. His comrades, tumbling into the hacienda just before dawn, had loudly praised the region's *aguardiente*.

Doña Anna flicked back a wisp of hair trailing from her tidy bun, and Charity thought she would have shaded her cheeks flushed, her smile self-satisfied.

Intent on their hearty meal, the twins leaned back in their chairs, relishing the lull in activity. Since daybreak, Anna had relegated them to the position of servants, carrying orders and cauldrons of food from kitchen to courtyard to house.

Nicolas she would have sketched with stiff fingers. Erect and still, garbed in black and white, he might have been chipped from ice.

She'd be damned if she'd feel sorry for him. Why wouldn't he trust her? What stopped him from confiding the glorious truth?

"Señora, you're not ill after that long walk to the shore?"

Charity caught her breath as Don Carlos's voice summoned her.

"No, Don Carlos, I loved the walk. But, in spite of the sea air and exercise, I—didn't sleep well."

"I saw candlelight streaming from beneath your door, very late," Barbara reported as she nipped a rolled tortilla.

"And why did you stroll the halls 'very late' last night, sister?" Arturo wagged his finger at his twin.

"I was looking for Princessa. I'm always afraid one of those dogs of yours will eat her if she escapes into the courtyard," Barbara said.

"As they should," Nicolas muttered. "A more useless animal does not exist."

*Ha! Princessa had crouched next to her as she'd embraced Halcon! And the little cat avoided men at all costs. All men except Nicolas. Hadn't Princessa even batted the nightrider's arm?*

"I was up late, writing," Charity admitted.

"Adding to your Halcon research?" Barbara pushed her plate away. "It's so amusing when Charity reads me her notes," Barbara told her parents. "Do you know—"she caught Nicolas' wrist, "that she suspects he is an hidalgo by day—"

200

"Charity's proof," Nicolas drew out the word with sarcasm, "is no doubt the same sort she's concocting to support this theory of female wolves selecting their own mates."

Charity almost lurched from her chair. Was she insane? Was she frothing-at-mouth mad, to believe his sneering lips had kissed hers last night? But he had, she knew he had. He must be very afraid to attack her so.

And if he'd attacked her in anything else—her appearance, riding ability, social ineptness—she would have allowed it.

"My proof—" Charity's voice quaked with fury and she brushed off Freddy's cautioning hand, beneath the table. "Nicolas, when I publish, my proof and supporting research will be above reproach."

"And what scientific process is it which allows you to project human qualities onto wild beasts?" Nicolas folded his napkin into a perfect triangle. When she couldn't marshal a response, he continued.

"Like most of your sex—" Nicolas glanced at his father for support, "you think with your feelings."

Nicolas smiled for the first time all day. It was a condescending smirk she itched to slap from his handsome face.

The screech of Charity's chair legs on the adobe tiles preceded Don Carlos's low reprimand.

"Nicolas."

Nicolas' inclined his sleek black head to his father. "Forgive me, *Padre*," Nicolas's regret seemed genuine. "I've reached the age when I need my sleep. Or perhaps I begrudge the time I must spend going over accounts before tonight's fiesta."

"I did enjoy our ride back, though, amigo." Freddy winked at Nicolas and for a moment Charity felt bewildered. If Nicolas had been in Los Cielos this morning . . . "Did you hear any more of Santana's horse?"

Paloma! Of course, the horse stamping behind Halcon hadn't been black.

"I'm sure we'll hear more of it tonight. I feel certain the gossips will contribute valuable evidence to your notes on the outlaw, Señora," Nicolas's aside seemed calculated to provoke her.

"Sneer now, Nicolas," she took a deep breath and set her jaw. "But I am sure," she continued smoothly, seeing Don Carlos unclench his fist at her moderate tone, "that my research will be of such value, the alcalde will wish he had done it himself."

Arturo glanced from her to his father. Don Carlos shifted uneasily.

"Pardon me, Charity, but it's unlikely Guerro will be interested in the scribbling of a schoolgirl." Nicolas pretended to camouflage his smile behind a raised water goblet. Clearly, he meant her to see. "His strategies, poor as they are, exist on a slightly higher plane."

"Enough," Doña Anna's slashing gesture told her son she found his biting cynicism inappropriate for the *sala*.

Charity flinched when Freddy pinned her hand to the tablecloth.

"I wish I understood what happened between you while I was gone," Freddy's melancholy face turned from Charity to Nicolas. "I vow"—he shrugged to the other Carillos—"I never saw such close friends as these two were in Boston."

Charity tried to believe it was embarrassment that made tears threaten. Freddy's assessment of her friendship with Nicolas touched her so that she hardly bristled when Arturo assessed her behavior as he would that of an unpredictable pet.

"They get better and then they get worse," Arturo told Freddy. "They talk well enough of horses, and wildlife—though not today. Even," Arturo lowered his voice and pretended to glance about for eavesdroppers, "they even discuss the plight of our *Indios* in a civilized manner. If Santana isn't about.

"But mention Halcon," Arturo continued, "and, as you see, they bring out the worst in each other."

"Oh, and they do well enough when they're fencing," Barbara looked up from the orange she'd begun peeling. "Nicolas leaves his den flushed and happy as a boy!" Barbara bumped her shoulder companionably against Nicolas's, then squealed her irritation at his stiffness.

"Oh! You're like hugging a tree—" she fumed.

"How about some fencing, then?" Freddy suggested. "I haven't seen you two spar—with swords, that is—since I returned. I used to love to watch. Doña Anna, could you spare Charity from her decorating chores, later in the day, perhaps?"

"Anything, if it will enable them to behave in a civilized manner," Anna agreed.

"I have the books to do—" Nicolas began.

"You'd be doing me a favor, amigo," Freddy insisted. "Perhaps the added exertion will tire Charlie so she may," Freddy cleared his throat pointedly, "sleep, tonight."

Nothing improper showed in Freddy's tone, but Charity pushed up her glasses and hoped sheer will could control her stomach's quailing. Probably she imagined his implication. This time.

There'd been nothing veiled about his outright—and justified, she must admit—suggestion, day before yesterday, that taking a glass or two of wine before bed might make his life—and their cock-eyed, yes, that was what he'd called it, "their cock-eyed marriage"—easier.

Nicolas's nod of assent and appointment of an hour made Freddy beam.

If she had any backbone at all, Charity told herself, she'd protest. Not one of them—not Freddy, Nicolas, not even Arturo—had consulted her. But, she felt again that flush of heat, faint compared to last night, but dizzying just the same, and muttered grudging consent to cover her excitement.

*Sangre de Cristo,* Charlie's research was truly impressive. Nicolas looked quickly over his shoulder. A scratch had sounded outside her closed door.

He closed his eyes to listen. Down the hall, Barbara and Pilar squabbled like hens over the placement of a table. Charlie would be with them.

A shovel rasped on rock from the courtyard where Freddy's

booming laughter accompanied the layering of seaweed and clams into a fire pit.

Playing outlaw in his own home was risky, but worthwhile.

Charlie's map of the land from Monterey to San Diego was surprisingly accurate and marked with x's indicating sightings of Halcon. She'd used black ink for reliable sources, her footnotes said, and blue for those she considered less reliable. She'd listed every source by name, too—Santana, Arturo, Barbara, Don Carlos and a host of helpful vaqueros.

He moved the map aside and regarded what appeared to be lists, headed "Appearance, General," "Attire," "Horse(s)," "Speech," and, in large capital letters, "BEHAVIOR."

*Dios,* had she missed a thing? No wonder she'd taken offense at his harranging. Nicolas ran his finger down the sheet titled "Horse(s)."

"1) Black horse, probably stallion. Moorish/Mustang cross? 2) Chestnut—unsubstantiated because of light. 3) Dun—unsubstantiated, source has preference for duns."

He flipped to the next page.

"Voice: whisper, but us. silent. Uses gestures, etc. Source 6: Halcon speaks w/*Indios*, vaqueros."

Nicolas rubbed his forehead vigorously. Was he more talkative with *Indios and vaqueros?*

The scratching at the door came again, accompanied by Princessa's nasal meow.

The useless beast would keep at it, too, until he admitted her. Nicolas took a long step to the door, scooped up the cat and cradled her with one arm as he continued to read.

*Ah, here, she proves me right,* he smiled. *This is where she shows that females are poor scientists, no matter their sharp minds.*

"Appearance: wide shoulders, narrow hips/horseman's carriage. About six feet tall (comp. to ht. of horse—other estimate: 7 ft., Source 12, S. del Valle) By all accounts Handsome! Dashing! Protector of helpless. No companions. (Source 8: Indio outlaw Salvador?

Source 7—lapsed priest in Santa Barbara?) Source 2: no mustache. Disguise? Valid? Flashing smile. Eyes: brown or dark, merry in most instances."

Beneath these citations, she'd used dark, sweeping pencil strokes to sketch a windswept portrait of the outlaw, sword raised in mocking salute.

"*Carumba!* He resembles Halcon as much as you do a cougar, eh, Princessa?" Nicolas mocked quietly. "Cast your eyes on this hombre's legs? Do you blush, Princessa? Tell me, why would such a one need a horse?"

He turned the page sideways to read a hastily scrawled notation.

"Source 7 (Esperanza Ortez): menacing mien. Valid?"

If he were any kind of a renegade his devoted fiance would bear the weight of his "menacing mien." Esperanza had been pointedly absent since Halcon's theft of her betrothal ring, but Nicolas had no doubt the garish replacement would stir his fiancee's passion. He should feel no guilt. Esperanza whored for money and position; he would use her accordingly.

The hell of it was, he didn't desire Esperanza. He wanted Charlie. He'd almost given up attempts to banish such thoughts.

How much longer would he spend on his knees in confession if, just once more, he pictured Charlie naked? If, just once more, he felt the avid softness of her leaning into his arms?

How many *ave marias* redeemed a patriot lusting after his best friend's wife? How many "our fathers" for touching her breast? Princessa bit his tightening hand and plummeted to the floor.

Charlie would hate him for destroying her labors, but the papers were too damning to exist. Especially the last page, which she'd headed "Nic/NH."

Charlie had taken each category from the preceding pages

and compared him with the bandit. My sweet *scientifica*. He gave a low whistle and shook his head. He remembered Charlie studying a Latin text in their Harvard dorm room. Hair chopped short to curve around her face, she'd leaned excitedly over the book, flushed and eager to absorb.

Halcon's passionate *Caridad* had not been in charge when she penned these pages. It had been Charlie, thirsty blue-stocking scholar, and Charlie hadn't missed a thing. From horse to hat to opportunity, she had him. The only aspect of Halcon's existence that puzzled her was what she called "habitat." She didn't know of Refugio. There, at least, God had been merciful.

He folded the three largest pages together and slipped them inside his vest. He rolled his shoulders back to settle the black coat, and smoothed his lapels.

He'd light a candle in his study and burn the papers, but first, he wanted to read these over again. Perhaps Charlie could help him plan one spectacular event to galvanize the *Californios* into action, so he could quit this charade.

And do what? The question slammed through his frame as if he'd lunged his sword point into a boulder. While the fantasy here existed, Halcon could court Charlie. Halcon could kiss Charlie. Halcon might even bed her.

Christ! His sanity wavered, elusive as smoke.

Charity stepped into the doorway of Anna's sewing room to catch her breath. The headless mannequin, dressed in pinned scraps of red silk, regarded her.

When would she shake this feeling that someone just around the next corner snickered at her attempts to be female? Not Nicolas. Not Arturo, nor Don Carlos. Barbara and Anna had smiled at the opal brooch fastening her new shawl, this morning. Freddy had applauded the coffee and cream striped gown she'd worn in place of riding skirts.

Her head ached and her stomach felt as though someone wrung it like a wet towel. Why must it be time again? She'd counted herself lucky to avoid that beastly process her embarrassed father couldn't speak of, that Aunt P. had haltingly explained, only after Charity questioned the tidy rectangles of cloth left discreetly on her nightstand.

Other girls mastered the inconvenience, just as they learned to move gracefully among their skirts when whalebone crushed the breath from them, just as they inclined their heads cunningly when a suitor bored them past endurance. They learned the knack of smiles which promised or denied.

Barbara, for instance, would know exactly how to signal a man that her yearning for him surpassed friendship, propriety—even the laws of man and God.

Well, no, probably she wouldn't. Barbara would never flout such absolutes, but Charity knew she must.

In spite of everything, she wanted Nicolas, and she must convince him to—take her. Iron determination had taught her fencing, Spanish, and horsemanship of a sort. All that determination paled next to what she had decided to label "physical need."

She'd never guessed longing could be so fierce! No wonder deer clashed antlers, horses slashed with ripping teeth and wolves, once mated, sidled so close they tripped each other to the earth.

Last night had been a revelation and a relief. Finally she knew her desire flared for one man, not two. Her body had recognized Halcon/Nicolas long since, but her mind had refused, until she compiled the list.

But the solution had lead to another problem. What of Freddy, her husband?

"I won't force you," Freddy had promised the same night he'd urged her to drink a second glass of wine. "But I want to resolve this—" he'd swallowed and pursed his lips and finally turned away from her, "this *situation*, during our voyage to San Diego. We'll only sail for a day or two, but I'll tell you the truth, Charlie. I can't take much more. I'm getting itchy as a hound."

Tomorrow the ship would sail for San Diego.

Last night, at the crest of her wildest imaginings, Charity had erased the mistake of touching Nighthawk's mask. In her imagination, they'd shone golden in the candlelight, making love before Freddy could have her as a virgin. Her waking dreams were so sweet, she'd resisted sleep, staring at the tongue of candle flame long after her vision blurred.

Now, she pounded her fist against the black trousers she wore for fencing. Nicolas could not make love to her here, in his parent's house. Even coupling beasts required a certain amount of privacy. Besides, the partners involved were usually on speaking terms, and the only words he'd awarded her today had been critical and demeaning.

Self-indulgent ninny. Charity yanked the cuffs of her white silk shirt, as she strode from the sewing room. Piratical in cut, she knew it was silly and impractical for fencing, but it tucked neatly into the waistband of the black trousers, baring her neck. She prayed the sight was provocative.

She hesitated in the doorway. Why did she feel an undercurrent of weakness in this feminine stalking? She stood, resisting the lure of the high ceilings, the honey-colored light and the faint scent of honing oil.

Go engage his blade, she urged herself silently, it's likely the most of him you'll ever have.


Nicolas had known Charlie would be there first. If she came at all.

From the doorway he watched her lunge at a wall target, one leg bent, one stretched long and firm from toe to waist. Her combative posture, viewed from the rear, cleared his mind of patriotic gibberish. He wanted nothing more than to bear her to the floor, to fall on her and enter her in the fleeting afternoon sunlight.

"Your back leg isn't straight enough," he barked.

Charlie didn't flinch at his voice, didn't give any sign she'd heard, except that she launched another lunge, nearly perfect, then turned with folded arms, blade angled toward the ceiling. She didn't smile, only held his eyes, warily.

She'd worn white silk and black trousers as he always did

when fencing. And her hair fell over her shoulder in a tight braided queue. Why had she made them twins?

"We don't have a lot of time." Nicolas selected a light sword from the rack and heard her footsteps follow him. When she still didn't speak, he glanced over his shoulder before examining his weapon's grip.

What did it mean, her silence and half-smile? One thing was sure, Charlie looked pretty. Not healthy and energetic, not impish or teasing—pretty. His mother and Barbara had made it impossible for him to ignore, this morning. The cream gown had been nice enough, but the shawl, something like the color of a ripe peach, had fired the copper of her suntanned cheeks until he had to leave the room to keep from staring.

Nicolas pulled on his glove. If that's what a sleepless night did for her, he would gladly provide more of them.

No.

He swiveled his wrist in a figure eight, letting the sword slash the disciplined song of Nicolas.

He turned, elbow bent, and she came immediately *en garde*. She'd indulge in no social chatter, said her narrowed eyes. He snapped her a brusque salute, wondering if she meant to punish him for the morning's unforgivable jibes.

"Don't crouch, Charlie. Relax into your legs, there," Nicolas tapped her blade with his. "Remember that back arm is for balance. Not too stiff. Better."

Advance, retreat, advance. Charlie danced forward and back, lighter on her feet than ever before. The white shirt billowed as she retreated, then clung as she advanced. He could almost see the shadow between her breasts. He retreated again, again, reeling her closer.

Her furrowed brow told him she suspected his retreat. She sensed a trap, never guessing he was the prey, tempted past discretion each time he won a glimpse beneath the fluttering shirt.

Nicolas tilted his blade to leave one side unguarded. She sought his eyes.

"Are we playing or training?" She advanced as she questioned, but her frown remained.

"Come on," he snapped, impatiently.

Two short running steps and a lunge brought her close, but he deflected her blade like a feather.

"Don't ask permission, Charlie. And don't signal your lunge so far ahead. Surprise me."

Her lips compressed into a line and she stood out of position, arms folded once more.

"What?" Nicolas recoiled at his own peevish tone. *Cristo*, why must he bully this girl?

"I just want to know what we're doing, Nicolas." She strolled past him, arms folded. He had to turn to see her.

"Are you giving me lessons," she asked. "Or are we fencing?"

If the idea weren't so farfetched, if Charlie weren't so opposite to subterfuge, he'd think she had decided to control this moment.

She waited, black hair plaited so tight her eyes slanted at the corners, arms cinched hard against her waist.

"I'll make you a bargain, Charlie." He strode close enough to touch her and almost faltered when her eyes examined him like a specimen. "I'll fight you left-handed."

Her lips twitched. Because he'd called for a fight or because he patronized her?

"Left-handed, but I'll give you no quarter."

"I don't know what that means."

Charlie shrugged as if she didn't care, either, and her breasts rolled beneath the silk.

" 'Quarter' is a military term, *pequena*," he settled into position and prowled around her, "It's the mercy you grant a surrendering foe."

Charlie couldn't swallow back the smile, but she tried, as she gave his blade a quick beat and moved closer.

"So if I ask for mercy—" she began.

"There will be none."

She narrowed her eyes, licked her lips and glanced pointedly past him, but the smile still curved her lips.

"I'm for you, sir."

Charlie laughed and wheeled around backwards, taunting him to come after her. *Dios,* she was quarry worth chasing.

Her smile had vanished when she faced him again. Trim and light, mistress of delicate finger work on the grip of her sword, she used both mind and body to place the tip where she wanted it, but she lacked the strength to best him in close quarters. As soon as he pressed the thick part of her blade, she retreated or feinted low.

Exhilarated each time they closed, he considered teasing her that the shirt, not her sword, was her best weapon. He could not keep his eyes from the material, now yawning, now concealing.

She feinted low again, and as he lazily dipped his blade to meet her, there was no contact, no metallic clash. Charlie's blade vanished, and her sword tip pricked his shoulder before he parried and trapped her blade with his.

She held him there, resisting so close he saw perspiration gather on her brow.

"No quarter," she grunted. She used both hands on her grip to push his blade away, before she skittered backward, far off balance, but out of reach.

Metal rang on metal as she attacked again. Charlie parried every riposte, huffing like a winded horse, and he knew she'd been careful, until now, to avoid his blade at all costs. He heard, too the creaking of *carretas* and barking dogs in the courtyard outside. He'd have to finish before his father sought him out and scolded him as a bad—

*Cristo!* He'd had to deflect her attack into the floor. Sloppy. The defense of a juvenile.

"Very well," he muttered. He should be ashamed that he gloried in her widening eyes.

He caught her in one lunge.

He trapped her blade high on her left, at neck level. She tried to parry, but he'd found her weakest quadrant, and he locked the hilt of his sword against hers.

Charlie refused to move, pressing until she had nothing left but will, into the thick part of his blade.

"No quarter," he whispered.

She launched one desperate thrust off her back leg, fighting with all she had. If he released the pressure now she'd fall.

They were close enough that their breaths mingled.

*Give up, Pequena. You can't always win. Give up to me.*

He pressed a little harder and her arm trembled, but she only bit her bottom lip and strained closer. With a twinge of remorse, he saw her lip bleed. He'd become an animal. He wanted to kiss the blood away.

A moan, she relaxed her grip and his sword slipped past, leaving a slash along her neck.

"God, Charlie!" He let his sword fall ringing to the floor.

He pulled off his sash for a bandage. She kept staring at him. Could he have hurt her that badly? It appeared to be only a scratch. The wound remained a thin red line, not pulsing, not dripping.

"Charlie!" He dabbed the sash at her neck and held her face in his other hand to turn her chin toward him. She tripped forward a step and pressed her lips over his.

Nicolas told himself that even if he hadn't heard footsteps ringing down the hallway, he would have moved off to arm's length. Charlie's chin dropped to her chest as tears of humiliation squeezed beneath her eyelashes.

*Charlie, Charlie, what do you want from me? What can I do? Will you reach into my chest and wring my heart so hard you jerk me to my knees? Will you kill me with your clumsy kisses?*

"Well Freddy," he said as Charlie's husband swore and jogged toward them from the doorway. "I fear I've given your wife more of a fight than either of us wanted."

# Chapter Seventeen

She did not want to be a bride.

"You insist on wearing spectacles?" Pilar ignored Charity's agitation, tapping a forefinger against her lips.

It was too late, months too late, but she wanted out. She could not go through this travesty of a celebration.

"I insist. You've taken over every other preparation for this fiesta. So please, leave me my sight!" Charity wheeled on the Mexican woman, unsatisfied with raging at her mirror image.

"That cream muslin dress would serve. I brought it to be my wedding gown. But no, you must dress me in Doña Anna's cast-offs." She glared past the glass disks, wishing they clarified this merciless alien world.

"I think no mantilla, then." Pilar ignored the outburst, and brushed Charity's hair. "You were a bride two months ago, after all, not yesterday."

Two months ago she'd been so sure of what she wanted. Her plan, conceived in the brain-numbing days sans Father, John, and Nicolas, called for marriage to Freddy. He *owed* her for ending her stint at Harvard, and his letters had proven him amenable.

She'd pictured them striding up and down California hills during the day, transcribing her notes and examining her sketches each night. But her plans hadn't worked.

Betrayed by both mind and body, always before her allies, she found herself bewildered.

Never had her mind conjured the possibility that she and Freddy would have a falling out over—marital relations.

"No, no, Señora. Keep your head level."

If only she could.

Pilar yanked the plait to keep her from burying her face in her hands. Charity couldn't recall falling into such a pose ever before, yet she'd stood so for nearly an hour after Freddy had grabbed her and stormed from Nicolas' den.

"What happened? Damn it, Charlie, you *will* tell me!"

She'd refused, and he'd finally decided his stubborn wife had only suffered a blow to her pride.

"Hellfire, Charlie, you let me blow off at Nicolas, let me cuss my best friend, and for what?" Freddy had paced across the room, then pounced back. "If you don't tell me otherwise, I'm assuming this injury is half, *at least* half, your fault."

He'd peeled back her shirt collar and she'd leaned her head to one side so he could examine the mark, again. If Nicolas had touched her so, she wouldn't have felt dull detachment.

And then Freddy's blue eyes had clouded with sympathy.

"Are you just homesick, Baby? Is that it?"

She'd swallowed, closed her eyes and leaned into his broad chest. Even as she'd felt the softness of well-worn corduroy against her cheek, she'd known only a selfish brat would seek comfort in his familiar hug when he'd believe she wanted more.

"We'll have a good time tonight," Freddy had said, rocking her. "You put on that Spanish lace Pilar jabbered about. I'll wear the blue velvet *ranchero* suit Arturo convinced me to wear—Lordy won't the boys hoot?—and we'll be the fanciest pair of *Yanquis* California ever saw.

"There's the smile I've looked for," his knuckle had nudged one corner of her mouth. "A little trembly, but worth the wait.

"We're going to be happy, Charlie. I promise. Starting tonight. The Eagle sails on the early tide and I'll show you the time of your life in San Diego.

"We'll do some business, too. I won't presume on the

214

Carillos' hospitality forever. I've even written ahead to set up appointments." Freddy had winked, then taken himself off to apologize for the tongue-lashing he'd given Nicolas.

She'd resisted Barbara's probing, too. She might have given into Arturo, but Nicolas, thundering and imperious, had driven his little brother away. She must face her misery, alone.

She'd felt desolate after Father died, but this heavy gloom felt most like the November afternoon when Aunt P. had had Critter crated up and donated to the zoo. For days after, her chest had ached with tears.

"Ladies often keep pets to occupy their affections," Aunt P. had recommended when Charity complained of loneliness. "They keep kittens, spaniels . . . Why, Mrs. Laughton even has a dear little monkey who chatters to her while she does needlepoint."

So, Aunt P. had approved her decision to adopt the sleek-coated baby racoon. Things had gone well, at first. Ladies who called for tea clapped their gloved hands in delight, calling Critter "cunning" when she washed a sugarplum or tart crust in the dish of water Charity provided. A "dear little thing," they'd agreed, when Critter nibbled her own refreshment, rotating it in her paws, glancing at Charity, but never lowering her shining black eyes from the perfumed creatures who pointed and cooed.

Critter had reached one year, when Mrs. Graver's niece Theodora, a cake brain in violet silk, clutched the racoon by the scruff and sought to lift her like a house cat. Critter's spitting growl drowned in Theodora's shriek. Then the animal vanished and Theodora held aloft a bitten, bloody finger.

No good had come of Charity's attempts to explain the idiosyncracies of wild creatures kept captive. Each word only intensified Aunt P.'s outrage.

She didn't visit the zoo after that, and often wished she hadn't watched as the carriage carrying Critter pulled away, leaving her to press her nose against the window's frosty glass.

"Surprise me," Nicolas had teased. "Don't ask permission." She'd felt confused, but when he explained "no quarter," she'd decided he was flirting, speaking of more than fencing. She'd convinced herself—how mortifying to remember!—that he'd meant she should—that he'd been referring to last night, and that she should kiss him!

Their rapid, unrestrained swordplay had echoed, at least for her, the passion of the night before. Truth be told, she'd never felt the sword cut. He'd loomed above her and she'd seen only his eyes, black centers widening, spreading until they swallowed her and she lost the strength to hold off his blade.

His arm had caught her as her knees buckled, and his shouts came from faraway. By then she only knew he held her, and she had kissed him.

"Be still now." Pilar adjusted Charity's collar. "I do not want to disturb your bandage. Perhaps this shawl will disguise young Nicolas's handiwork," Pilar spat the last word.

"Don't blame him," Charity began.

"Of course not," Pilar snapped, fist closed over a pair of silver brooches.

Pilar tugged Charity's white lace bodice until it met the lawn skirt, then draped the peach shawl over her shoulders and the coin-sized bandage on her neck. She crossed the long ends of shawl over Charity's breasts and secured them at her waist with a gold satin sash and silver brooches.

"I still think the spectacles—" Pilar wheedled.

"I won't negotiate about the spectacles." Charity took a last shuddering breath, weary with fighting off tears.

Her wedding fiesta proceeded without her on the patio. She smelled spicy red sauce and the salt tang of clams pit-baked in seaweed. And she smelled roses.

The scent enveloped her as she spotted Esperanza. Nicolas's fiancée wore crimson satin and scores of serpentine ribbons that shivered amid jet curls as she laughed up into Guerro Santana's enchanted face.

"God." Charity moaned, stepping back from the window to tread on Pilar's toes. She'd thought the woman gone.

" 'God comes to see without ringing the bell.' " Pilar winced, but her eyes had followed Charity's and the grimace might have been for her toes or Nicolas's bewitching *novia*. "He comes. Wait and see if He doesn't, *chica*."


"I love my ring, Nicolas," Esperanza purred as she rubbed the oversized ruby across the small of his back.

Santana had recalled urgent business with Freddy Larkin at Nicolas's approach, and now Esperanza took advantage of the bushes behind them to snake her hand beneath his vest hem, beneath his shirt, to the waistband of his breeches.

Hot as he'd been last night, Esperanza's public invasion of private flesh should have been titillating. Instead, he bristled that she tried to play him for a puppet.

"Esperanza, what did you say that so amused Guerro?"

Her pout accompanied the snappish withdrawal of her hand.

"You and I were not speaking of Guerro, Nicolas," she said. "Although it was he who sought after my last engagement ring."

Married to this one, a man would do well to guard his *cojones*. Esperanza would need no knife to geld her husband. Not as long as she could speak.

Had he been insane, weeks ago, when he'd believed Esperanza an advantage of his royalist pretending? Or was he insane now?

*Quien sabe?* Who knew and who cared? There'd be time enough for philosophizing, soon. His mother had promised to concoct some homely errand to take him away from the rancho and allow him to range further to sow revolt. And escape Charlie.

Just now, his fiancée had called him a coward.

"You question my manhood, Señorita?" He caught her hand. Damp from its station on his back, it repelled him.

Esperanza raised her arm so the back of his hand grazed her low-cut neckline. Her lidded eyes glittered with the same flat sheen of the ribbons in her hair.

"Not your manhood, Nico. I vow, you look so well in these breeches, one would have to be blind to doubt your manhood," she glanced about, certain her words would intrigue anyone nearby.

"Never that, my love, but your attentiveness," Esperanza's petticoats rustled as she pressed her hip against his and lowered her voice even more, "It's been weeks since you've been *with* me."

"The season—"

"Don't tell me you denied yourself during Lent!" Esperanza spat. "You go to chapel everyday with your dear Mama, si, but your mind is filled with schemes and politics!" She tapped his temple with her fan. "You and Guerro, both. It's all you think of—'Oh! A letter of commendation from the governor! I am truly blessed!' " She crossed a clenched fist over her breast, eyes closed in mock pride, " 'Ah! Another night spent riding the dark hillsides, seeking the devil Halcon! What patriotism!'

"Well, I, for one, think Guerro finally has the right idea." Esperanza smiled past him to waggle her fingers at the approaching Arturo. "Guerro plans to trap the bastard and hang him."

"Esperanza, you curse like a soldier." The cold condemnation came not only from proper Nicolas Carillo, but from his heart. He wanted to yank the diamond from her finger and fling it far as he could throw.

"Oh! Arturo has brought me a rose." Esperanza turned away to greet him. "Nico, you could take lessons from this handsome little brother of yours."

"Never, Señorita," Arturo bowed from the waist. "In all things, I but mirror Nicolas, and," he swept the flower past Esperanza's fingers to press it on his brother. "Since *mi hermano* is more adept at handling such prickly blooms, I'll allow him to affix this," his gaze flicked over her taut bodice, "Wherever you like."

"And here comes the little guest of honor," Esperanza traced a finger down Arturo's sleeve, "And her husband. How fortunate Doña Anna conducts this fiesta in the courtyard, no? That *Yanqui* is too big to have in the house.

"Oh! Her spectacles are unfortunate, are they not, Arturo?

218

She looks like an owl tangled in the laundry, rather than a bride in wedding lace."

Esperanza tittered behind her hand, threw a kiss to an acquaintance, then confided to Arturo, "Your brother, I am told, nearly cut her throat today! When does the clumsy thing depart and leave you in peace?" Esperanza asked, but moments passed before Nicolas answered.

Esperanza was right. Charlie had allowed Pilar freedom to decorate her like a pet dressed in doll clothes. The tiara of white daisies might have been lovely, but it faded amid the clutter of glasses, crisscrossed shawl, gaudy sash and brooches.

Fencing whites and an intense expression, those suited Charlie.

Christ, now she'd stumbled on her white lawn skirt, hauled it up at the waist and wobbled ahead on heeled slippers, clutching Freddy's arm for support.

Clumsy? Yes. Sweet Charlie, who fenced with the grace of an angel, tripped on her own anxiety when forced to be a lady. And yet, he'd wager on her swordplay against most men. Intensity had made her almost dangerous this afternoon.

How her eyes shone when she saw him. No coyness, no subterfuge, only love, beaming unchecked.

*Oh Charlie, yes, you're dangerous. I'd be safer suffering an hour with your swordpoint at my throat than I would be losing an instant in one clumsy kiss.*

"Nico, I asked you when?"

"Tomorrow, Esperanza," Nicolas caught the jeweled hand picking at his sleeve. "Señora Larkin leaves tomorrow, on a honeymoon voyage with her husband."

"It's your fiesta, Charlie. Relax."

Her fiesta, indeed.

"It's all very well for you to say so."

Freddy's dark auburn hair and suntanned face provided a startling contrast to his suit's sky blue velvet and silver lace.

"You've never looked handsomer in your entire life!" She pummeled his arm in mock irritation and watched him preen.

Charity knew she'd never looked worse.

219

The "little house party" swirled with señoritas in flounced scarlet, green and purple. Colorful embroidery, spangles of gold and dancing rainbow ribbon lavished hems and hair and sleeves. Only she wore her decorations like a circus horse.

All because Pilar had insisted on hiding the cut on her neck. People would talk, Pilar had insisted. As if Freddy's bellows had not attracted every household servant.

Not that she cared. Tomorrow she'd sail away. She'd never face these people again. Freddy insisted he'd open his bank in San Diego. Or Monterey. True presidio cities—unlike Santana's trumped-up headquarters—attracted Americans. Americans would be eager to stockpile gold with the Larkins of Boston.

Freddy promised as soon as the bank had sufficient workers, they two would ride for the Sierras. There she'd catalog mountain beasts never seen by a white woman. She should be ecstatic.

"Freddy!"

Arturo, turned out in an ink green jacket, shattered her dark musings by enfolding her and Freddy in the same hug.

"Amigo," Arturo warned Freddy as he released them, "Your wedding fiesta is the proper time for me to do what I've dreamed of since I found your charming wife in our courtyard!"

Arturo wound an arm around Charity's waist and swept her close.

*"Con su permiso,"* Arturo sighed, but without Freddy's permission, Nicolas's little brother bent her backward in a dramatic kiss.

"Arturo!"

Barbara's shocked voice and the high whistles and warbles of approval from Arturo's comrades, nearly distracted Charity from his fumbling hands.

"That accursed shawl looks terrible," he muttered against her mouth.

Charity broke away, laughing, and when he displayed the shawl, flaunting it like a prize, her protest was weak.

"Pilar thought, because of—"

"They're looking anyway, *querida*," Arturo breathed. "Let them see your beauty."

Her nervous laughter trailed off under the gazes of those who'd gathered around. Nicolas held Esperanza's arm. Barbara and a girl in pink ruffles held back a bevy of dressed-up children. Charity caught the blue-gold glitter of Guerro Santana's uniform and the flowing white mane of Don Carlos. And wasn't that woman in topaz taffeta Doña Ronda—her chaperon on the cattle drive?

"The señora looks far more bridelike this way, don't you agree?" Arturo turned her toward Freddy, who snatched her as if she were a bone between two dogs.

"I do. And though I don't recall granting permission for that kiss, I admit, I find this sword wound rather rakish—"

Freddy nuzzled her neck, unashamedly.

"—and decidedly attractive."

Charity's face grew hot and red and she knew her freckles stood out like beacons, even before her eyes sought Nicolas.

Past Freddy's shoulder, Nicolas's face looked stern, but his gaze rested in the V of her neckline. She'd forgotten that the gown's white lace bodice—where it wasn't underlined by her camisole—allowed skin to show through at her neck and arms.

"Señora Larkin," Esperanza's voice pulsed amid the laughter.

Thank God, she'd never face the girl as a rival. Esperanza's gown crackled like flame, and Charity had no doubt who'd tucked the crimson rose in her sash.

"Señora Larkin—Charity, I have a surprise!"

Bless Don Carlos for rescuing her from whatever question Esperanza had been about to pose.

"I've found you another American!" Don Carlos bragged, before he introduced Joseph Chapman, a lanky native of Maine.

"Rubio Jose," someone behind her remarked familiarly, and indeed his mustache was straw-colored and a few strands of blond hair showed beneath the man's roguish black scarf.

"I'm something of a local curiosity," Chapman admitted at

Don Carlos's urging. "A few years ago I fell in with bad companions in the Sandwich Islands—"

"He was a pirate, Charity. That's what he's trying to say," Arturo interrupted, delighted as his father.

"Not as colorful as all that." Chapman shook his head in denial and Charity saw a gold loop twinkle in his ear.

Her eyes flew to Nicolas's and she saw him fix Chapman with a glare.

"I was shanghaied, actually, and then stayed around for the free food, but they were a bad lot. Black Max of Duxbury—an Englishman who came to have followers in Argentina. Do you know of him, Mrs. Larkin?"

*Mrs. Larkin.*

No American tongue had addressed that name to her. She shook her head at the reality of it.

"He thought he'd just sail up the coast and conquer California," Chapman's rueful smile charmed Barbara, who rolled her eyes and shivered as she elbowed Charity.

"He did well enough further south, sacking and burning." Chapman shifted to Spanish as guests gathered to hear the favorite tale, "But without the element of surprise, he lost. Now that I'm a Californian myself, by religion and marriage to my Guadalupe, I realize his attempts were doomed." He smiled at Don Carlos.

Nicolas's father clapped him on the shoulder.

"You must tell the rest, Don Carlos," Chapman demurred.

"No, no, the girl is eager to hear the voice of her countryman," Nicolas's father insisted.

"I left Monterey on the Santa Rosa, and just above Santa Barbara, I was ordered ashore with a pair of half-naked Sandwich Islanders. We were told to scout the area—"

"And that's where Father became an avenging hero!" Arturo shouted it like a refrain and joined several of his friends in a high yipping yell of celebration.

"An avenging hero," Charity repeated. Her mind grew still and a line of thoughts clicked into place like cards laid deliberately, on a table, one by one.

*Ah ha,* she thought, trying to catch Nicolas's eye. *Ah, bloody ha, Nighthawk! Heroism is in your bones.*

"Not really a hero, Señora," Don Carlos protested. "I was in Santa Barbara visiting my brother, who served as sergeant at the *presidio.* When word came of the sacking of the capitol, and then of the landing party—" he spread his hands wide and shrugged.

Nicolas had been a young, impressionable boy. Charity narrowed her eyes past Esperanza, who listened as intently as all the others. Nicolas looked steadfastly away.

"We rode to the shore with our swords and reatas, and one of the little naked ones challenged us." Don Carlos's chin lifted, "So we shook out our reatas—"

"I took to my heels at this point," Chapman admitted. "No hero, myself, I saw these two centaurs spurring ahead, ready to ride me down, and the sea looked damned safe by comparison."

"And we roped them," Don Carlos shrugged.

Just as Nighthawk snared the false alcalde. Charity remembered Santana's cut-short shout and the spraying sand. She saw Nicolas shake his head, almost imperceptibly.

*Oh no,* she thought. *Don't bother to deny evidence that makes perfect sense, Halcon.*

The guests who'd gathered for the tale went on to praise the reformed pirate. Chapman's logging skills had helped construct Los Cielos's new church. His amazing medical skills served when a friar was absent. If pressed, the man could even blacksmith.

Conversation shifted and eddied. Someone mentioned the recent arrest of Ibarra and deCelis. Their fines for trading with foreigners had, some said, been all to the good, since the monies defrayed the cost of new altar cloths. The remarks seemed so light-hearted, Charity wondered why Sanchez and Joaquin Tiburon—a darkly handsome man with glass beads trimming his black vicuna hat—regarded each other somberly at the exchange.

Freddy hailed Ambrose and Sergei, and together they drew

Sanchez aside to bemoan the past evening's disastrous game of *monte*. They reviled Arturo for his unbearable good luck.

"Not so lucky, I fear," Doño Anna's crisp voice accompanied a gentle pat on Arturo's shoulder. "My *niño* will have to take his brother's duties yet again for a few days."

"What's this, Mother?" Arturo asked.

"One of your cousins, Arturo, Sandoval Ayende, has had a most bizarre accident. I just had word." Doña Anna made a vague gesture, toward some departed messenger.

"Sandoval insists on digging pits around his borders," she explained to Sanchez, "against wildcats which snatch his calves. He set out to check them with one of his hounds"—she sent Arturo a pointed glance—"When the dog stood barking at the brink, it fell in. When Sandoval drew too close, he, too fell in."

"Excuse me, *Señora*." Ambrose's drawl silenced the speculating listeners. "But was the cat still in the pit?"

"Apparently not." Doña Anna shrugged.

While others nodded, relieved, Ambrose's face fell in disappointment. *Despicable man,* Charity thought.

At her elbow, Barbara talked of the baked clams. She'd just seen them revealed from beneath their blanket of seaweed and detailed for an acquaintance how this delicacy had been stalked.

"Shall we eat?" Freddy asked, guiltily.

Charity realized that while dusk had settled, beyond the *luminarias* and torches, Freddy's conversation with the trappers had held him spellbound. She should have noticed.

"Arturo was right," Freddy said as they strode toward a table loaded with beefsteaks, "the gown looks far better, now."

Freddy's eyes, too, followed the V of the neckline.

"Oops, back this way!" Freddy wheeled her with such alacrity, Charity tripped. "Santana. Sure as hell, he'll ask if we've applied for citizenship."

Charity sighed. Deep within, where she kept pictures too dear to sketch—hillsides swept with mustard, poppies and lupin, wild-horse bands swift and wide-eyed as deer, and sleek

224

# O GET YOUR
# 4 FREE BOOKS
## MAIL THE COUPON BELOW.

## FREE BOOK CERTIFICATE

### GET 4 FREE BOOKS

**Yes!** I want to subscribe to Zebra's HEARTFIRE HOME SUBSCRIPTION SERVICE. Please send me my 4 FREE books. Then each month I'll receive the four newest Heartfire Romances as soon as they are published to preview Free for ten days. If I decide to keep them I'll pay the special discounted price of just $3.50 each; a total of $14.00. This is a savings of $3.00 off the regular publishers price. There are no shipping, handling or other hidden charges. There is no minimum number of books to buy and I may cancel this subscription at any time. In any case the 4 FREE Books are mine to keep regardless.

NAME

ADDRESS

CITY                                    STATE                        ZIP

TELEPHONE

SIGNATURE                                                           ZH0194

(If under 18 parent or guardian must sign)
Terms and prices subject to change.
Orders subject to acceptance.

Heartfire Romance

# Heartfire Romance

# GET 4 FREE BOOKS

HEARTFIRE HOME SUBSCRIPTION
SERVICE
120 BRIGHTON ROAD
P.O. BOX 5214
CLIFTON, NEW JERSEY 07015

AFFIX
STAMP
HERE

beaches reflecting back the stars—inside, she'd long since sworn allegiance to California.

Just the same, she allowed Freddy to steer her toward the clam pit.

A lively group thronged the area and Charity struggled to balance a platter-sized tortilla full of clam meat. The taste was salty, the texture oddly chewy. Strangest of all was the dip in her belly as she looked toward the pink-orange sunset.

She couldn't see it settling into the ocean, beyond the grassy bluff and the path to the shore. But the memory, fueled by the clams' sea scent, made her yearn for Nicolas and the beach.

"No sighing allowed, *Caridad*."

She jerked around to see Arturo. Her heart pounded high in her chest and she swallowed against a throat that felt swollen.

"I'm sorry, Charity. I didn't mean to startle you." Arturo looked helplessly at Freddy. "I am sorry. She's gone all white."

"See what happens when feisty little girls grow up?" Freddy kissed the tip of her nose. "Charlie's not as tough as she used to be. But there are other compensations."

Charity ignored the teasing and let her eyes search the crowd for Nicolas, before it was too late.

Tomorrow no one who addressed her in Spanish would expect an intelligible answer. Tomorrow she'd be Mrs. Larkin. She might just as well be a housewife in some Boston neighborhood.

Damnation! Why didn't Halcon gallop through the courtyard gates, snatch her up on his plunging stallion and sweep her away?

Charity swallowed again. Her throat ached, full and tight. That's what comes of living in fantasies, girl. Halcon won't come, you pining, daydreaming goose, because he's standing across the patio, watching Esperanza flaunt her diamond ring under Guerro Santana's nose.

How, how, *how* could Nicolas endure such duplicity? How could he pretend friendship with a man who blocked his dreams for California? How could Nicolas pretend affection, his fingers caressing Esperanza's forearm, when it was Charity he wanted?

Oh, but look at him. She rubbed her eyes. Look how his brown velvet trousers snugged to his thighs as he crossed the patio with Santana. Nicolas nodded stiffly at Joaquin Tiburon and the handsome ranchero passed him, without recognition. Certainly a trick of torchlight made her think a twinge of hurt crossed Nicolas' face.

Santana didn't speak directly to them, never mentioned citizenship, but Charity clutched Freddy's hand as the alcalde addressed Esperanza's father, nearby.

He spoke of his plan to capture Halcon, and though it was Freddy's hand she squeezed, the eyes she held, once Santana hit his stride, reveling in his own high-flown language, were Nicolas's.

"Yes, my trap for Halcon is based on a wolf-hunting trick learned from my sergeant. A strong, brawling sort of man, but terrified of wolves. The trick is designed for use in the cold country, but he says it works here, as well."

Freddy's hand loosened as soon as it became clear Santana wouldn't issue a formal requirement for citizenship.

"One fixes a slab of meat, bloody meat it must be," Santana cautioned, "Atop a knife, stuck in the dirt. When the wolf comes to eat it—they're little better than scavengers, you know—he gets the taste of blood in his mouth and keeps eating."

Charity's hand went to her own mouth. It took little imagination to see where this trick led.

Nicolas still watched her. In spite of his frown, she thought his eyes slid sideways, as if he'd soothe her.

"Soon," Santana gestured widely, "the beast's tongue has reached the knife, but still he tastes the blood. He keeps licking, and licking, and though the meat has disappeared, still there's that tantalizing flavor."

Nicolas's hand reached out spasmodically, as if he'd touch her, and Charlie wanted to press both palms over her ears before Santana explained what relevance this horror had for Nighthawk.

"At last, the stupid wolf's tongue is flayed to shreds and he bleeds to death: a victim of his own appetites.

"And this, my friend, is what we will do to Halcon."

How could Santana look so handsome? Sunlight among the gathering shadows, he passed a hand over his golden hair and aimed a smile at entranced Esperanza, before he continued.

"The Indians, the poor helpless *renegados*—"Santana's voice thickened with sarcasm—"are his weakness. Protecting them—when *Dios* knows the only masters they serve are Thievery and Sloth—is his obsession, as the wolf's obsession is blood. It will be simple enough to threaten Indios and watch him ride to their 'rescue.' And with no cost to you, amigos—" he bowed to his audience, "but a few useless red skins."

A choking cough died in her throat, but it was enough to make Santana turn.

"I am quite determined in my pursuit." He pretended the words were meant for everyone, but his pointed stare held Charity while she gasped for breath.

"You are unusually silent about your favorite topic, Señora Larkin," Santana taunted when she didn't take up his provocation.

Freddy tugged her hand, but she wanted to speak. She wanted to challenge Santana's analogy and scorn such cowardly murder. She wanted to, but the patio spun around her and she felt herself sinking in its vortex. All speech, even scorn, shimmered beyond her reach. If she were very lucky, though, she might be able to place one foot before the other and hurry from his presence before she lost her dinner on his spit-shined boots.

Abruptly, she turned her back.

"Jesus Christ, Charity," Freddy whispered.

Nicolas's face swam before her eyes. Why couldn't she breathe? She fought the weakness, scrubbed her hand at her eyes and swallowed against a throat so thick she feared it had swollen to the size of a fence post.

Panic and nausea surged as one.

*I can't breathe,* she thought. *I can't.*

"Nicolas—" She reached a hand toward him and he hesitated. Yes, she should cling to Freddy, yes, but something was very, very wrong. Her throat—

Freddy and Nicolas pressed close, then rushed her inside. She choked and felt brandy burn in her nose as they forced her to drink. Wretched black dots swarmed, then clotted before her eyes.

In her room, naturally as if he carried a breakfast tray, there appeared blond Joe Chapman.

"Have you eaten clams before, Mrs. Larkin?" He squatted next to her bed, intent on striking up the oddest conversation.

Charity choked on the answer, certain she would be sick at any moment. Why couldn't they leave her alone?

"Your throat feels thick, does it?" Chapman placed a shallow basin on her bedside table.

She nodded vigorously at the basin. They'd said he knew doctoring; he could stay, but she refused to vomit before Nicolas.

"Does it itch?"

"Yes. And I've had clam soup—" she gasped. "I think."

"I've seen this happen twice," he spoke over his shoulder to Nicolas and Freddy. Behind them stood Doña Anna. "Once with crab. Once with abalone. Never with clams. Still—"

"Your diagnosis is appreciated, Jose—" Nicolas's brusque tone echoed the one he'd used at Harvard.

Oh God, her stomach rolled like—

"But I must know what to do," Nicolas insisted. "Must I send for herbs, for wine—?"

"Only thing I know for it is being sick. I used a feather to tickle the back of one tar's throat, though someone suggested charcoal water—"

Charity groaned and crushed both arms over her squirming stomach. When Freddy ushered Doña Anna from the room, she wanted to cross herself in gratitude.

She lurched upright and hovered above the basin.

"Get out," she gasped loud enough to disrupt their discussion. They stayed in the doorway.

"We'd better," Chapman conceded.

"Forget it, hombre," Nicolas snapped. "I saw her fading before my eyes. She couldn't breathe. I'll stay until I'm satisfied she can."

*Take your nobility down the hall, can't you, Carillo?* She wanted to bawl in frustration, but she only swallowed back the acrid rising.

"There's always the chance, too, that she's pregnant, *verdad?*" Chapman whispered.

"That's a question I'd give anything to answer, amigo."

Nicolas's voice rang with irony, and though she'd never heard irony made a suitable emetic, Charity vomited until she thought she'd broken her ribs with it.

# Chapter Eighteen

Carmen, a mission runaway wearing a man's white smock and looking like a waif atop her huge charcoal gelding, had ridden across the path of raised bows and muskets to save Nicolas from Salvador's *renegados*. For a moment, he wondered if the girl should have risked it.

Spurred by the conviction that he would ruin Charlie's life and his own if he stayed at the rancho, Nicolas had spent two solid days riding. His usual liaisons with the *renegados* had vanished. At Mission San Gabriel, then Mission San Fernando, he'd been offered only whispered half-clues to Salvador's whereabouts. Something was afoot.

Finally, in the oak-studded foothills outside the bounds of Mission San Buenaventura, at dawn of the third day, Nicolas rode Hamlet toward a wisp of smoke so faint it might be illusion, and blundered into two hostile riders and Carmen.

"No, no, don't shoot him."

Riding bareback, thin legs athwart the gray, she crossed in front of two warriors, her hand ordering a halt.

"What have we to fear from one lone white man? Besides," she toyed with a tangle of beads, shells and a silver rosary wound about her neck as she studied him. "This one only pretends to be a proper hidalgo. He is Halcon."

Nicolas almost laughed at how deftly he'd been identified, his great deception unraveled by a girl.

The men, both bare-chested with black hair loose behind their shoulders, lowered their weapons.

230

The girl's complex dialect of Gabrielino passed in a blur. Though Nicolas credited himself with a fair understanding of the Indian tongue, this girl's accent almost defeated him. In snatches, he heard his name, that he was a supporter of the *hindas*—the mission runaways—and a friend of Salvador's.

Carmen addressed the others with authority, saying it would only cause unnecessary noise to wrest the sword from Halcon. Though she didn't smile, her face radiated an openness that tempted him to guess her Indian name as something like "Lark". As Hamlet picked his way along a high trail to the village, Carmen glanced back over her shoulder, eyes full of the same cocky assessment he'd received, of late, from Charlie.

"What kind of specimen have we here?" either might have asked. Charlie, however, had not sounded her sassy self when he'd ridden out.

Rubio Joe Chapman had sworn her physical danger was past, and speculated that Charlie's sudden rash of weakness—fainting, "sniffles," as he'd called them, and the sensitivity to clams—might have been stimulated by climate and diet differences between California and Boston.

A sensible explanation, but Nicolas's mind couldn't avoid that awful barrier to Chapman's logic: Charlie might have died.

*Cristo!* He'd rarely worried over her. Charlie's confidence and sense, her intelligence and ability to blend with nature, shielded her as she rode the countryside. Even when she'd provoked the grizzly attack, she'd dealt skillfully with the consequences, dropping to the earth and playing dead. Truth be told, Charity O'Dell y Larkin, was in little need of a hero.

So, who would guess such a little thing as clams, a *food,* could come close to taking her?

Terror. He'd seen it in her eyes and felt it roar in his ears, when she couldn't breathe. And she'd reached for him. *Him,* not Freddy. And in that moment, some primitive instinct—Halcon's instinct—had sworn she would be his, regardless of vows or politics. Like a beast, he'd burned to drive off intruders and take his wounded mate to his lair and growl eternal protection.

Marriage ceremonies and friendship be damned. What if she had died Freddy's wife, never knowing he loved her?

Reason, of course, reasserted itself.

Nicolas Carillo did not act like a beast. He didn't snatch her off to Refugio; he issued orders for her care. He didn't inform Freddy that Charlie was no longer his; he talked with his friend, politely lowering his eyes when Freddy wondered aloud whether the illness was a reaction to seafood or a complication of early pregnancy. Schooled to be a civilized and reasonable man, Nicolas Carillo ignored the urgent desire pounding behind his eyes, at the back of his throat, in his heart and loins, even as he realized the truth: Desire this strong would not sicken and fade. He must kill it.

An hour after Charlie had fallen asleep, he'd left Freddy at her bedside. An hour after that, pretending to serve his mother's whim that he aid her injured cousin, Nicolas walked out the hacienda doors while the sky still wore stars.

He'd already swung into his saddle when he heard stirring in her room. Telling himself he dismounted to tighten his cinch, not eavesdrop, Nicolas placed a flat palm against his horse's shoulder to still it.

"You're as tough as nails, Charlie. Sleep all the way to San Diego if you want, but don't tell me you're too sick to travel." Freddy's low snarl came from between his teeth.

"My head hurts, my chest hurts, my eyes are so swollen things are blurred. My stomach aches from vomiting! Freddy, can we just wait a day more?"

"The ship sails at first light, Charity."

Nicolas had waited through the pause, through the echo of Freddy calling her by her full name. Nicolas pictured Charlie fidgeting with the bedclothes, fighting weariness because she trusted her quick mind to formulate a solution. Freddy gave her no time.

"Charlie, you're not keeping your part of this bargain. I got you out of Boston—"

232

"I got *myself* out of bloody Boston! This was *my* idea—"
Charlie's voice had faltered after its burst of vehemence.

"It was, and, I'm not mad at you, Charlie. I just don't know what you expect."

Nicolas waited, frozen lest he miss her weak answer.

"You never used to refuse a dare—" Freddy taunted.

*Oh, this is not fair.* Nicolas felt something coiled in his belly unwind in a whipping motion. *Freddy, you do not fight fair!*

"—well, Charlie, I dare you to be on that ship in two hours, to keep your promise and work this thing out."

Charlie never refused a dare. Nicolas had no doubt she'd be gone when he returned. And if she'd still been a virgin when he kissed her last, she would not be when she returned.

Oh, they'd meet again. California was not so big, really. He'd glimpse her—or someone like her—at the occasional grand *baile*. That frosting her Aunt P. had applied, the surface decoration that made her seem a lady, that frosting would harden into Mrs. Frederick Larkin, while his friend Charlie shriveled to nothing but a memory.

Hamlet's ears flicked back. An Indian pony had tripped on the trail above, but that hadn't caused Hamlet to listen. Nicolas wondered if he, ice-blooded hidalgo and dare-all patriot, had moaned.

Weakling! Nicolas touched the sword on his hip and felt the stallion gather with snorting eagerness. Nighthawk should have cut Charlie out of his heart, long since. And if he couldn't—no, if he chose not to—he should end the obsession. He should have taken her to the shore, riding wild on Santana's palomino, and made love to her on the beach.

Entering the makeshift village, his senses retracted as if he'd walked from the dimness of a cave into harsh sunlight. The acrid scent of burned hair mixed with the smell of horses. Bay, black and dappled haunches gleamed from behind tents and trees. And everywhere, standing, squatting, working wood, grasping flints and arrowheads, bending over blankets of drying jerky, were Indians.

At his approach, three mothers—not frightened, but cautious—swooped up their babies. The children were equally brown and naked, but their mothers reflected a strange mixture of cultures. One woman wore mission white, one displayed a flurry of beaded leather strings flaring around bare hips, while still another wore a fur apron beneath her rough gray rebozo.

The men who squatted to play *chuchrki* were too intent on their game to give him more than a glance. In teams of four, they faced each other, shaking and exchanging little markers. Even in this small group, he noticed the short thick-bodied Indians of one tribe, mixed with tall men who wore sea-gull feathers braided into their hair.

"Halcon, you don't fly so silently," Salvador, sunlight glinting on the gold stud in his slashed nostril, strode from a copse of oak. "We've heard of your search for two days, now."

Why hadn't he noticed Salvador's approach until he stood before him? Salvador was right to worry over his clumsy seeking, and yet his friend's expression held only concern, not criticism.

Never, with Salvador, was he greeted with an *abrazo*, no hug or pounding of shoulders. But always, their eyes locked in a connection Nicolas missed when they worked apart.

They shared the same goal, working toward it in similar manners, and Salvador's wry acceptance of his own importance made him stronger in Nicolas's eyes.

"I'm not a hero," Salvador had protested once. "I can lead men, have a talent for strategy and I do so enjoy stealing horses."

"You ride your black," Salvador said, now. "How disappointing. I heard you had tried your hand at theft." Salvador smiled, lowering his eyelids against a shaft of sunlight slanting through the canopy of branches as they walked through the camp.

"Halcon grows weary of subtlety, and seeks to waken the Californios, however he can." Nicolas thought his sigh sounded like a weary old man's.

"I have word that the true alcalde, Don Emelio, has left Mexico City—"

"Yes?" Nicolas wheeled to face Salvador. If Don Emelio re-

234

turned, Santana would fight. He'd not relinquish his growing power easily. Now California opinion must swing against him. Now Santana must be discredited.

"You know as well as I, such rumors may mean he left two months ago, or will leave two months hence," Salvador cautioned. He motioned Nicolas into a clearing to sit near a dead campfire.

Rein in your feelings, Halcon, he told himself, settling cross-legged. He concentrated on the ashes as if the fire still danced, seeing only the variation of grays: pale silver to thundercloud dark.

Forget Charlie. See the mighty oak branch burned to softness a finger could destroy.

Forget Freddy. See the black charring of a stick that escaped the heart of the flame.

Nicolas's shoulders loosened and his eyelids drooped. In his mind's eye he recreated the wavering heat of orange embers dusted with white ash. This peace, this feeling of controlling yet being totally insignificant, flowed from Salvador.

Salvador's fight, and Halcon's were worthy, magnificent, historic.

Esperanza? Arturo? Guerro Santana and Nicolas Carillo? Breeze sifted ash. Floating. Nothing.

"Your camp is full of horses," Nicolas said, wetting his lips.

"They serve two purposes, my friend." Salvador nodded as if Nicolas had waited an instant, rather than half an hour, to speak. "*Hindas* come from a hundred far places to join our revolt, and it takes a dull man not to realize it is easier to ride, than walk. Also, one who brings horses can be fairly sure of welcome."

Sun shimmered through the oak branches, marking midday, when they shared a skin of water. They spoke of revolt, Nicolas mused, as if it were a business like banking or selling foodstuffs.

They analyzed Halcon's forays into Santana's presidio and the bodega. They discussed Salvador's rescue of an Indian woman whipped near to death because she poisoned a priest who punished reluctant novices with starvation. Salvador questioned Halcon regarding a rumor Santana planned to destroy Indio vegetable gardens, so all would be dependent on the missions for food.

"Most padres would turn my people into penitent pets. They would rather starve. But there is one priest for whom I have the highest hopes. Father Juan Alvarado, who was maimed by the Pirate Bouchard. It is said he rode one-armed, reins in his teeth, as leader of the northern *renegados*— Los Lobos." Salvador stopped.

Together, they weighed the potential value of this priest who knew Nicolas Carillo, but not Halcon. They considered the use of Jaime Tiburon, of the talkative messenger from Monterey. Then Salvador bragged of a new asset—Carmen, who could assume any disguise or accent—a jewel beyond price for spying.

Perhaps, Salvador had speculated, she and Halcon's freckled swordswoman—

"No," Nicolas slashed his hand in the space between them. "Charlie is gone. We need to talk of the one grand episode which will discredit Santana with all *Californios*, royalists and independents alike."

Salvador blinked, his only recognition of his friend's abruptness.

"True. Don Emelio is not so strong, though he tries to be fair. Never would he have allowed an attack like that against the Chowchilla. There was gold, you know, in Chowchilla." Salvador nodded. "But the soldiers who came for it only found a few rocks within the village. They slaughtered those who knew where it had been found. A rare joke on the Mexican soldiers."

"Rare," Nicolas agreed. "A mistake I don't think Santana would make. The man craves gold, but only, I think for its power, for the way it makes him appear to his superiors. The messenger I spoke of believes Santana will buy the good opinions of officials who will return him to Mexico or, at worst, make him governor."

Salvador cut his eyes toward a disturbance in the camp,

looking back when they'd identified the sound of spilled soup sputtering on hot coals. "It's happened before."

Interrupted by the delivery of corn cakes, beans and fresh skins of water, the two leaders sketched out strategies and discarded them. In the end, their plan was two-pronged, relying equally on the *renegados'* strength and Halcon's knowledge.

First, Salvador's renegados would humiliate Santana.

Carmen and Miguel would seek out a blacksmith in Los Cielos, requesting a lump of gold be made into a cross. A present, they'd swear, for the good mission father who'd marry them.

"You have met Carmen, and Miguel you would recognize because of his vigilance. This one," Salvador explained, "feels his responsibility so strongly, he pricks his eyelids with nettles, so there is no chance he will fall asleep on guard duty.

"Also," Salvador said, "Miguel wears a thin string of buckskin around his neck. It was a custom in his village, for the swiftest runner to be so honored."

Nicolas suggested the blacksmith, Gonzalez, as their pawn. An intimate of Santana's, Gonzalez had been among the Mexican soldiers who witnessed Salvador's whipping that day in the plaza. The irony pleased them both.

"Gonzalez will ask these simple Indios where they found the gold, and Carmen will allow herself to be convinced. She'll mention Las Calderonas," Salvador smiled.

"When Gonzalez tells Santana of Las Calderonas' hidden wealth, he will seek it," Nicolas warmed to the idea.

"But the only gold hidden there will be my warriors, ready to seize the horses and leave Santana and his band to make their way home, afoot." Salvador rubbed his palms together.

"If anything I overhear should endanger our plan, I will send word. Although your contacts are so well disguised—"

"They will find you, should you need them. Also—" Salvador squinted against the new risen sun, "We will broach Father Alvarado," Salvador's smile bound them together, "We will remind him of his own wild-riding youth and the fires which drove him."

Hoarse from a night of talk, they breakfasted on acornmeal mush and berries, and there was no excuse to remain.

"Will you stay another night, Nicolas?"

Nicolas swallowed and grasped his friend's forearm. Salvador's use of Halcon's true name proved the request more than politeness, but both knew he would go.

The camp recognized Salvador's acceptance of him, and his importance to their cause, but Nicolas felt the warning of a hundred glares. Even Halcon was an unwanted stranger, here.

"*Gracias,* no." Nicolas glanced at the sky. With the long May evenings, he still had many hours of daylight.

"You ride to your refuge, yes? It's good to have your own things around, I think. They remind you of a self beyond—" Salvador motioned fingers across his eyes, sketching a mask.

Nicolas recalled his volumes of Cervantes, the nobly inscribed broadsword and the cool earth scent of Refugio. But it was Charlie he needed to remind him who he really was. She knew, and admired him all the more.

How quick she'd been, seizing that tale of Father's bravery at Santa Barbara! Fired by those images of pirates and reatas, of men protecting their land, he'd become Halcon. She'd known, immediately.

"You're sure she's gone, then? Your student of wild things?" Salvador asked.

Nicolas caught Hamlet from where he cropped grass with the other horses, before unclenching his jaw to answer.

"Si, and a good thing." Nicolas bridled the black. He'd long since given up questioning Salvador's ability to read him. "She'd started stalking Halcon, keeping notes on his identity—"

Gone. Charlie would never have rejected Freddy's dare. Gone.

"You know amigo, it is easy for these young ones," Salvador gestured to a group of warriors gathered around a cooking pot. "They boil down gall to the thickness of honey. They coat their arrows and shoot. Maybe they kill. Maybe they get killed." He shrugged. "They don't think past tomorrow. For us, it's not so easy. We must focus on the horizon, even when, underfoot, there are snakes like Santana. Even when we are nipped by insects, like padres who would help if they knew how. Even when wild flowers abound." Salvador paused as Carmen came to stand near him. "And we have no time to enjoy them. Who would chose such a life, Halcon?"

Hamlet protested as Nicolas swung aboard. He reared and neighed at leaving fresh grass and company. Nicolas spurred the stallion lightly before turning back to return his friend's rhetorical shrug.

"*Quien sabe,* Salvador? *Quien sabe?*"

# Chapter Nineteen

"I will never be like you!" Charity lay on her belly amid a tumble of rock and weeds. She put her spyglass down with enough energy to shatter the lens, and enough anger not to care.

Nicolas lay beside her on the ridge overlooking Sable's valley. Only moments ago, they'd been close enough to kiss and she'd flushed with a shameless desire to grab Nicolas' shoulders, and force herself against him.

They'd met by accident. Charity had been charting mustangs in Sable's valley when Nicolas had ridden into the circle of her spy glass. She'd started back in surprise, at first, then watched him rope his chestnut from the wild band before releasing the black horse.

Off seeing to an injured cousin, indeed! Vaqueros and passing visitors had gossiped of Halcon's activities, but many accounts were too fanciful to credit. Halcon now rode with a beautiful Indian girl, both dressed in white leather, reported a man named Salazar. Halcon had captured a messenger on El Camino Real and left him naked and horseless, swore three men who'd been searching for horses which had strayed from the bodega rail.

She'd recorded neither incident, and yet, here rode Nicolas, brazen as the sunlight glittering on his sword hilt, astride Halcon's black stallion. And the wild horses hadn't scattered at his approach. That meant—the significance broke over her like the scent-filled *cascarones*—he did this all the time.

She'd heard herself chortle, knowing if she were patient, he'd lead her to his hide-out. He must have one. Where else did he keep his costume?

"What is it you find so amusing, *chica?*"

Doña Ronda, extraordinary horsewoman and stentorian snorer, had remained at the rancho after Charity and Freddy's ill-fated wedding fiesta, then offered herself as temporary escort for Charity's excursions.

At forty, Doña Ronda wore neither cosmetics nor frills. She pinned her hair in a tortilla-sized clump, and galloped the grasslands as she pleased. Proper ladies covered their mouths in horror, but Don Carlos granted her grudging admiration.

In spite of her husband's death six years ago, the Doña's rancho produced fine cattle and fields of corn, beans, melons and pumpkins—all cultivated by *paid* Indian labor.

There were moments Charity found such praise unbelievable. The Doña began each day at a gallop so reckless Charity prayed more fervently than she did in chapel. But, soon as the sun rose to midday, the hellion on horseback vanished.

As Charity worked, Doña Ronda slept in the shade, propped against the forelegs of her horse. She did so now, since the answer to her query about Charity's amusement came too slowly to keep her awake.

Luna nickered and flicked his ears toward the back slope of the ridge. Doña Ronda's Arab did the same. A rough hedge of manzanita bushes shook. A blazed chestnut forehead emerged, and then Nicolas.

Adobe smeared his white sleeve, unshaven beard shadowed his face. Disheveled and dirty after his days as Nighthawk, he had never looked so handsome.

Nicolas's jaw clenched with a strength that made his skin pull white and his eyes, quick and dark, searched her face as if he couldn't believe she sat there.

"You didn't go."

The flood of feeling his words freed couldn't have been stronger if he'd said "I love you."

241

"No," Charity said. Strange lethargy flowed through her muscles, making it impossible to stand, impossible to do anything but sit up, and watch as he slipped from the chestnut, eyes widened in relief that she hadn't followed Freddy, but stayed with him.

In one long stride, still trailing his brigand's spell, Nicolas moved close enough to engulf her, then stopped. Doña Ronda shifted in her doze and he glanced at her, then turned back to Charity and revealed his affection in a manner, to her, more telling than kisses.

Nicolas Carillo's sole infraction at Harvard had been taking *daily* rather than weekly baths, but instead of riding home now, to cleanse himself of trail dust, he collapsed beside her, asking to join her observation.

He didn't ask if Freddy were truly gone, didn't question her recovery from fish poisoning, or remind her of her accusations regarding his identity. He stretched on his side, next to her primly tucked up legs, and paged through her sketchbook.

"This is splendid, Charlie!" Nicolas had stabbed one drawing with his fingertip.

"Yesterday, the leader of this band challenged another stallion," she explained. "I watched the battle, but, I did this while he was showing off for his new mares."

Nicolas's admiration shone clearly. She felt embarrassed, but willing to let the easy acceptance lay between them. Then, Doña Ronda began snoring, in earnest.

The piggish snorts, combined with the joy of Nicolas's praise, triggered a volley of giggles Charity couldn't contain. Brown eyes glinting, Nicolas pulled her, belly down, beside him, and gestured for her to continue her study.

She couldn't. They were virtually alone. Neither spoke and they avoided each other's eyes, but Charity knew he felt his knee brush her skirts and collide with the leg swathed within. Perhaps he'd even done it on purpose, because he didn't shift away. The pressure of his knee remained.

A dream. The gold-hot afternoon had quaked around her like a vision of paradise, until he told her Santana's secret. Santana planned to destroy Indians' gardens, starving some, making Mission chattel of others, and Charity watched, gratified, as censure and sympathy crossed Nicolas' face.

He asked her to carry food from Aguas Dulces to the Indians and she gloried in this melding of their beliefs, until Nicolas qualified his request.

"You understand, this must be done secretly, Charlie."

She understood. Heaven forbid Santana should discover his "friend" betrayed him.

She didn't want to do it alone. Fear was no deterrent, she simply longed to ride with Halcon, and, bloody hell—she wanted Nicolas's trust!

"Will you do it, Charlie? Take them the supplies?"

He flattened his hand over hers.

Surprising pleasure wove up her wrist as he pressed her palm into the warm earth.

"I know you're sympathetic," he'd wheedled, "And it would help so many . . ."

"Then you do it," Charity challenged. They lay together, connected by touch, by purpose, surely he'd confess.

"I can't." Nicolas glanced back at Doña Ronda, then laced his fingers between Charity's and slid them back and forth, stroking. "Charlie, don't you understand anything except animals?"

His tone joked, but veered too close to condescension. How *could* he? When he touched her like that?

Damnation, she'd sidestepped this knowledge from the first, but it couldn't be avoided. At his core, Nicolas was as closedminded as any white-haired *ranchero*. He couldn't accept that a female, might think, might be trustworthy!

"Guerro would find out," Nicolas enunciated, "Do you see?"

Charity cautioned the hussy screeching in her brain, but each instant it became harder.

"I understand bravery, Nicolas." Slowly, slowly, now. "What I don't understand—"

Words spewed like lava, beyond the control of any, save God.

"—is why you are such a coward about Santana."

Nicolas clenched the fragile bones of her hand. His sword hand could crush hers, and it didn't. But he loomed so near, he blocked the sky.

"You called me coward once before, remember?"

Nicolas' mustache quirked at one corner, but he was not amused. In still instants like this, wolves chose to flee or attack, men decided to reason or fight. Charity didn't move.

"How did I answer you then, Charlie? What did I say?"

As before, she felt the weak-strong spurt of energy Nature gave creatures to escape. That day by the river, knee-deep in mustard and primitive terror, she'd known he was the predator, she the prey. Affection was swallowed by fear.

"You said you'd show me—"

"Yes, I should show you."

She waited. When he shoved her wrist away, separating them, she gulped in relief. And disappointment.

"I won't do it, though it would serve you right! Do you know how my father—how any *ranchero*—"

He was only Nicolas, and he threatened to "show" her nothing more menacing than how to keep quiet.

"You're not even listening! Women do not act this way, Charity. Do you know how any hidalgo would discipline a shrew like you?" Nicolas broke into rapid Spanish she couldn't follow.

"Damnation, Nicolas, speak English, so I understand your bloody insults!"

"A shrew, s-h-r-e-w, Mrs. Larkin. I called you one. Perhaps you'd understand better if I'd chosen 'fury,' or virago, or yes, of course, a witch! *Bruja! Comprende, Señora?*"

He still hadn't released her hand, but his sarcasm hurt worse than his fencing-hard grip.

They lay still, poised up from the dirt on their elbows. If Doña Ronda roused, they'd slump in defeat. If either mocked in word or gesture, they'd rejoin the battle. Their pulses pounded together, shaking their hands.

When Nicolas finally spoke, she bristled at his amusement.

"Charlie, you're as much a coward as I. As much a hypocrite. Because that's what you mean, isn't it?"

"Hypocrite?" Charity hissed, then deflated in silence.

"What else, *Mrs. Larkin*, do you call a married woman who lounges in the dust, yearning to kiss a man who's not her husband? Nothing nicer than a hypocrite, surely. What name would you give a "devoted biologist" led astray by her throbbing heart? Hypocrite seems right enough."

Even this skirmish over ethics and cowardice had little to do with bravery, it had to do with love.

Three strangled neighs rent the valley below. Charity scrambled for her spyglass, but Nicolas lifted it, first.

"What is it?" She asked.

"You don't want to see."

"Of course I do. Are they mating? I've seen it before," Charity glanced behind at Doña Ronda.

"Not like this—"

Nicolas lowered the eyepiece, holding the glass out of her reach. He gestured with it.

"This is how I spotted you, you know. The sun on your glass—"

"Give it to me," she growled. "Damnation Nicolas, you are the most infuriating man." She rammed her shoulder against his and snatched the instrument.

The red stallion, leader of the wild band, appeared to mount the black mare he'd won, yesterday. But his storming approach drove her to her knees. The mare scrambled up, ears flat, teeth bared, defiant.

She wasn't in heat, then, Charity reasoned.

The stallion bucked and neighed, stirring yellow roils of dust as he launched a powerful kick against the mare's belly. She staggered, rib flesh sliced bloody by his hooves.

Tossing her head in protest, the mare fell. The stallion lashed her belly, once more. She fought to rise, scrabbling with frantic front hooves, before she lay flat.

Without lowering the spyglass, Charity cut her eyes toward Nicolas, unwilling to ask for an explanation.

The stallion circled at a triumphant trot. A breeze lifted the downed mare's mane. She flung her neck back, along her side, teeth snapping.

"In your opinion, why did he try to kill her?" Charity kept her tone level.

"If he were trying to kill her, would he strike for her belly, do you think?" Nicolas' calm voice pointed to some other truth.

"Then what—?"

"*Vaqueros* say that when a stallion takes a new mare, if she's pregnant with the old stallion's foal," Nicolas weighted his words, "he makes sure she loses it."

Charity examined the explanation. If she blocked out the black hide smeared with blood, if she ignored the vaunting neigh, it made sense. The mare selected the stronger mate and carried *his* seed.

At what cost would the breed improve? Contracting in a mockery of labor, the mare writhed to slough off the foal.

"Charlie," Nicolas's whisper made her nape tingle as if he'd touched it. "Joe Chapman said your illness, the night of the fiesta, might have been caused not by clams, but pregnancy."

Her inner arms stung with the gliding sluice of fear. He cared, but refused to admit it, except in hints and clues.

"Are you?" Nicolas asked.

"Does Joe Chapman claim to be a midwife, then, as well as a physician?" Charity collapsed her spy glass into itself.

"Are you, Charlie?"

What made her want to punish him?

"Do pregnant women often stop breathing, Nicolas?" She glared at him, frustrated near to screaming when his hold on her hand softened.

"You're not, then."

"Of course, I'm not. But what if I were? What has this," she gestured toward the valley, "To do with me?"

"I meant no comparison." He released her hand.

"Truly, Nicolas, what if I were?" Charity sat up, brushing dust off her skirt. What must he say to satisfy her?

"I would do nothing," Nicolas said with exaggerated calm. "Your lover Nighthawk might."

Shock robbed her of speech. Could a man be jealous of

246

himself? *Your lover Nighthawk.* Insane. No explanation showed in the tanned planes of his cheeks, the even stare of brown eyes.

Doña Ronda's snores ended in a snort, but Nicolas continued waiting, watching Charity warily as an animal lured to hand.

A devil danced in her brain, daring her to walk her fingers up his wrist to his elbow. Let him see she wanted both: Halcon who'd pressed her nightgown sleeve high and kissed the veins, there, as well as the man who lay in the dust beside her.

He shuddered as if she'd doused him with river water, but said nothing that didn't befit a gracious host, as Doña Ronda rose to her feet, beating her skirts clean.

"You're back then, Don Nicolas," she yawned. "Just in time to escort us back to your *rancho* for a cool glass of wine."


Cold coffee, cold tortillas and purple grapes. A pitifully simple offering to a woman he meant to seduce.

Seduce, of course, only her mind. And that, only because he'd promised Salvador he'd set Charlie to the task of warning Indios of Santana's plot. On the hillside, he'd failed, but Charlie's inexplicable temper had cooled.

Adjusting her hat, then pushing her spectacles up her nose, Charlie had left off haggling about bravery. If not for her black braid, tassel dangling above her breast, anyone would have taken them for boon companions, trotting home side by side.

Now Fate, in the guise of an ailing cook, offered him a second chance to convince her. If Charlie resisted logic once more, he knew how to win her.

Nighthawk had made Charlie tinder to her emotions. His touch had burned away analytical thoughts. Passion had consumed scientific processing.

Nicolas Carillo wouldn't use lust, exactly. At worse, he might crush her arguments with a single kiss.

Their sparring, half debate, half frolic, sprang from their

Harvard friendship. Withstanding that bond was simple. Another feeling threatened, one which had nearly unmanned him that last night in her room.

A simple clutter of objects at her bedside—a quill, gold spectacles, a turquoise hair comb and an adobe jar stuffed with wildflowers which scattered their petals over all—which felled him with tenderness, when he thought no dying.

Tenderness had no place between them.

This chance to maintain a cordial friendship and no more, occurred as she helped him unsaddle. Doña Ronda had sought the cool house, but when they followed, Anna announced the cook had returned home. She'd prepared midday enchiladas, first, but Doña Ronda had just consumed the last of them.

"If you linger in the yard like vaqueros," Mother had scolded, "You must fend for yourself until dinnertime."

Far from provoked, Charlie bowed to Pilar's demand she change clothes, and promised to meet him in the *cocina*.

The air stirred behind him and Nicolas turned. Charlie, dressed like a most alluring maidservant, wore a white *camisa*, embroidered with yellow and blue flowers. It fell to her ankles and her feet were bare. *Bare*, as if Boston's propriety had been bleached away by the California sun. He ordered his eyes not to peruse her like a serving wench, even though she dressed as one.

Faint wet splotches made him certain she'd washed her hands and swiped them dry on the fabric over her hips. Christ, he'd wager his horse Charlie wore no camisole underneath. The peasant gown hung suspended from the very tips of her breasts, and Charlie's yeoman stride, allied with her missing undergarments, made her a sight to provoke a saint.

She cleared her throat, recalling his eyes to hers. Face still damp from her ablutions, Charlie flushed and pushed up her spectacles. Before she spoke, Nicolas traced a water droplet's wet path from Charlie's chin to the underside of her throat, down the column of her neck.

"Nicolas," she said taking the plate, placing it on the plank table and settling on the facing bench, "We'll compromise."

And though the chit looked reasonable, face mild and hands folded, the accursed water droplet, settling in the hollow of her throat, as she tilted her head to swallow coffee, distracted him.

Still, he thought he explained, with some flair, Santana's blind spot for Indian affairs and the patriotic role Charlie might play. Alone. As the water droplet vanished inside her neckline, he assumed her silence meant agreement.

"And if Santana, who trusts you," Charity asked, finally, "required you to do something you consider wrong, to prove your loyalty, would you do it?"

God's blood, the girl could think.

"You wouldn't, would you?" Charity dared.

Wide behind the flat disks of glass, her eyes burned with faith. Her fingers dropped the tortilla, and the empty hand reached toward him, then withdrew beneath the table.

He wanted to hold her, kiss her for her trust, take her to Refugio and prove to her, Halcon and Nicolas Carillo, together, could make a whole man.

"Why are you sure I wouldn't do something 'wrong' to protect my own skin—and my family's?" Nicolas cleared his throat against the rustiness in his voice.

Her smile—what a simpleminded ass he'd become!—felt like sunrise.

"Because heroism is in your blood, Nicolas. It's as elemental to you as your black hair," Charlie said. "Even at Harvard you protected me—"

"You can't compare a squabbling bunch of schoolboys to an *alcalde* appointed by the Emperor of Mexico, Charlie."

"It's the same instinct," she insisted, leaning forward until her breasts pressed the table edge. "It's why you can't help being—"

Halcon. He held up both hands, palms toward her face.

"—good."

Her impish smile, like rebellion, must be crushed.

"Charlie, you're the only one I can trust."

He'd cursed Freddy for unfair fighting, but a carrion bird had more care for its victim, than did a hell-bent patriot.

249

Nicolas wolfed down a tortilla and drained his coffee.

"You're right, Nicolas, you can trust me. I'll ride to the Indiada tomorrow and explain. However—no, you mustn't look so relieved, my fine puppeteer—" Charlie waggled her fingers as if dancing a marionette. "A compromise, remember? I'll ride to the Indiada, alone, but *you* will accompany me to the mission, to inform Father—Alvarado, was it?—of Santana's plans."

"Charity, that would defeat the entire—"

"Pretend to go on rancho business," she waved off his protest.

"You'd ask me to lie?" Nicolas pressed his chest in mock horror. "The woman who chastised me as a hypocrite encourages me to tell a falsehood?"

"It wouldn't be the first time, Nicolas."

Charlie slid from the bench, rounded the table's end and stood behind him. Nicolas remained seated, eyes fixed on the whitewashed wall. Her body radiated heat through the camisa. The prickling at the base of his neck, instinct born of a hundred gallops through darkness, told him his smallest move would bump his leather bound hair against her breasts.

Kitchen heat had curled the tortillas' edges. The corner of his eye burned from dripping perspiration. He should want Charlie further away. Instead, he wished she'd embrace him.

Charlie tapped his shoulder.

"It wouldn't be the first time," she repeated, "would it, Nicolas? That you've lied?"

Ah, yes. When he turned, his eyes *were* level with her breasts. Nicolas nearly upset the bench in his rush to stand.

"You may be right," Nicolas admitted.

"Right? I'm right? You couldn't possibly be conceding a point in this debate!" Charlie clapped her hands together. He wanted to rumple her hair like he would a pup's ears. He wanted to span her waist and feel that flexible spine bend backward to accommodate his body against hers.

*My little roommate. God, I want you.*

Charlie avoided his look by pushing her spectacles up her

nose, and brushing a crumb of tortilla from his shirt. Her fingers grazed his neck, and he nearly grabbed her.

Like a boy, a randy, out-of-control adolescent, his desire was so obvious, Charlie stepped back before she spoke.

"I'll help you, Nicolas. I'm smart enough, brave enough and I'll do it."

Charlie's noble little speech still vibrated in the *cocina* as her sandals slapped away down the hall.

"God help California," Nicolas muttered, gathering the remains of their lunch. "And God help me."


Climbing from her window, into the midnight courtyard, Charity formed a guilty prayer of thanks that Doña Anna didn't believe in locking young women in their rooms. Don Carlos disapproved his wife's liberal view and Charity feared Barbara would be forever captive if her parents discovered this escape.

By daylight, the patio appeared swept clear of stones. By night, her bare feet found the ground littered with them. A warning bark stopped her. Charity fumbled to pull on her slippers as a stiff-legged shape approached.

Lobo, the most wolfish of Arturo's yard dogs, licked her hand, then rolled over for a belly scratch. She complied and moved on, hoping Luna felt as agreeable.

Though her equestrian skills were improving, she didn't know where saddles were stored, feared she couldn't lift hers if she found it, and, most embarrassing, didn't understand how to fasten the cinch.

Hackamores hung on nails in the stable wall. With luck, she'd balance with her reins.

"Luna?"

A gray shape detached from the shadows. Arturo had said Indians breathed into horses' nostrils, so their mounts knew them by scent. Charity did it, and though Luna nudged her face away, he accepted the bit, and stepped off only when Charity sat, wobbly but upright, astride him.

Nicolas had appointed her to spread a warning to the nearest *Indiadas,* she thought. And while he'd probably imagined she'd plod about on sunny afternoons, instead of riding like Paul Revere or Halcon, he hadn't specified when and how, had he?

She bounced crazily, until Luna jarred from a trot to his rhythmic canter. Then, smugness, fear, everything but Luna's rocking chair gait, ebbed. Charity pressed low on the gray's neck, breathed the wind with him, let her hair blend with his mane, made her silhouette his, but soon she paid for her exhilairation.

A stone struck Charity behind the ear when a boy, set to guard three ragged sheep, halted her galloping approach to the first camp. Her stuttering explanation, translated by a boy who recognized her from the rancho, was accepted in bemused silence.

The second group of villagers stood in a half-circle outside their shelters, as if they expected her, but at her last stop, she almost lost Luna when a gust of wind snatched her cloak, wrapping it like a blindfold over Luna's face. A soothing set of hands at Luna's head and a second pair buffeting her hip as it sagged to one side kept her from falling.

But even humiliation couldn't ruin her night. Safely astride, free of the scent of campfires and people, she once more filled her lungs with green scents, hoof-churned earth and mist. Liberty like that she'd felt her first California night, crested like a wave inside her.

Charity squinted against the wind, letting boulders and manzanita groves pass in a blur. This was worth anything.


"*Gracias,* Arturo, for showing us the well where your father chills his wine." Charity felt her tongue brush the roof of her mouth, and thought she should always speak so precisely.

"Anytime, *cara.*" Arturo wore Nicolas's half smile as he steadied her arm. "Are you girls enjoying your picnic?"

He trailed through her doorway and held her arm more warmly than she should allow. Curse this clumsiness which made her stumble against him.

"We are, Arturo. Really having fun. We put the other bottle in the fountain. In the garden off Barbara's room? And we've been talking. Why can't I find my pen and paper?"

"This is only a guess, Señora. However, I would say it's because you've had too much to drink. Here's your paper, Charity, right on top. And your ink."

"Your opinion is absurd, Arturo." She held a wave of hair from her eyes. "That white wine is like water. Clear, sweet, water. And it's so hot outside!" She fanned herself with a sheet of paper. "I have to go. They're waiting."

Instead, she collapsed on her bed.

"I'll tell you something else, Arturo. And it isn't that you shouldn't be sitting on my bed with your arm around my waist. But you shouldn't, of course."

"I'm afraid you'll fall off, if I don't, Charlie. Shhh! Mother will be home any moment. If she hears you giggling. . . . Hush now, what will you tell me?"

"Just that Esperanza—" Charity stood, straightening her blue skirts, "is not so bad as I thought."

"Oh, you are drunk," Arturo chuckled.

"What?" She stamped her foot, then grabbed his arm to steady herself.

"*Borracho*. Drunk. What did Nicolas say once—'foxed?' If you think Esperanza is 'not so bad,' perhaps I should detain you for a nap."

Arturo's face loomed quite near, and she tapped his cheek with her pen.

"Barbara and Esperanza are going to teach me something."

Charity swallowed against the sing-song quality of her voice. Possibly, Arturo was right. The three of them *had* finished a large bottle of wine and uncorked a second. There'd been a picnic, too, but she couldn't recall what she'd eaten.

"Those two peahens could teach *you* nothing," he said.

"What about," Charity took a deep breath. Even wine couldn't buffer her embarrassment. "Seduction?"

"Charity—"

253

"You needn't look shocked, Arturo. I am a married woman." Charity braced her forehead against her fingertips.

Damnation. She dissembled so poorly. She'd convinced Esperanza and Barbara she needed advice to lure Freddy home. She'd better escape before she blurted the truth: Charity O'Dell would seduce the seducer. She would lay with Halcon the next time she met him, and let sensible Nicolas sort out the mess.

Arturo frowned. "Perhaps I should be with you."

"I. Think. Not." She punctuated her words with backward steps.

"Señora, be merciful."

Arturo's smile told her he expected no such thing, but his merry eyes darkened and something melancholy swam through their depths. Surely, she was just deceived by the wine.

"They won't let you listen." She shook her head. "But, Arturo? Will you help me practice?"

She skittered down the hall, her steps so light she heard Arturo's whisper.

*"Que lástima!"* he said. "What a pity, Charity. I should have met you before either of them."


"We've decided there are at least four things you should know."

Barbara, legs tucked beneath her yellow cotton skirt, cocked her head and set her earrings, clusters of tiny silver bells, jingling.

Esperanza perched on the fountain's edge. Charity wondered where Nicolas's fiancee would land, when she slid off. Her unsteadiness seemed to guarantee it.

Princessa bit Barbara's confining hands and bounded toward Charity, batting her ankles with sheathed claws.

"Going to hamstring me, little cat?" she murmured. "I could use the rest," she whispered. "I rode all night, but oh," she touched Princessa's sniffing nose, "I did a good job of it."

254

"She will spend the afternoon talking to your cat instead of us." Esperanza yawned.

"No, I brought my things, so I could write down what you say? See?" Charity sat next to Barbara, poised to write. "Just tell me the four things—"

"Maybe five," Esperanza fretted.

"—I must learn so I can have my way with a man." Charity giggled, covering her mouth at her own daring.

"I knew you hadn't done it yet," Esperanza exulted, reaching into the fountain to snag an earthen jug. After pouring, she shook water from her hand and regarded the other two. "What?"

The fountain prattled, until Barbara spoke. "Esperanza, that *was* rather coarse."

"Barbaracita, we *are* talking of seduction," Esperanza leaned back, offering her face to the tree-stained sun.

"I suppose," Barbara's lips twisted, "the first thing, we agreed, is—are you listening, Charlie?—play as if you don't care for him. You must seem to like someone else—"

"Or many others," Esperanza put in.

"—so he is eager for your attention." Barbara choked on a sip of wine, then continued. "When you pet one of Arturo's disgusting dogs, don't all the others gather around?"

"Of course," Charity marveled at Barbara's apt example.

"Myself," Barbara said, "I think you've done a fair job of that. Half the time, you treat him no different than you do my wretched twin."

Guilt scorched Charity's cheeks at her friend's accuracy, as Barbara held up a second finger and took a deep breath.

"Next, be attentive to all he says. Even if it puts you to sleep. Say, for instance, he talks of—"

"—horses," Esperanza filled in.

"I'm interested in horses," Charity dipped her pen.

"Or drought, or politics." Barbara said, raising herself to watch Charity dab excess ink from her pen.

"Now if he spoke of Halcon, Señora Larkin would not be forced to feign interest," Esperanza teased.

Charity's heart thudded against her chest wall.

"I find all California politics fascinating," she said.

In her head, the words sounded level and cool. *Don't let her guess, don't let her guess, please, God—*

"Well, then, it sounds as if we've nothing left to teach you." Esperanza shrugged a dismissal and stuck out her tongue.

"She can't do *this*," Barbara leaned forward until her nose touched Charity's, lowered her eyelashes and peered up.

"And it melts their hearts," Charity sighed with admiration. "But you're right, I couldn't do it."

"Not until you practice. Esperanza, more wine for my student."

Barbara paused as wine splashed to fill Charity's glass.

"Barbara, you could be an actress." Charity told her.

"What is it?"

"In Boston—"

"I have no stomach for more Boston," Esperanza snapped.

Charity watched Esperanza's tiny waist twist as she replaced the jug in the fountain. When she turned back, no sneer marred her perfect lips. Perhaps she'd imagined the mockery.

"Practice that look," Barbara exaggerated a blink, "in front of your glass, so we can continue your lesson. Mother could be home anytime, and I think it's best she find us in our rooms, napping." Barbara's chatter broke off as she regarded Esperanza. "Will you be fit to ride home?"

"Nicolas will assist me." Esperanza trailed her hand in the water, a feline smile visible, even in profile. "Although it's getting late. He might have to spend the night or risk riding home in the dark."

The girl raised a dripping finger to her lips. Sickening! How could Nicolas enjoy kissing her?

"I think Nicolas is up to the challenge." Charity clamped her lips into a benign smile as Esperanza's cloudy eyes focused.

"What did you say?"

"Nicolas is a—a superb horseman who can ride home in the dark. He's accompanying me to the mission tomorrow, you see, and he said . . ." Charity's voice faltered.

Oh, it was easy to be cocky when she spoke without thinking, but now Esperanza drew herself up. She was the queen bee, the reigning lioness. She fluffed out her hair, rotated the rubies in her ear lobes and crossed her white-stockinged ankles.

Charity regarded her own ankles—bony, bare and scored by Princessa's claws. "He—Nicolas said he wanted an early start."

"All the more reason—" Barbara drew her index finger over the dried line of writing, "that we hurry. Oh, he would beat us, Esperanza, if he thought we filled Charlie's head—"

"Have you drunk the rest of that whole bottle?" Barbara broke off as Esperanza bumped onto the blanket beside her. "Saints, Esperanza!

"The third thing, Charlie, is easy, but very important." Barbara held Charity's chin and enunciated. "Be happy all the time. Even if you feel sick, worried or hungry."

Charity laughed at Barbara's earnestly puckered forehead.

"My turn," Esperanza drained her goblet.

"Barbara, you have told the señora to be coy," Esperanza touched one index finger to the other, "to hang on a man's words, flutter her eyelashes and be happy."

Esperanza's fingertips scurried the air like white mice.

"This is all very well for an innocent, but Señora Larkin is *married*. She needs more than flirting to keep her husband. I mean, how long since he returned? A week? And already, he's gone? Batting eyelashes, *amiga mia*, will not serve."

Dread and excitement coiled in Charity's stomach. This girl, whose curly head barely reached her shoulder, who couldn't read a word and had no desire to, knew it all. Her languid posture—head flung back on the fountain's edge, one knee drawn up under her swishing skirts, legs exposed to the knee—she knew things no mother told her daughter. The secrets of Eve.

"Esperanza's right." Charity put on an expression of studious concentration.

You pretended to be a boy, she reminded herself, for

weeks. You can, by God, pretend Nicolas is no more than a friend, pretend not to care what she's learned from him.

"First, meet him in a romantic setting, but you mustn't let him know you find it so." Esperanza instructed. "A garden like this, perhaps during a fiesta—public, yet private, si? Or he might see you to chapel. It is dark and quiet, and two people may sit quite close without arousing suspicion . . ."

Charity drew a breath. "Garden," she lettered carefully, then "chapel." Really, she needn't be a baby about this. Esperanza instructed like a schoolmistress.

"A riverbank is somewhat primitive." Esperanza wrinkled her nose. "But the first time I lay with Nicolas—"

Barbara's gasp sounded like ripping silk.

"By all that's holy, Esperanza! I am not at all sure—no, I correct myself. I am quite sure, there are some things I do not wish to know about my brother!"

Barbara's carefully modulated tirade continued, but Charity heard it only as a background for her mind's jeering.

*God. Did you think he hadn't? Did you think because he's intelligent, charming, a skilled swordsman—oh! that's rich, Charity!—that he wasn't a rutting beast like any bull, like that brutal stallion?* "What do you want me to do?" *he'd pleaded on the twilight beach.* "You're married." *Oh, he'd tugged her heart with his melancholy eyes, and all the time he'd been cleaving unto—onto, into—*Her thoughts hammered and slashed until she came to the worst one of all. *Primitive? Esperanza complained her lover was primitive? Oh, does he nip at the palm of your hand, Esperanza? And does it make you as weak-kneed and helpless as it does me?*

"Truly, for one willing to perform under such conditions, Nico is strangely gentle." Esperanza's voice slowed and her lazy eyes measured her words' impact.

"P-R-I-M-I-T-I-V-E," Charity drew the letters with precision, but her pen point bit through the paper.

"I had no wish to offend," Esperanza leaned over to kiss Barbara's cheek and the girl fanned her hand, as if scattering wine fumes from Esperanza's breath.

"Once a man is interested," Esperanza continued, "his maleness takes over. Your willingness to stand near him, near enough he can smell your perfume," Esperanza circled her hand near her bosom, stirring the attar of roses, "and your inadvertent touches—steadying yourself upon his arm, brushing his hand as you open your fan, bumping against him in the pattern of a dance—all of these show you welcome his closeness.

"*Dios*, it is hot! Barbara, I am half tempted to wade in your fountain."

Humidity stuck Esperanza's black curls to her forehead, cheeks and white neck. Perspiration dotted the points of her upper lip, and she closed her eyes, rolling her head from side to side. Charity wanted to smash her fist into that pretty mouth.

Barbara tucked her chin into her neck and smoothed up the back of her upswept hair. She glanced first at Esperanza, then Charlie, and her silver earrings chimed with the movement.

"Is there any more advice?" Charity's words sounded stilted, as if they'd been pried from her throat by a wooden spoon. She lifted her pen from the paper where it had formed a black puddle.

Outside the garden walls, a dog yapped. The following chorus of barks drew squawks from yard fowl as riders approached.

"One last thing." Esperanza stood, taming her ruffles into position. "Now, Barbara, don't give me that look! You never were such a prude before.

"Is it so different that I talk of Nicolas instead of some faceless *he?* I am his *novia*, after all," she cut across Barbara's protest. "Before so many priests came, all California's *gente de razon* did it. It was expected. Ask your parents."

"As if I could!" Barbara stood, testing her balance before she bent to retrieve the blanket. "Oh, I'm light-headed. Charlie, are you?"

"The last thing," Esperanza insisted, "is not to act too innocent. Not you, Barbara, but the señora. A man wishes to be the only one in your bed, but he hates to feel the *despoiler*, the instrument of your ruin." She spread her hands wide, and

259

Charity thought her expression changed from brazen to bitter.

Esperanza rustled away, leaving Barbara and Charity to fold the quilt. It took that long for Charity to gather her nerve.

"I want you to pierce my ears."

"Charlie, what are you—"

"Si, you have it, *chica!*" Esperanza laughed from Barbara's room. "Make him think he's come home to another woman."

"Barbara, will you?" Charlie clutched her friend's arm.

"Perhaps Pilar—"

"No, I want you to do it, right now. In your room."

"Charlie, I couldn't! They do it when girls are babies!"

"How hard can it be, Barbara? Use your embroidery needle. I'll sit still," she wheedled, "I won't cry or tell on you."

A little more pain wouldn't matter, and she'd have something from it.

"Please, Barbara?"

Nicolas' little sister bounced her head from side to side, weighing the question.

"Please? What's the worst thing that can happen?"

"I suppose you're right," Barbara conceded. "Come inside. I already hear Mother telling the vaqueros how to unsaddle a horse, so we'd better hurry. Saints, I wish we had another bottle of wine."

# Chapter Twenty

"I know what you did, Charity. I believed you were smarter than that."

Skeins of silver fog still streamed over the rancho's roof and the black-green cock had yet to crow, but Nicolas had lost all patience with Charlie.

*Ay Cristo!* To gallop from the rancho to the Indiada at midnight—! Her horse might have snapped a foreleg and stranded her. She might have been "arrested" by Santana's men. Unhorsed, she might have stumbled into an arroyo, broken her neck and lain cold and pale, beyond help, instead of squealing the front gate as she'd returned.

Charity needed a master. Until Freddy rode through those gates, he stood as that master, and he refused to allow such dangerous behavior.

Her eyes darted to the hacienda, then the corral, wondering who'd betrayed her. Little innocent. In addition to the gossip of vaqueros and housemaids, he'd been notified by half a dozen worried Indians.

"Do you mean the wine?" Charlie asked, still as a cornered rabbit.

"No, although in that escapade you might have considered Barbara. Father will confine her for months if Arturo decides to tell."

"Arturo told us where—"

"I consider it unlikely he'll tell," his voice rolled over hers. "He enjoys holding threats above his twin's head."

Nicolas cleared his throat against amusement. Quickly, his mind showed an image that guaranteed solemnity: Charlie, drunk.

Silly, instead of studious, Arturo had said, and affectionate beyond belief, cuddling like a kitten.

"The earrings, then?" She offered another transgression.

"No," he said. Nicolas tipped up the brim of her hat. With one finger, he lifted draped hair, glossy as a crow's wing. Her ear lobe, swollen and pink, held a tiny gold cross.

The earrings looked sweet and female. He clasped his hands behind his back and frowned.

"Why did you chose to mutilate yourself, Charity?"

"If you weren't scolding me for the wine or earrings," her voice flared too loud for the drowsy dawn. "What was it, Nicolas?"

"You rode out in the middle of the night, no doubt mimicking Halcon. You have heard the expression, 'foolhardy?' It's you, Charlie," his voice picked up momentum like a barrel rolling downhill. "The words should be emblazoned on your garments. You dare all, with no judgement. Furthermore—don't talk, Charity! Listen!—you returned your horse hot."

Her outcry ended when he mentioned Luna. She took off her spectacles, held them at arm's length and peered through.

"His coat was stiff with sweat and his muscles so sore he could barely walk, because you didn't bother to let him cool down before shutting him in the corral."

"Is he all right?" Charlie whispered.

"Each time I rode in yesterday, I asked Toro. But, each time, no Señora Larkin had not been to the corral.

"Why should the Señora care? The Señora drank herself silly, laughed at ribald stories, but—"

"Nicolas, I'm sorry," she apologized.

Worse than corsets and confinement, he knew Charlie hated to appear stupid. And yet she didn't fling excuses, didn't dodge his accusation. Foolhardy, rash and thoughtless, but never a liar.

*Dios,* what were you thinking when you made her a girl, instead of a man?

"Always before, there's been someone," she mused. "It's no excuse, no excuse for poor Luna. I didn't know I had to cool him down." She rubbed her forehead to force the knowledge inside. When she looked up and found no forgiveness, her tone strengthened. "I feel terrible, all right?"

"Lower your voice, please, Charity." Nicolas glanced toward the corral. "I merely want you to understand, I won't tolerate such behavior."

"My behavior," she swept the hat from her head and slammed it against her thigh, "is not for you to tolerate or not tolerate. My behavior—"

"Charlie, if you insist on performing for the entire rancho, I can't talk with you."

Her fists threatened to split her deerskin gloves. But she didn't storm away. Seeing no one in the yard, she flung her hat at his feet.

"Damnation, Nicolas! Why do you do this?" She spoke through gritted teeth. "Why do you cause a rift, just when I've helped you, when we're becoming friends, again?"

He shrugged, knowing it would provoke fresh fury.

"You can't stand me to get close, can you? We were at school, but—you're not even close to your own *novia!* I expect you bed her well enough, but—" she sputtered, bit her lip so hard it whitened, then stripped off her gloves, as if to fight.

"Well, I won't let you goad me into saying it!" she shook her finger under his nose. "I won't tell you I can't bear your company riding to the mission. I know it's what you want! And, another thing, I'm not going to cry!"

"Why should you, Charity? Over an abused horse?"

"Nicolas, if I were a man," she flapped her gloves close enough that he drew back. "I would slap you across the face and demand satisfaction in a duel."

"Whatever for? I haven't smirched your honor, Charlie, just asked you to be more careful. Why would you challenge me?"

"I—" she snatched up her hat and squared it on her hair.

"I don't know. I only know it's not even six o'clock in the morning and you've ruined my entire day."

"Excuse me, Doña Ronda." Charlie's sprint to the hacienda bumped the older woman.

Adjusting an orange rebozo over her hair, Doña Ronda stopped beside Nicolas. *Ay Cristo*, he recited more lines than a priest.

"Good morning, Doña," he greeted. "This time tomorrow you will be asleep in your own bed."

The old harridan ignored his pleasantry.

"That girl seemed more sensible when she first arrived," Doña Ronda said.

"California isn't the place for everyone," Nicolas shrugged. "Besides, she's a *Yanqui*."

Doña Ronda considered this as she walked toward the cocina.

*A rift.* Nicolas stalked to the corral, wishing to hell his spurs and conchos tolled his mood.

In one cast, his reata snagged the docile bay Pilar favored. Charlie had harmed her own mount. He'd defy her to go adventuring on this nag.

A rift, and he—of course, *he*—caused it. But *he* hadn't received a letter, yesterday.

A gentleman's tongue should shrivel before prying into a woman's correspondence with her husband, so he'd given no hint he noticed the red-scarfed messenger delivering the letter.

In his own mind, he'd made excuses. Charlie had needed time to mull over the letter's contents. She'd been weary from night-riding. She couldn't believe—what a welcome fancy!— Freddy had left, forever. But this morning Charlie still hadn't spoken. She had *Diablo's* own audacity blaming him for causing a rift.

"Don Nicolas, which horse for Señora Larkin?" asked Luis. Dressed in calico neckerchief, purple sash and neatly braided queue, Luis could scarcely wait to visit his parents, who lived on Doña Ronda's land.

264

"Just catch the doña's animal, and take my chestnut for yourself. I'll saddle this cow for the Señora."

"Wake up, beast." He leaned against the reata circling the animal's neck. "You might as well have *your* day spoiled, too."

When Charlie reappeared, five horses stood saddled before the hacienda. Four to ride, one to lead, since he meant to leave Penance at the mission.

No reddened, tear-blotched face marred her. Charlie stepped onto the porch, hands twined through Arturo's elbow, laughing.

"Which mount is mine, Don Nicolas?"

*Don Nicolas.* Because he'd reprimanded her, she pretended subservience. A subservient Charlie, a contrite Charlie, even a polite Charlie was unbelievable.

"The bay," he replied.

She looked past Penance, past his chestnut and the black on the lead rein, to the mule-eared animal. Charlie's glance stopped at Doña Ronda's bay, a deep-chested stallion with mane to his knees, then tracked back to Pilar's favorite.

Charlie's hands came to the hips of that awful too-tight habit, and she whirled on him.

*Come on, Charlie. Have at me. Come on. I'm spoiling for a second round!*

"Ah," she pushed her spectacles up her nose, then stepped close to rub the bay's muzzle. For that, she had to lift its head by the bridle. "He's less spirited than Luna, sí?"

Charlie plucked up the reins, vaulted aboard and arranged her legs into the sidesaddle. She urged the bay to walk.

Nicolas pretended to check Penance's cinch, keeping Charlie in sight, over the pinto's back. He could count ten between times the bay lifted a hoof and set it down.

"The padres get back a better horse than the one they loaned," Nicolas muttered, clapping Penance's shoulder before mounting.

"Charlie, come down off that sullen creature," Arturo instructed, "Let me make the old cow dance."

Sash flapping, Arturo swung up behind the side-saddle.

Funneled through front teeth, his shrill whistle made the other horses side-step and snort. The bay continued plodding.

Arturo sat erect, legs intent on rousing the horse. His arm whirled at the edge of the animal's vision, hoping it would shy and he could spur it into a trot. It slowed, then stopped.

Arturo pulled a comical frown.

"This one is dinner for my dogs, *hermano*. And not good enough for that."

"Pilar likes him," Charlie protested.

"She'd like him even better stewed." Arturo swung his right leg high over the bay's ears and jumped to the ground. "Charlie, ride my Tigre."

"And get herself killed?" Nicolas blurted.

"It would be quick." Arturo thrust his lower lip out, then squinted, as if considering. "Better than dying of boredom."

Sassy rooster. *Cristo*, Arturo had done it again. Flaunting his immature manhood, he'd strutted to Charlie's rescue. Should he hand over Halcon's mask and sword, too?

Charlie had the sense not to laugh. She stood silent, as if witnessing a fight between grizzlies, not brothers.

Grizzlies. Thank the saddle's creator for the leather hump blocking his crotch from view! He didn't even *like* her this morning. Her ride to the Indiada had been childish, her reaction to being caught, insolent. Yet he wanted her more than food, drink or his soul's salvation. In hell, *Diablo* would taunt him with grizzlies, forcing him to relive the feel of Charlie, always unattainable, writhing beneath him.

Nicolas snorted in disgust. Hell might not be so different from Earth, after all.

"Charity, please, take my chestnut for the journey. Luis—" he turned in the saddle to see the vaquero wave an arm in assent.

"My grulla will be ready in *uno momento*, Don Nicolas."


For hours he thought like a *ranchero*—not a patriot, nor a lovesick boy. He surveyed his lands, assessing the legacy of drought.

In early summer, these grasslands should be verdant, but plants parched and killed last year, hadn't reseeded. Spring rains, little more than mist, had moistened the low spots. Old riverbeds and cattle trails undulated with grass, but in many places it had already been grazed to a gold stubble. Only the distant hills showed blue-green threads.

Oppressive stillness closed him in a drawstring pouch.

"Earthquake weather."

Until now Doña Ronda had addressed only Charlie, identifying wild flowers and chaparral, pointing out Sangriento creek and Monte Negro, describing a ravine favored by fugitive Indios, outcast bulls and rabid coyotes.

"Indeed?" he covered his skepticism.

"It's true. In the last hour, have you seen any wild things? Heard any birdsong?" Doña Ronda asked.

Nicolas waited for more arguments, but Doña Ronda fell into a smug reverie, and he heard only Luis's bit-rolling grulla, and Charlie's wordless reproach.

At first, she'd been absorbed with controlling the chestnut. Just onto the Plato, the horse feigned terror at a rabbit, and bolted. Nicolas's fear turned to admiration as Charlie all but sat on her reins, then, when the chestnut failed to respond, turned him in a tight circle until he shook his head, snorted and resumed his jog.

Bright pink with pride and exertion, Charlie had turned to him for approval. He'd stared past her. Foolhardy.

She must not compare herself to Halcon. He rode for a cause, not for the thrill of galloping by moonlight. Even if she wanted to help, Charlie lacked the skills.

Her horsemanship was adequate—for daylight hours and predictable terrain. Her swordsmanship was fine—for his sunlit den or a Boston lawn. Her subterfuge, her ability to hide her thoughts—pitiful.

Charlie's feelings colored her face like Esperanza's rouge. He might protect her as long as she only suspected his secret. Once she had proof, Santana would read her easily.

Horse*man*ship. Swords*man*ship.

267

"Charity," he might gently turn her own language against her, "You cannot be Nighthawk. Only Nighthawk's woman."

From the tail of his eye he caught Charlie watching. He returned her stare, but Charlie only winced, lifting her chin from the chafing blue collar, shifting her legs in the horns of the sidesaddle.

Since she'd commenced her studies of wolves and wild horses, she'd ridden astride a stock saddle. Why, now, did she perch in that waist-twisted, bosom-thrusting position?

"I expect you bed her well enough—" Had Charlie really said that?

He hadn't bedded Esperanza at all, for over a month. Not since his proxy marriage to Charlie. Wrong, Carillo. Not since *Freddy's* proxy marriage to Charlie. You merely facilitated their joining. Like a ring.

*Had* he bedded Esperanza well? Before?

Penance shied at a bleached rib bone, and Nicolas swayed, trying to picture Esperanza's body.

He'd only seen her in fragments. She'd allow him glimpses of her soft, small legs and then, "*Por favor*, these skirts are new, darling, be careful." She'd place his hand at her decolletage, encouraging his touch, but if his fingers broached her underclothing to dip her breast free of restraint, "Peel down only the bodice, love, so I may cover myself, if someone comes."

The glimpses had stirred him, and he'd set upon her, fired by the concealment. Now she seemed no temptress, only stingy.

Esperanza's fire and ice were contrived. She only burned—clawing his vest, rolling her hips in a precisely circular motion—until he'd unlaced his breeches, committing himself to the act. Then she cooled, staring past his shoulder with eyes vacant as glass. The first time he'd seen them so, fixed in unearthly detachment, he'd wilted to the size of her little finger. Esperanza hadn't noticed.

*Had* he bedded her well enough? Hardly, and yet last night, after her afternoon of drinking, she'd rubbed against him like a bitch in heat, promising a lusty detour if he'd see her home.

"I'm required here," he'd begun.

"Don't think you can break our betrothal," she'd hissed, the cloves no cover for her wine breath.

"I have no such intention," he'd replied, but her words had kindled a vaunting hope.

"I want no other man in California. My father would settle for no other. Except," Esperanza had taunted, "Guerro Santana, perhaps. Power can be as intoxicating as love, *verdad?*"

The bitch and the hell hound. California would reel under the curse of such a mating, but Guerro's graft could supply Esperanza's jewels. The price of her ruby still galled him. The gold would have fed Salvador's renegados all winter. But until Halcon rode for the last time, Nicolas Carillo needed a royalist fiancee, and that fiancee craved jewels.

Nicolas glanced at Charlie's left hand, light on her reins. No bump peaked beneath her gloves. Would Freddy ever give his bride a ring? Nicolas touched his thumb to the shank of his Harvard band.

Oh, sweet mother of Christ, why? Why had she married Freddy?

Charity stood in the dim room Doña Ronda had designated hers. Arms wound around her ribs, she stared at the letter she'd flung to the floor.

She'd force herself to read it again, word by word. But, unless she'd suddenly lost her ability to comprehend English, there was no point.

Freddy wanted to go home.

With her.

To Boston.

Laughter flowed from the hacienda's courtyard. Luis greeted his father, slapping his back. Nicolas's spurs rang beneath the gaiety and snorting horses. He joked with Doña Ronda's vaqueros as they unstrapped bedrolls, saddlebags, and unbuckled cinches. Within, Doña Ronda badgered her cook.

Charity turned the gold earrings as Barbara had warned

her, to ward off inflammation, and accepted the resulting twinge. Flesh pain could be borne more easily than heart pain.

Moving as if she were underwater, Charlie took up the letter and stood close to the window, using the day's waning light.

> Charlie,
>
> I was Wrong to leave you. So unfair. You were Sick and I know you were not being Contrary. Although I think You might Excuse Me for thinking Such A Thing.
>
> San Diego is not ready for an American Bank.
>
> It will be best to return to Boston. We are not Ourselves here.
>
> Your Loving Husband,
> Frederick

Chattel. All her study, all her intelligence came down to this: her husband was ordering her back to Boston.

And what of your beloved Sierra? She flapped the letter toward the window. What of the wild, roaming life you promised?

Freddy couldn't force her to go, of course. He wouldn't beg the *alcalde's* assistance. He wouldn't bind her hand and foot, and fling her on the next Yankee trading vessel.

She paced the narrow room, cutting the air with the letter as she weighed her choices. She could stay on with the Carillos, causing them endless embarrassment. She could hire out as a duenna to some less respectable family. She might convince a priest to cut off her hair and christen her a bride of Christ. Poor choices, but each would keep her in California. Near him.

She ripped the page in two pieces, then four.

If only Nicolas had given her one word of encouragement. Who but gossips cared if an American spinster became an outlaw's mistress? She'd gallop away, her silver Luna beside his black stallion, and never look back. But she had nothing more than his aching question, from the beach, "What would you have me say? You're married."

Married. Nicolas linked that cold ceremony with his loyalty to his church, to his friend, to honor. What right did she have to lever him away from values that ruled his life?

Charity pressed her hands against her breastbone. To keep her heart within? To keep it from breaking? She shook her fingers to restore the blood flow, wishing she could laugh at herself.

And Halcon. In his way, he'd encouraged her. His hands, his arms, his consuming kisses—but no words! Lips that made her insensible to anything but their bodies offered poor promises.

"Señora, are you finding everything you need? The chamber pot—" Doña Ronda asked.

"I can't stay. I must leave. Now. Before dark."

She'd do it. What Esperanza and Barbara had taught her. Seduction.

"Is something wrong with the room, Señora?"

Doña Ronda stepped inside, squinting at the perimeters of the floor, under the bed.

"No, I'm sorry. Nicolas and I have to leave. Tonight."

If he wanted her, she'd stay. If he lay with her and honored his betrothal to Esperanza, she'd go with Freddy. And remember Nicolas, feel Halcon, love them both, always.

"There, there, Señora," Doña Ronda crooned, smoothing Charity's brow. "You're still not recovered. The fish—and it is as I said. The weather, no? You feel confined? Come with me—Maria! You useless wench, brew the Señora a calming draught of Manzanilla—come out to the patio and sit."

She heard boots, spurs, the gentle chinging of conchos as they brushed edges at each step.

"Nicolas!"

"Don Nicolas," Doña Ronda insinuated herself between them, glancing back at Charity with a nervous smile. "Señora Larkin is suddenly quite desperate, quite—"

Charity dodged around the woman and grabbed Nicolas'

271

forearms. She looked into his eyes, trying to transfer her thoughts to his mind, without words.

"Charity?" Nicolas coaxed, using the tone he reserved for bewildered young horses. "What is it, *pequena?*"

Oh, he'd take her. He had to.

"I must leave. I've—" Damnation! Already she was breaking the rules! "I've had some bad news."

Be happy, Barbara and Esperanza had ordered, and the very first thing she'd done was babble of bad news.

"How could you have had bad news, Señora?" Doña Ronda tried to catch Nicolas's eye.

"A letter. I didn't read it, until now."

"The drink, Doña," a girl hovered with a cup.

"Take it away—no, leave it. Oh, Don Nicolas, explain what a good hostess should do?"

His brown eyes were still, but a dozen shifting shadows crossed within them.

"The señora and I will ride on to the mission, tonight. You have need of the *padre*, Charity, is that it?"

She nodded wildly, her mind skidding out of control. Would she go to Hell for involving a priest in her falsehood?

" 'Beads about the neck and the devil in the heart,' " Pilar had scolded when Charity fitted two small gold loops, Barbara's, into her ears this morning. At Charity's bewildered expression, Pilar had sniffed, "Beads, earrings—it is close enough."

And so she'd substituted the gold crosses. Did they damn her doubly?

Nicolas hadn't even known of the letter. Was he helping her lie or did he believe she needed spiritual comfort?

"Will you take a meal, first?"

Doña Ronda's face showed confusion, but no suspicion, no sign she'd taken offense. Charity threw her arms around the woman, nestling, and for an awful moment, Charity thought she might cry.

"I'm sorry," she began.

"Visit another time," Doña Ronda waved off the apology. "You were only staying until dawn, anyway." She took a sip

272

of the drink before offering it to Charity. "You really should try some, Señora. It will settle your nerves and you wouldn't, after all, want to scare the horses."

Charity gulped the warm liquid. Over the cup's rim she saw Doña Ronda brighten.

"The horses," Doña Ronda nodded. "Yours will be wearied, Don Nicolas. Please be kind enough to choose two of my blacks."

Doña Ronda boasted of her manada of Moorish blacks. The fleetest, most beautiful animals in all of California roamed her pastures. And each one gentle as a house cat.

"I would be honored, Doña," Nicolas gave a half bow. "Luis will return them in a few days and resume the visit with his family."

"Shouldn't he—" Charity swallowed. Luis. Her amateurish seduction could not stand an audience. "Couldn't he stay?"

No gentle questions flickered through Nicolas's eyes, now. Blatant suspicion skewered her.

"But Señora—" Doña Ronda clucked her tongue.

"I appreciate your concern for my reputation, Doña. But I am a married woman, so truly, I don't need a chaperon, do I?" Charity's breath jerked through her chest.

"We will reach the mission by moonrise," Nicolas assured Doña Ronda. "I'll select new horses and tell Luis he may remain.

"Charity, eat something before we leave."

It sounded like a dismissal and Doña Ronda didn't linger.

"Maria!" Doña Ronda called, rushing from the room. "Quickly! Where are the *antojitos* I asked for? Maria!"

Her voice faded and Charity, seeing the menace in Nicolas's eyes, would have followed if he hadn't snatched her arm.

Nicolas's gloved index finger stabbed toward her. Twice he growled beginnings of harsh speech. Twice he shook his head. The second time, the black ribbon holding his hair slid off.

"*Ay Cristo*, Charlie!" He reknotted the ribbon so violently one end snapped loose. "Be ready in ten minutes or—" he stormed from the house, gripping the satin fragment and muttering.

Nicolas supposed he must take the blame. Unable to maintain his *hidalgo* hauteur, ramrod posture and incessant fury toward Charlie, he'd relaxed. Perhaps the restless longing of a summer night stirred whatever youth still lingered in his blood. Whatever caused it, cantering into the purple dusk on a stallion called Cordoba, Nicolas forgot duty, forgot riding directly to the mission, and offered to show Charlie Las Calderonas.

The horses snorted their uneasiness, negotiating a sloping defile so narrow it admitted only one animal abreast, high sides making it so dark, they rode blind. Nicolas refused to think of Salvador's *hindas* who might have arrived early for the attack on Santana and might consider any white man worth killing. He refused to mourn the night raid he'd planned, even packed for, which must be aborted since Charlie rode with him.

Charlie had learned to flirt. Chirping like the most feather-brained Californiana, she twittered questions about his responsibilities as a *ranchero*. She'd kept her horse stirrup to stirrup with his, watching his lips answer, nodding at each word. If he spoke of marking cattle, her eyes widened until her eyelashes curled back. When he explained how he must balance the number of hides traded to the missions against the number offered to the munificent trading ships, weighing religion and practicality, her brow furrowed in concentration.

Her raptness led staid Nicolas Carrillo to joke about the vanity of California horsemen. From blue-blooded hidalgos to Indian vaqueros, all the same, choosing to spend their gold on horses and trappings.

" 'His spurs are silver, but his wife is barefoot,' that's what Pilar would tell you."

Charlie's gaiety, though quite out of proportion to his jest, made Nicolas smile.

And so he shouldn't have been surprised when they

274

reached the end of the steep defile, rode into the moon-washed box canyon and Charlie gasped.

"Where is this?"

Steam from a score of hot springs wavered, silver as spirits. They floated behind each rock and tree, ghosts of girls whose heaven was this, eternal dancing in the moonlight.

"Las Calderonas—The Kettles—but really, they're hot springs," he explained "The water bubbles up from beneath the ground, hot as a bath."

"We must stay."

Charlie's voice rose like steam. She didn't know what she was asking. But he didn't refuse, or question, didn't even tell her another hour of riding would have brought them to the mission gates. He slid off the horse and helped her dismount.

She explored, and he listened to her movements as he unsaddled Cordoba. He crouched at the stallion's hooves, securing the reata in cross hobbles, when Charlie's hand flattened on his back.

"How hot?" she asked.

"*Que?*"

"How hot is the water? Could I really bathe in it?"

Her brows rose in the same flirtatious expression she'd worn on the trail, but her own huskiness lurked beneath the chirp. And she spoke of bathing.

"Some are right for bathing . . ." he licked his bottom lip and reminded himself Nicolas Carillo, not Nighthawk, straightened and stood next to Charlie. Alone. With no likely interruptions for a week. A *week*.

". . . some will boil the flesh off your bones."

"One could watch the horses, don't you think, and judge which pools were safe?"

Charlie nodded toward her mount, as yet unhobbled. The horse had waded into the water, collapsed with a contented grunt and rolled, splashing.

"Other wild life would serve, too," she speculated, "and probably the vegetation if one knew what to look for."

Charlie shook her head. Although she'd been shoved aside

by the naturalist, for just a moment, Charlie the coquette looked back at him.

"Well, shall we go in? Shall we swim?" She laughed and touched the laces at the throat of his shirt.

*Jesu Cristo,* what was the girl about?

"I think you'll be wet enough after you catch that horse so I can hobble him. And I'd better make a fire to keep away cougars. Then, we'll eat."

Twilight didn't quite disguise the trembling at the edge of Charlie's smile before she flounced after her mount.

*What in hell?*

Nicolas gripped his knife and squatted. His blade shaved a branch until mounded wood curls, enough to kindle a blaze, sat before him. He arranged a circle of rocks, thinking he'd use the largest as a griddle. A safe thought, far less risky than the fragrance of Charlie's hair as she crouched beside him.

"I hobbled him myself," she boasted.

He cut his eyes toward the horse's feet and nodded.

"As long as you're sure of your knots," he said, striking a spark into the shavings. "Cordoba might not carry us both."

Flame caught with a hiss that almost covered her whisper. ". . . could just stay . . ."

He closed his eyes, feeling the fire's heat and seeing the red through his lids, refusing to look up and see her features in the firelight. It didn't make sense. Charlie was no tease, no brazen, practiced—

Of course. Now he had the sense of it, even though disappointment struck his chest like a lead weight. Barbara and Esperanza had coached her. He regarded Charlie with amusement.

"What?" she asked, accusing.

"I said nothing, *pequena.*"

Charlie's fingers smoothed back the hair at her temples and she swallowed. The high collar bobbed over her throat.

"But you looked—"

"If you get the blankets I tied on the back of your saddle, you'll have a place to sit while we eat Doña Ronda's supper."

Charlie nodded and he watched her scurry off. Those girls

were idiots. Esperanza and Barbara had no business teaching her to encourage men. Might as well hand a child a primed musket.

"You were so smart to bring these," Charlie praised, smoothing blankets onto the ground she'd cleared of stones.

A mooncalf. He thought of her that way before, but she had never been one, until now. Did they tell Charlie she must act brainless to attract a man? What idiocy! And yet—he bit back a rueful laugh—hadn't he cantered along, joking and thinking what a delightful companion she'd become?

"A vaquero is always prepared to spend the night on the range," he shrugged off her praise.

"But you're not a vaquero. You're a *hacendado*, the boss." Pragmatic Charlie pointed up his error.

"But a vaquero, too, Charlie. With my reata and knife I could survive on the range quite well."

When she didn't answer, Nicolas rocked back on his heels. His resolution not to see her by firelight was stupid. Where would he turn his eyes the rest of the night? He looked up from his makeshift bed and saw her, rose-gold and beautiful against the black night.

Still, he didn't like what he saw: a smile so artificial he wanted to shake her. What could he tell her? *Fight with me, Charlie? Show me that daring I shamed you for this morning?*

He'd made a mess of things. Be sweet, Charlie. Be tough, Charlie. And he had no right. Worse, he couldn't hug her and confess his stupidity. He couldn't—

A squeaking sound, then a cough, came from her.

"Charlie, what are you doing? Charlie?"

Her breath raked from her breast.

Nicolas jumped past the campfire to steady her against a violent cough. He pried a brandy bottle from her fingers and patted her back.

"It burns," she choked.

"I daresay it does," Nicolas sighed his relief then swished the container before sniffing at its neck. "It wasn't full?"

"I was so thirsty."

"It's brandy, Charlie. You can't gulp it like water."

"Doña Ronda said you liked it."

"I do, but it's a drink you sip," he said, squeezing her shoulder. "It would be best, I think, for you to eat."

He pressed food on her like the most concerned father, watching her chew the corn colache, the cold beef and fruit.

"Careful," he cautioned, passing her a rock-warmed tortilla, "Don't burn your fingers."

Solicitous, oh so solicitous, he mocked himself, keeping the fire between them, but he didn't feel paternal. Charlie had loosed several buttons on her habit. Down the back, out of sight, but Nicolas remembered Arturo's assessment of Charlie, drunk. Kittenish, he'd said. Very friendly. And Esperanza and Barbara had planted seduction in her mind. Those wicked girls.

Nicolas Carillo might possibly be a patriot; he was not a saint.

*Stop.* He rose, stretched and walked to Charlie's side of the fire. *Go back. She doesn't know the difference between seduction and flirtation and you're not, tonight, the man to teach her.* Charlie, pink and gold with the back of her ugly gown gaping to show her chemise, looked up at him.

She flinched, startled by the fire popping and settling.

"Green wood," he explained. *Filthy lecher. Return to the other side of the fire before you both get burned.* Nicolas settled on the blanket beside her.

"Oh, yes," Charlie sighed, easing against his shoulder as if melting.

*Oh no. I am not gelding enough to make this mere flirtation.*

"Charlie," he cleared his throat, but the gruffness remained. "What was in the letter?"

Her eyes sprang wider than when the fire popped.

"Oh, nothing."

"You were very upset, then, about nothing."

Her lip trembled before she shook her head, not once, but over and over, until he caught her face between his hands and kissed her.

Something rose up in him, crested and his mouth widened over hers. *Ay Cristo, only one kiss. I promise, God, only one. One.*

278

Blindly, his hand found the nape of her neck, laced over with fallen tendrils of her careful, ladylike hair style and he pressed his mouth down, harder.

She struggled to breathe and he released her. A bargain with God must be kept.

"I didn't mean—" Charlie leaned toward him, eyes still closed.

She'd forego breathing, for kisses. But he wouldn't let her.

"The letter," she sighed and folded her hands in her lap. "Freddy said he's taking me back to Boston."

"No! I—Charlie, you like California. And Freddy, what of this talk about the Sierra? What is he thinking?"

Nicolas told himself to be silent. For Halcon's purposes, Freddy's proposal couldn't be better. Thousands of miles away, Charlie could neither distract him nor hurt herself.

"So, you see, this is probably my only summer in California," Charlie said.

She squared her shoulders and held her arms out to him. Poor little bride. He took her under his arm and held her against his ribs. Long ago, he'd promised her a land of wolves and wild horses, swords and free riding across the plains. Adventure. What cruelty to snatch it all away!

Charlie wriggled under his brotherly arm, struggling to reach his lips.

"Charlie, no."

"Why?" she demanded. "Why can't you kiss me?"

She pulled away and stood, glaring down with her hands on her hips. He couldn't see her face. Only her angry form, silhouetted black against the fire's gold.

"What would it hurt, Nicolas? What?"

What, indeed? He started to fork his fingers through his hair and then kept the hand there, squeezing his temples with strength enough to make his mind function. For the life of him, he could think of no reason not to kiss her, not to make love to her. Freddy would never know. No one need know, ever.

"Nicolas, I'm going into the cauldron."

"What?"

Charlie had walked the dozen steps to the nearest spring. And she had done it in her chemise and petticoat.

"Where's your gown?"

It was an idiot thing to say, but his mind stuttered, grappling with the task of *not* gathering her close, *not* stroking long bare arms flowing from the sleeveless chemise.

"It doesn't matter, Nicolas."

Would she make him run mad?

"Come with me."

She poised for just a minute, arms crossed over her chest, frightened by her brazenness. A ribbon coursed, dark and light, through the lace of her petticoat. She turned with a jerk and jumped, feet together, into the spring.

It wasn't very deep.

"Damnation!"

Splashing, then the thudding of flesh on mud, sent the hobbled horses plunging. Nicolas waited until the liquid slaps settled to a quiet lapping, until whirlwind vapors swirled in a silver fog.

"Are you all right, Charlie? Charlie?"

The firelight reached far enough that he saw the water barely covered her lap. Her wide-spread knees, draped with the sodden petticoat, cocked up at angles out of the pool. A snatch of hair lay wet against her cheek and her eyes blazed. She looked like a half-drowned kitten. A wildcat maybe, or a lynx, but still pitiful.

Suppressed laughter might have choked him if he hadn't seen her nipples pressing against the wet chemise. He knelt at the pond's edge.

"Besides checking for temperature, I suppose one should check for depth," she said.

"I suppose," he answered, cursing himself as his hand curled around her shoulder.

Soft. *Dios*, softer than anything he'd ever touched and smooth, no doubt, when it wasn't covered with gooseflesh. But it felt so tiny, undisguised by taffeta or silk, so vulnerable. He lowered his lips to kiss it before his vow resounded in his mind.

"Nicolas."

If he'd never been right about another thing in his wretched life, Santana had been right about Charity's magnetic, throaty voice. Nicolas brushed his mustache slowly, delicately across her shoulder. *It's not a kiss, God, see? Not a kiss. My lips barely touch her.*

"Nicolas."

She held her breath after his name, and it swelled her chest so high, dark cleavage appeared between her breasts.

"I'm not a virgin, you know."

"Ah," he said.

And then he waited, trying to identify the feeling vibrating within. Relief? Disappointment? Anger at that bumbling Freddy?

"No, Charlie, I did not know."

"You wouldn't expect—"

"Of course not."

"So then, it doesn't matter." Charlie's voice stopped and her shoulder shivered under his hand.

"It matters that. you belong to someone else. By the law and by the act that—Ah, Charity, it makes you one, si? You and my friend, Freddy." He closed his mouth before he could say more.

"But he won't know! How could he?"

Her eyes filled with tears and he saw how much she'd staked on this argument.

God, he'd wanted to believe Charlie and he were, somehow, married. Some demon whisper had tempted him to believe, because of the missing ring, or because Freddy was no Catholic, or because there was a God in Heaven—He'd wanted to believe she could be his.

"Do you remember, Nicolas," Charlie turned in a fresh wash of water, "on the beach, when you asked me what I wanted to know? What I wanted you to say? Do you remember?"

"I remember, Charlie, but—"

"I want to know if you—-"

"Stop, Charlie. No, *niña*," he raised his voice, refusing to

281

give in, refusing to let her humiliate herself. Because he would never confess he loved her and she mustn't be allowed to ask. "Charlie, stop."

She pressed her hands on each side of his face and he hoped she'd only kiss him, but she drew his head down to her breast. Disarmed he couldn't stop her whisper.

"I want to know if you love me."

Her heart beat sounded in his ears. His hands trembled, his arms, his entire body. Another instant and he'd do it. Ruin her. Or humiliate her. Which, Carillo? Which?

"And even if you don't love me, I want you to—"

"Charity."

Nicolas grabbed her wrist and removed it from his hair. He raised his head from her breast, and stood.

He focused his eyes just to the left of her head, past her tiny gold earrings, past that scrawny curve of shoulder.

"If you're going to seduce a man, you ought to know enough to let down your hair. And pose nearer the fire, next time. Don't sprawl in a puddle."

If she'd gasped, or thrown a rock, or sworn her great, loud "damnation," he might have stormed away. He might not have felt like his torso had cracked at the breastbone. But Charlie didn't make a sound.

No honorable path—Cervantes be damned, this hurt worse than being shot—stood clear except the one back to his bedroll. By dawn, she might have recovered the dignity he'd shredded. He wouldn't speak to her until then.

He tried not to listen as she slogged in wet petticoats from the pool to her blanket, but her chattering teeth and audible shivers forced him.

"You should put on something dry," he said.

"You should—" her voice caught on a sob, "keep quiet, Nicolas."

He waited for her to thrash around, to keep him awake with furious huffs or scathing accusation. But Charlie cried.

Never before, not during her expulsion from Harvard, not when a grizzly mauled her, never had Charlie cried. The sobs ripped, as if torn out by long, long roots.

Nicolas lay on his back, forearm blocking the stars. He loved Charlie. He was doing what was best for her. Then why did he want to die from it? Poor little girl.

What would it hurt?

What would it hurt if Nighthawk gave her—if Nighthawk, unscrupulous despoiler, thief of treasures rarer than rubies— what if Nighthawk gave her what she wanted? Was he insane that it suddenly made sense?

Charlie's sobs came muffled from the blanket pressed over her lips.

A gentleman would not let this go on. A gentleman would give the lady what she wanted. And Nicolas Carillo was nothing if not a gentleman.

# Chapter Twenty-One

Had such a hopeless failure of a female ever been born? Had death been merciful in taking her parents before they could see the she-monster they'd spawned?

Charity drew her knees up against her belly and huddled her face against them. If she pulled in tight enough, maybe she'd disappear. She clenched her teeth on the blanket, until her teeth grated, and her sobs raged in silence, only jerking against her chest.

Never again. She'd gone too far to ever win him. Would he kiss her goodbye, even, or be too wary of her animal lunging?

She wasn't so stupid that she hadn't understood the intent of his last remark. He wanted to wake her, set her away from him. Even though the words were awful, he'd clearly hoped to save her from making a worse fool of herself. And she would have.

That faint falling away at her stomach, which she'd felt with Nighthawk and hoarded like a miser, had returned. Before, it had felt like missing a step coming downstairs. Tonight, when Nicolas rubbed his mustache lightly on her shoulder, she'd plummeted off the highest mountain in the world. Falling, but turning, just short of the bottom to surge up. She'd trembled, inside and out, and she'd been so sure he had, too. But, oh God—the humiliation made her want to scream against the cloth in her teeth, that feeling—she'd done it to herself.

She remembered her "wedding night" with Freddy. He'd

touched her, fumbling with her clothes in a generous attempt to make her a real wife. Now she knew how he'd felt when she'd pulled away, laughing that it wasn't working, was it? His face had been red, angry and embarrassed. "It sure as hell was working for me," he'd blurted. And yet she'd forced Nicolas to inflict the same humiliation on her.

Sexual congress in animals consisted of brief sparring, gentle battles meant to inflame, and then the thrusting, the squealing, and they were mated. Why couldn't humans be so straightforward?

Charity O'Dell. The ultimate seductress. She ground her forehead against the hard dirt beneath her blanket, trying to wipe out the images. "I'm not a virgin," she'd boasted, all yearning and trembling while Nicolas remained a shocked observer.

Begging, grabbing—oh! She stuffed the cloth past her lips to stifle the groan, and kept her head tucked, afraid she'd heard him move.

Please, don't try to comfort me. Please just forget. Believe me tomorrow when I blame the brandy for my headache and memory lapse.

No, the sound had probably only been sap popping from a branch. Green wood, he'd said. Green wood, and then she'd grabbed his face and forced him to kiss her. When his mouth widened, trapping hers, she'd felt certain, to her bones, that Nighthawk and Nicolas were one. Her mind had known before, but tonight her body had believed, had rejoiced that Nicolas's mind and Nighthawk's passion fused in one man.

Dismal, dismal failure. They gelded horses. Was there an equivalent punishment for mares who weren't worth breeding? For women?

She sniffed and shivered and her teeth chattered. Spite kept her swathed in pounds of wet underclothes. Her yawn ended the chattering. A shame, really. If she could only die of pneumonia, she'd never have to face Freddy, never feel the disappointment of his caresses and know, really *know*, what a failure he felt, certain his hands would never rouse her. If she could only die of pneumonia, she'd never see Nicolas by sunlight, and cringe before his pity.

She spit the cloth from her mouth, rolled onto her side away from the fire, and prayed to the Virgin for a second grizzly.

Awake completely, she knew the paw on her shoulder, wasn't. It was a hand. Legs, bent at the knee, close enough to brush her eyelashes, were sheathed in leather.

The campfire burned too dim to show his eyes and she saw just dark hollows. But, below the mask, his smile flashed quick and bright.

"Halcon!"

He raised one finger to his lips and nodded behind her, past the campfire. Nicolas's sleeping form humped up the serape he used for a blanket.

"But you're not—"

"Señora," the rough whisper was barely audible.

Halcon slipped his hands beneath the blankets, beneath her arms and drew her to sit, facing him.

"Do not confuse me with that weakling."

She wouldn't argue. She wouldn't use her mind at all. She only wanted to know how, in one deft movement, his hands raised the hem of her soggy chemise to just below her breasts.

No. Her mind shrilled the alarm of all prey. No. That touch is invasion, control, death. But a soothing purr came from his throat. Yes, Charity, and have you never heard a cat, so delighted with her captive that she sings to it?

Halcon's hands rested, still and patient, and she didn't speak. Rib flesh warmed under his touch, and her drive to push him away, faded. Her teeth clacked together as a breeze shivered oak leaves above, chilling through her rumpled chemise.

Halcon inclined his head in question. Her fists closed in resistance as he eased the clinging fabric up. The chemise passed her chin, her nose, then blinded her.

She could see again.

Could, if she had nerve enough to open her eyes. But she did not. She heard flames sort through the twigs for fresh fuel and a horse lipping grass. She smelled steam dancing through the canyon, and the blend of leather and green herbs that meant Nighthawk. She felt night wind tickle wisps of hair around her neck and around breasts never exposed to a stranger's gaze.

His hands were gone. A dream. If she lifted her eyelids, she'd be sitting half-naked and alone, with Nicolas likely staring across the campfire.

But no. Halcon still sat before her. Behind her, asleep, lay Nicolas. If this were a dream, so be it.

Halcon beckoned her to stand and she did. Strange that the cold clung only to her soggy underthings. He held her fingers in his, waiting, letting her feel that the breeze, swirling mist around them, was warm.

His right hand pressed her a step close, tugged twice at the back of her waist. Again he waited and Charity felt a gust of impatience. He'd—what? Untied the drawstring of her petticoat *and* her drawers? if they hadn't been so sodden they stuck like skin, they'd have fallen to her ankles. She'd be naked.

It must be what he wanted.

He touched the small of her back and lowered his mouth over hers. Gentle and slow and searching, it began. The tips of her breasts brushed his leather shirt, and she jerked away.

Hell and damnation, Charity, wake up. You're half-naked, alone, and some savage who may or may not be Nicolas, is *touching you*.

She sighed against his mouth as one of his hands cupped the back of her head and one slid from her waist to her breast. His lips must have been closed, before, because they opened as her nipple shocked to his glancing touch. Heat that slashed from her breast to between her legs made her certain this was no dream. Nothing she'd read, theorized, or guessed had prepared her for that connection.

She wished it were a dream, wished it truly, because if the way that slash had made her arch—involuntarily, like a reflex—against his leather trousers were any indication, she might act shamelessly. And, if the way she sucked in her belly and twisted to accommodate his fingers as they peeled loose her petticoats *and* drawers supplied further evidence, she might not stop him until he had her naked. And worse, far worse, she loved the feeling of wind spiraling across shoulders, past breasts, around waist, swirling at hips and thighs and ankles.

She felt his body cant before his arm scooped under her knees and lifted her off the blanket, and still she hadn't stopped him. When would she?

Sanity rushed back like rain, pattering incessantly, maddeningly.

Halcon, fully covered in leather, carried her across the canyon, past several hot springs. He appeared normal, for a scoundrel; she appeared naked as an egg. Charity stiffened her legs straight and kicked.

"I want down. Now."

Good, Charity, quite persuasive. At least you amuse him,

"Shh," he whispered against her ear.

A scoundrel, certainly, but one possessed of sympathy. She nuzzled her head into the curve of his neck, sighed, and drew a deep breath to speak. The scent of him flooded her. Before she could think, or use thought to stop herself, Charity touched her tongue to the side of his neck.

Halcon stopped as if shot, and just as fear told her to escape, run, flee, he kissed her. Charity's knees jerked tight over the arm cradling her legs. He swayed. Surely he swayed, and then he knelt and lowered her, twisting and protesting when her bruised bottom first felt the water, into a spring.

Darkness like none she'd ever known, closed around her, and though the warm liquid circled drowsily, though she heard Halcon's boots scuff just behind, she felt exposed and abandoned.

A plop sounded beside her and she jerked away before realizing she'd only lost a hairpin.

A hairpin.

"You ought to know enough to take down your hair when you seduce a man."

Is that what she wanted? Her fingertips pecked and searched, grabbed and discarded until her hair collapsed over her shoulders and spread, webbing over the surface of the water.

Seduction. Did she want it? Not in a Boston bed but on a canyon floor in New Spain? Her mind refused to respond, noting his dark form joined her in the pool.

He didn't move closer. Wavelets rushed to her, from his entrance, but, for five minutes, at least, she stood alone on her side of the pool. Faintly, she heard his breathing, then felt the underwater ripples as he stirred.

She felt for a submerged rock, and when she found the perfect concave boulder and seated herself, starlight showed her his smile.

"I know you won't answer," she began, but her mind suggested he might. Hadn't he already mocked Nicolas? "But I must tell you—I'm leaving. I don't know how soon. Tonight—" her voice faltered. "Now, might be the last time I get to see you. Well, I can't see you really, but you know what I mean—"

She felt compelled to chatter, to fill the darkness with sound.

"I'm glad you came, I mean, because—"

His ankle caught hers and yanked, but she gasped and maintained her balance atop the rock. Did he mean to duck her? Caress her leg with his? Silence her? Play?

"It's just that my husband could make me go, anytime. And what you do is so very dangerous." She wondered why she'd never thought of it before. Muskets belching sparks, swooping saber blades, Santana's treachery. "I'm afraid for you. Santana is a bastard, a bastard."

She felt the tears again, trickling down her cheeks, and she swallowed to keep them from her voice.

"And that's why I'm so glad—"

She heard him launch from across the pool, felt the water rush toward her, and then he stood, black against the darkness, stars beyond his lowering head.

He kissed her temple, her cheek, and then, tracing his fingers before his searching lips, found her mouth. He didn't have to pull her to stand. Already her toes gripped a clear space on the pool floor. Already her arms reached for his shoulders.

Her lips met his collar bone, then the hollow of his throat as water lapped her waist. His skin, naked as hers, felt firmer, charged with more warmth. Power and weakness flooded through her.

Could bones melt? Halcon's kiss, as he pulled her flat against him, as his hands pulled her hips forward and she felt him seeking against her belly, melted her very bones.

Their lips opened together, and his tongue touched hers, edged away, and slid along the inside of her cheek. Tension twisted in her belly until she couldn't tell whether to pull him closer or push him away. She did neither, and felt his thumbs roll over the points of her hip bones.

Trees sheltering the pool fluttered in a gust of wind, and she shivered against him. She tried not to, afraid he'd stop. She could bear wind, snow, ice, easier than parting.

Her traitorous teeth chattered.

His hands left her hips, lifted her hair, then dropped it across her breasts. He climbed from the pool, snagging her hand as he passed, but she hung back.

"Don't go. Please, not now."

He laughed, a bewildering chuckle that threatened to stop her heart.

"Please," she whispered, disgusted with her begging, but too weak to be silent, "Please don't go."

Without the water between them, his arms felt harder and his grip closed tighter.

"Not yet, *querida*, not yet."

Words, she thought. She followed him toward the camp-fire, almost at a trot. Everyday she heard words, but from him they were treasures.

He snapped her black cloak against the night. Like a wing it floated and settled on the ground. Without smoothing it, he took them down, one of his arms bent beneath her head.

Eye to eye, she surged toward him, rubbing her cheek

against his mask, measuring her length to the flat shins that met her toes. When he kissed her again, she darted her tongue to touch his. His hand smoothed her throat, flowed down her arm, back up to touch the abraded ring left by her too-tight collar, down the slope of her breast to the curve of her waist and back to cover her breast.

His mouth held hers, but his hands made her restless. Her legs churned, unable to stay still. It was impossible to concentrate on his lips, now gentle, now rough, when his fingertips dusted her belly, skimmed lower, and ignited, again, that slash of heat that made her gasp aloud.

Stop now, stop now, stop now. Her brain forced her to struggle sluggishly.

He let her go and her own hoarse pants assaulted her ears. His breaths silently fanned her neck, but they came fast and he held her hand so hard it hurt.

"Damnation!"

Shivers, ruining everything, racked her shoulders. Stupid, weak female failing, but then he rolled her to her back and covered her.

Oh blessed, blessed shivers, and lovely chilling night banished by his warmth and size and weight. Overwhelming, yes, but right, fitting them together at each rising breath.

She put her chin in the side of his neck and he did the same to her. She stretched her arms wide, and he mirrored the movement, wrists passing her fingertips. She spread her legs wide, pointing her toes in a stretch, but he didn't follow. He shuddered closer. His hips ranged against her and she felt him.

Merciful heavens, she wanted to see! Wanted to touch him, at least, but Halcon shook his head. Ignoring him, she slid both hands down his lean sides, probing under, slowly. But he caught her wrists and trapped them on the ground, above her head.

He kissed her slowly and she responded savagely, pressing back so hard she moved his body. He returned her force and her lips softened while she trailed her instep up his calf, high as his knee.

291

His hips ground into hers in a fierce rhythm she met and matched until her head felt full of blood and she thrashed to get even closer.

"I'll never tell," she vowed, lips brushing his ear. "Never, never, never."

With an uneven breath he slid off, to lay beside her. She rushed to face him, to keep her breasts against him, her eyes on his face. He lifted a long lock of her hair, high as his arm would reach. He let it fall strand by strand, and as he watched, Charity saw his proud hidalgo jaw jut forward, and loved him. She tried to kiss that lean line of bone and flesh, but he forced her slowly to her back.

"I must see you."

He swept aside the flap of cloak slanting across her shoulder. Reverent fingers touched her chest, her ribs, and she closed her eyes, embarrassed by the fire's brightness. She kept her eyes clenched closed when he stroked lower.

Then she knew.

All bewildered curiosity flowed away. Nature left no questions at this juncture. She knew how he would enter her. She knew where. She throbbed with the knowing.

Her legs trembled, but not from cold. She halted his tentative touch, grabbing his hand away. Her knees shuddered together as she moved from her back to her side again. He sucked in a breath, but didn't resist, didn't jerk from her grasp as his tightened muscles threatened.

Can you do this? Can you? Her heart throbbed deafening loud and she searched for his eyes. Oh God, he could take off his accursed mask, couldn't he? Now? She wanted to see him, wanted to meet his eyes when he did this.

Charity raised his hand to her mouth, biting gently as he had, in the high grass above the fiesta, at her bedroom window. He convulsed toward her, and his knee shoved to spread hers.

Flame gleamed off his skin, red-gold and sweating, and the part of him that had nudged and urged, stood out from his body, demanding.

*You're a biologist. You know. You've seen.* But suddenly it seemed so separate, she tensed away.

His hands gentled her trembling thighs in long strokes, down, then up until he brushed her there again, and when she sighed, he talked to her.

"You're sure, *Caridad?*"

She nodded and then tossed her head back as his fingers touched a slickness she couldn't have guessed, couldn't resist.

"Tell me," he insisted.

"I'm sure, but—"

His fingers stilled.

Like the pendulum of a clock, blood and words pounded in her head.

"B-but . . ." she stuttered. "I can't think. It doesn't matter. Don't stop."

She arched her spine, forcing his fingers to touch her again, but he didn't move.

"But I lied about . . ." Charity groaned when his hand covered her, *protectively,* not exploring like it had a moment ago. He moaned in denial and she opened her eyes to see he had raised himself on one elbow.

"I am a virgin, really."

He lay as if turned to rock.

"I shouldn't have lied, but I was afraid you wouldn't want to spoil me."

He rolled away from her. They didn't touch.

"But I want to be. I mean, it won't spoil me." She crawled to stroke the wet hair on his cheek. Ink-black, soft, wet hair, making him look vulnerable "I love this, I do. It's better than anything," her voice reached out as he moved beyond her arms.

"Don't let me ruin it." She held her hands up, "I'm sorry."

He rolled close again, patting the cloak over her skin.

"I'm sorry. Let me take it back, what I said, please."

He shook his head as if it weren't her fault. But it was, oh damnation, it was!

And when he left, when she was alone, staring into the

ashy remains of the campfire, Charity wished the blame would rise up and choke her.

The sun burned an hour above the horizon, and still she slept. Nicolas squatted at the far end of the canyon. He'd been there all night, ignoring tendons that burned from his heels to the back of his knees. The pain was bearable, and he deserved it.

For hours, he'd scratched a twig in the dirt, trying to understand why he hadn't taken her. Charlie had wanted him as Nicolas and Nighthawk. But he'd resisted both virgin and wife.

There was no sense to be made of it. He'd stopped. Incapable—like a gelding, a steer, a eunuch.

Finally he'd stood, determined to go night raiding, catch the ghost of the old highwayman and see if Cordoba could dodge as nimbly as Hamlet. He'd been dressed for hell-raising, and primed, God knew, hot as a dueling pistol. But if he'd been followed—

*Jesu Maria*, she'd made him a coward! No one would have followed. And if someone had, he could have led them away from her. From her. And in that moment, he'd known. That protective jump of his mind proved he wanted Charlie as *his*. Not as part of anyone else. As long as Charlie was Freddy's spurned or reluctant bride, he couldn't possess her. She couldn't be completely his, and only that would do.

Even now, he sat like one of her infernal wolves, guarding his mate in their den.

There! She sat up, and he had a boot in his stirrup before he decided to lead the horse. He'd give her a little time.

She used both hands to push hair back from her eyes.

That mane of hair had surprised him. He'd yearned for her body, guessed well at its mixture of softness and strength, but her hair, always confined, pinned high or woven in braids, had awed him. Last night it had flowed everywhere, wild and lush. He'd wanted to wake with it flowing over his eyes, his throat, his chest.

Black cloak over her shoulders, Charlie knelt before her saddlebags, pawing for something. No sleepy contemplation for Charlie. She glanced down the canyon and her abrupt, angry movements told him she marked his approach. She'd seen him, all right, and searched for something. With luck, it wasn't a knife.

Charlie flung her arm out to stir up the fire. Something rank burned on it. Flame shot erratically from thick roils of smoke as the awful blue riding habit smoldered.

Well. He bumped his hat up with the back of his hand, regarding her crossed arms and combative stance. He had perhaps ten more steps to walk, and though Charlie's attitude was clear enough, he couldn't quite comprehend the message.

"Would you like some breakfast?" he offered her turned back. "I have jerky and—"

"I'm not hungry."

She faced him, tucking a turkey red blouse into the waist of her leather riding skirt. Her brush rasped through tangled hair, snagging time and again, as if she groomed a horse's tail.

"The mission is a short ride, only an hour and a half away. The padre will be glad to have us eat there." He bent to douse the fire.

She matched his steps, breathing hard, hair half braided, half waving loose.

"An hour and a half? A short ride away?"

Swollen and puffy as if they might burst, Charlie's eyelids glowed red. Pale patches sagged underneath blue eyes that seemed oddly green. Her lashes spiked out in stiff clumps and her weary face reproached him.

"Ah, Charlie," his hand touched her shoulder before she whirled away. "I should have told you last night."

"It's a little late for that," her voice cracked.

"That brandy . . ." he mustered a jest, placing his hands on her stiff shoulders, ". . . it's an evil drink, *verdad?*"

She nodded, still facing away from him.

"Charlie, I'm sorry."

Brisk and efficient, she snagged her hackamore from the ground and shrugged.

"At least I got to see this," she gestured at the springs.

By day, the canyon seemed a valley of smoke, the air thick and humid, smoldering gray as the remains of a chaparral fire.

She raised her thumb and middle finger to her lips, whistled, then strode on. Doña Ronda's other black pricked up its ears and trotted a few steps toward Charlie.

"I've never heard you do that," he laughed and hefted her saddle from the ground, hurrying to keep up. "How did you know it would work?"

"He has no idea what I want," she shrugged. "He's just curious."

Charlie glanced back over her shoulder, meaningfully.

*Oh no, my love,* he followed her, shaking his head, *believe it if you must, but you weren't just feeling curious last night, and neither was I.*

# Chapter Twenty-Two

Virtue and honor might feed a man's soul, but Nicolas thanked Dios that Father Juan was not a Jesuit who proved his devotion by setting a paltry table. Lean and brown as a piece of jerky himself, he fed travelers with the generosity of a lonely host.

Father Juan Alvarado hid his past well. A few rancheros suspected the one-armed priest's antiroyalist leanings; Nicolas knew Juan Alvarado had once been murderously so.

The year before Harvard, Nicolas and Father Juan had been left bleeding, in a burning mansion, by Spanish Governor Jesus Serrano. They'd taken their revenge on colonial rulers in different ways.

While Nicolas's mind conceived Nighthawk, Juan assumed leadership of the northern *renegadoes*, leading raids with his reins in his teeth, good arm clenching a rifle.

He'd been in charge the day Reynaldo, Nicolas's brother, fell in an ambush. Finally, Juan made peace with the God who'd let him be maimed, and he'd returned to the church. Though Nicolas trusted the man, he couldn't say he liked him.

Charlie halted her horse and shaded her eyes.

"Are those mustangs, do you think? Or a tame herd?"

Nicolas squinted at the horizon, then frowned at Charlie. "They could be cattle, from this distance!"

She shrugged, and he mused that for a girl who wore spectacles, Charlie saw wondrous well. This morning, she'd sighted him down the length of the canyon. Now, this.

"Charlie, why do you wear spectacles? Obviously you have no need of them."

"I need them!" Charlie moved to push them up, found her face bare, then unbuckled her saddlebags to probe for the wire frames.

"But not for seeing."

"No," she admitted. "Not for seeing, for my research. Be truthful, Nicolas. I look smarter in spectacles, don't I?"

"Charlie, people don't *look* smart or slow—"

"Do I look prettier without them? Quick! And none of your hidalgo flattery. Do I look prettier without spectacles?"

*Carumba!* He felt a gush of happiness that her cheeks were flushed instead of pale.

"If I must, I'd say, yes. Without your spectacles, I can see your eyes." He stopped, a dozen sentences tumbling in his head. As a young caballero he'd swooned over a hundred girls' eyes, comparing them to limpid pools, warm brandy, and cold sapphires, but he couldn't tell Charlie how he loved her eyes—how they offered up every thought crossing her mind, how they told him that while women like Esperanza were fire and ice, Charity O'Dell was always fire. She only burned hot, or hotter.

Before she could pursue her thesis, Nicolas pulled up Cordoba and motioned Charlie to follow his charge up a gently rising hill. As they rode, she accused him of dodging a challenge. She gasped for breath when they stopped, and he swung his arm in presentation.

Orange-gold poppies ran meandering streams through the grass, swooping in an S-shape, then clustering in a pond before spreading among spindly mustard and purple stands of lupin.

Beckoned by nodding heads, flickering from hot orange to shining silver, Charity slipped from her saddle, into the widest pond of poppies. Her skirts made a canopy over them, and one arm curved behind with her hackamore rein.

Nicolas memorized her, this Charlie, graceful as a dancer,

who had nothing in common with the girl who tripped and stammered at fiestas. Here, squatting to examine the poppies' fernlike leaves, Charlie's gawkiness disappeared.

"Don't pick them for me, Nicolas, ever. They wouldn't be the same out of this meadow," Charlie straightened her knees and twirled, flinging her free arm toward the mountains.

She had resilience. Last night he'd drained her pride, but now she whirled in childish abandon.

He had no armor against her. No, Charlie, he thought, I won't pick poppies to die in a goblet at your bedside, anymore than I can pluck out my love and offer it as tame marriage. Away from this sun-flooded meadow, poppies fade and die. Away from silver-splashed midnights of leather and steel, Nighthawk would die. California wouldn't have me, and you wouldn't want me.

"I won't then," he promised. "Not a single one."

The sun behind his head made her squint as she looked up at him.

"We're almost there," he said, and wheeled his horse away.


*"Amar a Dios,* welcome," the priest, in gray sackcloth and a wealth of beaded necklaces, transferred a long notched stick, from his mouth to his hand in order to greet them.

The yard was crowded with horses, and they'd passed masses of the animals just outside the mission gates.

Nicolas dismounted to speak. Charity acknowledged her introduction to Father Juan Alvarado, but continued watching Nicolas. She saw more than the boot fringe dancing along his tight rider's calves, more than the broad shoulders which might bear the marks of her fingernails. She saw, in the angle of his head, his respect for both priest and church. Nicolas Carillo was a good Catholic, an honorable man. Why must she interfere with him?

"—it's up to Señora Larkin."

Both men looked up at her and Charity felt a hot blush.

"I apologize," she began. "I admit I was watching the horses, Father. You must have hundreds."

"Four *manadas*, with twenty mares in each," he explained, and for a moment Charity saw a strange attentiveness in his eyes.

Standing against a background of cactus tortured into a fence, the priest looked—too confident.

"—for a meal, or stay and watch the threshing?"

"I'd enjoy watching," Charity saw her answer made sense to them. "And, perhaps later, you will hear my confession."

"Of course."

The priest's cowl slumped forward as he nodded. Over his tonsured head she glimpsed Nicolas' alarmed face.

Charity glanced over her shoulder to see a young Indian, arms laden with brick-laden forms. He wore the typical neophyte garb of muslin. Only a thin knotted leather string, tied around his neck, marked him as different. Had he provoked Nicolas's distress? And if not, was he afraid of what she might include in her confession?

The mares, Alvarado explained, were herded into the *hera*, a fenced area covered with grain, and forced to run in circles.

*"Yegua! Yegua! Yegua!"*

Mare, mare, mare! The Indian vaqueros swung reatas, cracked whips and yipped as they forced the four bands to stampede.

Doña Ronda's blacks laid back their ears and bucked.

"Charlie—" Nicolas grabbed the reins beneath her mount's chin and jerked. "Get off."

His words were abrupt, but she obeyed.

The mares swept past, heads extended, eyes red-rimmed, mouths agape, scattering chaff from the grain beneath their hooves.

Father Alvarado shouted and the vaqueros whirred loud birdlike trills to set the mares running in the opposite direction.

*"Yegua! Yegua! Yegua!"*

Go this way. Go that way.

You're a bad girl. You must go home—from Harvard. You're a bad wife. You must go home—to Boston.

Charity squinted toward the high-humped roof of the white

300

cathedral. The bell squatted in its tower, catching the sun's flare to make her squint.

Speed and confusion caused mares to crash the fence each time they circled. Charity stood on the third rail and looked down on the plunging backs, brown and gray and golden.

"Charlie, get down!"

When a huge mare slammed the rails beneath her, tossing clots of white foam from her open mouth, Charity complied.

The priest shouted again, then crossed toward her. Nicolas disappeared and she felt a dull satisfaction that he'd gone.

Wind blew a gritty lash of chaff into her eyes. If only she had her glasses! Charity scrubbed her fists into her eyes. She blinked and tears squeezed from between her lids.

"I hope you're all right, Señora," the priest said. "You see why we thresh on windy days. This way the mares do the work for us, even separating the grain from the chaff."

Another horse slammed into the fence nearby.

"They're getting dizzy," Charity blinked and looked down.

The priest wore thick leather sandals. A wooden cross, engraved with the crucified Christ, swung at the end of the bead and chain rosary looped through the cording at his waist.

"Si, that's why we keep changing directions."

"Why," she looked up, sniffing as if she'd wept. "Why do all of them have their manes and tails chopped short?"

"For horsehair, Señora. My vaqueros braid beautiful reatas and hackamores," he pointed out the headstall of a passing saddle horse. "The mares are willing to make the sacrifice."

Charity crossed her arms in protest, but kept silent. It didn't hurt the mares. Besides, the day was hot and still, and perspiration seeped into her eyes.

Charity flipped her hat off, letting it hang down her back. She ruffled her fingers through her too-tight hair and regarded the sky. Morning's blue had faded to an eerie yellow-gray. She wished it were black, pricked with stars, and she were asleep.

Charity yawned. The flat bronze circle of sun wasn't even at its zenith. For hours, she must stay awake, apprise the padre of Santana's evil plan, and suffer girlish love pangs. Her head ached from the glare of the gargantuan bell.

Siding with mares against the Catholic church was beyond her strength, just now. Then she saw the stallions, locked in individual corrals.

"Padre, the stallions still have their long manes and tails. How can that be?"

"Ah, señora," the priest seemed to joke, "There is but one stallion for each *manada* and the vaqueros tell me that mares hate the stallion if he is not beautiful!"

Charity stifled her groan and Alvarado, laughing, gave the sign to turn the mares, yet again. As he raised his arm she noticed, that his other sleeve fluttered loose and empty.

"*Uno momento, Señora.* I will put my *mayordomo* in charge and escort you to dinner."

Waiting, she spotted Nicolas. Far past the corrals, Nicolas talked with a group of Indian vaqueros. Legs wide apart, but loose, hands resting on the sides of his thighs, he and the others regarded the ground. Occasionally one man would scuff his boot in the dirt and glance up at the others, then return his gaze to the earth. Nicolas did the same.

Although his deep-bred dominance infuriated her, she admired the way his head came up in a brief bark of laughter at an Indian's joke.

*I love you, Nicolas/Nighthawk.* She sent the thoughts at him, aimed like an eagle-fletched arrow, but he turned away to watch an Indian mount a rangy brown horse.

"Ready, Señora?"

The priest shortened his stride to accommodate her, as he described the mission's inhabitants.

"We have, in all, nearly one thousand souls, half of those pledged to Christ, but—" he looked up to gauge her reaction as they passed the huts lining the paths toward the church, "the Indians lose position in their tribes when they are baptized, so many stay—unofficially.

"They cook, they clean, make bricks and tile, butter and soap. They fashion harnesses and furniture, farm, tend the Church's herds. The little ones gather eggs and carry messages. All for the glory of God!" Father Alvarado took a breath. "Although the alcalde says they stay for the food."

"Santana." Charity said, and she saw the first link forged between them. Alvarado didn't claim to be a willing servant of the Mexican government, and she didn't hide her pleasure at it.

But now, they passed a small adobe structure that showed a Mexican flag, and a laundry line that held a uniform.

"And the alcalde, doesn't he, too, use the mission for food—for his troops?" Charity asked.

The priest nodded. "Of course, but from the alcalde, we receive sheets of paper redeemable in gold in Mexico City."

"It's a long ride to Mexico City," she blurted.

The twitch of humor on his lips made her feel a favorite teacher winked at her astuteness.

Alvarado greeted a teenage girl, her cheeks painted red. "Sarita is in love," Alvarado explained, "So her aunts paint her cheeks with red ocher. It's not allowed by the church," his sidelong glance dared a comment. "But I see no harm in it."

Before Charity inquired further, the priest looked pointedly at her bare left hand.

"Señora, you rode out with Don Nicolas. Without your husband. Unchaperoned?" His voice implied that rules which might be ignored for Indians did not bend for her.

A wave of unsteadiness swept Charity. No doubt a combination of heat and embarrassment, but perhaps she could avoid an answer by pretending to swoon.

"Doña Ronda, my chaperon, lives nearby—" Charity blinked and covered her stomach with her hands. She needn't feign infirmity. "Forgive me, Father. I feel suddenly rather sick."

Alvarado hardly noticed. His eyes scanned from one side of his mission to the other. Dogs yelped and howled. Chickens squawked. Crows, preening on rooftops minutes before, circled and cawed.

The wind—?

The Indian on the rangy brown horse rode past, but his

303

mount capered sideways and he fought to point it toward the gates.

"Something—" Father Alvarado began.

Charity put her foot down and the ground was gone. She could see it, but, like a boat swooping off a wave crest, it dipped away from her shoe. A faint rush of sound, also like the sea, pressed against her ears.

"Earthquake!"

The priest snatched her arm, rushing her past a black kettle swinging over a cook fire. Stew slopped over its lip, hissing on hot rocks below, then flaring as fire caught the fat and consumed it.

Earthquake. But one could always trust, if nothing else, the earth beneath her feet. Couldn't she? A hundred human voices, low, high, screaming, calming, joined the cacophony of animals.

And then it stopped.

The earth's shifting stilled. The animals grew quiet and only the mission bell clanked dully in its tower. Charity swallowed and listened to the incessant braying of a donkey. A bunch of young boys, dressed in tunics that barely reached their knees, jeered and strutted before the huts, brandishing sticks and boasting how *macho* they were, how unafraid.

"Well, we certainly have nothing like that in Boston," Charity heard the trembling in her voice and looked past the priest, searching the milling Indians for Nicolas.

*"Cuidado,"* a Mexican woman, gray threading her black hair, shooed children out into the open. She knelt next to the priest, near enough Charity could smell garlic on her hands as she shook her index finger back and forth, cautioning, *"Cuidado."*

Be careful.

Of what? Charity stood and stamped dirt from her boots. Why did so many people still pour from their huts, crouching and regarding the sky?"

She slapped dust from her leather skirt. And why in creation did that damned burro continue braying, fit to split his lungs?

The rush that had sighed like far-off waves built again. It roared like pelting rain, like lions gone mad in a storm, and the earth snapped out from under her feet.

Her chin smacked rock and grit and her hands clawed into the earth as if she could hang on. This time the screams were joined by something worse, a long-drawn moan—of people, wind? She couldn't tell.

The mares neighed unceasingly, then there was a crack as the fence broke and eighty terrified horses swirled about them, running, stumbling, shying from dogs and children and the thatched roofs tilting and tumbling from the huts.

*Please God, please God! Oh Mary, Mother of God, let Nicolas be all right. Protect him.*

Charity heard her prayer drowned by wailing voices, saw Father Alvarado rise, his fingers telling beads before he clutched the shirt of a child who'd fallen near that swaying black kettle.

Cracking like thunder, the plastered front of the bell tower sheered loose. It slid straight down like a guillotine, baring the church interior before vanishing in swirling dust.

*Think, Charity. Had anyone been standing in front of the church? Picture it in your mind. If anyone had been under it—*

"Nicolas!"

Her shriek rang among too many. All around her sounded the cries of children begging, "Mama! Mama!"

Charity tried to rise. If she could hold one babe until its mother was found—but the earth's jerking pants had turned to rolling, and still she couldn't stand.

"Mamaaaaa!"

She pressed her hands against her ears and fought the strangling panic that made her want to join the cry.

The ground beneath her quieted, and she moved her hands, only to hear another hellish shout.

*"Fuego!"* the voice yelled, and her reeling brain wouldn't translate until she followed a pointing finger. Fire.

She saw him then, for a minute. Nicolas bent low. He shouted, motioning men toward the mission's central well.

The dust before the chapel hadn't settled when another

splintering crack drew all eyes back. Charity looked in time to see the bronze bell arc free of its tower, pitch through the air and hit, then tumble end-over-end, clanging madly until it smashed the well wall.

He'd been standing right there. Nicolas had been at the well. No. He emerged on the other side of the bell, holding his shoulder, shouting. Then he was surrounded by tunicked Indians, hair flying as they swarmed after buckets. He bent once, seeming to fold in on himself and Charity tensed. If he were hurt—

But he couldn't be. He joined two Indians pushing against the bell's side, striving to release a trapped reed basket. Why? She heard a baby's whimper. Reed *baby carrier*, not basket. Oh God, someone's infant had been struck by the awful missile.

Tenderly, painstakingly, with a rebozoed woman hanging on his arm, Nicolas extracted the brown doll-like creature from its basket. Charity stood rooted, waiting. A shout, and then Nighthawk's white smile split Nicolas' dirt-streaked face.

"She's all right, Señora! For the love of God, she's all right!"

A brigade of men with buckets separated them. And then the mad, circling mares wheeled through the square, and she saw the blowing manes of stallions who nipped and herded them.

"Señora Larkin, you must help me if you can," Father Alvarado gripped her shoulder.

"Of course I can. I—"

"Stop bleeding first, wherever you see it. I will seek those who might be buried in the wreckage. Señora?"

Charity reviled herself. Perhaps if she quit nodding like an imbecile he'd stop addressing her as one.

"Yes," she answered, pulling away. Lord, the grip of his good hand was strong enough for two.

By dusk, Charity judged she'd ripped a hundred white tunics into bandages. She'd ordered dozens of men, whose language she couldn't speak, to scavenge blankets and help her fashion an outdoor hospital with beds on the ground.

"Truly," she told Father Alvarado when he reappeared at

her side. "There were not so many cuts—mainly those who were in the huts when the roofs collapsed and those from the church," she shuddered, as she had all day, at the sight of the faceless sanctuary. It frightened her more, than even the careful line of bodies, arranged inside it. "They were cut by brick—"

"*Gracias a Dios!* In His wisdom He never granted my requests for window glass," Father Alvarado moaned for the first time. "When I think—"

"Oh, the burns, Father," she stooped to a stack of green plants. Here, she'd had children pile spears of aloe vera, like lengths of fire wood. "Burns, everywhere." She used a machete—where had it come from, this wicked, heavy weapon?—to hack through to the gelatinous interior of the plant.

"Don Nicolas and the others have been putting out fires all day," the priest protested.

"I know," Charity let her hands rest on her hips as she scanned the rows of injured. Which one had she been going to?

"But, many were burned by cooking fires, and the blacksmith and his helper, they were—terrible. The cook, from your *cocina,* her tortilla griddle flipped, she said. I think that's what she said." Charity rubbed her eyes, jabbing her face with the aloe's spines before she remembered she held it. "I never did get my breakfast, you know, Padre."

"Food?" the man looked horrified for a moment. "Oh yes, it was the last thing on my mind. Food—"

"I was joking, Father." She patted Alvarado's cheek. "Some ladies, mothers, asked if they could cook again. They'd nursed their babes, but the older children were crying from hunger. So I said, 'yes.' They promised to bring soup for the injured. And for me, I think."

Charity held the aloe spear before her face, as if it could remind her who she'd been going to tend when the priest appeared?

"Padre!" A man about her age rushed up. "The horses,

they're back, and they're eating all the grain we threshed this morning. We'll have nothing for the winter if they eat it all."

Father Alvarado clutched up one side of his habit and ran to follow.

Nicolas reeled away from the man who'd collided with his injured shoulder.

*"Cuidado, cabron!"* Nicolas snarled. Stabbing pain bent him almost double. His hand shielded the ripped cloth where his shirt's shoulder seam and a good portion of his flesh had separated under the bell's glancing blow.

He looked up at the man he'd cursed and found himself glaring at Alvarado.

"Padre, I'm sorry," he began. Add swearing at a priest to his misdeeds. Christ! But the Jesuit was past him, showing no hint of recognition.

*So, if you are not caught, Carillo, there's no crime?*

*I'll never tell, never, never.* His breath caught, not with pain, but with the memory of Charlie, black hair lashing side to side. Hell-bound already, he might as well be condemned for lust as well as blasphemy.

Nicolas rolled his shoulder against the pain. If only it had been the other side. The bell's blow reminded him he'd barely recovered flexibility from the grizzly attack. A man who prided himself on wielding swords with either hand couldn't afford such accidents.

He took two steps before he realized. Ah, there are limits to your he-goat lust, eh Halcon? Images of Charlie and the grizzly attack caused only the faintest rising! And it took only the mother of all earthquakes and near amputation of your arm!

At least Charlie was safe. Three times he'd passed her makeshift hospital. The first time her face had been bloody, and if she hadn't been so intent on bandaging an old man's fire-blistered feet, he would have dropped the slopping bucket and gone to her.

The next time he'd passed, the blood had dried in

scratches along her nose and cheeks and she'd been shouting orders in a garble of Spanish and English. Her hands moved fast as her tongue, and twenty Indians hurried to help her move debris and spread blankets.

An hour ago, she'd been kneeling in the dirt, splinting the leg of a yellow pup. Having abandoned Spanish altogether, she used classroom English to teach a wide-eyed Indian girl, how the bone would knit back together.

*"Café, Señor?"* A woman, serape draped over her head in spite of the airless summer night, offered him a pottery cup.

*"Gracias."* Nicolas drained the liquid in three gulps. Hot off the fire, it scorched his tongue.

"Pardon," he addressed her, "but might I have a cup for the señora?" He tilted his head toward the makeshift hospital.

"Oh, si," the woman answered. *"La señora es una angela."*

An angel. Charlie. He stifled a snort of laughter and explained, as the woman poured, that he wanted to pull Charlie away from her toil and find her something to eat.

Eating. There, God. That's one thing we can do together, *verdad?* Nicolas shook his head. Praying was pious. A healthy admission of one's limitations. But holding conversations with the deity? Some might think he needed more help than could be rendered by a plate of beans.

Charlie stood alone, the only upright form in a sea of blanket-swathed bodies. Skirts smeared with blood and dirt, turkey-red sleeves rolled above her elbows, she stood with legs apart. Someone had tied a grape-colored scrap of cloth low on her brow, like an Indian headband. In one hand she held a plant, in the other a machete.

No one had ever told Charity O'Dell she didn't know how to run a hospital, so she'd capably stormed ahead and done it.

"Dulcinea," Charity muttered as he drew near. "I was going to change her dressings."

On such a day, perhaps even level-headed Boston girls were allowed to talk to themselves.

"Dulcinea?" he asked.

"The weaver," Charity muttered, not looking at him. "Her frame fell on her head—oh Nicolas!"

She pounced and Nicolas caught her under his arm, hardly spilling the coffee. Naturally, Charity chose his bad side to cling to, but she stuck there like honey, sweet and melting. He'd let the shoulder putrefy before he asked her to move.

Nicolas lowered his chin to her head, breathing the scents of smoke, and dust, but underneath, a hint of hot springs, and a girl whose hair spread black in the moonlight.

"Is that coffee? Is it for me?" Charlie sprang away and drank the liquid as quickly as he had. "I'm so hungry. But someone's bringing something. What I could really use—"

Charlie paused for breath.

"Don't raise your eyebrow at me, Nicolas Carillo. The situation is much too serious for that. Besides, I thought—" She looked down at her boots. "Besides," her hands went to her hips and her chin jerked high. "You had your chance last night."

She jammed the machete dangerously quick through her belt, and marched toward her patients.

"Señora," he mocked, following in her dusty wake. "I have no idea what you mean. The earthquake. Perhaps, it rattled your brain, *no?*"

"No doubt," she muttered, not turning.

*Cristo,* he felt hot. Hotter than she usually made him. Feverish, almost, and ashamed for joking in the midst of misery.

In the crook of her elbow, Charlie cradled a woman's head, trying to give her water.

"I could use that brandy of yours, is what I meant," she glanced at him as the woman coughed.

"If I could find Cordoba, it's in his saddlebags. But, I fear he's halfway home by now. With what you left of it." He laughed.

"I don't understand what's amusing, Nicolas. I have no medicine for these people." Her voice cracked with irritation. "Nothing for pain. And only aloe vera for the wounds. I don't know what else to use."

"Father Alvarado must have medicines."

Charity ripped a piece of cloth, dipped it in water and moistened the woman's lips.

"He has been too busy, and last time he was here, I forgot."

"You're tired and hungry, *querida*."

God, had he called her that? Beloved? He must have, because Charity swayed toward him, eyes soft in spite of the nest of blood-brown bandages curled stiff around her. An angel.

"Don Nicolas, Señora, come quick!" a boy tugged at his shirt. "The hide shed! Some men were working there when the earthquake came. They are buried, but the Padre, he thinks they're alive."

Nicolas found it hard to believe anyone buried under a ton of ox hides could survive. But two of the six men still lived.

Harder to believe, was Charlie, ramming her shoulder against the stacked hides, grunting like a work horse, as an Indian pulled at the lifeless hands, below. Strings of muscle and blue veins reared from her neck and sweat darkened the headband before dripping off her jaw. She strained so, until all six were dragged free.

"Outside," she ordered. "I can't stand the smell in here."

She squatted next to the first man, found his arm stiff with death, and scooted to the next. Her thumb peeled up his eyelid before she made a tsking sound and pressed her fingers at his throat. She closed her eyes, concentrating. She waited, shook her head and moved to the next man, motioning Father Alvarado to offer the last rites.

Charlie and Nicolas sat alone, with the two men who breathed, when he gathered the nerve to speak.

"Charlie, doesn't this bother you?"

She stared as if he'd slapped her.

"No," she snapped. The centers of her eyes expanded so wide her eyes seemed black. "I'm a biologist, remember? I know a little of how the human body works. And stops working."

He thought her sarcasm must burn her tongue, but Charlie

only leaned her cheek low over her patient's lips, seeking the brush of his breath.

"Besides, I've used up all my tears for this week, *verdad?*" She didn't even glance up. God, he felt awful.

Nicolas pitched to his knees, a black shrilling fog encircling his head. Hot, he felt so hot.

"Nicolas!"

There was nothing cool and scientific about her now, except her hands, rolling him to his back, fluttering about his eyes, his neck, his shoulder.

*"Ay, Cristo!* Charlie, don't touch it!"

Ripping. She ripped his shirt with that tree-sized machete.

". . . fever. Hell and damnation, Nicolas! You and your damned nobility! What good are you dead? Father Alvarado!" she shouted before gripping his jaw. "Open your eyes, Nicolas Carillo. Dear God, I should slap you.

"What was it? The bell? The accursed bell? I thought it missed—Nicolas! Oh, damn you."

But still, her hands felt cool.

"Señora Larkin, you must let us take him inside my quarters."

"No." Charity shrugged off the priest's hand and continued passing the cloth over Nicolas's forehead.

"The danger of earthquake is past."

"How do you know?"

"Well, usually—"

"Father, I know how to treat a fever. If a roof should collapse on him, I don't think I could help."

Charity closed her eyes in prayer, squeezing the cloth until she felt water trickle over her fingers. When she opened her eyes, Alvarado had gone, and she recommenced her rounds. Water for each patient. A change of bandages for some. For three men, a fingertip taste of the Padre's miraculous powder. One of the three was Nicolas.

Dozens of Indians helped, and Father Alvarado felt sure

Los Cielos would send aid when they learned of the mission's plight. Plenty of help, but nothing seemed enough for Nicolas.

Once, near dawn, he'd spoken. Hot with fever, he mumbled, and she tried to understand, fearing he hurt inside. But she'd understood nothing, until a moment ago.

His mouth worked and she leaned close, ear almost touching his lips.

"Halcon is an ass."

No problem unraveling that.

Cocked up on one elbow, head bandaged, a white-haired man seemed the only one who hadn't heard.

"*Que?*" he queried.

"He's delirious," Charity explained. "Out of his head. *Loco.*" She made a circular motion near his temple.

The old man settled back to his blankets, whereupon his nearest neighbor, an adolescent girl whose foot was swollen three times its normal size, explained what Don Nicolas had truly said.

"That girl is well enough to go back to work," Charity muttered, sponging Nicolas's brow and cheeks. "Just the same, me lad," she whispered to him. "You'd better keep your voice down."

An hour later, Nicolas opened his eyes.

"Nicolas," she touched his forehead. Hotter, but he looked lucid.

"Kiss me, *querida*. Kiss me."

Charity looked about her. Most of the injured dozed after midday bowls of broth. She knelt next to Nicolas and pecked him on the cheek. His eyelashes fell closed. Bloody stupid bell.

His mumbling ebbed, then returned at renewed volume. Most was still unintelligible, but she heard names: Santana, Don Emelio, Esperanza, Arturo, Charlie and Halcon.

"Whistle up Hamlet. In the herd, hombre," he thrashed, wiping his lips with the back of his hand. "We'll give Santana a taste of cold Toledo steel. Halcon will make him dance!"

The words were damning. And almost as clear as before. What else could she do for fever? One of the women had suggested sweating, but he seemed wetter each time she touched him. She needed to undress him and bathe his entire body with cold water.

Father Alvarado returned, sat next to the girl with the swollen foot and talked with her. In a moment his voice rose, as if he wanted Charity to overhear.

"Si, Maria. I'm sure it was only a dream," the priest glanced sharply her way. "People with fever sometimes have the oddest imaginings. Go to sleep now. Rest."

He moved toward Charity.

*"Now* will you move him?" the priest demanded.

"I had just decided it might be a good idea," Charity agreed. She stood, and for a moment the dirt squirmed beneath her. She looked wildly back toward the church.

"You only stumbled, Señora," Alvarado's voice softened.

"Will you please call me Charity?" She masked her fear with irritation.

"Of course. I think you, Charity, should also get some rest. Inside. Don't be guilty of pride, now. I see them, all your patients, but they can be nursed by others. Those who can't—are beyond earthly help."

"How many?"

"Eleven," Father Alvarado sighed, gray around his mouth.

"I would have guessed fifty. Or a hundred," she closed her eyes, then opened them when she swayed once more. "I'd never seen a dead person before today."

"Yesterday, Charity. The earthquake struck yesterday morning."

She watched his lips. He spoke slowly, as if to a child.

"And last night Nicolas became feverish. And now it is almost six o'clock, in the evening. You have done the work of a doctor, of three doctors, and you must go inside, with Nicolas. I will send Santiago, my most trusted neophyte, with you. He will bathe Don Nicolas while you eat."

Before entering the kitchen she passed a room of blackened brick. Three metal hooks held huge carcasses. She stared dumbly, horrified and immoveable until Santiago whispered.

"Meat, Señora. Here we smoke meat, sometimes."

314

Charity devoured tortillas and shredded goat. She dozed with her forehead in her hand, between the time the cook took her plate and brought a cup of chocolate. She wakened with a jolt that cramped her neck.

Father Alvarado hadn't ordered her to bed. He hadn't questioned her concern for Nicolas. Concern? You should be so controlled, Charity. Frantic worry, perhaps? Or panic?

Santiago nodded her into the room. Clean, with spartan furnishings, it must be one of the rooms in that long row of arched doorways. Nicolas had explained that since California had no true hotels, the missions, placed a day's ride from each other, offered hospitality to travelers. Clean and comfortable, this room, but empty.

"Nicolas? Where is he?"

Panic roared in her ears as loudly as the earthquake. Dead? His body removed?

Santiago gestured at the closed door across the hall.

"But there, Señora. And see, I've left you things for washing. And a dress."

*"Gracias."* Charity smiled politely. She waited for the young man to depart, then she sat down on the bed and wept.

Tears didn't bring the great wrenching sobs she'd suffered before. They ran in endless sheets down her cheeks. For pity's sake, Charity Ann, Aunt P. would say. For pity's sake.

But Aunt P. would never see stiff brown arms thrust through smashed roof tiles, never see a vaquero's disbelief at a roping hand crushed flat as soggy bread. She'd never see Nicolas's elation, holding high that baby girl.

For pity's sake.

She sniffed and looked at her own hands, almost muddy from grime and tears. And she'd eaten with them. Ugh. And tended the sick. She made quick use of the pitcher and water, braided her hair, and slipped on a much-washed pink calico gown. Sleeveless and made for a larger woman, judging from arm holes gaping open over her rib cage, it felt lovely, soft and clean.

It would be good to sleep in. And when she sat in the chair

at Nicolas' bedside and saw how peacefully he drowsed, she knew she'd sleep, too. After one last look at his wound.

Santiago, bless him, had washed Nicolas and left him on his belly. Turning Nicolas's limp weight alone, without hurting him, would have been beyond her. Too, it gave her a chance to study the strange swelling on his back. The cut across the top of his shoulder, where the bell had slashed clear to the bone had festered by daybreak. After cleaning it, she'd asked a Mexican women to sew it closed.

"You do it, Señora," the woman had demurred.

"If you had seen my needlework, you wouldn't suggest such a thing," Charity had assured her.

Tiny stitches, drawn tight, tracked a black row across his shoulder, but a fresh scar, still pink and shiny, slanted over his back. Charity frowned and traced her index finger over the heated swelling between the two injuries. Self-taught biology had limits, she decided; she could only offer Nicolas her best.

Her best did not include poring over his form like the basest voyeur. Charity snatched the binding of the white sheet, intending to cover him. Nicolas would hate anyone to see him so defenseless. With his mustached face buried in the mattress and his damp black hair braided into a fresh queue, the sides of his neck curved smooth and bare as a child's.

He'd wake if she kissed him on the muscle ridges sloping from his neck to his shoulder. Fencing, riding, and roping had forged those muscles that had lifted her into his arms. She deliberately drew the sheet to his nape, arranging his queue atop it. Wakefulness, not kisses, was the best medicine she could offer Nicolas, and her drooping eyelids signalled even that simple remedy might be out of reach.

Charity's head snapped up from a doze when Nicolas moaned.

"Shh," she whispered, stroking his uninjured side. "I'm here. Shh," and it seemed, as her eyes closed again, that he slept more soundly.

* * *

"Charlie. I'm so cold."

The words struck as if she'd never drowsed. Nicolas lay on his back, and one of his hands gripped her wrist.

"Nicolas, you're awake."

"I'm so cold," his teeth chattered, his eyes had no sheen, and he looked embarrassed.

"I'll get more blankets."

Feverish thrashing had displaced his covers, so she pulled up the sheet and rough gray blanket in a single tug, then pawed through the pine chest at the foot of the bed. Nothing.

"I'll be right back." She crossed to her room, stripped the blanket from that bed and hurried to tuck it around him. His eyes followed her and she swallowed at the burden of such trust.

But if he were cold from fever, would the blankets do more damage? Damnation, how was she to know?

"Santiago?" Her call echoed in the still hallway.

By Saint Mary, this was not fair. She, alone, should not be expected to play the role of doctor, nurse, and chemist. Who, in the name of all that was holy, had elected her to be in charge of a critically injured Nicolas?

Charity's mind conjured an image of her cocky self, hunched over Nicolas, one hand tipping water to his lips, the other tossing off Father Alvarado's advice.

"Fools rush in where angels fear to tread," Mr. Pope had written, and Nicolas had by God, characterized her well, when he'd labeled her foolhardy.

Nicolas's teeth chattered into her instant of hesitation.

Damnation! She threw wide every door on the corridor, stripped the blankets from each bed. Charity yanked a wall hanging, a poorly executed and suffering saint, and added it to the blankets. Now, pillaging holy works to cover her beloved, after she'd cursed him in the mission courtyard, she thought it possible love wasn't always gentle and sweet.

She staggered under the load of blankets and weavings, then layered them on Nicolas until they were a foot deep.

*"Querida."*

Candle flame, stretching and shrinking from her frantic

317

movements, showed her Nicolas's eyelids fluttered, but remained closed.

Charity held her cheek against his. Hot, still too, hot. His black hair stuck to his forehead and though his skin was pale, his cheeks blazed dry, rough red. Black and white and red, and too beautiful to suffer like this. Beautiful. The devil Halcon, wicked swordsman and rider of the wind, and so beautiful. Charity swallowed hard and kissed his temple.

"I love you," she whispered against his skin.

His eyes opened, dazed with fever. His lips moved and his tongue licked out.

Ninny. Incompetent child, to let his lips dry and crack while she slept! Charity gathered the basin and looked for the cloth. Gone. Had she dropped it under the damned bed? What an idiot she'd become. Not under the bed, but she bumped her head on it—hard enough to rock a gasp from him.

She paddled her fingers in the water and stroked them over his lips. His tongue flashed out for the moisture and she did it again. Hypnotized with the repeated movement, she felt her shoulders sag, and closed her eyes, for just a minute, with one wet index finger still on his lips. He sucked it into his mouth.

"Nicolas!"

Half shocked, half laughing, she stared as he suckled the finger like a lamb.

"Nicolas! Are you sick? Or playing?"

His smile curved around her finger, but he kept sucking. His tongue circled her finger and her body's reaction made her jerk her finger away, with a pop.

"I think I'm sick," he croaked, but the smile lingered.

It disappeared when the shivering shook him. Irritation and worry battled for her weary mind. Would this go on all night? Weren't there limits to punishments for foolhardiness? Weren't fevers supposed to break at midnight? At dawn? Old wives' tales, probably. What wouldn't she give for a knowledgeable old wife?

Charity wet her palm and lay it on his brow. A choking in his throat sounded, to her, like a plea for his mother.

Oh God, oh God. Two men, crushed 'til they looked like rag dolls, had called for their mothers before they died.

"Nicolas!" she thought his eyelids revealed a slice of brown before clamping shut with shivering. "Nicolas, it's Charlie."

"Q-q-querida," he smiled, though hammering teeth.

"Nicolas?"

He lay motionless at her sweet question, so she snapped.

"Nicolas! I'm weary of nursing you day and night. Tell me what I can do to help you."

He'd lost consciousness again. Only his body jerked in response, then he whispered.

"I . . . kept you warm."

He kept her warm.

Charity turned the words in her mind. Was this more delirium, like his talk of Hamlet? He kept her—

Las Calderonas.

"You want me to get in with you?" Charity fought the logic of it. When she'd shivered at the hot springs, his body had covered her, warming her from wrists to ankles. "In the bed with you, Nicolas?"

He couldn't be pretending. His skin burned fiery red, in spite of that devil's smile.

"I'm not taking my clothes off," she whispered, closing the door and placing her chair in front of it. "And there's no sense moaning, either. I might fall asleep, and if someone came—Damnation Nicolas, there must be another way." She crossed her arms and waited for a response. "What if I make you too warm?"

Charity paced the room's width, twice. When his teeth clacked louder, she gave up, crossed herself, and crawled under the blankets. The bed was ungodly hot.

"Be still or you'll hurt yourself even worse."

He moved quickly to his side and curled toward her. She put her lips to the side of his neck and kissed him. Tremors brought Nicolas's hips against her skirts, and once he'd encountered them he pressed nearer with a will, then cast a leg over hers.

"Nicolas!"

319

"S-s-shrew," he chattered.

His trembling slowed and finally he found a fitful sleep. Charity didn't.

"I can ride. I can ride half-dead, if I must. I can ride, damn you." Nicolas muttered, time after time.

It wasn't only that his delirium disturbed her. Nor could she blame her body, simmering into awareness. She lay awake because her biologist's brain, schooled to observe and record, prodded her, exulting at its hard-won solution.

"I kept you warm," Nicolas had admitted.

Wrong, my love, she might have answered. Nighthawk, not Nicolas Carillo, wrapped me in his arms. That hard, insistent face over mine wore a mask.

"I've snared you now, my wild bird," she whispered. "And I love you, even if you are a liar."

# Chapter Twenty-Three

"Doña Anna, your son's room is just down this corridor. Santiago has not yet been in to see if he is awake—"

Damnation!

Charity's feet slapped the dirt floor. She limped past the tumbled blankets, past the door scraping the chair she'd propped there.

Charity arranged herself at Nicolas's bedside, hands fluttering to her hair. Braid still tight, but her skirt—the pink rag of a dress wadded around her waist. She tugged it down, fluffed it up, and the door opened.

Father Alvarado's eyes went wide. Nicolas, half wakened by sudden noise, bolted upright in bed and grappled at his hip for a sword, before pain felled him and he lost consciousness, again.

"Doña Anna!"

Fear, anger, light-headedness, had coursed through her at the woman's name. But now, Anna's aristocratic bearing, her proper green gown spilling lace from throat and cuffs, and her absolute competence, made Charity crave nothing more than sleep.

Charity leaned against the bed post, trying to swallow her yawn as Anna's eyes raked her dishevelment.

"I think his fever has broken, Anna. Not long ago. Perhaps an hour or two." Charity glanced toward the window. "I know the sky was graying. Before that he was delirious, and he shivered."

"That would be the fever burning itself out," Anna plucked off her gloves and rounded the end of the bed. She lifted the mass of blankets. "You did your best to keep him warm, I see."

Charity cleared her throat and nodded,

"Father Alvarado? If someone could bring me a chair? No, Charity, no, you sit," Anna said. Then, as the girl placed both palms flat on Nicolas' bed, trying to maintain balance, the woman added. "Or go to bed. The padre explained how you've worked with him, side by side, tirelessly, until Nicolas fell—sick."

The cool voice broke under that one word.

"I hardly knew what to expect," Anna shaded a hand over her eyes. "The padre's message said Nico had been injured, and when I jumped my horse over huge cracks in the earth near Doña Ronda's, and rode through the gates and saw the devastation—I admit my faith faltered." She repinned one side of her perfect bun. "That huge bell struck him, did it?"

Charity saw the horror in Anna's eyes. The bell might have crushed Nicolas as easily as it struck that babe in its carrier. For all his strength and daring, Nicolas had been Anna's baby.

"The wound is healing well." Charity pointed to the neat stitches. "He called for you once, last night," Charity added.

Anna stroked her hand across her son's forehead.

"He must have been delirious. This one hasn't needed me since I left for Spain. Before that, even."

Anna's voice faded and the priest withdrew. Suddenly Anna revived, speaking with forced lightness.

"We've had word your husband is returning from his most recent expedition," Anna looked down as Nicolas stirred beneath her hand. "You will have tales to tell Freddy Larkin, no? His mountain man stories pale beside this."

Nicolas caught his mother's hand and brought it to his lips.

*"Mamacita."* Nicolas's voice sounded rusty with affection, but as she knelt at his bedside, Nicolas sent a frown over Anna's tight black bun.

Charity returned to her courtyard hospital, to find she'd

been supplanted there, too. She offered water, and salved on aloe vera, then nothing remained for her to do. When she stood, hands pressed to the small of her back, she counted seventeen patients. The dead had been buried. The babble of moans had been replaced by querulous complaints and the far warbling of a meadowlark.

Nicolas would live. Freddy would return. And she must sail for Boston. Amid the rubble and destruction around her, she battled the old need to smash something.

A riderless brown horse shambled past. It stumbled, leaning off balance, eager to thrust its muzzle into the well.

"Señora!" An Indian snagged the brown's reins and motioned her to come. "It's Miguel!"

Hiking her skirts to her knees, Charity ran. The young Indian who'd spoken to Nicolas, who'd ridden away as the earthquake struck, clung to the saddle horn.

No. His fingers were stiff and clawlike and a hank of horsehair rope bound his wrist to the horn. Another strip held his right ankle, but his left—

Charity crossed herself.

"A knife! I need a knife!" she shouted, but the man who'd summoned her had already sawed through the rope. Another eased Miguel, his eyes open and scanning the yard, to the ground.

Ruined fragments of tissue and bone protruded from the cuff of linen trousers soaked red-black to the knee.

"A musket ball," Father Alvarado mused from beside her. "Miguel, a musket?"

The young man nodded.

"Don Nicolas?" Miguel asked.

"Nicolas is fine," Charity soothed, not daring to touch him. "I must speak with him."

"First, we must see to your leg," Charity's lips twitched. The injury was far beyond her skills. Why hadn't he bled to death? Anna said she'd sent to Santa Barbara for a doctor. Charity gave Miguel a sip from a water bottle and prayed the doctor would ride through the gates before sundown.

"No. The leg can wait." He rinsed the water through his

323

mouth and then spat, splattering the pink gown. "I must speak to Don Nicolas."

"Can't you tell me? I'm his friend—"

"Only Don Nicolas. Before nightfall."

"Get a litter," Alvarado said. "Take him to Don Nicolas."

"But Nicolas can do nothing for him—"

"Fine, Señora," Father Alvarado lowered his voice and rounded on her. "*You* tell this strong young man he can die with his important message. *I* cannot find such words. Call me when I may offer his last rites."

The priest stormed across the yard, and Sarita, the girl with red ocher fading on her cheeks, whispered to Charity,

"He hasn't slept since the earthquake, Señora. He hasn't eaten, either. You must pardon him."

Charity nodded. She couldn't find the words to deny Miguel, either. She directed two men to carry him into Nicolas's room.

"If the sky falls, hold up your hands."

She'd heard Pilar say it before, and the words had never seemed more fitting. But damnation, her arms were getting tired.


Charity slumped against the hallway wall as Miguel was deposited in Nicolas's room. Eavesdropping was not her intention, but her legs buckled beneath her, rejecting another step.

Face pressed to the bowl of her hands, Charity heard Miguel repeat his tight-jawed demand that he speak to Nicolas, alone.

"But I am Don Nicolas's mother, and even if you could rouse him I feel sure he'd delegate anything you required to me."

"No. Leave us, Doña."

"Señor, you must trust me."

"No."

"He trusts me to know everything."

"No."

324

Charity thought the colliding wills had jammed to a standstill. Then she heard Anna's whisper.

"Even as Halcon must trust *his* mother."

Hell and damnation. Charity's hands flew up to smother her gasp. Doña Anna knew. She knew and must be helping him every step of the way. Nicolas's proper lady mother was a rebel.

When Anna appeared, tardily moving to shut the door, Charity had no hope of scuttling away, unseen.

Anna met her eyes.

"Call back the men to carry his litter. This young man won't be able to talk long," Anna instructed. Then she closed the door.

Anna, who hid books under her needlework, also hid the night raider who was her son. Incredible! Charity ran to seek help.

Even after Miguel was carried to the courtyard and delivered into the experienced hands of a midwife who'd ridden from El Pueblo, Anna sequestered herself in Nicolas's room. Charity squatted in the hall, drinking coffee, rubbing the scabbed scratches on her nose and listening to Anna pace. Nicolas's mother, by Charity's count, crossed the room forty-two times.

Forty-three. She'd make her patience last until the fiftieth crossing. Then she'd push her way inside, assure herself Nicolas still lived, and declare her intention to help, whether Anna wanted her or not. The door opened.

"Señora Larkin."

Anna's voice and manner were silky, as if receiving Charity for tea. With a glance back at Nicolas, she closed the door, then crossed the hall and motioned Charity into an empty room.

"You know of Nicolas's unusual political dealings."

"I know he is Halcon."

"Yes," Anna sighed, steepling her fingers and tapping them on her lips. "What has he told you of his work with Salvador?"

"Nothing. I don't know Salvador."

325

"And yet—"

"Anna, Nicolas won't admit he is Nighthawk," Charity sunk into a leather-backed chair. "But all the facts add up."

"They do. How lucky that Lieutenant Santana can't see past his own ambition," Anna's face clouded. "Nicolas seeks to protect you, of course."

"It doesn't matter. Let him protect—" Charity faltered and her hand spun in empty circles as she groped for words, "the Indians, the peons, his California. I'll take care of myself and I'll do whatever you need, whatever he can't do now."

Charity meshed her own fingers together, see-sawing them back and forth. God, but she wanted to go back to his room, to touch his still face and measure his breaths with her own eyes.

Anna repeated Miguel's account of the renegades' plan and its failed execution.

Miguel and Carmen had gulled the blacksmith with the story of their gold discovery and allowed themselves to be tricked into confiding its location. But the Devil's own luck had sent Santana into the smithy before the Indians could leave, and the blacksmith insisted they retell their story.

"Miguel felt certain they were believed, until Santana arrested both Indians and called soldiers to shackle and jail them. With nothing to lose, Miguel and Carmen bolted for their horses. Carmen rode ahead of him, when Miguel was shot. He clung to his horse's neck, and when he next looked, she was gone.

"Trusting the animal to run home, Miguel tied himself to its saddle, planning to accompany Halcon to Las Calderonas, tonight."

"Why Las Calderonas?" Charity asked.

"You know it?" Anna's voice and expression intensified.

"Nicolas showed me the hot springs on our ride from Doña Ronda's."

Anna paced, then stopped, facing the window.

"Could you find it again, in the dark?"

Charity rocked against the chair's leather back and let her

eyes trace the beam overhead. She recalled, of that morning, the heaviness in her chest, more clearly than landmarks.

"I think I could. Nicolas said the ride from Las Calderonas to the mission was an hour and a half," Charity closed her eyes, conjuring the terrain, "It would take me longer. Why?"

"You could warn the *renegados*. Santana and his men won't come tomorrow, as planned. They're riding now and Miguel thinks they'll arrive by midnight. He insisted I tell Nicolas, but there's no question of that."

Charity dismissed the idea with a gesture, but she couldn't help wondering if Nicolas's fevered mind had guessed at the plan's failure. "I can ride, I can ride," he'd muttered. Even in delirium he clutched at his responsibility.

"The ride would kill him. We both know that, and for once, he's unable to challenge us." Charity said, irritated by Anna's skeptically curved eyebrow. "I don't care how angry he is!"

"You have not seen him so mad, *chica*," Anna shook her head. "You had better hope this excursion is kept secret."


Foolhardy. Nicolas had branded her rash and foolhardy. This headlong dash would doubtless prove him right. Charity's uneasiness grew at each galloping step away from the mission.

Such a foray required days of planning. But how could she refuse, when Miguel swore Las Calderonas would be carpeted with camped Indians tonight? How could she refuse, when she imagined Santana's soldiers riding and slashing, dealing death undeterred because the Indios slept. Who else, if discovered, would protect Nicolas's secret? Who else could Anna send, but her?

Allowing ample time to compensate for darkness and error, Anna predicted that even if Santana arrived before midnight, the Indians would be gone. Charity should be safely in bed before Nicolas woke.

"I'll sleep when I'm old," Charity murmured, patting the neck of Doña Ronda's black. But her promise was weak.

Last night she'd shared a bed with Nicolas, but the heavy blankets and his radiant fever had made her restless. The night before, she'd nursed earthquake victims until dawn. And before that, she'd nearly made love to Nighthawk.

Coyotes yipped at her passing, and Charity kept her knees hard at the black's shoulders. Daylight dimmed.

If this worked, Nicolas would have Anna to thank. Her talent for subterfuge verged on genius. Because Anna paid Alvarado for a special thanksgiving mass, with all in attendance, Charity rode away unobserved. Because Anna sighed that poor Nicolas suffered great pain, Alvarado granted a few more grains of white powder, guaranteeing he'd sleep past the time for protest.

"That old fox isn't fooled, though," Anna said of Father Alvarado. "There's something to all those rumors."

Charity jerked on the horse's mouth, causing him to shy, but the stick which had looked like a viper, stretched across the faint path, was only a stick. She couldn't afford such foolishness. She'd come to the last and most dangerous part of the journey. Navigating the steep defile into the box canyon, she'd have to slow the horse to a walk.

The chorus of coyotes followed her, yipping and howling, drawing closer until they encircled her. Suddenly she knew they were not coyotes.

Indian riders blocked her descent into the canyon. The black shied and bucked and Charity wondered if she'd dash her brains out on the rocks before she could even speak.

The horse subsided, and even in the darkness she felt it. These were not helpful mission Indians, resigned to bringing cups of chocolate and shoeing oxen. Nor were they the noble savages of Mr. Longfellow's "Hiawatha." The jostling silhouettes tightening around her were men too proud to bear the Spanish yoke. They would rather die. Or kill.

"I must talk to Salvador."

Damnation, with little enough chance they'd speak Spanish, why had she quavered her request in English? And why didn't someone light a torch?

The black tossed his head at the press of Indian ponies.

"I am Salvador."

Another shape—no different from the others except that his horse burst from cover, scattering the other riders who parted without protest—spoke Spanish.

Charity poured forth Miguel's message, adding details as they emerged in her mind. Finally she stopped.

"Santana has Carmen still, *verdad?*" Salvador asked.

"Miguel thinks he does," Charity said, squinting to make out features which might render the shape more human.

"She will be executed if there is trouble for the soldiers?"

"That's what Santana said."

"And if there is no trouble, but also no gold, what then?" The inflection that raised the question also raised his arm. Starlight glinted on the Indian leader's spear.

"I don't know," she said. "We didn't ask Miguel."

"What do you think?"

"Me?" Charity gasped. The man must be joking, must surely be making sport of her for the amusement of his followers. Why else would he ask *her*, a female, a foreigner, to predict Santana's actions? Charity's heart thundered in her ears as she tried to sort it out. She must have misunderstood.

"You are the one who studies animals, si? Nighthawk's woman. What do you say of the animal Santana?"

Like a mantle of iron, responsibility fell on her. Her brain must work more clearly than ever before, or men might die.

Her fingertips chilled until she had to scrub them on her skirt. She needed to think before answering, but the tall Indian with the spear didn't appear patient. Surely, a seasoned leader wouldn't make decisions based on her opinion. But he had asked.

"I think anyone here, when Santana comes, will be sorry," she faltered as a warrior sneered and spat. "I think Santana is a vengeful, petty man with no honor and I don't think he'll . . ."

Finishing the thought was unnecessary. Salvador motioned two warriors to dismiss her. Spears smacked the black's rump, the horse bolted and for endless minutes the wind tore tears from her eyes and whipped the scarf from under her hat.

329

When the horse slowed, snorting, Charity was alone on the empty plain.

The encounter had lasted, how long? Five minutes? Ten? Had she left them angry? Afraid? Had her words verified Salvador's suspicions, or did he scorn her? Would they stay and be slaughtered, or ambush the Mexican soldiers?

She prayed they would melt away into the darkness and wait for another moonless night.

The black stood still, trembling. Her busy thoughts had allowed him to slow to a lope, a jog and now he stopped.

*Nighthawk's woman,* Salvador had said. If it were only true! Charity tightened her legs and clucked her tongue. The black's skittering refusal tested her waning energy.

"Oh, no, horse. Don't do this to me."

She turned him in circles. Arturo's trick had never failed. Until now. The horse ran a few steps then bucked.

"Why, you pigheaded beast? Why?"

Then she realized the streamed slanted downhill, toward Doña Ronda's rancho. The black wanted to go home.

"Tomorrow, boy," she coaxed. "Another hour and we'll be back at the mission and you'll be eating fresh-threshed grain."

Mincing sideways, the horse seemed to comply.

Charity felt the stiffness in her neck, the ache beneath her shoulder blades and the ankle rubbed raw from poorly adjusted stirrups. How easy it had been to crave adventure amid the ferns and crocheted shawls of Aunt P.'s Boston parlor.

Too late, she felt the horse lunge. Standing in the stirrups, she sawed the reins, but he ran wide-mouthed against the bit, dashing toward a crack blacker than the ground, galloping headlong toward a yawning fissure. And then he jumped.

". . . child. Sergeant, you're right. It's Señora Larkin."

Dazzling gold hair and mind-sapping blue eyes swam before her, as a hand raised her from the ground.

"Are you injured, Señora?"

"Those Indians, the scum—"

330

Charity interrupted the second voice, opening her eyes enough to take in Santana and his column of soldiers.

"No, I fell from my horse," Charity said, tossing back the hair which had escaped from her braid. "Then I walked a while and crawled up here to sleep."

Charity surveyed the place where they'd found her. Last night it had looked like a haven, but it was only a hump of ground crowned by a few rocks.

Santana watched her. "The Lion of Castile," he'd been mocked, but the title fit. Huge and golden, prowling and suspicious, he stepped around her, examining her attire, scanning the terrain, blue eyes narrow. Charity felt every inch the mouse to Santana's calculating cat.

Sounds of fighting, faint and borne on the wind had inspired her to concoct a story, last night. Nighthawk's woman, he'd determined, could do no less. But what had that story been?

"Lieutenant, I rode out to meet the doctor."

"Doctor?"

"Yes. You know about the earthquake, of course, and a doctor's been sent for—"

"But surely vaqueros survived, Señora." Santana speculated. "They might have saved you a dangerous journey."

Like feral dogs, the soldiers sensed their leader's dark mood and slunk closer, taking his skepticism as permission.

She heard the tone, but not the intent of a sniggering remark from one of the soldiers. She followed his leer to her skirt. The green skirt she'd borrowed from Anna had ripped, revealing a glimpse of petticoat.

Charity's fingers itched to pick up a stone and skip it off the soldier's nose, but her mind warned her to stop.

She needed the leader of this pack on her side. And she'd learned at least one lesson in California. She could put no name to it, but it had to do with men and women, with California chivalry, and she'd had it from Nicolas, Arturo, Don Carlos and even Nighthawk.

Charity pretended to cringe with embarrassment. She stepped closer to Santana, slipping behind him.

331

"Lieutenant, can't you make that man—"

Santana drew himself up to shield her. He rapped out a series of orders that straightened the column and sent it trotting away before Charity unravelled his words.

"You must accept my apology, Señora. They are coarse men, fit only for the frontier."

Santana's flushed as he took a leather lace from his scabbard and fashioned it into a loop.

"You will ride sidesaddle, before me, Señora. See," he used both hands to test the knot, "This will serve as a stirrup after I place it around the saddle horn. I will ride behind."

Embarrassment, this time, didn't have to be feigned.

"I don't believe I can do that, Lieutenant."

The man would be sitting a hand's breadth from her buttocks. To be that close to Nicolas, in the darkness, was one thing. With Santana, it was quite another.

"But Señora, the cantle of the saddle will be between us for modesty. I assure you, it is done all the time." Santana smiled at her reluctance. "Truly. I would not compromise you."

"I don't mean to sound prudish, Lieutenant, but I can imagine that it's proper." Charity could scarcely believe the words were hers.

She didn't approve of Santana and his tactics, but he had never threatened her. He was an attractive and intelligent man, charming, in fact, on the day she'd toured his Presidio.

Santana smoothed his hair, then stood next to Paloma, making a step of his hands, coaxing.

"Please, Señora."

Still dubious, Charity used his hand, his shoulder and the leather loop to clamber up.

"I'm not sure I'll fit," she fussed.

Santana chuckled from his position at the palomino's head.

"Señora, please. You are slender as a doe."

"But not nearly as graceful."

She settled between the saddle horn and cantle and Santana swung up behind, his silence unbroken by spurs or conchos. He kept his arms bowed away from her as the palomino walked.

332

"Not so bad, is it?"

"I feel childish," she confessed.

Guerro Santana, she shamed herself, was no stalking cat. He even smelled better than most men. His clothes held only the faintest hint of trail dust; they'd been fresh hours ago. And his face smelled of soap. Undoubtedly he'd shaved this morning.

"No, Señora, not childish, merely modest."

They rode in silence until Charity realized he kept the horse to a walk so that he wouldn't bump against her.

"Lieutenant, you may let the horse proceed. I won't fall. At this gait we won't reach the mission until noon."

"Or the rancho till nightfall," he said, touching the palomino into a lope.

"But we aren't going to the rancho."

"Of course, Señora. I would not leave you at the mission. Especially Alvarado's mission," he sniffed. "And not today."

"Lieutenant, Doña Anna expects me back with the doctor, and although I haven't found him, she will worry if I don't return."

"Doña Anna Carillo is at the mission?"

"Of course, she sent for the doctor. For Nicolas. Lieutenant, didn't I say that before?" Charity glanced up, then lowered her eyes from his nearness.

"You mentioned the doctor, Señora, and I did wonder why such would tend the *Indios*—" he paused, frowning.

"Why," he asked, "Are the Carillos at the mission?"

Charity closed her eyes. Anna's skill at subterfuge, at social fibs, would have spun a deft second lie. Instead, Charity jabbered a tale of dust and destruction, of blood and fever, and hoped it would distract him.

Santana shifted the palomino toward the mission and Charity sighed as the column of soldiers shrunk to a wormlike line on the horizon, continuing away, west.

"Is Nicolas badly injured?" Santana demanded. "By the Madonna, I will go seek this doctor myself."

Charity reassured him, and as Santana relaxed, she felt the

corded tendons in her own neck loosen. Guerro Santana'
most endearing trait was his friendship with Nicolas.

When they were both quiet, her mind scrabbled for an
other distraction. If Santana recalled she hadn't answered hi
question, if he demanded to know why they'd been at th
mission, what would she say?

"I should not tell you this," she began, "but my friendshi
with Nicolas goes back years, to the time he was away a
school."

"Si?"

"If I tell you, Señor, I must have your word of honor yo
won't repeat it. I was young, and far too impetuous."

At his assurance, she continued.

"Would you believe, Lieutenant, that I passed myself off a
a boy?"

Santana's delighted disbelief fueled their conversation unt
they sighted the mission.

*Lion of Castile, indeed,* Charity scoffed. She'd emerged un
scathed by Santana's claws. Guerro was no more than
house cat, and she was leading him back to Nicolas, on
leash.


"Look out the window, Nicolas. I told you she'd be fine,
Doña Anna said, as if Charlie had been out for a canter. "A
ter all, the horse would have returned, if there had been
mishap."

The horse wouldn't have. After a lifetime around horse
his mother knew that as well as he. But he hadn't the strengt
to argue.

Chickens cackled over the voices in the mission courtyard
Nicolas let his weight fall against the window ledge and wille
the riders to pass before him.

Nicolas had envisioned a hundred horrors since dawn
when his mother had explained Charity's absence. Salvador'
young hot-heads were barely under control. They might ki
her outright, or send her mutilated body back athwart he
horse.

334

And Christ, the audacity, the arrogance of his mother, to confide in Charlie, to put her in the gravest danger, when the girl could no more hide her feelings than fly!

Santana's palomino carried double. Not Charlie, at all, damn it, but a laughing girl with loose hair. Guerro clasped her waist, brushed her bodice—a transparent grope, Lieutenant!—in helping her dismount.

It *was* Charlie.

"Mother, get my pants, if you would."

"Nicolas, I'll do no such thing. You shouldn't be out of bed and I won't help you leave this room. No, I said."

He snatched the trousers from a chair, grinding his teeth against the roll of nausea. He collapsed backward, onto the edge of the bed, sure that lowering his head to pull on one leg at a time would dizzy him into falling. Prone, he squirmed into them.

*Jesus Cristo!* Hair loose, pillowed on Santana's chest, gleeful as a tavern wench—what did Charlie think she was doing?

He pulled on his soft boots and commanded his fingers to close the concho buttons over his legs. He'd wager Charlie had deception in mind. She didn't know she was the worst liar born.

"Lieutenant Santana is something too forward with Mrs. Larkin," his mother spoke tartly.

Nicolas used both hands to thrust up from the bed. Killing heat flared from the pit of his stomach to suffuse his face. Santana pretended to help Charlie with her hair. She'd raised her arms to knot it, and Santana, gold fringe swaying, solicitously fanned up tendrils from the nape of her neck.

Nicolas meant to slam his fist into the adobe brick, meant to shatter the wall or his hand or anything except his "amigo's" leering face, but he only grabbed the window grating for balance.

He could allow fever weakness to be no more than a temporary inconvenience. Nicolas rolled the shoulder muscle and pain zigzagged like lightning down his back. Tender, but healing. If it hadn't disturbed two older wounds, he'd have no ex-

cuse to stand here, letting Charlie think she could lea-
Santana around by the crotch.

If Charlie believed that, she was sadly mistaken. Even
practiced Jezebel like Esperanza couldn't do it.

Lust, for Santana, meant power. He craved power like th
injured craved that white dust his mother had admitted givin,
him. Santana's drug, his love, his Madonna, was power. If th
Spaniard let Charlie believe she exerted influence over him
he did it for a reason.

"I'm going out."

Nicolas picked up his coat and then dropped it. *Dios*
Mother might have brought him another jacket. Not that hi
shoulder would twist to negotiate the sleeve, but this one, th
one he'd worn that morning, riding from Las Calderonas int-
the hellish earthquake, was a tattered, bloody ruin.

"Nicolas," Anna's voice flowed with infuriating patience
"You'll put her in worse danger if you go roaring ou
there—"

"I have no intention—" Nicolas slowed his words, an-
steadied himself against the door frame, "of 'roaring ou
there.' And Charity is not my primary concern. I mus
know—" Nicolas swallowed the bile at the back of his throa-
"what's become of Carmen, and Salvador, must discove
what happened while I've been sleeping off Alvarado's infer
nal powders."

Nicolas made it as far as the mission courtyard. He leane-
against a pillar, hoping he'd stop panting in time for his pos
to look like indolence, not exhaustion.

Oh, Charlie was full of herself! A forelock of black hair rip
pling and swirling to her waist, green gown ripped and show
ing a handful of petticoat, Charlie tossed her head so her gol-
earrings glittered. She twitched her hips as if she were a gyps
and Santana her dancing bear.

Charlie's strutting pride meant she'd reached them in time

Nicolas shifted to hang a thumb in his waistband. Charli
swayed closer, smelling of horse and dust, reeking of victor
She couldn't be allowed to remain so—thinking she could b
a desperado in her spare hours, but *Dios*, what if, someday, h

could make love to her in the sun and see her eyes light like this, sky blue and shimmering with satisfaction?

"Ah, amigo! Your hurt is not so bad as I feared!"

Santana strode past Charlie and Nicolas saw her brow crease. Already her pet had slipped its leash.

Nicolas extended his left hand, maneuvering to avoid an *abrazo* which would surely fell him, screaming, to his knees.

"I'm sure Señora Larkin overreacted, as females are wont to do," Nicolas said. He forced a lazy smile.

Santana chuckled and awarded Charlie a fatherly pat.

"Yes, we had a very scared little girl out there, on the plains. Thrown by her horse in Indian territory." Santana sucked in a breath and shook his head. "It could have been very bad, indeed, if my troop hadn't happened past."

*A scared little girl. Ay Cristo!* Nicolas looked, though he didn't intend to. Charlie's jaw dropped.

# Chapter Twenty-Four

If Charlie's pride dimmed, Santana's blazed. He gloried, in proving this bespectacled biologist was still only a woman.

"Your sergeant rode in not an hour ago, but he said nothing of the Señora, only demanded the padre produce an Indian. Juan? Or Miguel?" Nicolas feigned irritation at the request.

He turned toward the cool mission *sala*, fighting off weakness. "I expect he's out in the Indiada now, your sergeant."

"He has orders. Francisco is one man who'll follow them," Santana matched Nicolas' steps. "He'll find the spy Miguel."

He might make as many steps as it took to reach his room, if there were no other delays.

A girl in black braids tilted her head from beyond an arch, curious at the intrusion. Santana snapped his fingers and ordered her to fetch a drink.

At the distraction, Nicolas glanced at Charlie.

She shrank inside the green gown, growing smaller and whiter as her thoughts expanded, as she thought of Miguel.

*What did you think, Charlie? That you were playing Halcon for fun? And what if you'd been in charge? Miguel would have been captured and executed. By the time you arrived, he would have cooled and stiffened.* Nicolas wanted to shake her. He wanted to shield her. Most of all, he wanted to turn her face to the wall so Santana missed her wide-mouthed horror.

"If we'd had troops here, the red scoundrel would already have told us what we need to know," Santana groused.

"No question," Nicolas confirmed. Charlie's face blanched ivory pale and her freckles showed dark as the day he'd caught her in a faint, outside his den.

Good. Soon enough she'd ask Anna, and his mother could reveal her cleverness in spiriting Miguel away with the midwife. Until then, he'd let the wench suffer. He'd let her swoon and gladly, if it taught her to stay out of this "game."

Charlie lurched into a low table, nearly upsetting brass candlesticks and a bowl of yellow roses.

"This is no conversation for ladies, even one as daring as you, Señora," Santana snaked an arm around Charlie's waist, then snapped his fingers at the returning servant. "Here. Girl! Show the Señora to a chamber. Christ, Carillo, these redskins have neither manners nor brains, to leave a lady standing."

Charlie's eyes signaled she was about to do something illadvised. Nicolas hardened his jaw and willed her to behave. *Go away, Charlie. Christ, for your own good, go away.*

"Your arm?" Charlie asked, hand hovering near his shoulder. "Nicolas, are you certain you've recovered enough to be up?"

"Quite certain," he said, making a curt half-bow.

Charlie's fingers brushed beneath the fringe of hair over her brow, then she wove from the room like a sleepwalker.

*"Diablo,* you're a rock, Carillo," Santana chuckled. "I know all about your principles, but you could pluck that one with the smallest kindness—a smile, or a piece of ribbon. She says she rode out to find you a doctor. A lady—or what passes for one in Boston—riding about in the middle of the night?" Santana shook his head, as they approached Nicolas' doorway. "Surely the girl took such a chance to gain your favor."

Smashing one's fist into a face required a degree of energy he didn't possess, but Nicolas thought he might have just enough strength to slit Santana's throat.

"She's not my sort at all," Santana admitted, then wagged his head with a sly smile. "Still, the entire time she rode on my saddle, I couldn't help noticing," Santana made a hefting feint toward his pant lacings, "that the lady biologist isn't *constructed* like a—scholar. Amigo, I see you're weary."

"Only of discussing her," Nicolas forced the words through his teeth. He leaned a knee against the bedstead and hoped it would support him. "Truly, Guerro, I'm most interested to hear of this ambush Francisco mentioned."

"Ambush," Santana snorted, then stopped.

Warning, an instinctive foreboding, vibrated from that conceited snort, but the room slipped, liquid, before his eyes and he knew he was about to swoon.

"What if I call for a wash and a meal, before we talk? I need your advice," Santana said, "But, I'd be a poor friend to ignore your illness. Rest, amigo. I'll return in an hour."

Colored disks flashed behind Nicolas's closed eyelids as he collapsed on the bed. Just in time, he thought, as Guerro's steps receded down the hallway.

A door closed. Somewhere crockery touched metal and wooden wheels crunched sand.

Thank God, Charlie had done no harm, and she was safe.

Nicolas's head flopped back and his lips parted in exhaustion. His chest swelled full, and he slept.


"Ambush," Santana snorted the word again when he returned. In an open-necked shirt and blue breeches, he exuded a pirate chief's arrogance, as he settled into the room's only chair. "From beginning to end, that 'ambush' proved a pitiful display. Clearly, this tawdry band didn't have the advice of Halcon."

The ambush hadn't seemed pitiful when they planned it. He and Salvador had called it shrewd strategy, though he'd been bedeviled with images of Charlie pinned beneath her legal husband and Salvador had been itching for Carmen, that lithe Amazon on a gray horse. Now, Santana held Carmen captive.

"Carillo, I tax you too much!" Santana stood, shirt sleeves aflutter as he protested Nicolas' silence.

"I'm fine," Nicolas cleared his throat. "Guerro, settle yourself," Nicolas motioned, with an abrupt backhand, for

340

Santana to slam the chamber door, and relaxed when the Spaniard obeyed.

Santana poured water from the carafe.

"I'm no nursemaid, Carillo," he said, proffering the cup, "But you look like the very devil, not your usual sleek self, at all. Still, I'll trust you to know best."

Gloating couldn't be curbed, for long. Santana launched into a description of the ambush.

"The two who came to the blacksmith were convincing enough," Santana said. "I believed them! I only gave imprisonment orders to clear my way. Anyone can find Las Calderonas."

Charlie *had* reached them in time. Hadn't she? He imagined his face encased in ice. Whatever Santana said next, he must remain unperturbed. Surely, she'd warned them.

He blinked at the sound of slippers in the hallway. Santana bragged on. He recounted the battle in detail, and still Charlie lurked in the hall. Nicolas knew it as surely as if he could see through the wall.

"And so, how many awaited you at Las Calderonas?"

"We counted a dozen corpses after the engagement. None escaped. What did they think?" Santana chuckled. "That we'd just come riding into a box canyon on a summer's evening? That we intended to allow ourselves to be slaughtered? Say what you will, Carillo. These vermin show cunning, but they don't have minds like ours."

"You may be right, Guerro," Nicolas mused. He shrugged his injured shoulder, making the ache fracture and scatter like glass along his nerves. "A dozen corpses, you say?"

Why in God's name had Charlie been so proud? *A dozen corpses.* Halcon never allowed bloodshed. He didn't need it. Stealth and intelligence always served. Until Charlie rode onto the scene. Now the plain was littered with dead.

Nicolas closed his eyes, as if in weariness or agreement, but he peered toward the bottom of the door and saw darkness that might be her shadow.

"A dozen, yes. A paltry group. Still and all," Santana took a considering sip of his drink. "They've played into my hand.

Those rumors of Don Emelio's return have been confirmed. A letter from El Presidente tells me I'll be relieved of my post quite soon. To secure my future, Nicolas, I must make an impact, now."

*A dozen corpses. What, in the name of every blessed saint, did Charlie think she played at?*

Guerro fidgeted with the cuff of his shirt, revealing an angry maroon welt.

"Before I return to Mexico City, two actions will mark me a man they can't ignore." Santana jerked his cuff back into place. "I will quell these *renegados*, and hang Halcon."

The scuff of slippers didn't escape Santana's ears this time, and he wore no spurs to warn her. Silent and swift, Guerro sprang from the chair, swung wide the door and grabbed her.

Twisting her arm high behind her back, he slammed Charlie against the wall before he heard Nicolas's roar.

The gale whistling in his head smothered thought. Only when Santana's throat wavered beyond the grip of his outstretched hands, did Nicolas listen.

*"Diablo,* Nicolas. I won't hurt her, but the wench was eavesdropping, and for whom?" Santana asked, releasing Charlie's arm. "We can't have that," he added reasonably.

Charlie didn't look scared. Santana didn't look scared. Both surprised, but not frightened. The room swayed. Had Nighthawk become a man to be gawked at rather than feared?

No, he stared at Santana's gold-thatched chest, heaving beyond his shirt laces, as if he'd been running. Perhaps neither of them had expected such reaction from Nicolas Carillo.

"You were discussing Halcon," Charlie challenged, as if that gave her license to prowl.

"Si. And if you heard anything at all, Señora, you understand that Halcon's marauding nights are finished. He's ridden for the last time, and all your cynical sniffs and hands on your hips won't change a thing. Nicolas," Santana said, "her dangerous fascination with this criminal must end. The bounty I've set on the blackguard stands, Señora," Santana said, counting off on his index finger. "In addition, I will offer

342

the *renegados* their prisoner's release in exchange for Nighthawk. The Indios are poor, and loyal. Make it easy on yourself, Mrs. Larkin. Go home to your husband and forget this romantic fantasy. Don't inflict on yourself the unpleasantness of watching Halcon dance his death at the end of a rope.

"Nicolas and I, we are men of the world. We would not think of mentioning your indiscretion to Larkin, would we, amigo?"

"Of course not." Nicolas agreed, deliberately stroking one wing of his mustache.

Santana's lecture clearly infuriated Charlie, but Nicolas watched with detachment as she rubbed her wrist and glared. Her irritation meant nothing. His rage had vanished like smoke.

Santana clearly meant to trick Salvador's band. Even if Nighthawk were delivered, bound and gagged, Santana would not free Carmen.

A dozen corpses might indeed gain him notice, but weak-willed trading of prisoners, wouldn't. If Guerro wanted Mexico City to marvel at his taming of frontier California, exterminating renegades and hanging a revolutionary might work.

"Allow me to double the reward," Nicolas offered. "Such an amount might pique the interest of a few land-poor *hidalgos.*"

Nicolas examined Charlie, thinking she looked distant, as if she stood at the bottom of a well, and he stood at the top.

A dozen corpses.

"Charity, I recommend you stay in your room until our departure, tomorrow morning," Nicolas ordered. "I'm to blame, of course, but you've overtired yourself, and cannot be held responsible for your actions."

Santana departed, practically on Charlie's heels.

Twelve daring warriors.

Blood and death were the contributions Charlie poured into his revolutionary cauldron. Blood and death. At last, he'd discovered witchcraft black enough to cut free of her spell.

\* \* \*

Nicolas rode at a lope between Doña Anna and Santana. The Spaniard rode far forward in his saddle, offering too much bright conversation and scanning the horizon before him. Trotting behind on a mission mule, Charity coughed on the rancorous smoke which had smudged the sky for leagues.

Cordoba squealed and shook his hind legs until Nicolas resorted to quirting the stallion to regain its attention.

"The ladies will want to ride on, Nicolas, though I'm sure you'll find the spectacle interesting, in a grisly fashion," Santana suggested.

Charlie kicked her mule into a stiff-legged shamble before Santana finished his sentence. Doña Anna followed.

Smoke shifted in a single gray column through air thick and still as the day of the earthquake. Perhaps the smoke, or the aches plaguing his every sinew, clouded his understanding, because Nicolas didn't make out the jumble of arms and legs until he drew rein, close enough to recognize their faces.

Not Salvador, he begged, seeing the Indians' muscled forms tumbled together like grotesque fire wood. He forced himself to look. Their bodies had not been burning long enough to char. Most still had flesh, rising in thin silver bubbles that swelled, then burst. None looked like Salvador.

Santana's agitation remained high when they'd passed the bizarre bonfire. Though the Spaniard claimed his demonstration of strength was meant for the Indians, Nicolas wondered.

They rode so near Refugio that Nicolas glimpsed Hamlet's wild herd, disappearing in wisps of dust that hung in space rather than whirling into the sky. Ahead reared the rancho plateau. In spite of the horror, Nicolas felt his taut nerves relax at the nearness of home. Then, Santana nodded toward Sergeant Lopez.

"Soon now, Sergeant. Fire when you're ready."

Charlie stiffened. Refugio, Nicolas thought. She must know, since she stared right at the cleft rock above his hideout. But no, she looked too far right, toward another cave. Santana and Lopez were looking for Charlie's wolf.

Charlie maneuvered her mule next to Santana's palomino.

"Lieutenant, you can't mean to let him shoot that wolf."

344

"I see no wolf, Señora Larkin," Santana replied. "But if one were to appear, why would I not?"

"You know," Charlie said, wetting her lips, "I've been studying that wolf."

Charlie's black hat brim stayed level. So did her tone and her gaze, flush with Santana's taunting eyes. Few vaqueros would stay so cool in the face of danger, Nicolas thought, and fewer would anticipate the alcalde's signal to Paloma, and match the palomino stride for lengthening stride.

"It seems you are more interested in studying Halcon," Santana chided, eyes fixed on the dark overhang to the wolf's den. "And you offer no respect for those who would end his reign of lawlessness."

"Lieutenant, I apologized for eavesdropping—"

"Señora, your transgressions surpass that prank. Since you arrived, you have asked many probing questions about Halcon. A more suspicious man would think you meant to take advantage."

Clumped tendons bulged at the turn of Santana's jaw. Nicolas had never seen him so angry.

"Lieutenant, how could I take advantage of you?" Charlie leaned back in her saddle, eyes wide as a child's. Santana mistook her incredulity.

"No more of your flattery, Señora. I trusted you."

"Trust," Charlie repeated, levelly.

*Ay Cristo,* the logical biologist faded as Charlie flushed.

"*You* wish to speak of trust?" Charlie's voice peaked. "*You* assured me how proper it would be to climb up on the saddle in front of you, Lieutenant."

"It is done all the time, Charity," Doña Anna interceded.

"It may be, but I—for all that I've made more than my share of foreigners' blunders—I tried to do what was appropriate. I was embarrassed," Charlie drew in her breath, "to ride that close to him."

"Señora, you are overwrought," Santana stiffened and his gold fringed epaulets shimmered above Charity's head. His haughty dismissal took the tremble from Charlie's voice.

345

"I believed you, Lieutenant, and then I overheard you talking to Nicolas of my buttocks—"

"Enough."

Santana's voice slashed across Anna's gasp. Nicolas felt a nudge of grim humor at Charlie's ability to pierce Santana's gentlemanly guise. But what would be the cost?

"Sergeant, you may have to bait the animal, or smoke her out, if she doesn't fall victim to her own curiosity."

"You'd kill something just to punish me?" Charity insisted. Santana ignored her. He turned to Nicolas's mother.

"Doña Anna, though you think me harsh, now, you'll thank me, later, for sparing you embarrassment. One animal is of little significance and this lesson will teach the señora to consider the consequences of her actions." He spoke over the rasp of Lopez's priming rod. "This lesson will last a lifetime."

Sleek-coated and bulging with unborn pups, Sable emerged from her den at the sound of hooves. She went rigid for a minute, assessing the number of riders, and breathing their scents. She had only begun her bowing ritual, frisking her hindquarters, then scratching the ground in greeting, when Lopez shot.

Sable yelped as the musket ball threw her sideways. She clawed herself upright and staggered toward her den. Dark red gouts veed her belly to drag the earth and she stumbled.

When the she-wolf offered no threat, Lopez, perspiring and sucking his breath through his teeth, kneed his mount closer.

Sable, using only her front paws, dragged herself nearer her den. Then, despairing at the soldier's nearness, she pressed her ears flat, slanted her eyes nearly closed and bared her teeth in a submissive grin. Wagging her tail frantically low, she fell again.

*Jesus Maria*, Lopez was a coward of the worst order. He reined his horse closer to the fawning wolf. Desperately, she rolled to her back, offering tribute to his superior strength, by exposing her belly. Mouth open, tongue lolling, eyes downcast, Sable submitted with every sign she could make.

His sword. In the time Lopez took to reprime his musket, Nicolas knew he could end Sable's misery.

346

Black smoke puffed at the corner of his vision, and the con-cussion of the explosion shuddered next to him as Santana's musket ball struck the wolf's head and killed her.

# Chapter Twenty-Five

Charlie wished she could slash the roots of ever[y] emotion—love, hate, fear, devotion. She wanted to feel noth[-]ing.

Nicolas might have studied how to hurt her, and not bee[n] so successful. He'd mocked her as a weak female to Santan[a]. He'd blamed her for the death of the warriors who'd disre[-] garded her warning and challenged Santana's troops. All [of] that she might have accepted as part of his act for Santan[a]. But Nicolas could not be so fine an actor that he gave her n[o] glance of understanding as Santana and Francisco murdere[d] Sable.

With each blast, her own entrails had blown apart. He[r] own head exploded into fragments. She'd needed the solac[e] of Nicolas's eyes so much, and he'd denied her. When she re[-] alized he wasn't pretending, she'd kicked her mule into a ru[n] and left the others.

Charity sat in the shade behind the *cocina,* back presse[d] against the whitewashed wall. No one would pass by on ran[-] cho errands. She'd be alone.

Two days past, she'd soared at his touch. Now, she'[d] crashed, like a stupid bird flying into a parlor window, whe[n] his eyes blamed her for those twelve corpses.

All night, she'd pondered what she should say to him, an[d] still she circled back to a single thought: those young brave[s] rode to meet Santana knowing full well he'd fight. Others i[n]

Salvador's band had escaped, those twelve could have followed. Instead, they attacked, and died.

They'd chosen martyrs' deaths. She knew it. In her heart and bones and bookish mind, she knew she was right. But Nicolas wouldn't accept harsh philosophy from her, she knew that with equal conviction.

Worst of all, Charity bit her knuckles, as if she could shock herself sensible, she didn't care if she was right. In fact, she didn't *want* to be right if he hated her for it.

Clattering hooves entered the courtyard.

Charity rocked back and forth, eyes fixed on the rafters supporting the tile roof. She breathed the scents of olive oil and corn meal, tomatoes and onions. Then, listening intently, like a horse pricking its ears, she heard Nicolas.

Ringing spurs and chinging conchos signaled his approach. He stopped. Silhouetted by daylight, Nicolas stood alone. Hands on hips, not even leading a horse, he surveyed the shadows behind the cocina, looking for her. Black garb turned his face waxen, and when he squinted, lines rayed from the corners of his sun-dazed eyes.

Her heart fluttered when she thought of what he'd lost. Not only had Nicolas's sword arm had been cleft to the bone, Santana had slaughtered twelve rebels, captured a hostage, and stood ready to execute Halcon. Santana held the power to crush the revolt Nicolas had nurtured for years.

Charity ran toward him, shrinking away from his injured side.

"I'm sorry, Nicolas, about the *renegados* and the—sword Santana has poised over your people," she whispered, speaking Spanish while she stroked the muscles beneath his velvet coat.

"I'll help you," she said, rubbing her cheek against his good shoulder. "Tell me what you need, while you're recovering, Nicolas. I'll do whatever you want."

He stepped back so suddenly her fingers caught in the neat black ribbon, snagging it from a bow to loose ends.

"Haven't you done enough?" Nicolas's tone remained cold as he enumerated her failings. "A country's freedom is threat-

349

ened, a young woman jailed and about to be hanged an
twelve brave men are dead. Even for an ambitious girl suc
as you, Charity, I should think that a lengthy litany of erro
and death."

She didn't know this frigid man, not did she want to. Cha
ity stepped to sidle past him.

"I'm not done with you," his voice cracked and he grabbe
her wrist. "You think you're not to blame, because you di
your best to save Salvador's band. *You did your best.*"

Nicolas' mockery lifted the corner of his mustache. Befor
she'd loved that half smile. Now it damned her.

"Your best wasn't good enough, was it, little girl? Yo
thought you could play Halcon, but you couldn't. You wer
wrong. You should have wakened me. I would have though
of Miguel. I would have known those young bloods woul
venture something stupid and Salvador and I could hav
planned a second attack."

A spitting sizzle came from the cocina, and Charity tried t
hear that, instead of his voice. Peppers fried in hot oil. Sh
tried to smell them, not Nicolas's scent of horses and leathe

"You weren't even a decent messenger," he sneered. "Fal
ing from your horse, arousing Santana's suspicion until h
trusts neither of us!

"Weakness and errors and death. That's all you've brough
me, Charity.

"You've emasculated Halcon. God, he's like a hen, flutte
ing about to protect you and worrying about saving his ow
wretched hide so you can get your hands on it," Nicola
scorned. "You made him forget what this revolution
about."

He pulled her a step closer and kissed the back of her han
so gently she almost believed his touch, instead of his word

"I think you're wrong to call that weakness," Charity whi
pered.

*Most men call it love,* she wanted to add, but she couldn'
She filled her voice with reason, to lure him back. "As fo
errors—"

"Shall I only list those of the past few days?" he asked, "W
350

ever should have been in the same place with Miguel or ven Father Alvarado. That was your idea, you'll recall, going to the mission together? Next, you never should have ridden ut alone. No lady would, to 'fetch a doctor.' I swear, *chica*, ou are the worst liar born. And you told him, he says, of our masquerade at Harvard. Do you think him so stupid hat he won't guess you could play your dress-up games, gain?

"No, no, Señora, don't leave now! The worst is yet to ome.

"Death. *Ay Cristo*, Charlie," Nicolas' voice broke and he hook his fist in her face. Then he let it fall to his side and owed his head like a man at prayer. "For five years, I've voided bloodshed, and now twelve deaths lay at my door."

"It wasn't your fault and it wasn't mine, Nicolas." She vanted to cup her hand over the back of his head, to comfort im. "Those men chose to face Santana—"

"Rather than face the humiliation of running away. Can't ou understand the coward's choice you offered? 'Run away, ow, boys, the soldiers are coming!' " his voice twirled in im-tation.

"Salvador had to protect the women and children of his and, so he fled. But no man, Charlie, no man—" Nicolas roke off in frustration.

"But then you're not a man, are you? You have pretended. Oh, how you've tried to look and think and act like one! But, ou will never understand."

Charity strained her arms toward him, not sure whether to close her hands around his throat or embrace him.

"No," his voice slashed like his latigo. "You may not touch ne, may not talk with me, may not 'help' anymore."

A booming laugh created a havoc of barking dogs in the courtyard and though the bond tethering them was anger, oth stepped apart.

Nicolas wiped away the perspiration ringing his lips, and mothered the groan from bringing his drooping shoulder evel.

351

"Ah yes. That is what I came to say." Nicolas dipped his head in courtesy. "Mrs. Larkin, your husband is home."

She rushed past Nicolas, praying he'd catch her by the waist and pull her back. But he stood, frozen, while she faced Freddy in the glaring sunlight.

Freddy whirled her around as he had the first day. The heat and motion made her queasy, but she remembered their parting, and held her tongue. Instead she tried to hug him, reaching halfway around his huge chest, and took comfort from his familiarity.

"That's what I've been waiting for!" Freddy's voice rolled across the courtyard so anyone could hear.

Was Freddy, then, what she needed? Freddy's loud American voice would never whisper words of love, but she didn't want them. She wanted that open affection shining from blue eyes. She wanted his raucous words, unshaded by suspicion.

Freddy held her back at arms' length. And, though she marvelled at his crisp auburn hair, his broad chest and wide shoulders, she felt no desire to touch them.

Gooseflesh pricked her scalp, sweeping down her neck and shoulders as the two men closed her in their *abrazo*.

Nicolas laughed heartily. God. He turned and turned, a more consummate actor couldn't exist. He joked with Freddy about the trials of chaperoning her and Freddy responded by cursing the autocratic port authorities in San Diego.

Meanwhile she stood with Arturo.

"Tell me what's wrong, *Caridad*."

"I couldn't begin to," she said, "But I can tell you, I can't stand to watch them grinning like jackasses much longer."

"You can talk honestly to me, *chica*, and though I'd rather receive your confidences alone and in darkness—"

"Arturo!" Charity's squeak incurred only raised eyebrows from Freddy and Nicolas.

"Don't mistake me, Charlie. I'm waiting for those two to kill each other, then I'll swoop in and have you to myself."

"You'll never get the chance, Carillo," Freddy interrupted as if he'd been half-listening. "As soon as it's socially appropriate," Freddy tilted her chin up so she had to meet his eyes.

352

"after dinner, I'd say, we are going to discuss our cock-eyed marriage, once and for all."

"Freddy, I am rather tired," she began.

"Not this time, Charlie." Freddy's merriment disappeared. "We'll have this out before daylight. And no matter if I have to tie you down—excuse me, gentlemen—" He wheeled her away from the other men. "If I have to tie you down and deprive you of food and sleep, we *will* have this out."


Charity sat tailor-style in the middle of her bed. She felt like a circus dog, in this ruffled yellow gown Aunt P. had deemed suitable for her wedding night.

She glared at her mirrored reflection. Summer flushed her cheeks, her nose still wore scabs from falling during the earthquake, and her hair waved like snakes.

Ugly as sin, but Freddy insisted they'd "have it out," and she knew that meant he'd insist on his husbandly rights.

"Ringed yourself with candles like a sacrificial virgin, have you?" Freddy slipped into the room, raising a hand to halt her words.

"I'm sorry, Charlie. That was totally uncalled for. Shall I go out and begin again?"

"I don't think that's necessary." Charity's lips turned in an involuntary smile. If only she'd trudged that midnight beach alone, and never met Nighthawk.

"It's all your fault!" she cried at the revelation. "Freddy, if you'd met me when my ship landed, I'd never—" she wagged her finger at him, delighted at shifting the guilt.

"You are mad, my dear." Freddy sighed in false despair. He settled on the bed, pulling her down beside him as he worked his boots loose and kicked them to the floor.

"You never were a delicate child, even scrappy enough to survive measles unscathed. And now you're driven mad because I didn't meet you," Freddy mused. "But," his face pressed so near Charity heard him swallow, "you're not a child anymore, are you?"

That darkling shift in his blue eyes, the lowering of his lids

353

. . . this time she recognized it and she wouldn't allow him to make himself so vulnerable.

Charity wormed her arms between them and pushed his chest.

"Give me a chance, here, Charlie," Freddy said, restraining her gently. "It might not be so bad."

She moaned, and he clearly didn't understand it was the sort of moan you uttered after you'd stubbed your toe for the third time in one day, because he kissed her.

Kisses, she supposed, he felt appropriate for a virgin, but oh what pale, watery things compared to Nighthawk's. She was horrible to analyze his kisses as if she'd describe them in field notes. Charity pulled her head back, but he only caught her hair in a gentle grip, and followed her rising mouth with his own.

Charity squinted up at Freddy's closed eyes. None of this was fair, but hurting Freddy for no good reason was most unfair. *Just do it,* she told him in her mind, *just do it.*

"Did you faint?" Freddy's voice cut the room's quiet.

"No, I just—"

"Disappeared. Not that it makes a hell of a lot of difference whether you're stiff as a board or doll limp. For Christ's sake, Charlie, what do you think, I want to rape you?"

The hacienda was so still, she heard the fountain outside, heard a mourning dove's plaint, heard a guitar strumming.

"No, I never thought you'd hurt me."

"That's comforting." Freddy nodded, then ruffled his hair into a coxscomb. "I suppose a nice fellow wouldn't even hint at what this does to an hombre's concept of his own manliness."

Charity jumped, startling both of them with her guilty reaction to the Spanish word.

"Which one is it? Nicolas or Arturo?"

He rolled her to her back, holding her shoulders down with straight arms.

"Freddy!"

"Not me, lady, clearly not. Or is it this mystical Halcon?

354

Which one's stolen you away, Charlie girl?" His mournful voice faded as he kissed her, with a loud smack.

"I hope you're joking, Freddy—"

He did it again.

"—because you're not making any sense," Charity rapped the words out between assaults.

"Charlie, the haughty 'examining-a bug-on-a-pin' look of yours doesn't fool me. I watched you cultivate it about the same time you starting affecting those silly spectacles."

His next kiss lingered, but his lecture hadn't ended.

"That's why I threatened to take you back to Boston. I know it's one of them, but I—"

A kiss so warm and deep should have been answered, but she couldn't do it. He drew back and sighed.

"What's the sense of fighting them if you don't want me in the first place?"

"Oh, Freddy—"

"Charlie, just shut up for a while. Every time you whine that drawn out, pitying 'oh Freddy' I want to shake you—or hang my head for being such a poor excuse for a lover. Maybe I should take up with whores and learn a few tricks," he speculated.

"Freddy!"

He let himself flatten atop her, expelling her breath with his unexpected attack, then raised his face far enough to cover her mouth with his hand. Charity watched his pupils, black surrounded by blue, widen and spread.

"Don't talk. I was joking, Charlie. I don't know any whores. I said, don't talk," he cautioned. "Outraged squeals don't suit you and I'm not moving my hand anytime soon. So hush."

Her lips were already numb.

"Now, you're going to think before you speak, Charlie. You've always known your own mind. I'll ask a simple question, give you a few minutes—unbroken by your own voice—to ponder your response, and then I'll require an answer. Understand?"

She nodded.

"Fine. Charity Anne O'Dell Larkin, answer me this: What do you want? Don't frown. It's a simple enough question."

She waited, then drew a breath when Freddy moved his hand.

"Most of all," she said deliberately, "I want to stay in California, and I want to continue my research."

He covered her mouth, again.

"I suppose I should respect you for not serving up some palaver about being a good wife, or conquering this aversion to my touch," Freddy said, "But, I don't like it much. Suppose we stay, Charlie, can you be my wife? In body and spirit and all that?"

Again he waited. When he moved his hand, Charity parted her lips twice before she could talk.

"I don't know, Freddy. I think I can."

And then he stood. He swung his feet to the floor so brusquely, she nearly bounced off the bed.

"Freddy, don't go. Can't you, please—I know it's selfish— but, please could you stay the night?"

"Sleep with you?" Freddy snorted. His eyes reflected a confusion of anger and amusement. "God, Charlie, you have the most bizarre talent for making me feel as if I *like* being punched in the stomach. That's a damned unfair request," he said.

Freddy cocked his head to one side, reminding her of some Boston neighbor's red setter dog.

"Still, if you're willing to put up with my choice of sleeping attire—or lack of it? Yes? And the remote possibility I'd paw you as I'm falling asleep—?" He raised his brows at her emphatic nod. "All right. I don't even care why you want me. I daresay you haven't a clue, yourself. Yes, Charlie girl," he said, reaching down and shaking her by both shoulders. "I'll do it."

Stance perfect, feet braced a shoulder width apart, Nicolas held the crouch until his thigh muscles trembled. Weakness set in just a minute short of half an hour. His legs, at least, proved dependable.

But his arm, *Ay Cristo,* his arm. *En garde,* it wavered before he counted thirty. It rolled inward well enough, protecting his belly and chest, but the slightest twitch outward, to deflect a side attack, pained him. Worse, its clumsiness wouldn't surprise a blind opponent fighting by the dark of the moon.

And extension? Straightening his arm in line with the blade, to threaten or lunge at an enemy, couldn't be held a five count. He flinched at the mere thought of impact at the end of the extension. *Weakling.*

Nicolas let his sword arm fall. He passed the grip from right hand to left and back again. Then, to ram home the lesson that weaklings, even his own muscles, wouldn't be coddled, he lunged full force toward a wall target.

His bellow echoed-from the ceiling, but he maintained his hold, refusing to forfeit his claim on this ally.

Charlie, Freddy and Arturo were a different story, but he'd survive their loss. Freddy had been a jolly friend who recalled the carefree Nicolas of school, but Freddy would soon be gone. Arturo would outgrow their rivalry; young bulls learned not to charge each imagined threat. And Charlie—

Charlie had never been his to claim.

He'd come upon them outside the *cocina,* home from a gallop, cuddling a wolf pup swaddled in Charity's black cloak, and he'd cut short their gaiety with a frown.

"Nicolas, it's Sable's baby," Charlie explained. "The others were dead—she'd already had them, you see. I got to thinking last night, how her belly looked enlarged, not swollen and full." Charlie held her arms wide, and for an instant he'd imagined her pregnant. When Charlie had a child, whose would it be?

"Surely you aren't bringing it into the house?" he'd asked.

"I am," she fired back. "Must I seek permission?"

"No, no," Arturo said, shaking his head. "We'll be hiding it for a while, *hermano.* It's a small enough sin, *verdad?*"

Nicolas shrugged as the pup suckled Charlie's fingers.

"Wolves make poor house pets, you know, Charlie."

"Wolves and guerrillas, he'd thought darkly. Bad house pets, and worse husbands.

Charlie had looked up from the pin-sharp milk teeth testing her finger, face carefully blank.

"Freddy remembers Critter. I'm surprised he'll indulge you in this second captive," he'd said, and then Freddy had been snarling, worse than the pup.

"Why the hell do you care, Carillo?"

"I did not question your authority, amigo," Nicolas began. Freddy had turned away, then wheeled back.

"And don't look as if—you know what's best for my wife."

An imp of perversity taunted Nicolas with thoughts that were clearly Nighthawk's. Nighthawk's scandalous vaunting rang through his brain as clearly as shouts. *Sí, Freddy. I know what's best for your wife. I know how to make her run mad with passion that has nothing to do with books and animals. I know how to make her unpin her hair, unsash her gown, unhook—*

But he hadn't said a word, only allowed the devil's own smile to lift one corner of his mouth.

Then they clattered out. And when Charlie's flush and the way her pup-encumbered forearm bumped her glasses back up her nose, made him yearn to follow, he resurrected his Indian comrades, burning, blistering, blackening.

Tonight, only for tonight, she'd hide him in her room. Sable's son gave the lie to Nicolas' doom-saying. The pup's eyes tracked Charity's milk-withered fingers as they moved from the basin to his greedy mouth. His oversized ears tipped forward, but he ignored the footsteps crossing the moonlit courtyard.

The boots belonged to Nicolas. She knew, because Arturo and Freddy gambled raucously in the *sala*. She knew, because beyond the boots, a sword blade sliced the night air, and silver hilt clanged on adobe tiles each time Nicolas dropped it. She knew, because she felt Nicolas's desperation: California's future teetered between democracy and monarchy and Halcon must ride or allow the balance to slip, overbalance and crash.

The pup's milky muzzle had ruined her skirt when Charity

judged him asleep, doused her candle and peered from the window.

She scanned the courtyard for his shadow. Had a man ever been more impatient with his own body? Four days ago, his arm had almost been lopped from his trunk. Four days ago, his fever-hot brain had woven fantasies while infection whee-dled away his life. And now he paced the courtyard, rending the air in swooping slashes, determined Halcon would ride.

After their snarling spat this morning, she'd left her bed-room door slightly ajar, hoping he'd come. At midday, he'd deserted his den long enough to get water. He'd strode down the hall, tilting his head back to drink from the mouth of the jar, when Princessa pounced from the shadows and wrapped herself, clawing and biting, around his boot.

With a long-suffering sigh, he'd disengaged Princessa's claws, then sunk cross-legged to the floor and matched re-flexes with the cat. Princessa reared back, arching and return-ing his right hand attacks, strike for strike, swat for swat.

At each withdrawal, Nicolas hurt. His lips twitched, or the line of his jaw hardened. Yet he repeated the game a hundred times, until Princessa grew bored, and flopped down to lick her belly. Only then did Nicolas return to his den.

Now, with no challenger but himself, he tossed the sword to his left hand and curved his right wrist behind his waist. He fought better with his left arm than most men did with their right. For him, though, it wouldn't be enough. Only perfection suited Nicolas, and he didn't have time to regain it before Carmen's execution.

Tonight was Wednesday. Carmen's neck would feel the noose at Friday's dawn.

Charity watched Nicolas pace, his activity spinning her thoughts as well. What would Nighthawk do?

Abduct Camille from the hangman's hands? No. The plat-form would be ringed by armed soldiers. Steal her from her prison. No. Santana's new jail was sturdy. Although some-thing in her notes, from that day, pecked at the back of her mind.

Was she arrogant to consider her improved horsemanship?

Was it prideful to recall her successful night ride? Nicolas would strike her for what she was thinking.

Charity tapped her fingers on the window ledge. Did she dare ride disguised as Nighthawk? He needed her help.

Charity watched Nicolas continue pacing, rotating his wrist, blade whispering in the summer night. Of course.

She silenced her lips with the flat of her palm. Lord, Charity, how many times must the hint be flaunted? For weeks, she'd searched for Halcon's hideout, when all along she'd had it in the circle of her spy glass.

Halcon's hideout must be near Sable's den. Three times, she'd made note of a lone black horse, running at the margin of the wild band that watered in that rocky niche. A bachelor stallion, her pen had labeled him, too mature to run with the herd, yet unwilling to challenge the leader.

Halcon must have schooled the black—of course! a man who rode like a centaur could train an intelligent horse to remain nearby, couldn't he?—to be near when his master called. Halcon's sanctuary must be right there. She had only to find it, and she'd find his costume. And his horse. Then she'd prove she offered him more than weakness and errors and death.

Outside, Nicolas stopped pacing as if he'd heard.

Give it up, *muchacho*, she shot the thought to him as he tested his sword point with one finger. Go to bed.

With one shred of her Irish father's luck, she'd be galloping away on Luna at dawn. With just a whisper of God's grace, she'd prove to Nicolas that he needed her.


If Irish luck allowed her to escape, common sense made her leave the wolf pup behind. Afraid he'd whine, alone in her room, she'd slipped the pup into the litter of Arturo's spotted yard dog. Charity had stayed while the mother sniffed, licked, then nudged the pup into the nest before flopping down, to doze.

Sighting the solitary black horse below her ridge, Charity tethered Luna and approached on foot. The black bolted long before she'd taken the last shaley step to the valley floor. But even without the horse to guide her, she felt drawn to the rocks camouflaging Halcon's hideout, certain as if she clutched a map.

The gray rock slumped toward a twin hulk which shielded Sable's den. Charity's eyes shifted between the two enormous boulders, sure they could have formed two halves with a missing center, if there had ever existed a force strong enough to cleave a stone big as a sailing ship.

She shoved through the screen of greenery, crossed the trickling stream, and faced the rock slabs which closed like an overlapping surplice. She wedged between, inhaling the dank earthy odors.

Standing in the darkness, she smelled no droppings or fur, but the tumble of fist-sized stones around her ankles created a mental picture of an animal, head down and digging frantically, spewing them behind as it dug this den.

Nonsense. She'd spent hours watching from the ridge. If there'd been a wild thing here, she would have seen it.

The wall behind chilled her back. The one in front flattened her breasts, and she turned her face aside so that the stone abraded her cheek rather than her nose.

Scuff one boot ahead. Drag the other to follow. Scuff apart, drag together. Gray light darkened to black. Her fingers inched forward across the uneven hardness, followed a crack and then clawed frantically as one foot scuffed forward and the other followed, into nothing.

She shuddered, spat dirt from her mouth and felt her heart shake her body. Calm down, she ordered herself, and listen.

Sifting sand, disturbed by her fall, slowed to a sighing shower. More deep breaths. Think like a scientist. Assess your surroundings.

The darkness seemed stable. No avalanche gathered around her, and, if she could trust the tapping exploration of one foot, no pit yawned nearby. Charity realized her eyes were closed. Methodically, she exhaled, then opened them.

"Might as well have left them closed," she muttered, and

the short hollowness of her voice, echoless and dull, hinte
this cave was not very large.

Shivering at their sticky tickle, she brushed cobwebs from
her face. The earth underfoot encouraged her to edge for
ward until her forehead collided with a wall. What kind o
scientist set off to explore caves without candles?

She patted the tunnel's sides. Walls opened away from her
hands and, as if she'd imagined it into being, she inhaled a
billow of wax and her right hand touched candles, flint and
steel.

Flaring, then fading out, the wick caught long enough to
show her ancient knotted roots, smooth earthen curves and
*books*. A bed, too, her mind chattered as her fingers fumbled
to reignite the candle. And a hanging blanket. She held her
breath as she struck the steel, carefully.

Flame stretched, then steadied, and the breath she'd held
rushed out. She took steps small enough to stay within the
candle's circle of light.

Three books stood together in a niche of dirt, but they
rested on a embroidered scrap fine enough to be an altar
cloth. Dried herbs hung in neat bundles. Light glowed back
from metal in a lower niche. She knelt to pry open a tin cask
which held three pristine white linen squares. Bandages.

Stupid that she should feel a stabbing of tears. Halcon had
chosen a dangerous route. He would need bandages.

Her eyes darted to the books, but first, she peeled back a
flap of greased paper protecting a packet of food tucked next
to the tin. Dried meat and fruit, enough for days. And here,
resting side by side, two bottle necks peered like gun barrels
from the dirt wall.

She lifted the rough blanket hiding a tree root he'd fashioned into a rack. Two swords, one thick and unwieldly, the
other Halcon's dueling piece, hung near a bridle. But where
was his costume? Urgency twisted her belly like hunger. She
needed the dark leather leggings, his shirt—

Charity gnawed the end of her braid. Had she invaded his
sanctuary for nothing? She knelt on the bed, willow and raw

hide by the spring of it. Still holding the candle, she wrestled loose one volume.

"The Complete Works of William Shakespeare," she whispered.

She opened the heavy cover and read the damning inscription. The cost of this book could be judged not in gold, but in blood if Santana found it, here amid swords, healing herbs and provisions.

"Oh Nicolas," she sighed. His full name, complete with intricate rubric, claimed the book, the refuge, the glorious, cause, as his.

Tremors shook her fingers and she gasped, letting the hot wax burn her fingers rather than mark the book in her lap.

"Damnation!"

Charity shook her finger in reaction, snuffing the candle. Delicately, she felt for the book's niche, replaced it, and pressed her palms together to pray.

Somewhere, Nicolas had surely cached a rosary, but Charity reverted to the conversational prayer which had suited her solitary moments in Aunt P's house.

"Lord," she began, "Some would take it as a bad sign that I'm too stupid to find his disguise and too inept to catch his horse," she whispered, eyes clinched closed. "But I can keep looking. And I can catch the horse, if that's what you want."

Charity waited. The silence seemed thick with the rushing of blood in her ears. The entire earth surrounded her. The earth held every answer to thousands of years of questions, but it offered no more than her silent God.

"Am I to simply do it my own way?" She tasted blood from biting her lip. *"Bueno,"* she said, for surely God, in Nicolas's refuge, spoke Spanish.

Charity stood abruptly and frustration tinged her words.

"No answer is an answer, too," she theorized. She winced as she rammed her head against the low ceiling. "If only I knew what it meant."

\* \* \*

Hoof beats, jingling harness and voices startled Charity from her plans. She pulled Luna to a halt and waited until Freddy and Arturo rounded a curve in the trail above the hideout.

"You look scared half to death, Charlie," Freddy's tone seemed half accusation.

"I didn't hear you until the last moment," she admitted.

The lull of earth and prayer and silence still muffled her senses so that the two men's conversation eddied around her, until one smattering of words stuck firm.

Freddy and Arturo were riding to San Pedro to book passage to Boston.

"When I return, I'll have the date we'll leave," Freddy said. His steady blue eyes begged a response, just as they had last night, when he'd slipped into bed late, and given her a wedding band. Her silence and stillness, then, had infuriated him.

"I'm beginning to believe it's not a man after all, Charlie. I think this godforsaken place has bewitched you."

Now, as he held his horse in place, reluctant to go without some word, Charity reined Luna close enough to squeeze his arm. And though Freddy left smiling, she knew she'd touched him from guilt. Her pulse raced with giddiness because watchful, restless Freddy wouldn't sleep beside her tonight. She could ride out unnoticed. This, thank *Dios*, was her sign.

# Chapter Twenty-Six

Luis strummed the final flourish of a romantic ballad and ducked his head to avoid looking toward Maria.

"Ay! Luis! You are the only two blushing," Toro guffawed at the younger vaquero.

Nicolas squatted on his boot heels in the kitchen courtyard. Dusk had faded from purple to black, but two lanterns, one from the porch, another at Luis' feet, kept the summer evening aglow. Vaqueros, kitchen maids and children—all told a dozen—lingered, too restless to go to their beds.

One round-faced baby, half covered by his mother's white blouse, nursed and dozed and roused again, between spates of singing and gossip.

"—*Dios* is kind to keep them away from this rancho." Lucia shifted the babe to her shoulder, patting his back.

"Who, Lucia? Who?" begged gap-toothed Angelica, who sat combing her husband's hair loose from its tight queue.

"The soldiers, of course," Lucia sighed.

"Rancho de los Palos Altos is ringed with them, I hear," put in a vaquero who sheltered a small girl under his arm.

Bedraggled braids laced with wilted daisies, the girl cradled Charlie's wolf pup.

"Because of the horse thieves, do you think? Sit still, I say, *hombre*, or this comb raps your thick skull, eh?" Angelica threatened idly, intent on her friend's gossip.

"What else could it be? Santana never took notice of patrolling, else," she lowered her voice as if whispering to the babe.

"And yet you'd think, wouldn't you—*Carumba,* woman! Even on a horse's tail you don't tug a comb through such knots!—" Angelica's husband snapped. "You'd think Santana would have need of his men here, to guard that Indian woman—"

Conversation faded as a boy borrowed Luis's guitar and plucked an intricate series of notes which tangled into discord.

"Give it back to Luis, *muchacho,*" Toro crowed.

Nicolas sipped his coffee, savoring the cinnamon in its rim. In the domed oven still hot from dinner, the cook had baked *dulces,* claiming the treat honored him, because "the young patron" so seldom sat out.

*This is what you're trying to save,* Nicolas thought, this blend of jobs and stations, yes, even races, melting together. For this, Halcon risks all.

His next, maybe last, great risk would come in a few hours. Nicolas raised his eyes to the moonless June sky. This time tomorrow, New Spain would have wakened. No fear flared at the thought he might not live to see a new age, free of colonial ties. In truth, he hadn't felt so relaxed, so relieved, since the shimmering hot day he'd become Nighthawk.

Salvador's primitively simple plan had built since the night his warriors died.

Tonight, Carmen would be freed and the Mexican army humiliated. Tonight, Santana died, as might Salvador and, if his luck ran out, Nighthawk. But the forces for independence would have taken a stand bold enough to rally every peasant, every Indian, every nonroyalist ranchero to their side.

Nicolas hoped it were so. A small voice in his mind whispered that the snatching of one prisoner—no matter how dramatically—might not wreak such havoc, but after the disaster at Las Calderonas, he must support the *renegados.*

"*La Palomita,*" urged the cook as she passed more pastries, "Play it, Luis."

Luis reclaimed his guitar, then plucked and sang a frivolous *jota* tune about doves and crows and lost love.

When something moved in the darkness, Nicolas's attention stopped short.

Past the pools of lantern light, beyond black heads bent to listen, in the shadow of the roof, stood Charlie.

Nicolas had seen her only once since he'd harangued her for rescuing the pup. Only twice since he'd blamed her for slaughter.

By lantern light, her gown seemed pale blue, reaching demurely high on her throat, before sweeping the wood walk. A contrast, he mused, to this morning's garb.

*Give it a rest, Carillo. You're past such thoughts. A patriotic saint, remember?*

He needed to contemplate this Charity Larkin as she stood, still and foreign. He needed to appreciate her as a man might a flower persistent enough to grow through a cracked adobe wall.

". . . thou art a diamond, for it has not been possible for my love to soften thee," Luis sang. "If I offer thee a caress, thou dost flout me, and then tell me I am a fool . . ."

*Don't touch me,* he'd commanded her. Christ, what arrogance! Nicolas swallowed the last of his cold coffee. If the woman poised in the shadows were *anyone* but Charlie, he'd apologize.

But Charlie would hear more than an apology. At least now she was quiet. Hurt, yes—Barbara had reported violet circles underscored Charlie's eyes—yet safe.

"But never mind, ungrateful one," Luis's voice soared against yipping accompaniment. "Some day, in thy dreams, thou wilt remember, that I was thy master."

Twice only, he'd seen Charlie mastered. Twice, when he pinned her beneath him, she'd been glad of his dominance.

If only—Charlie glided from the porch, beyond view.

*His* feelings were muffled with purpose. Regret—a faint whiff of it—yes, he felt that, but compared to the raging passion, anger and worry Charlie usually evoked, regret was a civilized emotion.

This morning, Salvador promised him Charlie would not see his corpse. Neither would his family. Disguised as a mission sheep shearer, Salvador had presented the plan without mention of the earlier fiasco, and promised, if Halcon fell under soldiers' guns, that his body would be flung over the withers of an Indian pony for Sierra burial. His family would never know, for sure, what had happened.

Standing in the chapel garden, next to a sundial that barely showed shadow, Nicolas had clasped hands with Salvador and felt comforted. Now, remembering Charlie as he'd spied her, on his way to meet with Salvador, Nicolas frowned.

An itinerant sheep shearer had notified Nicolas that the Indians' *jefe*, their chief, would speak with the young *patron*.

Nicolas had risen in darkness, certain the *jefe* would be Salvador. Only a thump from the far reaches of the hacienda, from his fencing den, had slowed his advance toward the garden.

Charlie's hair, black and copper at once, rippled past the waist of her white nightgown. Tamed by a ribbon, it didn't hamper her thrusts, merely flipped and swung with her movements. Light from her candle showed Charlie testing his dress sword, a valuable import from Aragon, also the lightest weapon he owned.

If Charlie had seen him poised in the doorway, she might have dropped the handful of skirt held high behind her, exposing one thigh as she advanced and lunged. Instead, she tsked impatiently, wiped her brow and knotted the ruffled hem.

In that moment, when she radiated determination, he'd loved her and known precisely why his love was doomed. Charlie refused to give up.

She wouldn't admit they'd never again fence. She wouldn't admit she'd be in Boston within the month. And she wouldn't admit, damn her, that she'd married a man who'd never give her cause to caress a sword hilt, again.

It was why, when he lay on his deathbed, whenever that might be, the girl would still live in his heart; Charlie didn't know when she was beaten.

Toro brought him painfully back to the present.

"Mooning for your Esperanza?" queried Toro, clapping Nicolas's bad shoulder energetically.

Nicolas forced a laugh, though his eyes remained focused on the space where Charlie had stood. A girl who didn't know when she was beaten might make a last, desperate bid at valiance.

The slamming pulse in his wrists, rose to his throat, then hammered his temples. What had she to lose, after all? Convinced he'd tossed her aside, convinced Freddy would sling her aboard a Boston-bound ship, convinced she could imitate a man—

*Diablo*. Nicolas walked deliberately to the kitchen and left his cup. Charlie's brand of bravery had led her to saunter among wild bears and gallop into Indian ambushes. Why wouldn't it spur her to disrupt a carefully planned rescue by cantering into the presidio to seize a renegado she'd never seen before?

Apologizing, smiling, nodding, Nicolas excused himself and strode toward the corrals.

"Where's the gray?"

Nicolas grabbed down a bridle even as he asked. The vaquero fanned away smoke from the *cigarito* forbidden near the corrals.

"Quickly, Pancho, where is Señora Larkin's gray?"

"Don Nicolas, she took him. I thought she might," the vaquero said. "Earlier, several days ago, she asked about preparing a horse for a long, fast ride. I helped her grain the animal, massage his muscles."

"She took him where?" Nicolas caught the chestnut and saddled it.

"I think she rode after Freddy Larkin to San Pedro. She meant, I believe, to surprise them." Pancho preened at his perception.

Nicolas jammed his foot into the stirrup and swung aboard the chestnut.

"Oh, Señor, don't tell her I told you—" the vaquero began.

The chestnut squealed when Nicolas spurred to a gallop, straight out of the courtyard.

Charlie was not tagging after Freddy. He wished to God, she were.

Nicolas rolled his spurs over his mount's ribs, sending the gelding toward Refugio. If Charlie was set on playing Halcon, he'd better have Hamlet beneath him, and a sword on his leg, even if he had to handle it with his left hand. Even if Nighthawk wasn't scheduled to appear until after midnight.

Tonight, hours before Carmen's execution, he'd have had help aplenty, three score Indians, and the hundred stolen horses guaranteed to create confusion as they stampeded into the presidio. But no.

By every blessed saint, why did that make him smile?

Halcon was a madman and worse. Lightning excitement and night lust let him relish the increased tempo of hooves—and flurry of hooves again, as he forced the chestnut to hurdle a clump of toyon he might easily have skirted.

Curse Charlie for tangling a plan that might have worked. If they both lived so long, he'd save Freddy some trouble. He'd shanghai the wench, himself, bind her hand and foot and sling her aboard a ship—be it bound for Boston, Canton or the Devil himself.


Given sufficient time for planning, Charity thought she'd make quite an adequate revolutionary.

Tanned leather trousers, purloined from Arturo's cupboard, closed around her legs with horn toggles. She'd sloshed her close-fitting white blouse up and down in a basin of tea until it stained a matching brown. Wound twice around her head and pinned, her long hair disappeared beneath a silk scarf. Best of all, she wore Nicolas's Aragon blade.

She could compensate for natural conditions, too. Fog had crept inland and no moon lit her way, so Charity drew rein and listened. It was worth the time wasted to be sure she wasn't followed. She touched Luna with her heels and loped on.

Her mind, too, carried vital tools: the map to the Presidio and the secret of the adobe cross, which should—if she'd correctly interpreted Santana's pride and that tinkle behind the center brick—give Carmen the key to her prison. Charity's brain also held a plan to flee to the Carillos' town house and shelter innocently with her husband, just as she'd led Pancho to believe.

Inside her camisole, she'd tucked a knife. She'd drop it through the high-barred window, in case Camille was bound.

Gone about in a precise and scientific manner, guerrilla warfare was quite simple. Charity checked the knife's position, patted her blouse back in place and squared her shoulders. After tonight, even Nicolas would have to admit that Mistress Charity O'Dell late, of Boston, Massachusetts, was an asset to his cause.

Something was wrong. She'd intended to tether Luna on the rise and creep between the guards into the presidio. But she neither saw nor heard guards. Gossip said Santana's forces were split, half patrolling against horse thieves, but when both Lucia and Angelica had shrugged when asked if Santana had gone, too, Charlie questioned the wisdom of using maids for informants.

Absent or not, Santana would have set a heavy guard on his valuable prisoner. Where were they?

Damnable darkness and fog disoriented her. *There.* Eyes closed, she concentrated on the feet stamping the open area where she remembered seeing guinea fowl and hens. The feet shuffled into less organized sound, scattered, and returned, she imagined, to their barracks.

She'd guess the hour at just after eleven o'clock. Perhaps the soldiers patrolled on the half hour?

The longer she stood here, the better chance she'd be sighted. Charity shifted forward and Luna tensed in answer.

"*Andale*, Luna. Let's hurry in and hurry out. After this night's work, Freddy Larkin's face will look near as welcome as Nighthawk's."

Luna entered the presidio at a walk, then froze, one foreleg stiff in midair, when a breeze stirred the presidio's bell rope.

371

She urged the animal toward the jail. In this darkness, it was visible only as the ground level to the whitewashed balcony Santana had appended to his quarters, above.

She could see neither the twisted wrought iron railing, nor the round red flower pots, but the scent of roses lay heavy on the fog.

"Francisco—"

The voice sounded close and clear as three hand claps.

"By my dear mother's heart, you are the hardest man alive. Let me sleep, I pray you, let me sleep."

A dry cough followed the request and Charity sympathized with any soldier who begged mercy from Sable's slaughterer.

"And so you *will* sleep. After your watch ends—"

"By the blessed Virgin—"

Francisco's rustic accent branded him uneducated, but he clearly had his standards.

"Shut your blaspheming mouth," he snarled. "The alcalde ordered thrice-hourly patrols."

Thrice? Damnation, she'd have no more than minutes.

Charity urged Luna close to the jail, wishing she were skillful enough to make him sidestep up the window.

"Carmen." Charity whispered, but the proximity of Santana's balcony made her voice sound loud as the soldiers'.

"Carmen, I'm going to drop in a knife, in case you're tied."

And what if she's asleep in the path of the naked blade? The thought came as Charity released the haft, and her fingers closed on air.

Slithering quick as a panther's spring told Charlie that the renegado captive had comprehended and rolled out of the way.

"It is I, Halcon," Charity's voice squeaked as if rusty.

"Not likely," the whisper came back.

Charity felt a smile lift her lips. Wavering light flashed in a crescent on the wall before her, but vanished before she turned. A soldier seeking the privy? A light from the barracks? She felt her scalp contract in wariness, perhaps one soldier held a torch while the other primed a musket.

She must, Charity lectured herself, convince Carmen to

follow her orders. Charity caught at the memory of another horseback night. A decent woman would have bleached her mind free of the name Salvador gave her.

"No, it's not Halcon," she admitted. "I am Nighthawk's woman, come to help you escape."

Luna's head lashed toward the presidio gate. His ears pricked forward to a single point, listening.

"Quickly, or I fear we're both discovered. Santana has hidden—" Charity closed her lips and eyes, praying for perception that would tell her she had *not* heard a board squeak overhead, that the far rushing sound had *not* been hundreds of hooves, beyond the gate.

"Feel for different bricks, here, under the window. In the sign of the cross."

*Please, sweet Madonna, please help us.* Charity crossed herself.

"Different," the voice repeated.

"I'm not sure—smoother? Rougher?"

"Smoother."

Charity forced her mind to recall her sketch, and the simple pattern of Santana's masterpiece.

"From the top of the cross—"

Damnation! That time, she'd heard jingling metal against leather. It could be harness or a sword buckling on.

"—count down three. No, four, four," she hissed.

"Get it right, *chica*. I hear them even now," Carmen prodded.

"Four down and three across. at the intersection—"

"*Que?*"

"Where they cross each other—"

Battalions of horses approached. Santana's troops returning? No, that pawing came from across the yard. Mounted men within the Presidio? Oh God. Luna tossed his head and swiveled his hind quarters against the prison wall.

"No need to break me out, *chica*. I—" the sly voice faded under the grating of brick against brick. "Ha!"

Exultation, like the snap of kindling flaring into flame, marked Carmen's voice. She'd found it.

Torchlight flared so suddenly Charity's eyes clenched shut before starting wide.

Horsemen ringed the yard. Jostling and grotesque in the flames held aloft by foot soldiers, they blocked the gate. And escape.

"Halcon!"

The cry so electrified her, she yanked back on her reins. Thank God, she thought. Thank God.

Luna reared, pale forelegs churning against black sky. Charity threw her weight against his neck, forcing him down, before realization struck.

The soldiers saw *her*. It had been a trap, a noose of horses and fire tightening around *her*. Not until her mask had been stripped away would they realize they'd snared an imposter.

As Luna's front hooves struck earth, she drew Nicolas's sword. A cry rose as horsemen galloped forward and one separated from the group. She recognized the wide torso and dogged position of Francisco Lopez.

Charity's spine straightened. Her body centered and balanced as she lifted her arm and cocked her elbow.

*Oh yes, Señora, and have you ever wielded a sword from horseback?*

The words flowed clear as if Nicolas stood behind her, arms crossed and brow arched in disdain. A nightmare. It must be, but her nape prickled with the mocking presence and she felt compelled to turn.

A candle inside his room, showed Santana lounging against the balcony rail, a puppeteer limned in gold.

Charity turned back, vowing to give a good account of herself. She could do it: Francisco's stocky mount lumbered, while Luna pranced with the hot blood of Moors. Francisco's cutlass hung thick and heavy, but Nicolas's dress sword swung like hawks' wings cleaving the air.

Let Santana watch and be damned.

"No quarter," she screamed, with Francisco nearly upon her. His eyes widened at her English words and her blade nipped inside his guard, tearing his shirt.

Charity drummed her heels on Luna's ribs, rushing past, then wheeling in time to duck Francisco's chopping blade.

Charity turned in a circle. Francisco's wrinkled shirt stretched before her and though no gentleman would slash a man from behind, the other soldiers were closing in. She whipped her blade across Francisco's back and hauled her reins in tight, sliding Luna on his heels, hoping Francisco would turn his bulk too quickly and fall.

He did!

Ha! she wanted to crow. Ha! for the mocking voice behind her. Ha! for Francisco, clawing for purchase and tumbling into the dirt. She gloried over his runaway horse and the sight of Carmen's figure vaulting onto the animal.

Chaos at the gate forced her eyes to veer. A black horse, and soldiers falling away. A babble of confusion, a horse down and a cry of pain.

"Halcon!"

This time it was.

Oh God! He couldn't ride through them all and live. If he came to her, they'd both die.

A grip like jaws closed on her knee and Charity felt herself yanked from Luna's back. The gelding's scream mingled with her own before she bit her lip against the female sound.

She heard the black horse plunge closer, but his rocking movements were far away compared to the tightening net of riders and Francisco's grasp hauling her upright, holding her shoulder and stripping off her flimsy scarf.

The roaring that filled her ears as the scarf spilled her hair down her back and across her face, drowned every sense but panic. She gripped the sword hilt with both hands and raised it over her head.

Charged with the power to strike him down to his knees, she almost missed Francisco's eyes rolling white as they turned up at Santana's voice.

"What think you now, Señora?" Santana shouted, gloating above the fray. "Witness your noble Halcon, cutting and slashing. Enough to stir your patriotic blood, eh? Watch him, Señora, this paragon, slaughtering soldiers whose only sin is serving their King!"

Holding the hilt against her lips, Charity stared after Santana's jabbing finger.

Nighthawk's sword fell like a hammer, slamming down right, then left. The patriot who had never shed blood, slashed a face, rent a shoulder, wrenched forth groans, bellows and prayers until he cleared a path to her side.

"Get up!" He shouted.

Impact made her stagger. Grassy breath steamed on her neck, and horse flesh struck her again. Looming above her, in crazy slants of red light, she saw Nighthawk.

"I can't lift you! Get up!"

His gritted teeth flashed white and she heard his anger, but Charity couldn't think how to mount. Halcon's blade blocked Francisco, but with no stirrup or saddle horn to grab, she couldn't mount.

The yard seethed with horses, eyes flaring orange amid torches which spun and fell in sparking showers.

Halcon's blade sliced a dark ribbon on Francisco's wrist and Charity pulled free. More soldiers charged, with a sound like a gathering earthquake. She must somehow get up.

"For the love of God—" Halcon spat, holding the stallion against a sudden tide of foot soldiers.

Charity jumped. Face down, legs scrambling against the black's shoulder, she ducked under his sword, flexed her right knee high as her chin and pulled athwart the stallion's withers.

"Stay low."

Her face and fists pressed into the stallion's mane. He darted and dodged, swiveling on his haunches. She heard swords clash and caught the smell of grated metal, shaved from impact. Grunts of effort that could have been Francisco's, Halcon's or the animals' swirled through the buffeting of bodies.

"Gold and an officer's commission for the man who takes them!" Santana's shout rained down the promise on his troops.

Halcon's right leg kicked Francisco before the soldier grabbed Charity's sash. Francisco sucked wind, but hauled her, hand over hand, down to him. Charity pelted him with her elbows, but slewed off into air. When she turned, she met Francisco's eyes for the first time.

No fear, no humanity burned there, just conviction that his commander watched. He blazed with satisfaction that he had Nighthawk's woman, the bait to lure a hero into a hell of plunging horses and fire.

Francisco's free hand reached for a grip on her shirt, but when his sleeve slipped up, baring his forearm, Charity attacked, sinking her teeth into his arm. Francisco recoiled, then locked his fingers into the flesh of her cheeks·

She twisted, thrashing her head aside, stretching for her sword, but there was no room. The stallion's neck and Halcon's flailing blade, pinned her. She struggled, but Francisco improved his grip, hooking his thumb, acrid and stinking of tobacco, into her jaw as grimly as if he'd hooked a fish.

Charity bit until her jaw muscles shuddered with strain. Nicolas's legs clasped her hips, all the help he could offer, but Francisco's relentless pull reeled her away.

A sword hilt fell ringing on tile, and she prayed Halcon was still armed.

Swallowing a gush of blood—hers or Francisco's, she couldn't tell—she sent a last inarticulate plea for him to be human. His eyes showed stubbornness and then surprise. His thumb jerked once and his groaning breath muffled Nicolas's shout.

Freed, Charity spat and wiped her mouth with both hands. Trying to regain her seat on the plunging horse, she pushed against Nicolas's boot, giving herself momentum to rise partway. But his straining torso twisted alongside hers, and finally she saw him clear: face contorted in vengeance, teeth bared, and eyes narrowed. His arm arched in a black crescent ending in Francisco's back.

Black, blue, red all shivered in the torches' hellish glow. Nicolas's hand locked around his boot knife. He jammed, and wedged it, leaning low with an enraged final roar as dark

377

blood spewed over his skin and sleeve where the blade buried deep in Francisco Lopez's back.

Santana's stage directions shattered into shrill orders.

"Take him! Take him!"

Charity turned rigid. Her head swung like an animal's from his blood-smeared knuckles to her shaking pale fingers. Revulsion gave her strength to shove the body away from them both. Nicolas's knife sucked free, and he pulled the black into a dizzying rear.

Gunpowder flashed, flaring gold on Nicolas' face. Smeared with blood or smoke, his head arched back in silhouette. He shouted something, raging wide-mouthed at the stars, and both arms, knife hand and free hand, raised high to the night sky, exulting in barbaric victory.

Mother of God.

An arm wrapped wet around her waist and then the stallion plunged toward the gate. The yard swarmed with horses, some carrying long-muscled, naked riders, who hung by handfuls of mane under the animals' necks. Lances glittered, and short knives, and one red-scarfed man aimed a musket.

There'd been a plan beyond her own. Of course. *Of course.* Weakness and error and death. Charity fought the bile in her throat at the horror of a dying man's flesh in her mouth.

She retched and choked, then lay limp except for fingers wound in the stallion's mane.


Salt marsh mud sucked at the horse's hooves. It echoed the pluck of a knife tugging free of flesh. But the horse wasn't plunging in terror. He trod slowly, lifting his knees.

"Will they catch us?"

"No one comes this way. It's suicide."

Devilish sly, sweet and joking, Halcon's voice banished horror. Charity worked her fingers free of wiry mane threads and pushed herself erect.

Halcon's thighs closed against hers and the stallion sidestepped at the strange signal.

"Shh, boy," Halcon comforted.

His hips shifted, sending the horse up a sheer dirt face before his heels ordered it to run.

The stallion's strides reached, rocked, and still the hard leather-clad legs held hers. Balanced between the stallion's neck and the man's chest, Charity leaned to meet the wet veil of fog, and let her fingers curve against his thigh.

He wouldn't notice, with the running horse, the pain in his shoulder, the fog and pursuers, but she wanted him to.

When her breast felt his fingers, she remembered the blood griming them, but moved forward against his hand. Her stirring made the stallion falter, and though Halcon's regathered his reins as a horseman should, he first snaked his arm around her waist and tugged her hard, against him.

"Won't they find your sword? You dropped it—" she shouted into the wind, thinking they should turn back.

"No one knows the weapon." His lips were at her ear, so close, she heard him well. They might have chatted in a drawing room, except that he'd killed a man, maybe many, to come to her.

"It's indistinguishable from a hundred others."

It would be. Halcon would have it so, in case. Buzzing like a vast swarm of bees droned just beyond awareness. Dark buzzing of what had happened. They kept it off by refusing to hear.

The tar-sharp scent of creosote bush invaded her nostrils. Had she dozed? When had his arm risen to wrap her ribs, instead of her waist? Why did Nicolas's right shoulder, instead of pillowing her head, slump downward?

"Ho."

The stallion halted.

"Can you slide down?"

Charity slipped from the horse's bare back and leaned, eyes closed, against the stone wall. The bit clipped the stallion's teeth and Halcon slapped the black flank. Hooves retreated. The bridle fell to earth with a slither of leather and he was with her.

Nicolas's arms thrust under hers, crossing over her shoulder blades to pull her full against him. For a heartbeat, his lips brushed gently, and then he invaded. Charity scrabbled for thought beneath kisses hard as the rock behind her.

When he released her, letting them breathe, her lips stung, torn from Francisco's grip. When Nicolas's mouth brushed hers, she jerked, wincing.

"Inside," he murmured. "Go, now."

Wedging between overlapping rocks, she crept into his refuge.

"Hurry."

"I'm—" Charity's voice rasped in her throat. "I'm afraid I'll fall."

"And so you would, if—" his voice broke. "You've been here before?"

Charity swallowed and kept shuffling her feet forward. She'd choose walking into a snake pit over confession.

"I should have expected it, I suppose," he sounded sober, but not angry.

Charity reached back, hoping to touch his face, and found it. The smooth curve of his temple, sharp shelf of cheekbone—this wasn't the face of the vengeful warrior. She breathed smoke and gunpowder from their shirts, but beyond there hid green herbs and leather, and she knew no stranger had pinned her against the stones outside. Nicolas. He kissed the finger that traced his mustache, then pressed her forward with a hand against her buttocks.

*It's going to happen. This time he won't stop and neither will I. Here, there will be no interruptions. Here, he'll forget our "duties." He won't stop.*

"Stop," Nicolas ordered, snatching her wrist. "Reach one foot in front."

"This is where it falls away," she gasped, and would have turned toward him if there'd been room.

"Si, but there against the side, feel it?" he asked.

"Footholds? That's incredible, I—"

"Stepping off into space is quicker," he mused, descending behind her. "But the floor provides a hard landing."

She reached around in darkness, until Nicolas ignited a

candle, dripped a blob of wax on a tin-lined niche and settled the candle upright.

*Now? Would he start now? How would he do it?*

Charity sighed, closed her eyes, and heard him light another candle. When she opened her eyes, he studied her face so intently, she stepped back.

"Sit down," he ordered, then added, "Please, I need to do something for your poor mouth."

Charity's hand flew up. She'd felt the stinging, when he'd stopped kissing her, but the flesh burned at her fingers' touch. Involuntarily, her tongue sought the inside of the ravaged lip.

"It will have to be the bed or the floor, Charlie. I have no place else to accommodate you."

Her eyelashes pricked back in shock. The bed—?

Nicolas' black-scarfed head bowed and his back flexed as he opened a jar of water and gathered cloths. He glanced over his shoulder at her stillness, then his brows arched up.

"*Cristo,* Charlie! I meant you'd have to sit—" he motioned at the bed. "For me to tend your injury."

Could a blush burn worse than torn flesh? Charity thought it could. She sank to the low willow bed and felt sick with shame. Only a trollop would think he meant to "accomodate" her carnally. And yet he'd known, right away, what she'd thought.

He knelt between her trousered knees, candle aloft in one hand while the other dabbed her lips with a folded white bandage. Her knees trembled with the effort of not touching him.

"Nicolas."

His name came in three clumsy syllables and she couldn't look away from his face. He hadn't removed his mask or scarf as he washed her bloodied lip.

Charity's arm felt weighted as she raised it. His scarf slipped loose with the barest brush, but she felt too weak to untie his mask. Her hands fell to her lap.

Carefully, he folded the bandage in half, then in quarters, then cast it away like trash. He jerked the mask's knot and when it resisted, tugged it off, baring his face in one swoop.

381

"Nicolas," she said again, but this time her hands surrounded his face.

He grabbed her hand away from his face and buried his lips in the center of it, then raised only his eyes, questioning so intently she feared his magic would drag her through the pupils of his eyes.

His lips moved to her wrist, and Charity's free hand curved over his hair, thick and curled with dampness. His mouth traveled past the cuff of her shirt, tracing the veins on her forearm and still his eyes held hers.

"Whatever you're asking—yes," she answered and Nicolas pressed her back, taking them to the bed, side by side.

The candle burned behind him, letting his face recede in darkness. He jerked her blouse free of the leather waistband, but then his fingers slowed, dusting the curve of her waist. Harsh or soft? Charity wondered how it would be, and he sensed her bewilderment.

Nicolas kissed the corner of her lips and made a promise. "I'll be so gentle with you."

"I love you," she told him, pressing her lips back, past the stinging, until she trembled with an insistent heat.

With a groan both frustrated and amused, he forced the kiss back, and Charity dizzied to that feeling of falling away. This time she might have stepped off a cliff over ocean. Nicolas possessed her from mouth to core, and though he caused her drowning, she had only him to cling to.

His mouth trapped her head against the bed and his hand loosened buttons, first hers, next his, then he kissed her and swore, and fumbled her shirt apart until it opened to her waist.

"Charlie, I'm—you're—" he took a deep breath, and his eyes roved her breasts, instead of her face. "I can't even decide which of us to undress first."

She meant to reach the lacings on her own trousers, but her shaking hand grazed the front of him, and before she made sense of the pressure swelling the leather pants, he rolled from the bed and stripped them off.

Beside her again, his hands slid everywhere. And everywhere he touched, she felt hot. Her pulse struck at her temples as Nicolas tried to ease her leather leggings free.

"Raise your hips," he said, one knee on each side of her legs and she thought she would faint with the heat.

The heat wasn't embarrassment, she'd realized. But when she raised her hips and his hands trailed from her waist to her thighs, sliding the breeches down, she turned her head. *That* was embarrassment. She closed her eyes against his rapt inspection, swallowing ragged breaths that sounded like panting.

"Charlie, look at me."

She opened her eyes and embarrassment fled.

"Charlie, I love you." Nicolas said the words insistently, eyes focused as if to brand his words upon her.

Brazen, but helpless against the impulse, she pressed her hips up to touch him. Before she cowered at her boldness, Nicolas's lowered eyelids and abrupt stiffening told her he wasn't thinking her brazen. He wasn't thinking.

He dragged her blouse off her shoulders and pushed it aside. His hands roved her from neck to breasts to waist and hips, and his knee abruptly separated her legs.

Charity's thighs shuddered and she drew her legs together, trying to roll away. Couldn't she think, for just a minute? He covered her mouth with his, kissing and breathing hard, and working his legs gently between hers.

"*Caridad,* it's all right."

His hand shook as he swept the hair from her face. He stayed still for a moment, only his chest heaving against hers, and the fanning heat returned, consuming and burning until her world narrowed to the hot patches where their flesh touched.

She twined around him, repeating his name until she no longer understood what it even meant.

"Nicolas, Nicolas, Nicolas."

She writhed, trying to push closer, past the boundaries of their skin. Even against the tightness and shock of his entry, she couldn't be still, and when she became aware that he seemed poised, waiting inside her, Charity's voice quavered.

"Don't stop, Nicolas, please—"

She opened her eyes to see him above her, shoulders blocking the candlelight, but gilded with it. His arms braced him apart, except where they joined. His muscled arms shook as he spoke.

"No, *querida*, it's too late for that. I won't stop."

And then his mouth fell, his body covered hers and his hands slid under to cup her hips. His thrusting increased until she arched higher to meet him, and higher still.

She opened her eyes to the cavern, to Nicolas, and she knew this sudden, dark mating could have happened nowhere else.

"I love you, Charlie, God help me, but I do," his voice wove hoarse, between desperate kisses, and then he shuddered closer yet, one last time.

He stopped, but was not still. His lips kissed the side of her neck and his arms crushed her to him, until she barely breathed.

"Charlie," he whispered, his fingers reaching down to weave between hers.

His tenderness, so opposite to the violent joining, made tears sting her eyes, and Charity told herself, that for the love of Nicolas Carillo, she'd give up anything else in the world.


"When did you know you loved me?" Charity asked the words against his neck, adjusting her body against his so that he pulsed inside of her, even though he was spent.

Spent. Weak. Nicolas had never felt so drained But she'd trapped him, legs wrapped around his, refusing to let him pull away. He had no desire to try. His body lay taut above her, and he couldn't stop his hands from roving—shoulders, arms, thighs—any more than he could keep from smiling at Charlie's self-satisfied sighs.

And now she'd made him confess he'd loved her, even when she was a boy.

"Once when we were fencing—" his voice curled around her.

"Here?"

"No, at Harvard, I'm afraid. There was a late afternoon, almost dinnertime, and you tried so hard, even though you didn't have the faintest idea what to do—" Nicolas gave a short laugh. "It's hard to explain. I dismissed it as admiration—the feeling, toward a *boy*, was distressing—but, I think, for me, it started there."

"And I loved you there, too, Nicolas," she ran her hands over his face. "For your stories of California. Of course—"

Charlie's hands circled around him, her fingers trailed the bumps of his spine. He suppressed a shiver which made him move within her.

"—I knew *you* were a man."

He kissed her, and the half-burned candle shed light enough to see her wide eyes.

"When did you want me for more than my stories?" He hid his embarrassment by lifting a section of her hair, high as his arm would reach, then watching it drift, as he slowly released each finger, in silky skeins back down to them.

"When you kissed my hand at the gates, that first night," Charity whispered. "And watching you ride. Nicolas, you are a wonderful rider."

He rolled them to their sides, letting his hands touch her breasts, as he revelled in Charlie. She remembered every sweet encounter. And she'd called him a wonderful rider.

On the back of a horse, perhaps. But he'd made an awful showing, with her.

Demons from the fight, from the blackness and blood and winning, had held him in thrall. And he hadn't taken her to blot out the horror. Nothing so noble. No, he'd done well enough until he felt Charlie's maidenhead, and then he'd claimed her. Like a savage. He'd hardly kept from bellowing she was his, *his!* Instead he'd branded her with his body.

Now, Charlie blushed, but kept talking as he cupped his hand around her breast and let his thumb tease her nipple. He hadn't taken a minute for that. He'd plowed ahead like a rutting animal, instead of coaxing her into readiness. He'd do it.

Then Charlie sighed as if she might sleep, and he rolled away, separating them, thinking he could wait, knowing he'd never felt so protective.

"How did you know—" he blurted the words, then shut them off, unsure Halcon belonged in this bed, between them.

"I don't remember," she said, wriggling up the bed to his eye level. "I'll think about it." She pulled herself to sit cross-legged, next to him.

Nicolas stroked his hand from her knee, along the inside of her thigh. When his hand slowed, reaching the center of her, Charlie's knees snapped together and she ducked her head. He didn't take his hand away, and she didn't make him. She leaned her forehead against his.

"Tell me when you decided to be Halcon."

"No," he whispered, thrilling his fingers until she caught her breath and pressed her forehead harder to his.

"Why not?"

"Later, Charlie." He ignored the shadow darkening his mind. He knew a sure way to banish that shadow, the legion of shadows clamoring at the boundaries of his mind. "Come here, *querida.*"

He pulled her atop him, smiling when Charlie propped her elbows on his shoulders and let her legs fall athwart his thighs.

"But isn't it difficult," she insisted, "to be two people, such different people?"

"Harder than anything," he admitted. How long had he wanted to tell someone? Five years? "So hard I gave Halcon permission to want you, to touch you, and Nicolas permission to talk with you. It made no sense," he admitted. "I was stupid to think—"

"Never!" Charlie sat up astride him, and although she crossed her arms over her breast, she clearly cared more for argument than modesty.

"In any case, my identity was bound to be revealed, to you, once I did that. Do you know, I had even decided Halcon might 'scare you away' by ravishing you?"

What an ass he'd been to consider it.

Charlie muttered something, face turned up to the cave roof.

*"Que?"*

She pressed her lips together, refusing to repeat her words.

"What, Charlie? Have you a comment to make about that splendid proposal?"

She cut her eyes up at him, looking through a tangle of hair, teasing and half shocked at her own daring.

"I said, 'I would like to see you try.' To scare me away by—" her hand twirled in the air.

Nicolas rolled her to her back before she thought of an appropriate completion. He kissed her neck, between her breasts and nuzzled her belly until she giggled.

God, he felt good. He felt young and strong just playing with her. He'd known their joining would be good, had known it the instant he'd seen her face down at the river in that pink calico dress—but this relief, this fun, was almost better than the lovemaking. Almost.

Even boneless with exhaustion, he couldn't stop his hands from seeking and smoothing her skin. When Charlie apologized, confessing an overwhelming thirst, he reached for the water jug, slow as if a spell had been shattered. Even then, he tilted the vessel for her, his thumb touching her face, and when she had finished, he sat next to her, shoulder to shoulder, thigh to thigh, until Charlie wiped her mouth with the back of her hand and faced him.

Her eyes narrowed. Twice she started to speak and broke off. She stared up at the ceiling, bit her lip and sighed.

"Yes, Charlie?"

"I—" she took a breath, expelled it, then lay back down, arranging her length against him as she stared over his shoulder, into the cave's darkness.

"Say it, *querida*," he whispered, lips grazing her ear.

With all anger shoved aside for this ultimate embrace, with so many questions left unasked, Nicolas thought his whispered encouragement might be the bravest words he'd ever uttered.

"Are you sure—"

He waited. *Dios*, there were a hundred heart-stopping ways that sentence could end.

"—that we did it right?"

Charlie burrowed beneath the serape before he could answer.

*Are you sure that we did it right.*

So. Nicolas stayed on his side, letting the hand that supported his head, massage his temples. From an experienced witch like Esperanza, the query would be criticism. From Charlie—

Hell. She might have asked much worse. He felt a lecture, just like the one by the river, gathering. Only this time he might demonstrate. Science had come to a sad pass, indeed, when a girl so innocent passed herself off as a biologist.

Nicolas scooted beneath the serape. She refused to face him, so he pressed against the curve of her bottom. Instinctively, she returned the pressure, then flinched away.

"Like this, you mean?" He netted her with his arms and legs.

"Nicolas!" she squealed.

"Your struggles only make things worse, little one."

She stopped, nipping the fingers that curled from behind to touch her swollen lower lip. Francisco had done a nasty night's work—cold, dead Francisco—and paid dearly for it. *Diablo*, the knife. Had he discarded it? Or did the weapon lie about the cave, somewhere, blade rusty with blood?

"I only thought," Charlie's voice rustled faint as the blanket brushing her skin, "that animals—"

"Si, animals," he encouraged, crawling to cover her. "Don't duck away from me, Sen—" he broke off to bite her neck.

Señorita? Señora? What was the proper form of address for the recently virginal wife of one's friend?

"Nicolas, I love you," her words echoed with surprise as she writhed against him, skin suddenly hot, fiery as before.

Did Charlie even guess how easily she wiped the world away?

"I love you, Charlie. Shh, lie still a moment. It might hurt, again, a bit."

"I don't care," Charlie said it quietly, at first. "I don't care!"

*Dios,* her voice rang off the walls and he laughed.

"Tell me, *querida,* if we were not doing it right, would you feel this way? Do you think it's an accident that we fit like this? That, poised above, I can kiss you, so?"

Nicolas wrapped his hand in her hair and she arched her neck backward, straining for his lips before he lowered them.

"What do you think, that it is sheer luck this arrangement allows me to touch you, so?" He savored her gasp. "I think we have it right, my love. We're one this way. One, Charlie."

"Forever," she said, fingernails scrabbling up and down his spine, "I'll love you like this everyday, forever."

He eased even further inside her and pretended his groan greeted the rise and fall of her hips.

Forever. If only it could be so.

# Chapter Twenty-Seven

Ash gray light filtered between his eyelashes. Nicolas judged the color fitting. Today he'd face the ruin of all he'd ever valued.

A man murdered. A virgin deflowered. A religion flouted. A friendship shattered. And those were only the most serious of his sins. He might also consider what would become of Charlie since he'd made her both an adulteress and keeper of his confessions. Ah yes, and what of his family's honor? All in all, a splendid victory for the devil. Santana had slavered for such a fall.

Nicolas massaged his aching shoulder, then drew back his ankle, trying to disentangle his legs from Charlie's. She made a faint mewing, protesting the waft of cold air, and wound closer, head burrowing beneath his chin.

During the night, her hair had swept back over her shoulders and twisted like a rope. Her face, neck, breasts lay bare to his gaze. Freckles, like pale beach sand, sprinkled her cheeks. If it had been the dawn following their wedding night—as it should have been when they woke so entwined—he would have kissed each freckle.

His hand trembled toward her and then he cursed and balled his fingers in a fist.

It was not such a morning. He had no right to seek more goldust freckles beneath the cover, no right to wake and rouse her. After five years of playing the intellectual hero, he'd fol-

owed his beastly instincts and attacked. Halcon's pure patri-
tism ran red with blood.

Charlie's breath stirred his chest hair and Nicolas felt thick
onging pull him toward her rather than away.

Some smug Spaniard had written that honor was prefera-
le to any love. De Vega? If so, the man had never lain be-
ide a girl warm and willing as Charlie. Nicolas ordered his
yes away from the dusky peach serape draping the rise of
er hip.

De Vega's veracity aside, Nicolas Carillo had sacrificed a
ood portion of his life on honor's altar. Only a weakling
vould allow one disastrous night to seduce him from his
ause.

Beneath the onslaught of action, his mind had clamored. In
his still dawn, last night's questions must be answered.

Wind gusted outside. He pictured wind-bent trees bowing
t the cave's entrance. He imagined wind whirling sand, spit-
ing against rock. Halcon focused on Nature, conjuring the
uestions to come again.

If he'd gone unrecognized . . . if Nicolas Carillo remained
ree . . . if Nighthawk continued harassing Santana, would
Californios support him? Could they revere a hero with
loodied hands? Could the church's sheltering wing shade a
urderer?

If he hadn't killed *wrathfully* . . . Nicolas rubbed his chin . . .
asn't that the condition Alvarado had set years ago?

His eyes dropped from the rock wall to the faint violet
ruise which tinged Charlie's chin, then flowed out of sight
own her throat. Francisco's sausage-fat fingers might have
renched Charlie's fragile jaw from her face.

Nicolas wheedled his conscience. Hadn't he only defended
he defenseless? No. Even his own mind scoffed at the lie.

Fury, not duty, had made him jerk the knife from his boot.
*If you'd only wanted to stop him, you might have pounded the knife
utt on his skull or slashed his forearm. But you didn't.*

Enraged by Francisco's trespass, he hadn't weighed the mo-
ality of killing. He'd gone hot, seared by a firestorm of fury.
*'How dare he harm what's mine!"* his blood had roared, and the

391

knife fell, not ripping and warning, but homing between shoulder blade and spine, hungering for the violator's heart.

The same raging power had goaded him all night. The *hidalgo* so controlled he lived two men's lives had died with the knife's descent. Nor had the mist that danced before his eyes like a million agitated red particles receded once he'd killed. It had brushed past murder and clamored with lust. And he'd fallen on Charlie.

He'd branded her his, forever. She might lay with a dozen men—a hundred!—but not even death would change the fact: he had been first.

Nicolas pressed a hand over his lips at the primal demand that bulled aside patriotism, honor and a Harvard education. *Jesus Cristo.*

And though he'd marked her forever, she was not his. Charlie wore a gold band that titled her "wife." She'd worn his ring first, but now Freddy's circled her finger. It caught the cave's milky light, twinkling it back at him.

Would Freddy understand? Trusting, gregarious Freddy? Nicolas's mind mocked him. "It's like this, amigo," he'd begin.

Curse them all! And yet, he prayed Freddy wasn't fool enough to force a duel. *I'll not have more blood,* Nicolas vowed, *not a friend's blood washing away an enemy's.*

Charlie purred deep in her throat. She reached her arms to him before opening her eyes.

Contrition counted for nothing if he compounded his sins. He refused to profane a second day. Nicolas swung his legs off the bed, turning his back on her. His splayed fingers gripped his thighs and he resurrected the trick adolescent boys used to banish unwanted arousal.

Think of something else, Carillo. Think, if you're not so degraded that thought is impossible.

*Honor is preferable to any love.* De Vega.

But Charlie had come to him so sweetly. Even when he'd pierced her maidenhead. There'd been a faint cry, sucked in breath and then she'd lunged toward him, not away, gasping his name and words he'd never imagined.

392

*The man without honor is dead.* Cervantes.

Si, and what would his days be without Charlie? Dull, leaden, endless.

*An ounce of honor is worth a pound of pearls.* Cervantes, again. Stuffy hypocrite.

Candlelight on Charlie's arms had touched her skin with opalescence surpassing the finest gems of La Paz. And those arms reached, yearning for him, now.

Nicolas set his jaws against a groan so huge he thought it would burst his chest. Charlie wiggled her fingers, beckoning him close, a half smile on her lips, though her eyes remained closed.

*Ay Cristo,* even the condemned were entitled to a last embrace.


A dull headache pounded behind her eyes. Her tongue explored the inside of a torn, swollen mouth. Charity's muscles stretched stiff as jerky and every inch of flesh ached with bruises.

But a sigh brushed her cheek, and Nicolas came into her arms. His warm, hard chest met hers, and he filled his hands with her hair.

"I love you," she said, turning lithely, as if twenty years' clumsiness had fallen away overnight.

She felt slim and beautiful, even graceful, returning a kiss that neither explored, nor demanded. She had absorbed the night's lessons deep as her heart, into her bones. This morning, she knew. Nicolas's kiss said he loved her.

Yet his eyes looked somber, turned down at the corners, like the ends of his mustache.

"Must we leave?"

He nodded and she cradled her head on the muscle linking his neck and shoulder. The taut ridge proved what he'd said last night. Their love and joining was no accident. Their bodies had been designed to fit.

"What will Santana have done since we escaped?"

"Scoured the countryside with soldiers, after the Indians left," he suggested, chest heaving a sigh.

Charlie saw it again: a moonless night lit by flaring torches, horses plunging everywhere. How much had Santana seen? Too much, she realized, tamping down a heart snatching hope where it didn't exist. Santana had asked her a direct question.

"What think you now?" he'd gloried in the deaths of his own men because his hate for Halcon was vindicated.

Charity squeezed her eyes shut, but opened them in time to meet Nicolas's, as he continued.

"Then, he might have sacked Los Cielos, looking for me—"

"For me," Nicolas had said. For Halcon. Charlie frowned. Didn't Nicolas know Santana had recognized *her*. Last night, Santana had given no sign he recognized Halcon, but he'd addressed her practically by name. Charity swallowed. Santana held her a criminal, but Nicolas didn't know.

"And what do you think he intends?" she asked.

"Execution, I should think. Hanging, probably. After all—" Nicolas's shoulder shrugged beneath her head— "Guerro's lost his Indio prisoner. He'll want some reparation."

"Won't there be a trial?"

Hanging. A dance of death, Santana had called it, but would she have a chance to defend herself, first, before a jury of level-headed hidalgos?

"A trial of sorts." Nicolas traced his finger behind her ear, then trailed it down the hollow, to her throat. "Not as you know trials. And I can't imagine it will count for anything."

"Nicolas, of course it will, the people—"

"—will be disillusioned with the bloody villain Halcon's become!" Nicolas bit off each word.

"No, no," Charlie corrected. She sat up and jogged his shoulder. "You were rescuing a female martyr, a girl alone against many soldiers. *That's* what your people will see."

"I wish I had your confidence in them." Nicolas said. "You don't understand the complacency of people who need only horses and fiestas to make them happy. As long as Mexico exerts control only on paper, what do they care?"

"Don't you see? That puts them with us." Charity assured him. "They'll love this rescue, and truly, I don't think Santana recognized you as Halcon," she paused as her mind churned.

Think. Analyze. Plan. She must escape whatever punishment Santana wielded. Yesterday, she'd flaunted herself like a scarf under a bull's nose, risking her life to save Carmen's. Today, she had too much to lose. Nicolas' love outshone the cold grave of a martyr.

"And if Halcon remains quiet for a time," Charlie said slowly. "The new alcalde will have come."

Nicolas was so still, she thought he considered the wisdom of her words. And then a thought flashed, brightening her mind like lightning.

"The new alcalde can annul my marriage to Freddy!" Charity sang, flinging her arms around his smooth shoulders.

When he remained motionless, she stroked fingertips across his brow, smoothing the wave of black hair that made him look like a melancholy pirate.

"I still think you should have your ear pierced. You look too serious, for such a daring blackguard," Charity kissed his ear lobe. "One day I'll convince you to wear a gold ring in it."

Convince him. She knew how she would do it.

Blushing so harshly her cheeks stung, she lowered her gaze to the hair veering from his chest to a dark trail below his waist. Wincing at her boldness, she found herself unable to stop fingertips that followed the raw summons.

"Bloody hell, Charlie!"

He hadn't sworn in English, for weeks. He jerked away as if she'd slapped him, but didn't leave the bed. She folded her hands together as Nicolas fixed her with pleading brown eyes.

"Do you know what I think," she chattered, refusing to consider the plea's meaning. "Last night, after you were asleep, I was thinking that Freddy and I might not be legally married at all," she swallowed, trusting that logic, not blind hope, had planted the thought. "I am a Catholic and Freddy isn't. Doesn't one have to be Catholic to be married in New Spain? Nicolas?"

"Heartsick" was the only name she could put to his expression. Nicolas wet his lips as if he would speak. Instead, he shook his head.

"Well, that's what I think," she insisted. "And I plan to consult Father Alvarado at first opportunity." She paused when he shook his head in a quick jerk.

"It only requires Freddy's statement that our marriage was not—" she faltered. What perverse modesty made her unable to name the act she'd already performed? "That we didn't—"

"Unconsummated. Your marriage was unconsummated," Nicolas supplied. "But Charlie, *querida*, no man would admit he'd slept with his wife and never enjoyed her."

"Freddy will!" She kissed the dubious twist from his lips. "Nicolas, I love you. I'll make Freddy tell the truth."

A knot of desperation weighed in her stomach. Oh God, he was silent. Nicolas had said he loved her. *He'd sworn it.* Over and over as they came together.

But if Nicolas loved her, why were his eyes full of pity and his mouth tight and grim?

"Even if we can't marry, we'll be together. I'll be Nighthawk's woman. That's what Salvador called me, you know—"

Wrong. Wrong. Wrong. Mention of Salvador must rekindle the fiery images for which he still blamed her.

Nicolas stood without touching her.

"Nicolas?" She swallowed the beseeching tone. He'd done nothing to cause such pounding panic.

He yanked on trousers, winding his sash tightly, smoothly.

Morbid fancy and nothing more sounded this alarm to fling her arms around him and pull him back to the bed before he moved beyond the boundaries of his promise.

*And just what, Charity me girl, what has your fine proper Nicolas promised? Marriage?*

No.

*And Halcon, did he vow to have you as his mate?*

396

No.

Someone else, some confluence of the two, a specter, had whispered hoarsely of love. And even he had offered no promise.

"Nicolas." She tried to catch his glance as he tightened the drawstring on his boot. "Please tell me what's changed. Last night—" she broke off, using widespread hands for emotions she couldn't describe.

"Last night I wasn't myself," he snapped, standing to face her.

"Then who were you?" she demanded, angered beyond endurance that her voice trembled when it should have cut.

"A murderer. A man you forced to kill."

"But I—" she croaked. "I was on the other side of the world when you decided to become Halcon."

Every word was steeped in truth, but it didn't matter. She and her truth sat alone in the cave. Nicolas Carillo departed in a soft chiming of spurs, and all that remained of Halcon was the cast-off mask crumpled on the floor.

Riding in front of him on the chestnut, she passed an hour—trying not to let her back graze his chest, struggling not to turn and let his unshaven cheek grate on her skin—before she saw them. Squinting against blowing sand, Charity noticed dust cones whirling beyond the gray rock and quaking brush. Riders.

"What will they do?"

"Just let me talk this time, Charity. Can you do that?"

She nodded. Nicolas halted his horse, letting the soldiers come to him. If he required nothing but silence, she could stay quiet. She'd sunk so deep in a morass of hate and love, dreams and fear, she hadn't composed a logical thought since sunrise.

Santana's palomino didn't lead the column, but they were clearly his men, dogged riders who knew their mission. Halting, they formed a strict line before Nicolas's chestnut.

She coughed from the dust and blinked so hard against the

grit and wind-whipped tears that the tightening of Nicolas's arm seemed, at first, a mere twisting of her clothes.

Then she felt it for an embrace, and wondered what it signaled. Should she tense, ready for a fight? Her heart beat faster, half believing she'd won him amid the whirling horses and gunpowder, half fearing she'd lost him there. Perhaps the squeeze was farewell. Could he believe the soldiers would snatch Nicolas Carillo? Santana's friend, an *hidalgo* gentleman—

With a dirt-smeared traitor on his saddle and no explanation for his whereabouts after midnight.

Charity straightened her spine and lifted her chin. If she were ruined anyway, she'd confess a bit of truth to Santana's henchmen. She'd say she was Nicolas Carillo's mistress.

A hot blush covered her face at the thought. Could she brag, bold as a brass spitoon, that they'd been together all night? Yes. Defiantly, Charity met the eyes of the lead rider.

"Señora Charity O'Dell y Larkin," the soldier intoned, so impressed with the gravity of his mission that her name ended an inaccurate mishmash. "I arrest you in the name of the Emperor Itrurbide of Mexico, by authority of Lieutenant Guerro Santana designated Alcalde of El Pueblo, Nuestra Señora de Los Cielos Azules, for the murder of Sergeant Francisco Lopez."

Horses shifted and stamped. Harness clanked, sand wailed on the wind and a soldier rubbed a liquid-sounding nose.

The corporal spoke no word of Halcon, no word of Nicolas.

They didn't know. *They didn't know!*

Charity's heart flew up. She turned to smile at Nicolas' astonishment.

"Pardon me, Corporal—" Nicolas began.

"No," she hissed, giving his arm a vicious pinch. Fate had handed him a chance and she would see he took it.

"—there must be some mistake."

"Quiet," she said between her teeth. Damnation, couldn't the man recognize salvation when it sat before him?

"No mistake, Señor, I assure you," the corporal said.

Nicolas had knotted a blue scarf under his hat. It ran aslant his brow and made him look younger. His eyes shifted quizzically, then widened with understanding.

She could buy him time. Oh Madonna, let him see that at least! He could set her adrift, a decoy for Santana to paw and nose, while Nighthawk rallied the *renegados*.

Surprise vanished from his face and Nicolas's eyelids sagged with boredom.

"I will convey her to the presidio, then."

"That will be unnecessary, Don Nicolas. This time," the soldier waved for a riderless bay to be led from the rear of the column, "we *expected* to find her 'wandering the plain, thrown from her horse.' " He delivered this last in sing-song falsetto, as if a simple-minded female would use the same ruse twice.

Throttle it, Charity ordered herself. Throttle the impulse to lunge for the corporal's leather chin strap and wind it until he turns red-faced and helpless.

All the litheness she thought she'd acquired overnight ended in a clumsy attempt to mount. Charity thought her boot toe balanced in the tapaderoed stirrup, but it skidded, jammed through the opening and trapped her ankle. Like a wounded stork, she flapped for balance, before collapsing on her backside.

The corporal silenced the jeering soldiers with a curt command, but when Nicolas offered to loop his scarf over the saddle horn as a sling for her feet, the corporal refused.

Forgetting all but their sniggering, Charity flung a leg over the saddle and mounted with a thump, astride.

The corporal uttered no order against the jeers and whistles that forced tears of humiliation to prick her eyes. She focused on the hooves of Nicolas's chestnut, unable to look at him.

Leather creaked as his hand grasped the hilt of his sheathed sword. Then she looked, head snapping up in fear.

No, she screamed with her eyes. Let them mock her. Leave them to their coarse fantasies and they'll forget the trollop didn't ride alone.

Nicolas seemed to expand in anger. His shoulders grew

wider, his chest broader and his eyes menaced. Then, he drew an audible breath, expelled it and withdrew his hand from hilt to reins.

"Ah, thank you, Corporal. You save me a great deal of trouble." Nicolas' gracious voice rang with relief. "I'll leave her *Yanqui* husband to unravel this story of—" Nicolas rolled his eyes and chuckled. "You did say 'murder'? Hard to believe."

Charity sawed her teeth against her lips. The soldiers weren't convinced. Fighting men, they hadn't missed Nicolas' instinctive move toward his sword.

"As you will, Don Nicolas. I believe the lieutenant is at your rancho, even now."

The column turned about face and Charity rode the bay's hammering trot only a few steps before kicking it into a canter. Her escort fit their horses snugly around hers.

Charity looked over her shoulder, forearm screening her eyes from the hair that whipped loose from her plait and watched Nicolas lope away without a backward glance.


*Dios* help them all if he'd started a child in her. Nicolas pressed a hand to his shoulder and moaned aloud. *Diablo*, it hurt! A babe bred of Charlie, if it inherited even a smattering of her foolhardiness, wouldn't survive childhood.

He rode home, unable to banish her image.

"Quiet," she snarled, then cantered off astride a strange horse. She'd ridden with passable flare, too, looking every bit the *hija del pais*, with her black braid snapping behind her.

As soon he entered the courtyard, Nicolas's senses focused. He dropped the chestnut's reins by the fountain and listened. No *metate* rubbed corn against stone for tortilla flour. No girls squatted, sorting beans for *frijoles*. No children sported with yard dogs. One speckled hen scratched her way toward him, then skittered and cackled into the roses.

Nicolas lived here, but it was Nighthawk who approached the *cocina*, stealth coursing through his legs. Seen, it would appear he only sauntered toward home, but Nicolas stalked the

400

soldiers who slouched in the doorway as surely as if he carried a gun.

"*Ay chica,* with such pretty ankles, you belong in Don Carlos' bedchamber, not his kitchen," taunted a voice.

Patting sounds told him the maidservant continued to flatten maize dough between her palms.

"Perhaps the lieutenant could offer for her," suggested a second voice.

A spate of laughter was interrupted by the padding approach of bare feet.

"Maria has a *novio,* you know?" asked a voice he knew for gap-toothed Angelica's. "His special skill is cutting a steer's throat without letting it bleed on his boots—"

Now two sets of hands patted tortillas, as Angelica baited Santana's soldiers.

"Tell me, hombres," she continued, "is it true you were hoodwinked by a girl, last night? A shopkeeper from Los Cielos—he who delivers onions—said Halcon has enlisted a girl to fight soldiers, while he trains his blade on worthier prey."

"Is that true?" asked Maria, of the pretty ankles.

"Si, the 'alcalde' attempts to interrogate Doña Anna, now, but she's having none of it," replied Anjelica.

"Watch your tongue, old sow," snapped one of the soldiers.

He'd heard enough. Nicolas stepped onto the porch and strode toward the sala.

"Mother," Nicolas began, stepping through the whitewashed arch. Deliberately, he breathed the scents of oranges and candle wax, centering himself, as if for swordplay. "Ah, Guerro!"

Santana returned Nicolas's handshake in place of an *abrazo.* The lieutenant's hat lay discarded and his golden mane, always dressed sleekly back, scattered in a fringe over one eyebrow. Beneath his left eye, skin jerked in nervous exhaustion.

"Something's wrong." Nicolas filled his voice with concern as he gripped the Spaniard's forearm.

"Indeed."

Santana didn't avoid the touch. Rather, he leaned into it.

"The execution—? It did not go as planned?" Nicolas asked, half turning to include his mother in the question.

Head bowed above the emerald collar of her gown, Doña Anna drew a strand of embroidery floss to the length of her arm. He couldn't be sure, but it seemed she raised one eyebrow.

"No, and it is about this fiasco I must question your *Yanqui* house guests, Nico. About the prisoner's abduction and a murder."

"Murder?" Nicolas let his hand fall from Santana's arm. "Surely not."

"Unlikely as it seems—"

Santana broke off at the peevish shifting of Pilar, Barbara's duenna, who sat in a corner with mending in her lap. Her finger tapped her lip as if she shushed the alcalde.

"That's what it was all about then," Nicolas mused. "I rode out to find Señora Larkin—her gray was missing—and your men swooped down and arrested her."

*"Bueno."* Santana sighed. "I'll explain, but I would not bore these ladies with repetition." He sketched a bow. "Perhaps you will walk to the corral and offer your advice?"

Santana had rearranged the facts to suit his purposes. Señora Larkin, mad *Yanqui* bitch, had freed the prisoner and stabbed Sergeant Lopez. She'd ridden alone, Santana claimed, but surely her accomplice was Halcon.

Nicolas's brow creased in puzzlement, "How could she have ridden into the presidio unnoticed?"

"It was a trap, Carillo. Ill-advised, but you were sick with the fever," Santana shrugged and lit a cigarito. "I had only peasants on which to sound my idea—"

"And the prisoner? You said she escaped?"

Santana struck his forehead with the heel of his hand and Nicolas noticed a chocolate-red smear on the alcalde's cuff.

"I told her how to do it! I practically *told* her!"

"Not the Indio, surely—"

"The *Yanqui* bitch, Carillo. Christ, don't bait a desperate man!" Santana's lip rose in a self-deprecating smile. "What an

402

ass I was to trust her, but—a silly foreign girl? *Dios!* Who would have thought she'd realize where I'd hidden a key!"

Santana's hands rose in a skyward appeal, but he fell silent when he saw his soldiers, ahead. He ordered them to ride on.

"Tell me what I can do Guerro," Nicolas offered, stroking Paloma's nose as Santana swung into the silver-mounted saddle.

"Help me wait. That's all. I don't believe Freddy Larkin knows, but his wife's Halcon's whore. No protests, amigo." Santana's hand swept the air as if flicking away flies. "Think. Think of the hours she spent 'studying wild animals.' What wilder beast than Halcon, eh? The bastard's nearly ruined my command, but he must have *cojones* like a bull to dare what he does." Santana thrust his hand before him in a fierce weighing gesture that revealed the gruesome hair bracelet.

Nicolas pushed back Santana's lewd assessments and considered the dot of spittle in the corner of Santana's mouth.

"And these tales of a new alcalde," Nicolas spoke with measured carelessness. "I trust they're only rumors?"

"Your trust is once more misplaced. A letter from the Emperor's secretary—on crested parchment set with his seal—has verified it. The new alcalde comes to replace me and I'm recalled to Mexico City pending a new assignment." Santana spat.

"No matter. Before he gets here, I will have Halcon."

Santana fixed his eyes on the horizon, fingers sawing the hair bracelet back and forth against his mortified flesh.

"The whore is irresistible bait. I'll keep her a little hungry, perhaps threaten to turn her over to my men—that should bring Nighthawk on the wing, eh?"

Nicolas forced his own chuckle to join Santana's, blocking the image of Charlie's face, in the disbelieving moment he'd breached her maidenhead, flashing through his mind. Biological studies hadn't prepared her for such invasion, and only his voice had drawn that expression of trust back to her face.

God would be good if he granted the death of Santana.

"Come to the trial, amigo," Santana urged. "You'll find it amusing."

When Santana had spurred from the courtyard, a whimper and scuffle made Nicolas turn. The yard dogs, first a yellow cur with one blue eye, then the spotted female and Charlie's wolf whelp, dragged themselves from beneath the porch. They shook off dust, yapped after the palomino, then trotted up to nose him.

"Beasts." Nicolas shoved them aside and turned toward the *sala*. Dogs at least used honest means of inquiry. His mother's cocked eyebrow promised trouble he was too weary to face.

Doña Anna sat as before, head bowed over a blue velvet jacket she worked with gold thread. Pilar had departed.

"Mother," he drew a lung-filling breath to begin. "I would speak to you about Charity."

Doña Anna draped the jacket over her green satin lap. She folded one hand over the other.

"Well Nicolas, you've proven you'll kill for her." Anna raised mild eyes from contemplation of her rings. "Will you die for her, as well?"

# Chapter Twenty-Eight

*Sunlight gliding on water, smooth as a drape of saffron satin on a table-top, pooled around Nicolas. Above a bare torso, his face stared, brown eyes resigned. Mirror still and encircling, the lake's golden clasp made him cease at the waist, vanishing beneath the water line. Slow as sea flowers, other men emerged behind him and beside him, fluid flowing past cheeks, down necks and shoulders, in amber sheets.*

*Warm light glinted on* cold, cold water.

Not water. Dirt and damp adobe. Charity shook off the dream, and sat up. She kept her eyes closed against waking, pulling her knees to her chin, chaffing palms up and down shins still encased in Arturo's trousers. Her tea-dyed blouse had been designed for overheated parlors, not nights in an earth-floored jail.

Just what did Santana hope to gain by withholding food and water, denying her so much as a serape for warmth?

Charity's tongue wet her lips. The tramp of passing boots drew her eyes to the high barred window. She rubbed finger-combed wisps of hair back toward her braid and remembered her last meal—chicken baked with red and green peppers, rice with golden bits of garlic and onion—taken at the hacienda before she'd ridden to free Carmen from this very cell.

Starvation wouldn't break her, yet why did Santana use such a weapon when he'd made no demands of her? No one had come near since she'd been locked up. Yesterday, every hoofbeat had made her heart lurch with hope Nicolas had returned, but he hadn't.

Not Nicolas, not Freddy, not Arturo and certainly not the sainted Halcon had arrived to bargain for her release. Neither Santana, nor his henchmen, attempted to extract a confession of murder or collusion, and that worried her.

She licked her lips again and let her head fall back against the cell wall. Amber light filtered through her eyelids, resurrecting the placid lake of her dream. It took no gypsy to puzzle out the meaning of Nicolas rising godlike amid golden serenity, invisible from the waist down. He'd been California's savior, infallible and incorruptible—until she'd tempted him.

"Blast and be damned—" she broke off, shocked at the crone's croak rasping from her throat.

"Señora?" the voice that queried behind her came from a soldier with lank black bangs and the rosy cheeks of a farm boy. Arm stretched between the bars, he proffered a battered tin cup.

"Thank you! *Gracias!* Oh, don't go. My legs have just fallen asleep. *Un momento, por favor.* Don't go, please." Charity lurched across the cell and grabbed the cup, cursing the eagerness that made her slop precious drops onto the floor.

She gulped half the water before she noticed he still stood watching.

"You don't have breakfast for me, do you?" she asked, then shook her head at her stupidity. *"Yo tengo mucho hambre—"* she began, but the soldier shrugged and departed.

Her biologist's brain judged it dim-witted to think a cup of water revitalized her, but Charity felt a surge of energy, as if the moisture coursed from throat to chest, out her limbs and shot warmth and intelligence through her mind.

She drank off the remaining inch of water and sent the cup ringing off the cell wall, just to see if it roused the curiosity of the farm-boy soldier. When no one ventured near, she paced.

Where, in this bounteous land of year round fruit, was the warming morning sun?

Why, in a land of such protective men, hadn't one of them come to her rescue?

How, locked in this bone-chilling cell, three strides in

ength and one and a half in width, could she construct a plan o counter Santana's, when he refused communication?

Was she to face a courtroom trial? Would she be fined or executed? If executed, would she face the hollow black muzzles of a firing squad or strangle in the hangman's noose? Would Nicolas's last sight of Charity O'Dell be a blood-spattered bundle or a rag doll dancing obscene antics at rope's end?

Charity stopped in mid-stride and buried her face in her hands, fighting tears that clogged her throat and darted her eyes. She didn't believe she'd die. But if she had to—God, what maudlin thoughts!—if she had to die, there were questions she must first ask Nicolas.

What is your beach like in winter? Silver and violet, instead of gold with green waves? How did you train a wild stallion to come at your call? With a master's discipline or pockets full of sugar lumps? Who will you be ten years from now? Brittle Nicolas Carillo, bitter with your people's blindness, or fool-hardy Halcon, handsome even in a daring death which would be told over and over in stories and song?

And yes, Nicolas, did it matter that I came to you a virgin? That I refused my husband because his hands seemed silly compared to a mere glance from you? And how did it feel to you, that joining that should go on forever, but ended in one night? And why, why, *why* are you casting me away forever when you said you loved me?

A sigh wrenched her chest as she remembered. *Three times.* First, they'd come together with the desperate grappling of long-deferred desire. Next, he'd laughed, smiled and used his body to taunt her innocence. But the last time, toward dawn, had been different. Instead of the rapid overlap of feelings, each sensation exploding past the last, like waves pounding close together, that time his coaxing had drawn her along in his wake.

His hands and lips promised even more than the thunderous power of joining. His touch had been sure, rather than wild. Nicolas's heavy-lidded patience and his pursuit of each

407

tender spot on her body had twisted tension anew, tempting her toward a delicate feeling, piercing as a shard of glass.

Enough! She slapped her palm against the adobe wall. Her cold-stiffened fingers felt as if they'd crack the flesh down to each skeletal member. She shook her hand and gasped at the pain.

She felt down her little finger and winced. It would serve her right if she'd fractured it. Sensible girls didn't snap the stems off wine glasses and slam their hands into walls.

What use was this love-lorn wallowing. She should stoke up her anger. She should scorn Nicolas for the mysteries his hands had promised but not delivered.

She nodded with grim satisfaction. Since she'd come to California, it had been the same. He'd lead her somewhere and then slam a door in her face.

Come fence with me, Charlie, he'd offer, but don't get too close. *Oh yes, he'd tricked her many times with that one.*

Marry with my good friend, but I'll hate you if you want him. *You injured us all with that, Nicolas.*

Flirt with the seducer Halcon, but keep a corner of your heart for cold Nicolas Carillo. *Would you ruin my brain as well as my heart, you cur!*

Leave on the next ship for Boston, but let me kiss you senseless, first. *Torturer!*

Let me declare my love, take all you have to give, but gird yourself for my scorn in the morning. *Swine! Despoiler! Liar!*

Charity stood in the center of the cell. Even if she lived, there'd be too many questions barricading a sweet future.

Spurs and silver conchos rung overhead and boots descended the stairs from Santana's quarters, just as she heard a flurry of hooves and Freddy's unmistakable bluster.

"Think again, soldier," Freddy's accented Spanish blundered. "I won't be put off. Lieutenant Santana told me to return this morning. I'm riding in—with your permission or over the top of you," his voice shambled into a confusion of two languages, then broke.

"Carillo!" Freddy's tone cracked with bitterness. "A man would think you'd have the decency to hide your perfect *hi-*

*dalgo* face. Or do you have better access to Charlie than her husband?"

Charity took three running steps across the cell and jumped for the barred window. She ignored the lancing pain in her hand and pulled herself up until her chin rested on the window sill.

Although she saw only his back, Nicolas's black-clad movements took on the fluid grace of Halcon. He stalked Freddy as he slipped off his still moving mount. But then Nicolas's black coat stiffened and his tone stung like a well-wielded whiplash, like the voice of Nicolas Carillo.

"Might we discuss this beyond earshot of common soldiers?"

Nicolas reached for Freddy's arm, but her cousin cursed and recoiled. Charity forced her trembling hands to hold her a moment more. Though she couldn't hear, she saw Freddy's wild gestures and saw his head snap like a barking dog's. Nicolas stood tall, coolly absorbing Freddy's fury.

Charity's fingers weakened as Nicolas broke his pose, cocked his head to one side and turned his face to gaze away. Freddy's lifted hands could have been a gesture of appeal or accusation.

Charity lowered to the length of her arms before falling. She huddled in the corner, blew warming breath on her small finger and tried not to imagine what they had said to each other.

Freddy stood outside the bars. He formed her name with a mix of relief and disappointment. She smelled lavender wafting from the folds of the yellow gown and felt the polished wooden handle of Barbara's hair brush as Freddy shoved both through the bars.

Yet she floated. Did hunger render her so dizzy and distant, as if she watched Freddy down the wrong end of her spyglass?

"You're all right?" he demanded. "They haven't hurt you?"

She watched herself nod.

"Barbara and Doña Anna are staying in the town house until your trial and they thought you'd need the dress and brush," Freddy shrugged. "I can stand watch while you change. Hell, they've granted you no privacy. How can you even—"

She saw him shudder at the smelly earthen pot in the corner.

Did he subside into silence then, or did she float off, before he erupted?

"Jesus, Charlie, is he worth it?" Freddy demanded. "When did it happen? Before I got back? Before that mockery of a wedding night? Open your eyes, damn it! Look at *me.*"

Charity clung to the cold bars. She shook her head.

"When, then? When we quarreled and I left for San Diego? And where?" his voice lowered to a growl. "In my bed?" Freddy grabbed her wrist through the bars or she might have sunk to her knees.

"I've always been a good sport, haven't I? Companion to a girl who'd dare anything for a taste of adventure?" He perused her tight trousers. "Santana won't prosecute for being *Don* Nicolas's mistress, so he says you're the paramour of a bandit. I'm sick to death of being a good sport, Charlie. Adultery is where I draw the line. You and my 'friend' Nicolas—!"

Charity craved water more than forgiveness. Her tongue touched the jagged flakes of skin on her lips.

"Nicolas didn't betray you," she started.

"Oh Charlie," Freddy's voice brimmed with disbelief, "Did you two agree on this story to save the blessed Carillo honor? It's a sham, Charlie. Whatever you're trying to foist off on me! A sham."

Freddy gave a short laugh.

"Do you want to hear the richest part, Charlie?"

It was the wrong place to nod, but her head wobbled on its stalk of neck, beyond her control.

"I finally had what I wanted, in the Sierra—I might have gone and forgotten all this—but Santana swears since he's locked you up for adultery, he can banish me for 'consorting' with you." Freddy yelled so loudly, Charity stumbled back.

An annoying hum droned in her ears and Charity blinked against the frenzied black dots obscuring her vision.

"Keep Nicolas away from me, Charlie. I want to kill him." Freddy huffed a self-deprecating laugh. "And we all know I can't do it in a fair fight!"

The humming rose to an ear-splitting pitch and Charity slumped toward the floor.


Apparently someone unlocked her cell, because she was choking, water dribbling from her nose and mouth, tears spurting from her eyes as she coughed. Freddy squatted next to her.

"You don't love me," she wheezed when she could talk. "Not like a husband loves his wife."

"That isn't the point, Charlie," he defended. "God, don't start choking, again."

Freddy's arm tightened around her shoulders as he glared at the soldier staring from the cell door.

"Here now," he snapped. "Could you grant us some privacy? Does she look like she's poised for escape? What's this purple bruise splayed over her jaw? And when did you feed her last?"

Probably the soldier backed away, because a warm quiet settled after her paroxysm of coughing. Outside, some military repair called for a chain to flow clanking through a metal loop and a mallet to tap wood. Freddy patted her shoulder, then drew back his hand and reached inside his coat.

"Oh, I nearly forgot. I brought you these," Freddy held out her gold-framed spectacles.

Charity set the spectacles on her face, but they seemed too big. She twisted the sidepieces closer to her ears.

"I killed Francisco," she lied, tilting her head to keep the glasses on her nose.

"Oh leave off, Charlie," Freddy moaned. "You're such a bad liar!"

"Nicolas didn't betray you," she added. "And if he had— would he deserve to die for it?"

411

Freddy's sigh rocked them both.

"You know I wouldn't kill him. But these damned Califor nios don't have a monopoly on honor, you know?"

"I know. And I think Nicolas is going to do something un bearably noble and stupid to make up . . ." Charity trailed off, afraid she had said too much.

"What? Drink this, Charlie, you're drifting again. No come on. Sit up. Prop your back against the wall, here."

"I had this dream . . ."

"You're not making sense. How about if you stand up and get dressed while your watch dog is gone?"

Freddy eased Charity to her feet. She swayed a moment then peeled off Arturo's leather trousers, aware Freddy gulped as she did. She tugged on the gown and stared back at him

Charity squeezed her swelling finger to see if pain helped her focus.

"Damnation! Ow!" Intelligence washed in and out, sharp then blurry. "Freddy, I want you to do something for me."

"What, little cousin? Slash my throat"—Freddy flashed a false, jolly smile—"So you and Nicolas can be together?"

His mockery focused her better than the pain.

"Nothing so dramatic." she answered slowly.

"I don't understand you, honey. We're talking about risking your life for—excitement." Freddy fussed with her braid, try ing to make her presentable. "In Boston, they'd lock you up."

Charity placed her hands on his shoulders, standing so close their noses touched.

"But, tell me what you want." Freddy uttered a long-suffering sigh, "I'll do whatever harebrained thing you ask."


Charity slept in a patch of sunlight. Freddy had pulled off her boots, and she'd dozed so soundly, she hadn't noticed when he came back in to cover her with his fringed saddle blanket.

The farm-boy soldier gripped her beneath each arm and hauled her, from deepest slumber, upright to face Santana. Charity's head swam and she gagged against rolling nausea.

412

"We'll see if Halcon takes the bait more readily when it's displayed in the plaza," Santana said.

Was he addressing her?

Charity compared the Spaniard's pristine blue and red uniform, shimmering epaulets and sleek blond hair with her own crumpled gown and snarled braid.

"Raise a crowd at the plaza ... shouldn't be difficult with the marketing ... herd them close to the church ..."

Santana issued orders over his shoulder while Charity picked horsehair off the calico.

" ... out of respect to the Carillos ... In fact, keep the rabble away from their townhouse, entirely."

Santana faced her then, his face registering distaste.

"What's it to be, Alcalde?" Charity tried to wring insolence from her thick tongue. "The pillory? A whipping?"

Santana's ice-blue eyes held the annoyed look he might flash a child tugging his coat hem, before he glanced away.

"I want the priest on the church steps, because this punishment is for a crime against the church—"

"Like murder, Alcalde? Like butchering and burning Indios for defiance?"

"—the military court deals with her civil crimes, tomorrow." He nodded dismissal to the soldier supporting her.

"I expect no trouble leading her to the plaza," Santana said, lifting her chin with one white-gloved hand and smiling when she didn't pull away. "Hungry, she's quite tractable, but that bitter tongue will apparently be the last to submit."

Charity's mind projected an image of old horses, dozing in the sun, as her chin settled into his hand. She strained to calculate the number of hours since she'd eaten. Three days? If only he'd given her more water. Four? Not such a long time.

How much had murder and lovemaking, interrupted sleep and half-formed plans, contributed to her humiliating weakness?

"You mention murder, Señora Larkin." Santana's voice lulled her, and his thumb stroked her bruised jaw. "It is an interesting charge, the one you'll face tomorrow in court."

Charity tried to raise her eyelids and failed. She imagined steam rising from a hot bath.

"You know I didn't kill Francisco. You were standing on your balcony and you saw," she insisted.

"Ah, Señora, but it was dark, *no?*"

On the black canvas inside her eyelids, she saw the orange-gold flaring of torches and shook her head in denial.

"You could make this easier, Señora," Santana urged, and Charity thought she heard again that undercurrent of decency.

"I think you must have been a nice man, once, Guerro." She sighed.

The sudden stillness of his stroking thumb made her eyes snap open. His blue stare flicked back and forth over her face, grudgingly kind.

"Just tell me how to make this simpler."

"By telling me who Halcon really is," he insisted.

"You've never even asked," she sputtered. "You charge me with murder and adultery, try to starve the truth out of me, and you never asked a single question."

"You'll tell?"

"If I had some food, I would certainly discuss it," she offered, then choked and recommended coughing.

Santana patted her back, distraught at the violence of her struggle for breath.

"No discussion, Señora," he warned, "no confession. Just a name. You'll get your meal in exchange for it." Santana shouted, "Private, bring a bit of food, *a bit,* for the prisoner."

No spoon accompanied the bowl, so Charity crouched in a corner, grabbed the accompanying tortilla and scooped beans into her mouth while Santana dismissed the private.

Her cheeks bulged and she hadn't swallowed when Santana snatched the bowl.

"And now, Señora, that name."

One arched brow conveyed his doubt. Swallowing, Charity, wondered just what she owed him for his moment of largesse.

"I did agree to discuss it," she admitted.

"The name."

"I can tell you he is no Indio," Charity began, but before she uttered another word, Santana dropped the bowl and his gloved backhand struck her, almost casually, across the face.

"Twice, you have tricked me, Señora." Santana locked his hands behind his back. "Twice, I believed your innocent face over my suspicious mind and twice, I was wrong. You see, how a 'nice' man grows stern?

"Private," Santana called, frowning at his soiled glove, "Conduct the Señora to the church."


They forced Charity to kneel on the stone church steps while a Mexican woman sheared off her hair.

At first, seeing the throng of people circling the plaza, she'd feared a beating. Barbara had told of public whippings inflicted on lawbreakers who were first stripped to their waists. But the intoning of the priest behind her made it clear there would be no whipping.

Charity licked the blood oozing from the corner of her mouth. It seemed impolite to bleed in public.

Heedless fingers unraveled her braid, jerking each snarl they encountered. Charity tried to ignore the jostling crowd, especially the buxom girl in red, who reminded her of Esperanza. Instead, she concentrated on the priest's words, which seemed to list Biblical punishments for adulteresses.

The step beneath her knees was cold and rough. A sidelong glance revealed shears that must have been forged for hacking wool from sheep. Huge sheep. The blades were the length of her arm from elbow to fingertips; the woman wielded them unsurely.

She grabbed a hank of Charity's hair, stretched it to its length and chopped. Charity opened her eyes and saw the black clump fall on the steps like some dead rodent. The woman yanked another handful, this time from Charity's crown, and clipped, slipping and grumbling as the shears gouged scalp.

Charity crossed her arms over her breast, closed her eye and bowed her head to pray.

When a pair of soldiers urged her to stand, she tried to re capture the detached trance she'd floated in while talkin with Freddy. She couldn't. How unfair that a mouthful o beans could rekindle feelings of fear and shame.

They herded her around the plaza and she tried to clos her ears to the voices speculating on her crime.

"They say she lay with Halcon."

"No, I heard it was with the *renegados*."

"Wrong, wrong, the *renegados and* Halcon."

She stumbled and wished Santana had given her time t put on the slippers Freddy had brought.

She nearly cried out when she saw Doña Anna and Bar bara, identical with white, drawn faces, crossing themselve and kissing silver rosaries.

She ducked her head. If the private hadn't held her arm she would have crossed them over her face. Still, her eye roved for Nicolas. She prayed he wasn't there. It would be su icide for him to intercede.

She recognized a face from her wedding fiesta and graspe for the name Arturo had told her meant "shark." Tiburon.

Joaquin Tiburon divided his attention, glancing now at he now scanning the plaza. A strong supporter of Halcon Arturo had declared, and a warm friend of Nicolas, grow cold over politics.

Suddenly a man in ragged gray stepped before her an spat.

*"Puta!"* He snarled, "Whore!"

She recoiled so hard she tripped, but a warm arm encircle her waist, and a black shawl, like a descending wing, covere her head and shoulders.

"Ah, Charity, I should have taken you away!" Arturo' clean mahogany hair bowed beside her as he arranged th black rebozo.

"Señor, I will thank you to remove your hands." Arturo snarled at the private.

"How does a nice girl from Boston get into such—No! N

416

crying. Keep your eyes down, and push your spectacles back up, but deny those pigs the satisfaction of humbling you."

The man who'd called her whore lurched into her path again, but before he screeched the words twisting his lips, Joaquin Tiburon grabbed him by the shirtfront and punched him.

"Bravo!" Arturo muttered. He sheltered her under his arm and tried to shoulder a path through the crowd, but Charity knew there was no escape, even before Santana's shout.

"Get away from the prisoner! Private, get that man away from the prisoner!"

Beyond the press of people, Charity glimpsed a head-tossing chestnut horse and black-coated rider.

"Oh God, Arturo, it's Nicolas! No, please."

She burrowed into him, trying to hide and knowing it was impossible.

"Just—let me go," she pushed at Arturo, but he didn't release her. "I'll keep walking and—" she looked up at him, then, making sure he understood over the tumult of voices. "Do what I told Freddy—Talk to him, and you do the same, please?"

"Listen, *pequena*, I'll be outside the jail, as close as they'll let me, tonight—"

"Promise me you'll talk to Freddy!"

The apple-cheeked private tugged her elbow. Thank God they'd circled back to the church steps.

"You scream if anything goes wrong. Charity—"

She gulped several times, painful sounds she couldn't stop, but she didn't cry.

"I will, Arturo. *Vaya con Dios.*"

## Chapter Twenty-Nine

Nicolas stood before the most splendid looking glass in Los Cielos. A stranger would be hard pressed to determine whether he'd dressed for his wedding or his funeral.

Nicolas Carillo often wore black velvet, but gold-threaded quilting lapped both shoulders of his jacket, and the conchos which ran from hip to knees, had been replaced by gold coins.

Tonight, when he confessed to Santana, he would cut a fine figure. Tomorrow, Santana would surely have him hanged.

Nicolas tightened the straps securing engraved silver spurs to his boots. His lips slanted in grim expectation that they would ring with final insolence as he hit the end of a rope.

He sighed and retrieved the hat which matched his trousers. Smaller gold coins dangled from the brim, glittering as he turned it. It would better suit a young dandy like Arturo. He left it behind, sure his brother would know it was meant for him.

Outside, he called for his chestnut and spurred toward the Presidio.

Nicolas had clung to the hope of rescuing Charlie until he'd seen her dragged away, shorn like a nun and ashamed. Now martyrdom appeared Halcon's best choice, if he could take Santana with him.

Two riders patrolled the perimeter of the presidio. Nicolas

drew rein and watched. Before they noticed him, he recognized Arturo's Tigre, and loped nearer.

"Halt—"

The windless night let him recognize the voice of Joaquin Tiburon. What in the name of St. Joseph were they playing at?

"Nicolas?" Arturo clearly hadn't recognized his brother until he was within four horse lengths.

His senses were ill-suited to replace Halcon.

"Si, Arturo, it is I."

"You won't approve," Arturo said, glancing at Tiburon. "But I hope your friendship with Charity means you won't reveal us."

"Of course," Nicolas agreed, but not before he marked Tiburon's short bark of derision.

"I promised Charlie I'd be nearby in case anything went wrong. She's only to call out—"

"And where is her husband?"

Curse Freddy Larkin!

"Freddy says he had washed his hands of her," Arturo explained. "He'll be present for her trial, but after that—"

Desertion. One could have a marriage annulled, especially an unconsummated marriage, if one partner washed his hands of the other. A priest would have to accept Charlie's assertion that union had never taken place. Still, it was possible.

"We'll also warn Halcon, if he rides to rescue her," Tiburon's voice dared his former friend to criticize.

"Halcon?" Nicolas sneered, "Murderer of slow, fat sergeants? Do Californios follow a 'patriot' with blood on his hands?"

"You didn't see the Señora in the plaza, did you, Carillo?" Tiburon's voice vibrated with fury. "Her lovely black hair all hacked off, her face bleeding from Santana's brutality—? I tell you, Nicolas, the people saw, and they know why Halcon fought to keep her from the soldiers."

Nicolas hoped darkness hid his smile.

"And if Halcon slips past you——" Nicolas said. "What if he surrenders to free the girl? What if he's hanged?"

Nicolas waited. Tigre feinted an ill-tempered kick at Tiburon's mount before Tiburon answered with a low chuckle.

"The citizens of California won't allow Halcon's death."

*Dios,* Tiburon might be the one.

"Si, and next you'll say they have the power of resurrection?" Nicolas mocked.

"If that's what it takes, Carillo."

Nicolas told himself it was poor timing that sent him back to his town house rather than up Santana's stairs. He told himself he'd make a stronger statement if he confessed during the trial.

In fact, he couldn't explain why he unsaddled his horse and brushed its coat free of dust.

His confession would free Charlie and there seemed to be an heir apparent for Nighthawk. What else could he want?

All morning, Charity sat in the stuffy room Santana called a court, listening to testimony from devoted Mexican soldiers. In some cases, their stories were so obviously scripted, they glanced at Santana for embellishments. Charity drained by nightmares which lasted until dawn, watched Nicolas.

A handsomer man never lived. Resplendent in black and gold, he seemed, for the first time, a perfect blend of Halcon and Nicolas Carillo. The rich clothing and reserved demeanor belonged to Nicolas, but that raised corner of his mustache, the amusement, surpressed by frequent glances down at his glittering spurs, those belonged to Halcon.

Plucking her short hair to curve against her cheeks, she willed him to look at her. Nicolas refused, but Freddy didn't. Seated behind Nicolas, he shifted, red-faced, waiting to play the part she'd assigned him.

Well, his blue eyes seemed to ask, *when?*

She shrugged and almost missed Santana's question.

"Señora Larkin, you stand accused of murder, treachery and traitorous acts committed in the guise of the outlaw Halcon." Santana's words sifted silence over the rustling courtroom.

"And yet," his merciful voice couldn't overcome the harsh set of his lips. "And yet, Señora, the court knows many of Halcon's misdeeds occurred before your arrival in California. And many attacks demanded violent skills no woman possesses."

She should have let the slur pass.

"I remind you, Alcalde," her voice piped, "I fought as a member of the Harvard fencing club."

Charity thought she glimpsed Nicolas clutch his temples with one hand. But when she looked, she saw no gesture of despair.

"Still, Señora, a court seeks motivation. These crimes were committed in the name of misguided patriotism and you are an American by birth and marriage."

When the rancheros' eyes shifted from Santana's face to hers, they struck like a slap.

"I admit it is strange." Charity raised her shoulders in a shrug. "But I've led a quiet life, Alcalde, except when I pretended to be someone else."

Before Santana's gavel silenced her, she pressed on.

"You'll recall I told you I mimicked a boy to gain admittance to college?" She paused as all eyes watched Santana jerk a nod. "Well, I thought it would be exciting to pretend to be Halcon. I never intended for anyone to be hurt."

There. She'd humiliated herself before the entire court. She hoped the silver disks of glass covered the shame in her eyes. And the irony of it all, she bit the inside of her cheek at the realization, the irony was—most of it was true.

Two dozen male voices rose as one, jeering a magistrate who'd continue such a trial. Charity sighed, relieved it hadn't been necessary for Freddy to implement her simpleminded plan.

Santana sat frozen in glacial fury.

Charity kept her eyes on her fingers, wound together in her

lap. Although she'd gambled that Santana wouldn't execute a woman, she saw his fingers flex, and knew he'd glory in the feel of her collapsing throat.

One rap of his gavel demanded silence. When order reigned again, Nicolas stood alone in the center of the courtroom.

"Alcalde."

Charity shivered.

Nicolas addressed Santana with chilling formality. No feet scuffed, no mouth opened in a soundless yawn. To a man, the court braced for what was to come.

"I confess to being the outlaw Halcon."

Eyes resigned and calm, chin raised high over black velvet and white linen, Nicolas' face radiated defiance. Charity couldn't look away from his beauty. Even though her plan meant his salvation, she felt regret. His sacrificial splendor was almost too fine to ruin.

Freddy heard his cue and stood. His shuffling boots were shocking in the wake of Nicolas' confession.

"Pardon, Alcalde." Freddy's Spanish sounded shakier than ever, "But my friend Nicolas only seeks to protect me. I ride as the patriot Halcon."

"Noooo . . ."

Charity thought only she was close enough to hear Santana's hiss as Arturo, too, emerged from the sea of men.

"Alcalde, *mi amigo* Señor Larkin and my dear brother, who everyone knows as a royalist," Arturo's voice lowered in condescension, "seek only to divert your suspicions from me—"

Santana rapped his gavel as Arturo's speech was interrupted by gloating Joaquin Tiburon, and Tiburon by Don Carlos. Soon the courtroom was filled with men claiming to be Halcon.

Charity knew she'd rescued herself and she'd rescued Nicolas. He wouldn't be executed for his confession. She'd also rescued the mythical freedom fighter, Nighthawk.

Herself, Nicolas and Nighthawk. It should have been enough.

But if it had been, she would have felt joyful and Nicolas

wouldn't have fixed her with the pained eyes of a man who had been robbed.


The blue silk gown hanging in Charity's wardrobe was her farewell gift from Doña Anna. When it became clear Santana would not rescind Charity's banishment, Nicolas's mother had presented the gift in place of a fiesta. After her public shearing and trial, it seemed best to leave quietly.

Freddy awaited her in Los Cielos, but Charity had returned to the rancho, with the excuse she needed to gather her notes and books. Truly, she'd hoped for a chance to be with Nicolas.

The hollow courtroom victory had convinced her that the time for childish pretending was over. She'd folded away her glasses, and decided she would act like, speak like, *be* the unconventional female she was. It meant openly pursuing biology. It meant telling Freddy she'd not tolerate a sham marriage. It meant confessing she loved Nicolas so much she wanted him any way he would have her. She would be his wife, his slave, his mistress—in secret or brazen display.

Nicolas had given her no chance. For three days he'd claimed the demands of sick cattle, of drought, of reviewing trade records before the new alcalde's arrival. She waited through the endless summer twilights, but he never returned until midnight.

Tonight, she would not be put off. Tonight he must accept her surrender.

Trunks packed and strapped closed, she memorized her last dusk at Aguas Dulces. Her fingers pleated, then smoothed the loose skirt of her linen gown. She smoothed down her short hair, washed with lavender water. She stared at her bedroom wall, patterned in shifting blue by the morning glory vines around her window.

Hooves, and then she heard Nicolas's exhausted horse blowing in the courtyard.

She stood silently, listening as the animal pawed eager for its dinner. Nicolas's spurs chimed each stride to the cocina.

His low voice thanked Angelica for warming a bowl of stew but urged her to take it, since he'd eaten with the vaqueros.

Nicolas's boot heels crossed the plank porch, then struck the sala's adobe tiles. Brandy gurgled from its decanter. She heard his quick intake of breath after he swallowed. More brandy splattered into the glass.

Last night, candlelight had bobbed beneath her door as Nicolas passed, but tonight he'd returned before dark. Instead of a candle, he swung the brandy bottle by its neck.

An uncharacteristic swagger marked Nicolas's approach. Princessa pounced from the shadows to greet him and he stepped over her. His unshaven, hollow-eyed visage contradicted his walk. As he drew near, Charity thought him a haggard replica of the man she loved.

When she blocked his path in the hall, Nicolas regarded her as if she were a ghost. Not, she thought, as if she frightened him, as if she were insubstantial and unworthy of notice.

"Nicolas, I leave in the morning. We must talk."

He started toward his bedroom, then turned and his eyes assessed her, outlining the contours of her breasts and belly as coldly as if he examined a cow.

"Are you pregnant?" he asked.

"I—no. I'm not. I'm certain."

"Then we have nothing to discuss."

He turned away and left her watching his silhouette fade down the corridor. She closed her eyes to listen. As soon as her ears told where Nicolas had gone, she'd follow.

In the courtyard, Arturo's guitar mimicked Toro's.

From Doña Anna's sewing room, a cup clinked against its saucer and Barbara's voice suggested a gown might fit snugger.

Outside, a salt breeze creaked the knotted rope hanger cradling a flower pot, and its swaying played background to Don Carlos' voice as he hailed the vaquero Pablo.

All the homely business of rancho life crept on as usual. Nothing set this summer dusk off from hundreds of other evenings, except that she'd never again enjoy such a night.

*There*. The air vibrated with the rattle of Nicolas pulling a word from the rack in his den.

Panting from the speed with which she sought him, Charity did not don fencing attire, did not find slippers. She ran barefoot, so quiet not even Princessa marked her passing.

In the den, Nicolas crouched *en guarde*, rotated his wrist, leveled the blade and, careful to avoid the crystal decanter on the floor, lunged. His sword struck the target and he lunged again. Settling back into the guarding crouch, he deepened the position, until his thigh muscles swelled beneath the twill of his trousers and strain painted his face with perspiration.

After several minutes, he rose, tucked the sword beneath his arm, and strode to the decanter. He shook back his loosened black hair and rolled his shoulders. Charity swallowed and her fingertips tingled with the desire to touch the shoulder blades showing dark against the sweat damp shirt. His loosely ruffled white cuff slid back as far as his elbow as he raised the bottle for a draught. He'd wiped his lips and started to drink a second time, before he noticed Charity pressed against the door frame.

"*Ay Cristo*, must you pursue me everywhere?"

"Not after tonight, Nicolas."

She might as well have kept silent for the pallid effect of her words. Nicolas didn't even shrug before he swallowed.

A sword. She could tie up her skirts. She'd done it before, and he'd never resist the lure of a duel. Charity darted past him, mind forming a hasty prayer that he wouldn't leave before she had the blade loose.

She needn't have worried. Nicolas tracked her movements and, when she stood before him, biting her lower lip to keep from trembling, he sighed.

Still clamping the sword beneath his arm, he stepped past her for the door, shrinking into himself as if to avoid an accidental brush of their clothing.

"You can't just leave, Nicolas!" Charity snatched his sleeve. "We can't part this way."

Nicolas looked down at the restraining hand, then quirked

425

an eyebrow at her insistence. Did she imagine interest flick
ered in his eyes, now that she couldn't think what to say?

"We have to—fix things," she told him.

Hope rallied as he leaned closer.

"Little girl," he whispered as the knuckles clutching th
bottle neck trailed along her cheekbone, "let me demon
strate—something that may help you understand. Watch
now," he cautioned.

He raised an index finger to catch her attention, the
rubbed the tip of it over her lips. Charity's breath shuddered
but the instinct telling her to kiss that hand was too slow.

Nicolas snatched his hand away, cocked the bottle high
showering brandy, and then flung it, crashing, to the floor
Sharp, faceted chunks of glass littered the polished planks.

Nicolas turned with hands widespread as if he'd performe
a magic trick.

"Some things, Charity, cannot be 'fixed.' Some things ca
be broken beyond repair."


No liquor seared hot enough to burn out his need for her
Gypsy ballads bemoaned this kind of love, passion so intens
every casual movement—pushing a ribbon through a hole i
had escaped, frowning as she deciphered a vaquero's collo
quial jest, inhaling the grassy breath of her favorite horse—
sparked lust. Linked with that fascination, and just a
passionate, was a darker truth: disappointment in the beloved
kindled rage.

No vaquero stirred. In the corral, only the horses lifted
dark-eyed heads, as if to question his panting breaths.

If Charlie were in his arms now would he wind her closer
loving her, shielding her, wanting her? Or would his hand
travel up her thin arms to close in a death grip on her throat

*Cristo,* the woman had driven him mad!

Nicolas snagged Charity's moon-colored gelding from th
corral. If he rode Luna, she'd have to stay behind. His chest
nut could only be roped, Don Carlos rode his bay an
Arturo's Tigre would eat her alive.

426

He swallowed the sour aftertaste of brandy and wished he ode Hamlet instead of this pliable beast. Hamlet tested his der at every turn. Only a man who wanted to end up walk-ig home let his mind wander when riding the black and God e was sick to death of thinking, sick with the rancor of the ame images circling round in dizzying circles. It would be a mple thing to ride toward Refugio and whistle him up, but ummer's long half-light lingered. It was too early and it was o soon.

Damned Charlie had hobbled him. He couldn't even ride ae horse he wanted, for fear of discovery. He hoped Santana id nothing to warrant Halcon's intervention, because every alifornio from Santa Barbara to San Diego gossiped of harlie's scandalous trial, boasted of Los Cielos's audacious aen, and every eye watched for the true Halcon to reveal imself.

Nicolas sent Luna shambling down the rocky path to the aore and sneered at his own understatement.

*"Hobbling" is a pretty way of putting it, Carillo. Pretty, but inaccu-te.*

Charlie's sly plan had unmanned him as surely as if she'd ashed his *cojones* with a knife. Oh, she'd thought herself so lever, hiding behind schoolboy's spectacles, admitting every-aing, until he'd seen confession was the only honorable path pen to him, after all.

Nicolas had lived through it all, before it happened, in the aoment he rose to speak. He'd imagined Santana's furious xpression of betrayal. He'd felt the iron manacles and jail ars. He'd seen Esperanza's outrage and Arturo's smoldering ride. He'd watched himself in Charlie's last bittersweet em-race, and clasped the strength of Freddy's forgiving hand-nake. He'd seen his own corpse, silver spurs singing as he as pelted with roses by mourners vowing vengeance.

Nicolas trotted Luna onto the white spit of sand between wo steep, grass-topped bluffs and watched waves foam round the gelding's hooves.

Si, in his mind he'd seen his fall and veneration as if view-ig a play, before Charity had turned his sacrifice to farce.

427

Nicolas had heard of men, rescued from firing squad
who'd so resigned themselves to death that their hear
spurned rescue, and stopped. In the same way, disbelief ha
dazed him, even when congratulatory back-pounding carrie
him out of court and into the streets, even when Father Juan
messenger brought a letter complimenting his artful humilia
tion of Santana and suggesting intercession with Rome on be
half of Señora Larkin.

*Señora Larkin.*

He'd won Charity O'Dell as completely as any mediev:
knight who'd had to slay a dragon for her. He'd won he
loyalty—as her friend Nicolas. He'd won her incisive mind—
with the patriotics of Halcon. And though he'd courted he
with Nicolas Carillo's badly disguised longing, with Halcon
taunting hands and lips he'd won Charlie's body and heart :
himself. Charlie had come open-eyed, to *him*.

Wooed and won and paid for in blood, and still he couldn
have her. She'd made him a barbarian, a monster. He'
killed and reveled in the climax of his bloodlust.

Nicolas stared at the chalky smudge of moon and felt h
throat swell with the need to bay—like one of Charlie
wolves. Bay and howl and mourn that she was leaving fo
ever, bearing the scars of love turned to hate.

His hand went to the hilt of the light fencing blade befor
he recognized the skittering sound as hooves descending th
path. The intruder rode an old horse with bad feet or an ar
imal out of control. *Ay Cristo,* it could only be Charlie.

How many times had he dreamed this, reliving that fir
night on the beach, with a strangely grown-up Charlie ridin
before him on Hamlet? The memory had kept him achin
and awake, through countless nights.

His hand remembered the bewildered flutter of Charlie
lips as he'd stifled her cry. His arms knew the boneless fragil
ity which turned to the desperation of a captive wild thing
His mind kept the picture of her at the rancho gates, kisse
hand held aloft, eyes following every galloping step c
Halcon's midnight stallion. She'd looked after him as if h
were the most perfect man in the world!

He could ride through this scene half asleep. If God were merciful, it would never end.

First he'd rein Hamlet behind a boulder, and wait in ambush until the cursed Francisco blundered past. The horse gathered himself, back feet churning, then exploded out to knock the heavy-footed army mount to its knees.

But it was pale Luna, not Hamlet, squalling outrage as Falcon's spurs struck. Luna who bolted. And the eyes that went wide were not Francisco's, but Charlie's.

Luna shied from Tigre's snaking head and bared teeth and, Nicolas saw Charlie sway and fall.

Christ. What kind of irresponsible sot let brandy think for him? What kind of madman rammed a galloping horse into an inexperienced rider?

Nicolas reined Luna around and watched for Charlie's prone form to rise. Tigre stood, reins trailing, nostrils distended as he inspected the beach. Charlie didn't move.

If she were acting out some Satan-spawned game—

If she thought to reel him in by playing as if her neck were broken—

Luna fought, jerking back and forth like a rocking horse, refusing to approach the dun.

*"Diablo,"* Nicolas snarled, sliding from Luna, stalking toward Charlie.

If Charlie's scrawny white neck weren't broken, he'd snap himself. Fear made him pant for air when her arms moved dark on the white sand, fluttering as aimlessly as a beached fish.

She gasped as he knelt beside her.

"Charlie?"

Her eyes opened and she gasped again.

"Can you breathe, *querida?* No, don't try to rise, just tell me, can you breathe?"

Charlie's knees drew up and she touched her ribcage with a griamce.

"Air—the fall knocked the air—"

He'd fallen to his knees beside her, groveling in the sand,

and she'd merely buffeted the breath from herself, like a boy playing tag with his amigos.

But her eyelids drooped closed again. Was the injury worse than she knew?

"Charlie, look at me," he directed.

Pain was not what shimmered from her eyes.

*No*, by the Madonna, he would not be trapped again. Since the morning after his trespass, he'd denied himself Charlie's smile, her approving eyes, even civil conversation. He refused to fall into the devil's snare now, in these last few hours.

Charlie laced her fingers behind his neck, pulling his head down. Waves of lavender floated up from Charlie's hair, short and glossy as a bird's wing.

God help him, for he couldn't help himself. Her body drew his lower, closer, until his lips nuzzled the black cap of hair and he closed his eyes and inhaled deeply as if he were the one who'd fallen.

God must have heard his plea, for Nicolas found he could straighten his arms to push himself away from Charlie's softness.

"Nicolas, please. What do I have to do?"

Her arms slipped under his, joining over his spine. Her legs twined closer, one insistently nudging his calf. His groin tightened as if it would burst and he knew this time he couldn't pretend disgust, because Charlie knew better. Her parted lips and slow, rolling movements reminded him: she understood seduction very well, because he'd taught her.

He shook free of her clutching arms, but it took his last flicker of logic to do it. When Charlie rose to grab him again, he surrendered, falling with her to the sand, pinning both her hands with his.

She'd jammed her sword through her gown's sash in imitation of him, and the two hilts rang together as he kissed her.

Charlie's hands swarmed up and down his back clutching, stroking, never still, and Nicolas trembled with a pent fury he couldn't articulate.

He wanted to tell her she was a fool to ride a dangerous animal like Tigre. Instead, he parted her lips and kissed her.

430

harder. He yearned to tell her how wondrous strange it was that after just one night, his body had missed hers so much, it seemed as if a chunk of his heart had been shorn away. Instead, his hands released hers and found the warm breasts beneath her dress.

Charlie's hands grazed the back of his neck, forked into his hair and she arched against him.

He knew he'd stop. He had to, but he let her hands drop to his waist, let her tug his shirt loose and ease past the waistband of his breeches. Only then, did he roll away.

Quick. He had to stand before—

His legs felt weak and he could not speak. She must have gelded him, indeed, for Charlie lay on the sand, soft and receptive, *his*. Her blouse gaped over one pale breast as she struggled up on her elbows. Her face accused him.

"You won't make love to me because I made you kill Francisco, is that it, Nicolas?"

"Charlie." He swallowed at the change. "You go too far."

He saw the hard set of her jaw and the glint of her gritted front teeth. She looked vengeful. How could submission flash into poisonous fury? He would not feed her anger by remaining.

Nicolas brushed the sand from his clothes and whistled. The gray gelding side-stepped away, rolling its eyes, but he strode after it. Nothing would be gained by staying. Falling into her arms had been a mistake, but not an irrevocable one.

Besides, the taunting heat of her voice, the open threat in her eyes made him wary. It was ridiculous, of course. He wouldn't have turned his back on her, if he really believed the prickling at his nape. Halcon's suspicion and battle-honed instinct shouldn't overflow to a girl who loved him.

And yet. His steps slowed and he listened. He'd learned never to ignore such primitive warnings.

His sinews recognized the hiss of a descending sword before his mind did. Charlie's blade slashed through his shirt and whipped his back before he rolled from its path.

"*I* go too far?" Charlie screamed through the still night. "Damnation Nicolas, I'm the despoiled virgin!"

Charlie came after him, making him jump to his feet and touch his own hilt.

"You've just found it convenient to forget, because then you can make me the villain."

Black hair slanted over one eye and she advanced with blade held high.

"Do you plan to wallow in your guilt forever? Since Francisco Lopez is dead? I can assure you he wouldn't have done the same for you," Charlie flipped the shock of hair from her eyes, but when he would have spoken she extended the blade.

"He would have accepted Nighthawk's death like a man."

Charlie's face dared him to argue. He ought to wrench the sword from her hand and leave her weeping. When he didn't she pressed her advantage, circling the sword above his chest.

"You know I'm right, Nicolas. He would have seen your fallen body as a regrettable, but natural part of warfare—the risk a soldier assumes once he buckles on a weapon."

He'd had enough. He needn't listen to this.

"And you, of course, know all about the smoke and suffering of warfare, of being a soldier and a man," Nicolas snarled.

Christ, she thought she was smart, to lecture him about manhood and daring, when she knew nothing of it, nothing.

"I don't have to be a man to see the truth."

He reached up to brush aside the blade and Charlie lunged, dropping the sword's tip and ripping the fabric over his ribs.

"Defend yourself, Nicolas, if you can," she taunted, tapping her sword point against his hilt before withdrawing a pace.

"Shut your mouth, Charlie," he drew the sword. "Shut it."

"And what if I don't, Nicolas? Tell me what I have to lose. Do you think your sword—" Charlie smiled grimly and swatted his blade with hers, "can hurt me worse than you have? Would you hear the truth, oh great Halcon?"

Her eyes clinched closed for a minute and her voice quavered on the verge of tears. He edged closer. He must snatch that blade before she injured one of them.

432

"No!"

Her sword snapped out, and even though the tears must have clouded her vision, she cut his unprotected hand. Christ!

"The truth, Nicolas is that it never occurred to you, when you set yourself up as California's savior, that you might get your precious hidalgo hands dirty." Charlie sucked in a sobbing breath and set her teeth in her lip, before continuing.

"You never considered that the path to patriotism might be covered not only with adventure and glory, but with blood!"

She screamed it, pointing the sword like an accusing finger.

"You're not angry because *I* made you kill someone. You're angry because you have to admit you are not a saint! You decided to carry a sword and break the law and finally you had to kill for what you believed in.

"A saint would have died first! A saint wouldn't have desired a woman who wasn't his, wouldn't have had her. But Nicolas, a saint isn't what California needs. It isn't what I—"

Her voice broke. Her sword drooped at a crazy angle and then fell, before she buried her face in her hands.

She looked at him then, peering between the bars of her fingers, beseeching him to hold her, to forgive the cruel words, but Nicolas did neither. He grabbed Tigre by the bit, leapt aboard, and rode up the beach, away from Aguas Dulces, away from Charlie.

# Chapter Thirty

Charity O'Dell Larkin affixed her signature to the second letter she'd written in three days. Father Alvarado's missives outnumbered hers, but he did not have to hire his messengers.

She rethreaded a bone pin through the purchased hair guaranteed to turn her boyish crop into a stylish coiffure, and gazed out the inn window onto what, in Boston, would have been called an alley.

Charity wrinkled her nose. Rats outside and a brass bed fit for a queen, inside. Californios had much to learn about inns. But who needed them? Every ranchero opened his doors, larder, stable and purse to travelers. Who needed an inn, but two banished Americans bound for Boston?

Freddy had delayed their departure, without cause, by her judgement. Under other circumstances, she would have asked why. But she'd caused Freddy grief enough. She had no desire to stir up the anger simmering beneath his excruciating politeness.

Besides, she could endure this hollow tugging that pulled her back to Nicolas and Aguas Dulces far easier than knowing she'd never see him again. Soon, her only view of California would be over her shoulder.

By fall, she'd be at sea and at Christmas she'd be ensconced in Aunt P's parlor, gazing through a lamplit window as snow piled up and she embroidered hankies with Freddy's initials.

Then an entire continent would bar her return to stubborn Nicolas Carillo.

She fanned her hand above the letter, hurrying the drying ink. After all, just because Freddy hadn't mentioned a time of departure, just because their trunks sat in a nearby stable awaiting an oxcart to San Pedro, didn't mean he wouldn't stalk through the door any moment, with just such plans.

She'd send the letter with the first available messenger, preferably, she thought, scanning it, before Freddy read it.

> Dear Father Alvarado,
>
> I cannot aptly express my Gratitude for your offer to intercede with the church and new alcalde. My husband Frederick, however, is satisfied with our marriage and so must I be.
>
> As you predicted, our banishment has been lifted. It is a great relief to learn one is no longer named Criminal. As I write, our departure for Boston is eminent.
>
> Father, I can think of no greater good, than offering the service of my hands to your mission, and I Thank God you think me worthy. My "physicking skills" are not nearly so fine as you say. Still, if not for the pressing duty of wife, I would join you.
>
> For all this, and for all you carry in your heart, I thank you and will remain most sincerely yours,
>
> Charity O'Dell Larkin

Charity stood. Biologist had no practice writing in veiled terms and she hoped the cantankerous priest understood the words which blessed him for saving Nicolas' life. She brushed back her midnight blue skirts, and stepped briskly toward the door.

Men's voices, just outside, slowed her steps. It took her only a moment to recognize the braying voice covering Freddy's.

"Go on, now! I'm sure the little she-cat will be tickled to be rid of you. After all—"

She hadn't liked that damned Ambrose from the first!

Charity jerked open the door, seeking to surprise Ambrose

and Sergei as they idled in the hall with Freddy. The movement felt particularly wifelike.

All three men wore new buckskins, soft and yellow as butter.

"Gentlemen?" Charity's voice was more inquiry than greeting, and Freddy's flush confirmed her opinion of just who Ambrose had labeled a "little she-cat."

She didn't have to unsheath her claws to lure Freddy inside. Freddy caught the gaping stares at her fading bruises and savaged hair and waved the mountain men away before closing the door.

"Charlie."

Freddy shifted from foot to foot. New boots, she noticed, thick soled and expensive. Freddy smacked his hands on his hips and regarded her, as if he would speak. He cleared his throat before motioning her back to the writing table.

"Sit down, Charlie."

She sat and deliberately creased her letter while she listened to Freddy's uneasy shuffling. He seemed torn between elation and dread.

"Charlie."

"Yes, Freddy?"

Charity caught his darting blue glance, and tried to steady it with her own as she folded her hands atop the letter. She composed her features in the mode of an attentive wife.

He studied her, riffled his fingers through the fringe on his buckskins and laughed.

"I could be dressed better for husbandly pronouncements, I suppose."

Charity joined his laugh just long enough to be polite before she had to ask, "Is that what they—" she nodded toward the hall. "—were talking about? Husbandly pronouncements?"

"Hellfire, Charlie!" he shouted. Freddy took two swinging strides across the room and when he turned back his frown didn't tell her if he was angry, disgusted or remorseful.

"I wonder if two decent people ever made a worse mess of each other's lives!"

Freddy walked behind her. She heard his hand slide along the brass bedstead, and then he stood silently. She felt herself blink as his palms perched on her shoulders. She waited for him to continue.

When Freddy's index finger trailed from the false bun to the bare nape of her neck, she knew she'd been right to sit motionless.

"Do you want to take that thing off?" he asked, prodding the borrowed hair when she dipped her head away from his touch. "There's no one here but me."

"It's all right," she said, "And I am sorry about—"

"I've heard your confessions, Charlie. It's my turn."

Freddy stepped back in front of her and leaned both palms on the writing table. His eyes greyed solemnly and his lips tightened as if he held back the words within.

"You haven't done a bad thing in your life, Freddy Larkin! Not that I didn't make you do!"

Freddy snorted and shook his head.

"What would you say if I said I'd been lying to you ever since you got to California?" He frowned at her smiling disbelief. "Before that, even. Before you proposed this arrangement."

Charity considered the possibility, then shook her head smartly. The false hair uncoiled and hung over her shoulder.

"I'd say you were trying to make me feel less guilty and doing an abominable job of it. But," she patted his cheek, "you're sweet to try."

A queer chill tingled through her when he leaned away from her touch.

"I never opened a bank in San Diego."

"Never—? But when you left in such an uproar, when I was sick—and you were gone for weeks? Where were you?"

"I rendezvoused with Ambrose and Sergei." He shrugged. "We made half-hearted plans for this trip. Since then, I've spent lots of money on traps and horses, clothes and food. Ambrose and Sergei have supplied the knowledge and I've put up the money."

He folded his arms over his chest, daring her to object.

437

"I suppose that's fair enough," Charity ventured. Inside she seethed. *Ambrose!* Better Freddy had pounded hundreds of dollars down a ground squirrel's hole than spending it on that vermin.

"That means we needn't travel to San Diego to see that the bank is running smoothly before we sail to Boston." She faltered.

She accepted his lie, but Freddy's straddle-legged stance and jutting jaw promised more.

"I'm not going back."

"Wonderful!" she clapped her hands. "Oh Freddy," she rejoiced, "you can't dream how I dreaded facing Aunt P! She never believed this marriage would work and—"

"Charlie, I said *I* wasn't going. You still—"

"No."

The chair screeched back from the table as she rose.

"Absolutely not. Why should you go off trapping and condemn me to Aunt P's drawing room? I'll cook your porcupine stew, mend your filthy stockings, even carry your detestable traps, but I will not go back alone."

Charity drew breath to continue, but hesitated when Freddy reached inside his shirt for a folded piece of paper.

"Another letter from Father Alvarado?"

"No." Freddy prolonged the word. He turned the document over, then end for end, regarding it as though it were completely foreign to him.

"What, then? Give it to me," she snapped.

"I don't know how to feel about this, Charlie," he admitted, extending the paper at the same time he rested a hand on her shoulder. "You told me," he cautioned, as she unfolded the top half, "the priest said, I only had to write that I didn't contest an annulment, that we didn't—make love." Freddy's voice faded. It rose again in a half growl. "Honey, for two years, I thought you'd be my wife. And most people believed you were. But I wrote that down for anyone in the world to read. I swear to God it was the hardest thing—I don't know how I did it."

438

Charity's eyes skittered from line to cursive line, trying to read, while her mind told her to listen to Freddy.

"You did it," her voice quavered, "because you knew it was the right thing to do. Because," she swallowed against a lump so big it hurt, "you don't love me. Not like that."

Freddy's eyes widened as if she'd slapped him.

"No," Freddy's voice creaked, "not like that."

She didn't look up, certain he'd misunderstand her tears.

"Ah, Charlie, don't cry! It's what you wanted, isn't it? For me to go off and for you to be with Nicolas?" he waited.

"Now, don't shake your head, God damn it, I know it's him, but—hellfire, I'm not *sure* what's right. I only know you haven't been happy. The only thing I've done right, far as you're concerned, is standing up for him in court."

Charity slipped around the desk and wrung Freddy's hands. Each time he'd mentioned Nicolas, she'd lied, but he wasn't fooled.

"Freddy, we would have had a fine life if Nicolas—"

"But Nicolas did happen. He rode up on his pretty brown horse, like something out of Camelot, and I never had a chance.

"And I'll tell you something, Charlie," Freddy squared his shoulders until he looked like the healthy blue-eyed brute who'd whirled her off her feet that first day last spring, "I've taken directions from other folks—my parents, John, you—all my life. Now I'm damn near thirty years old. I'm doing what I want. What I want right now is to kiss you like I should have three months ago. If I had, maybe it would've been enough."

Freddy blew out his cheeks, then expelled his breath just as he had as a boy. He caught Charity's chin and turned her to face him.

Buckskin brushed her cheeks as his arms dragged her in, then Freddy's kiss bowled her back against the desk. His lips pressed over hers. For a minute, regret and melancholy washed her.

"I still say I could have held up my end of the bargain." Freddy drew back with a lopsided smile. "Next time. Right, cousin? Now——" he cleared his throat and turned to paw through a stack of clothing, "I'll go meet Sergei and Ambrose and buy the strongest horse that'll have me." He winked and held up a fat money bag. "Then I'll gamble all night, and what money's left, I'll bring to you.

"Then you can tell me where you're going," Freddy mused, tossing the money pouch from palm to palm. "To Boston, back to Nicolas, and there's always the mission. Although an unlikelier nun," Freddy said, snatching the false hair from its last precarious pin, "probably hasn't been born."

Freddy stepped through the door, and had almost drawn it closed when he peeked back at her.

"In the morning, little cousin," he reminded, "and you better have a schedule drawn up. I have more gold, but I won't give it up easily."


Swathed in a black rebozo, Charity paced three circuits of the plaza, just as she had every day since her arrival back in Los Cielos. She'd done it in the belief that it would harden her against stares, snickers and the occasional tsks of pity.

Even if she'd married a Carillo, would they have forgotten her humiliation in the plaza, her outrageous admissions in Santana's court?

"Tamale, Señorita?" The youthful vendor, gangly and toffee-eyed, cocked his head sideways and smiled in a way she could only call flirtatious.

Señorita. Soon, she would be. No more Mrs. Freddy Larkin. No more Nighthawk's Woman

But why did this gypsy handsome boy look at her *like that:* Did some temptress like Esperanza stand behind her?

Charity checked over her shoulder, then returned his smile.

"That would be wonderful, Señor, but," Charity shrugged and held her hands wide to show she carried no reticule.

The boy straightened thin shoulders inside his embroidered shirt and glanced around, just as she had.

"For you, Señorita, I make it a gift."

"No, please." She gulped in embarrassment. Was she so poor at flirting that he thought she'd begged a meal of him?

"Señorita," the tamale vendor twisted husks over steaming cornmeal and meat, "for being a woman of *the people*. I insist."

Charity nodded her thanks, proud and smiling, before accepting the tamale and scuttling back to her room.

Another letter sat on the wooden table, beside Freddy's scrawled declaration.

Charity dragged the room's only chair against the wall and peeled the husk from her tamale. If she were indeed mistress of her own life, she'd eat when she saw fit, and right now hunger outweighed curiosity in the padre's newest letter.

Charity pushed back thoughts of Nicolas. She could live without him. She might despise her life. She might even become that hated self who petted only cats and other women's children, but she *could* live without him.

She bit the tamale savagely and decided biology might become her life. While she could walk and talk and breathe, she might serve science; suicide was a coward's path.

At least she wasn't an old maid. Not literally. Her lips twisted in a wry smile. The irony pleased her.

"Well, it shouldn't," she huffed to herself, dabbling her fingers in the chipped blue bowl that passed for a wash basin. "A maiden wouldn't know what she was missing."

Lacking a towel, Charity shook the water from her fingers before taking up the letter. The parchment was a finer, smoother grain and the letter was closed by the Carillo seal.

She popped the seal free and closed her eyes to pray, before unfolding the letter.

"Please God, let the letter be in Spanish, because then it comes from his heart, not from duty or obligation. And please let him say he loves me. Please."

She opened her eyes and the page she read was lettered in English.

Dearest Charity,
I am, in truth, no saint. I have proved it a hundred times over by my actions toward you. I apologize for

saying you forced Lopez's death. A sane man would have wounded, not destroyed. Seeing your danger, I passed beyond sanity. *I.*

Worse still, I apologize for making you fight for all I should have given freely. Your independence, your adventure and study and my love. Know as you leave, I wish you fullness of the first two and be assured that you take with you my heart.

*Vaya con Dios, Querida.*

Halcon.

Damnation. She'd choke on these idiot hiccoughs. Charity held the letter at arm's length and shrugged her shoulders, in turn, against each cheek, unwilling to smear the ink.

Who would he have trusted to deliver this letter? She rushed to the window and cursed the minutes spent eating and toying with her future, when she might have glimpsed him fleeing? Still clutching the letter, Charity whirled toward her folded riding habit. In hours she could be at the rancho, in his arms. She'd tell him her banishment had been lifted, Freddy had freed her, Father Alvarado would arrange everything—

She placed the letter face down on the desk.

Oh, Nicolas, why didn't you bring this letter yourself? Why didn't you just tell me? Why must *I* always come to *you?*

Even in apology he denied her himself.

He still might come. But in case he didn't, she'd trap herself into doing what she knew was best.

Charity knotted the black rebozo under her chin and slipped into the corridor. Too early, still, for most drinkers and gamblers, the *bodega* hosted only an elderly man and the landlord.

"Señor, I'll require my trunks be brought up. Can you arrange it?"

"Of course, Señora Larkin." The innkeeper raised his voice in case his customer failed to recognize the notorious guest. "But, are you departing, soon?"

"Tomorrow." She nodded curtly.

"And Señor, could you arrange to have my horse, the gray, returned to the Carillos?"

There. Charity nearly ran back to her room. She'd cut off her last chance to surrender. She closed the door behind her and leaned against it, knowing she should feel smug that she'd made herself act like the strong, independent woman Halcon had fallen in love with. She should feel proud that she'd decided to sit and wait. All night, if that's what it took.

It was after midnight when Charity unlocked her knees, wincing at their stiffness, and strained her arms to unbutton her gown. Nicolas wasn't coming.

She peeled the tight sleeves down and when they stuck at her wrists she yanked so hard one cuff ripped.

Damnation! What a foolish, soft-hearted mooncalf she'd been to really, truly believe he'd come.

Charity wrinkled her nose at the smell of her own perspiration. Better he hadn't. She'd sat for hours in this airless room, refusing to budge from her corner of the bed, for fear he'd run to the stable, hire a horse and ride to him.

She opened the trunk and regarded the folded clothing and stacked paper, ready for departure. She unwrapped a chunk of soap she'd left on top of her white nightgown, and bathed in water from the blue basin.

Damn you, Nicolas, she thought, shivering as a breath of air from the window chilled her damp limbs. Why did you write that letter? To absolve yourself of guilt? To keep me wanting you for the next thirty years?

Charity knotted the laces of her nightgown and mocked herself. The letter was a sop, a crumb Nicolas flung out of pity.

She refused to extinguish the candle at her bedside. It might burn down and the pooling wax might ignite, but it might also beckon Nicolas, if he rode past her window.

Charity slammed her head down on the mattress and stared at the ceiling. What an ass she remained, after all this, to choose hopeless dreams over safety!

* * *

A sword slipping from its scabbard sent her starting awake, pulling the bedclothes to her chin and straining her eyes toward every shadowed corner.

Charity parted her lips to ask "who?", but no sound came.

Lithe and leather-clad, the figure that detached from the darkness tapped its blade on the open trunk.

"Surely, Señorita, you're not leaving California so soon?" Nighthawk's rusty whisper, the one she heard when the grizzlies attacked, when he dismissed slumbering Nicolas at Las Calderonas, that rasping, magic whisper, teased her.

She slid out of bed and, feeling weak and frightened, she weaved before him.

"I don't want to," she admitted, curling her cold toes against the floor.

Nighthawk, masked and grim, stepped closer. Had the teasing tone been produced in her imagination? The last time she'd seen him, he'd deserted her on the beach, deserted her with a last look that bled hatred and accused her of murder.

Glinting silver in the moonlight, the sword tip rose from the trunk and whisked toward her throat. Charity closed her eyes. Let it be this way. What better time to die and what better executioner?

The sword tip flicked the laces of her throat, then, with a faint growl of irritation, the blade sawed upward, sliced the cloth, and the gown fell open.

Her eyes flew wide, then, and though he still didn't smile, her heartbeat quickened as the sword pressed against her breastbone.

Charity stepped back. The pressure continued and she took another step until the bend of her knees touched the bed.

"Your companion departs soon?"

Freddy. Could Freddy return even now? But her mind refused to think, only her eyes functioned, fastening on the flash of teeth that smiled from beneath the black mustache, beneath the leather mask.

Nighthawk's sword hand relaxed. The blade dipped lower to edge the gown's opening wider, and Charity's knees weakened with relief.

His left hand removed his mask, but when she stepped toward him, the blade snapped upright, cautioning.

"Señorita, do you remember one night we discussed the
expression, 'no quarter'? Just nod, Señorita, that will do
nicely."

Charity nodded. She must be hypnotized to stand like this.

"Ah, I had so hoped you did. Back one more step, if you
please."

She collapsed on the edge of the bed with a decided plop,
but it wasn't that sound that remained ringing in her ears.
Charity heard the sword hilt clash against the brass bedstead
as he dropped it. She heard the bed sigh under the weight of
two bodies, and she heard Nicolas's voice.

"Tonight, I will grant you no escape, no mercy, until you
promise never to leave. No quarter, *querida,* at least until
dawn."